OTHER BOOKS BY LONNIE BUSCH

Push Me; Feisty Stories of Love & Loss

Cargo Hold 4

Project Übermensch

All Hope of Becoming Human

Turnback Creek; a Novella & Six Stories

The Baldwin Hotel

The Cabin on Souder Hill

Turnback Creek

I0608051

The Anything Room

LONNIE BUSCH

THE ANYTHING ROOM

Cover Art by Lonnie Busch

ISBN: 978-1-964024-09-7 (paperback)

ISBN: 978-1-964024-11-0 (hardcover)

Library of Congress Control Number: 2024924499

First Paperback/Hardcover Edition, January 2025

"Nothing in the world is knowable. Knowledge is unflinching assertion."

— LYKOURGOS (FROM *THE WRECKAGE OF AGATHON* BY JOHN GARDNER)

For Nancy, the bright spot in my world

∾

The Anything Room

Part One

Chapter One

B*etter Put It Behind You Now.* Those six words echoed from the back of Martin's thoughts as he turned onto the dark, cracked street that cut the sleepy neighborhood in half. Lyrics from a song? A sentence from a book? Did it matter? Either way, Martin Moffett had to invent a new life for himself.

He wasn't very familiar with this part of South St. Louis. It seemed okay, maybe a bit desolate. After checking the address again, he creeped his car down to the end of the dismal lane, the smallish house sitting by itself at the end of a block of smallish houses, all with plenty of space between them, the closest neighbor at least twenty yards away. Martin was surprised there was no majestic, five-foot RELAX real estate sign staking out the front yard. Corporate could probably not justify their magnificent, expensive signage for this listing because the property was too low end to warrant such a grand statement of affluence. No profit, no point. Regardless, the size looked right, at least from the outside, and it was close to his office on Laclede's Landing on the Riverfront, no more than a fifteen- to twenty-minute drive to the ad agency.

After parking in front of the boxy, one-story dwelling, he got out to take a stroll around the property. The air was cool, and surprisingly fresh, quiet except for the chirp of peepers keeping vigil over the night. The house had a quaint but clean front yard, no fence, and a driveway that appeared to be in good shape, nothing a weed whacker couldn't bring into better focus. The backyard, no larger than the front, butted up to a vacant field, making it appear much larger than it really was (the backyard had recently been mowed while the field ran wild and rough with weeds, the demarcation between the two properties clearly defined). Railroad tracks ran beyond the field, maybe eighty yards from the house, far enough he should not be bothered too much by passing trains; he was a sound sleeper, at least that's what Noreen always told him, trying to wake him for work when the alarm clock blared on and on forever. In 1990, at the age of forty-one, Moffett lost his wife Noreen Ann to a car accident. She'd been thirty-nine. Noreen didn't die immediately, but wasted away in a hospital bed in a coma, finally succumbing to the slow ruin of her damaged organs after three months, leaving behind Martin and their son, Kenny, who was eleven. Martin vowed to raise his son on his own in the house he and Noreen had bought in Mehlville fourteen years earlier when they'd both agreed to use the last of their savings for the down payment.

Martin ambled around to the front of the house to wait for his real estate agent. For weeks she had shown him home after home, all too big, or too expensive, or too fancy. Martin tried to explain to Margaret that it was just him now. He was no longer in need of a split-level three-bedroom home like the one he and his wife Noreen had owned. Even when they'd bought it, they worried it was too much house for them back then. Nevertheless, they had lived simply, and with both of them working, had been able to double up on payments, whittling away at the mortgage year after year, until she died. They had managed to pay it down substantially, and adding to that the higher property value after twenty-two years, Martin hoped to buy something smaller, in a less expensive area, with a hefty down payment to give him a small monthly nut.

At one point, when Martin was explaining his situation, Margaret had asked about his son, Kenny. "Where will he stay when he comes to visit? Don't you want a bedroom for him?"

Martin and his son, Kenny, had got on just fine in St. Louis after Noreen died, Kenny attending a Catholic grade school, then a public high school, which he much preferred, ultimately winning a football scholarship to Rutgers University and leaving for New Jersey mid-

August several summers ago. Martin had told his son, that when he went off to Rutgers, he was going to try to sell their split-level three-bedroom home. "Are you cool with that, Son?" he'd said to Kenny. "Sure, Dad, it'll be good for us to move on from here," Kenny had said, and Martin believed him.

With Kenny on his own, Martin was thinking more of a *bungalow* maybe, something modest and unremarkable and small, one bedroom, a compact but comfortable backyard—big enough for a barbecue pit and a lawn chair or two—no garage, just a driveway. Margaret had grimaced and pressed her lips together so hard she looked like a duck. She promised, though her pledge was less than enthusiastic, to go back to the office and scour the listings, but told Martin that her company didn't normally handle such properties.

A week later Margaret called and said she'd found the perfect house for him, gave him the address, 352 Yurning Place, and said she could meet him there at seven that evening.

Margaret pulled up in her shiny gold Camry, the single street lamp near the sidewalk in front of the house sparking brilliant streams of light along the sleek contours of the new automobile. After a few minutes, still seated in her car with the dome light burning, perhaps rummaging her soft leather portfolio for some obscure data about the home to share with Martin, she popped out into the dimly lit street and shut her door, locking it with her key fob. She clicked across the street in high heels as Martin stepped forward to greet her. Her floral perfume reached him before she did. Margaret smiled, shook his hand, a set of keys dangling from her manicured fingers, then led him up the front walk to the concrete porch. A simple roof extended out over the edges of the porch, suspended on wrought-iron ornamental supports at the corners and on either side of the single step. Porches of this type were apparently fairly common in this part of St. Louis if the rest of the houses on the street were any indication. They all had the same porch.

After swinging the front door open, she fumbled her hand along the inside wall until the house exploded with light. Holding the door for Martin, she ushered him in with a sweep of her arm, then closed the door behind him.

Living-room-dining-room-kitchen, one unbroken statement that ran the full width of the front of the house. Luckily the builder knew not to divide this space with walls, which would have rendered each room useless. Margaret led Martin to the hallway—a decent size bedroom on the left, with the bathroom on the right, a shotgun affair, narrow, with the sink-medicine-cabinet-mirror, followed by the tub-shower combo, and finally the toilet bowl, with a small frosted window on the exterior wall, the toilet paper roll beneath it. Cramped but still plenty big for him.

Next, on the right, sharing a common wall with the bathroom, was a smaller room, maybe some kind of hobby room, too small for any kind of standard-sized bed. It was tiny, as it obviously had to sacrifice a third of its floor space to the adjacent bathroom.

Kenny would have no place to sleep when he came to visit. Martin wasn't about to share his concern with Margaret, as she had already warned him. Kenny would probably be good crashing on the living room floor.

Martin exhaled a bit roughly and walked back to the kitchen-dining-living room, trying to picture a futon instead of a couch, maybe a coffee table if there was room, then walked back down the hallway to the hobby room, wondering how he could build some kind of sleeping device into the small space, noticing for the first time the boarded-up area on the back wall that must lead to the field behind the house. The sloppy repair was almost the size of a door. Had the previous owner planned to expand the room out into the backyard. Why only a doorway? Why not knock out the entire wall? And what was behind the wood slats?

"What's the deal with this?" Martin asked, walking over to run his palm along the weird patchwork of horizontal boards, see if he could feel cold air leaking in through the chinks. For a moment he thought he had, but the sensation was altogether different than a draft, he realized, more like an odd sort of magnetism, something pulling at the air in his lungs. Folding his arms over his chest, he jerked back from the patch, giving it a hard look. Margaret fumbled with her soft leather portfolio a moment before bringing out some papers, then started to read.

"Not sure," she said. "No notes about damage here. I'm sure a little plaster and paint would take care of it."

The sensation eased, Martin no longer feeling the disturbing pull at his chest, figuring he had imagined it, maybe a pang of anxiety over buying the property. Noreen would have hated this forsaken place.

"What did you say?" Martin asked, realizing he hadn't caught a word she'd said.

"A little paint and plaster should take care of it," Margaret said again, her head tilted to the side.

Martin knew she was right, but would need some kind of compensation for the work, some adjustment to the asking price, even though he planned to fix it himself. It really was a simple job unless the hole went completely through the wall.

"Who were the previous owners?" Martin asked, listening to Margaret shuffle the papers behind him, trying to envision whether the walls were plasterboard, or the kind of plaster and lath common in older homes. He knocked on it. To him it had the more solid-rock feel of plaster and lath. No problem. Martin's father had been a plasterer for years. Martin picked up a thing or two growing up, though never wanted that life for himself. Graphic design had been Martin's calling, and his father had always marveled at his talent, though could never figure out where it came from. There were no artists on either side of Martin's family.

"Says here a... *magician*," Margaret said, bright-faced as a full moon, staring over the papers at Martin.

A bit befuddled, he shifted his attention between her and the wall. "A magician?" Martin was growing more perplexed by the second, trying to wrap that word around some career that could afford a man a house, even one this plainly inexpensive. "Like... for kid's birthday parties or something?"

Margaret shrugged, her narrow shoulders lifting the wrinkle-free fabric of her putty-colored blazer, her thin meticulously tended eyebrows rising almost comically, cutting neat little scimitars into her otherwise broad, rounded forehead. A tidal wave of reddish hair rose above her forehead, suspended, as if about to crash down at any moment. "Says here, Falco... Benjamin Falco, defaulted on the mortgage, the property went back to the bank. That's it." Margaret stated this with such conviction, as if this detail should explain everything— the haphazardly patched wall, Falco's odd vocation, the almost toy-sized scale of the bungalow.

Martin asked the price? When Margaret told him, he asked about any wiggle room, even though the price had nearly knocked him over, so low he could almost pay for the whole damn thing from the money he'd get from the sale of his and Noreen's house. He was already doing the math; he'd put a substantial down payment on the place, finally pay off all the medical bills from Noreen's hospital stay after the accident, and still come away with a small mortgage and even smaller monthly payments than he had ever imagined.

"Not usually on these bank defaults," Margaret said. "But we can try, you know, tell them about the damaged wall. They may make a small concession. But it's a pretty good deal as is."

That was it. Martin bought the house and everything went as planned, though he'd had no idea what he'd bargained for.

Chapter Two

The week after Martin took possession, Terrell Brandeshire, one of Martin's new neighbors, ambled over and found Martin in the backyard inspecting the outside wall. Martin was trying to determine if the inside damage poked through to the exterior siding, but he was unable to find any indication of a problem. Terrell lived three houses down, a widower with a white stubble beard, a pension and a pronounced limp. He hobbled over and introduced himself, a tall gangly man who seemed at first glance to be constructed of spare parts, the linkage between them never fully joined.

"Thinking of adding on?" Terrell said, his arms still moving, shifting his weight between the good leg and the bum one.

"No, no, I don't believe so," Martin said, smiling at the man. Terrell pursed his lips and took his dark eyes out toward the tracks.

"You know it was a magician owned this place years ago," Terrell said. "Nobody lived here since. Must be going on five years now."

Martin regarded the lean man a moment before turning his attention to the far tracks, both men staring toward the void beyond the field. It was odd you couldn't see the railroad tracks for all the weeds, and the trains roared across as if they were gliding on a blanket of air above the earth, untethered from gravity and physics.

"You knew Benjamin Falco then?" Martin said into the misty fog rolling in.

"Falco the Fantabulist," Terrell stated with the confidence of a tour guide. "He certainly was that."

Martin looked over at Terrell, who squatted down and plucked a blade of grass from the dirt and stuck it between his small yellow teeth. Terrell acted as if he knew what a *fantabulist* was. Martin squatted down next to the man and waited. Just then a locomotive rumbled past in a cloud of mist and wind, the force dragging down the tops of the weeds. When the train cleared, and the weeds became still again, Terrell, without looking over at Martin, started to explain about the elaborate experiments Falco performed in the backyard. He pointed toward the back wall of the house, explaining that that was where Falco had placed a huge glass tank, had it brought in on a flatbed truck.

"It was twelve feet high, six feet wide on each of its four sides, like an aquarium for Jaws," Terrell explained. "Had it three feet from that back wall of the house right there." Terrell cleared his throat, lapsing quickly into a coughing jag.

Martin wasn't sure what to do for the man, so he did nothing, waiting for his sputtering to pass.

"It must have cost a fortune," Terrell told Martin when he finally got his lungs under control. The way Terrell told it, the glass looked at least an inch thick. A couple firemen Falco knew, or had paid—Terrell had never seen them around before—came over one afternoon with one of those three-inch flaccid hoses from the firehouse, hooked it to the hydrant on the corner, and cranked it open. "Filled that gargantuan trinket box in about thirteen minutes." A day or so later, another truck, a heavy-duty utility vehicle, delivered a spool of electric cable, the wire thick as a garden hose and— "black as an otter's eye," Terrell said, squinting out at nothing.

Martin had never seen an otter and couldn't help but wonder where Terrell might have come across one in St. Louis. Terrell continued on, gesturing with his arthritic hands how Falco ran the electrical cable all the way out to the railroad tracks and welded the end to the side of the steel rail, then welded the other end to the metal frame of the water tank. But Falco wasn't done. With the tag end of the cable from the spool, Falco climbed the telephone pole on the north end of the field and attached it to the transformer at the top. Terrell had never seen anything like it, Falco up that pole with his portable stick welder dangling from a strap slung over his shoulder, black goggles, the ground clamp attached to the transformer housing, Falco wielding his torch, sparking fire up there like a madman.

"I thought he'd fry himself," Terrell said.

Before he finished up the pole, Falco welded a four-foot metal rod to the top of the transformer, then climbed down and dragged the other end of the transformer cable to the big tank and welded that end to the side of the metal and glass contraption. Martin could just make out the metal rod still attached to the transformer.

"Lord have mercy!" Terrell said. "I ain't no math professor or nothing, but it sure looked like Falco had created some kind of *triangulation* with those cables out to the tracks, then over to that pole and back to the tank." He looked at Martin. "You got any beer?"

Martin nodded and went inside to fetch a couple.

When he returned Terrell was sitting on an upside-down plastic paint bucket he'd found somewhere and Martin handed him a beer, then sat on the patchy grass next to him. Terrell was still staring out toward the tracks. After a few minutes of silence, tipping back the can a few times, he explained that after Falco had done all the wiring and welding and such, he came out the next morning wearing a swimsuit, a diving mask and air tank on his back, carrying some device with copper tubing, sealed tanks, valves and gauges.

"If I hadn't knowed better, I'd uh said it was a miniature still," Terrell said, then tipped his beer back as if the recollection had made him thirsty. Terrell said Falco sank down into the water with the device, then suction-cupped it to the base of the glass tank. Terrell had walked over to check his progress and there stood Falco in the bottom of the tank, animated, maybe upset, fiddling with the gauge. When Falco climbed out, he ripped off his mask and spit out the mouthpiece of his breathing tube, climbing down the ladder muttering to himself about water pressure, pounds per square meter, converting PSI into pascals, derivation and the atmospheric pressure of Earth at sea level, practically walking over Terrell, as if Terrell had been a ghost, and stomped into the house. After that Falco disappeared for several days, working mostly in the house, making himself a stranger to the outdoors. One afternoon, about a week after Falco had sequestered himself in the bungalow, the weatherman forecasted a huge electrical storm. That very night Falco came out of the house wearing some kind of rubbery frogman suit, completely black from head to toe, goggles and all, with a large breathing tank on his back. He leaned a ladder up against the glass wall of the tank, climbed up, and dropped himself right into the water. He stood on the bottom checking the gauges on his device, like Captain Nemo at the helm of the *Nautilus*.

"He'd asked me earlier that day if I could come over in case anything went wrong," Terrell told Martin. "But hell's bells, it looked like whatever he was about to do could go no other way *but* wrong!"

Terrell had positioned himself away from the tank, where Falco had told him it would be safe. Rain started coming in sheets by ten o'clock that night and Terrell could hardly see Falco anymore in that damned tank. Lightning cracked all around, illuminating the black clouds with an eerie green glow, steadily moving closer. Thunder rumbled along the ground, shook the flimsy houses straddling the street, and Terrell got soaked through his chintzy rain poncho, the ends blowing this way and that, the wind howling so loud Terrell couldn't have heard an atomic bomb go off in the front yard. It was a while later before Terrell thought he saw the lone headlamp of the 8:38 from Carbondale coming up fast. It usually passed through a little after 10:30. Lightning was cracking all around by then. Terrell wanted to check on Falco but was afraid to leave his post.

"Well, no mistaking the 8:38 from Carbondale, its big square iron nose and steely wheels dragging a line of coal weighing hundreds of tons, the ground shaking, lightning shooting down from the heavens, that single headlight on the front of that rig like the very eye of Satan hisself," Terrell told Martin, squinting as if to bring the memory into sharper focus. Terrell leaned forward on the paint bucket and stared out over the weeds and said it all happened quite literally in a *flash*. The train was passing as lightning struck the telephone pole and all the cables crackled and sizzled with blue electricity and the chlorine, burnt-wire stink of ozone and, "*BAM!* like Hiroshima, that tank of water exploded, lit up like a hundred suns! Water blew out in all directions, glass flying through the neighborhood, slivers and shards embedded in everyone's asphalt shingle siding and roofs. A hell of a thing..."

Neighbors figured Falco had done ripped a hole in the fabric of time and space itself with that stunt. "No way Falco survived that," Terrell said, then twisted on the bucket looking toward the back of the bungalow. "Blew a hole clean through the back of the damn house. Right over there." The men were both silent for a moment.

Terrell took a long pull at the can, then wiped his mouth with his sleeve.

"Vaporized for sure, that's all I could figure," Terrell said. "Until I seen him at the daggone Piggly Wiggly a week later. Fit as a fiddle. Couldn't believe my eyes." Terrell was rocking back and forth on the bucket, almost anxious, as if he had something to add that wasn't very pleasant. "I caught me a piece of glass right here in my leg," Terrell added, still rocking, rubbing his thigh. "Severed a nerve and I ain't walked right since, but I guess it was all right. Falco paid all the medical bills."

Terrell fixed his lips into a thin line and glared out over that field like it was the enemy of all humanity. When Terrell finished the last of his beer, he stood up and crushed the flimsy aluminum can between his palms, then stuck it in the pocket of his trousers. He looked over at Martin with eyes so black and lifeless Martin had to turn away.

"Never looked the same though, Falco didn't. Not after that night." Terrell hitched up his droopy, belt-less jeans. Then, as if the memories were coming like vague images in a dark theater, said, "Something surely died inside him that night."

A couple days later, Martin saw Terrell at the street reading his mail fresh from the mailbox. Martin was curious so he walked over and asked when was the last time he saw Falco.

"Not much after the "Big Bang" experiment," Terrell said. "Kept to hisself mostly. Some nights his windows'd burn so bright I thought he was in there splitting atoms... beams of light shooting out every daggone pane of glass like a UFO taking off..."

According to Terrell, Falco lived like a pauper, but was very wealthy. "Hell, every week or so one of them big black stretch limos would glide right up the street silent as a shadow and park in front of

Falco's bungalow. A minute later, here comes Falco and his girl, Mitzi, all gussied up like daggone Hollywood movie stars, Falco in his sleek black tuxedo wearing a black top hat and shoes so shiny you could see 'em from outer space. Mitzi on his arm, in one of those skin-tight red miniskirts and glittery high heels, her blonde hair in one of them bouffants like a queen, wearing one of them sparkly silver tiaras. Man, it was a sight for sure." Mitzi evidently had been Falco's girlfriend and stage assistant. "The eccentric ones always get the gorgeous gals," Terrell had told Martin. "They went everywhere together." Falco and Mitzi had finished a show at an exclusive nightclub called The Glass Menagerie on Washington Avenue. They had a few drinks and left the lounge laughing and were waiting for the limo to pick them up on the street when a gang of thugs demanded Falco's wallet. Then Mitzi's pearl necklace and silver tiara. Falco handed his wallet over and when one of the thugs reached for the tiara, Mitzi kneed him in the groin. Two of the muggers jumped Falco before he could intervene, when the other punk Mitzi had kneed, lunged forward stabbing her to death. The gang left them both for dead. "Falco was *eccentric* up until Mitzi was killed that night, but after that, he turned bat-shit crazy. That's when all the really nutty experiments started."

"What finally happened to Falco?"

Terrell gave Martin a hard look, then took his eyes to the envelopes and advertisements in his hands. "Not rightly sure," Terrell said after a few very long seconds, shifting through the mail to see who he owed money to. The way Terrell told it, the black limo never returned, and Falco's mail, after a while, just started spilling out the mouth of his mailbox … and, well, that was it—Falco was gone. "His last great magic trick," Terrell said, his face bright as if proud to have known the offbeat magician. Then added: "Falco the *Fantabulist!* That feller lived up to his name, I have to give him that!"

Chapter Three

Terrell had never given Martin a physical description of Falco the Fantabulist other than to say that in his tuxedo, Falco had the stature and radiance of a Hollywood actor. To that, Martin had unwittingly assigned more specific features to the enigmatic magician—jet black hair oiled back in the tradition of big screen film stars, with a Clark Gable regal-thin mustache, standing tall and stately, notoriously handsome. And Mitzi, of course, with her long slender legs and pinched waist, would have the striking, unblemished beauty of a 1940's pin-up model. They must have been quite a sight, Falco and Mitzi, strolling out to that long, sleek black limo—its dark, mysterious windows, the white-gloved chauffeur poised to open the door—shining like some otherworldly transport on that drab, run-down dead-end street Martin now called home.

By the end of the second week in his new bungalow, Martin managed to get everything moved in and arranged so the place didn't have the cramped feel of an overstuffed closet. He'd selected a nice futon and a small, but comfortable, chair for the living room. Satisfied with how everything was coming together, he went grocery shopping and stocked up on food, filling the kitchen cabinets to the limit. He purchased the smallest full-size refrigerator he could find, and a simple but functional small wooden kitchen table with two chairs. He should have been content upon finishing the move, but the absence of purpose only left him with more time to think, and a burgeoning lone-liness, missing Kenny away at school, and longing for his life with Noreen. He was miserable and knew he needed to make himself busy.

Martin drove to the hardware store and bought everything he needed to fix the wall in the *Anything* room; that's what he'd decided to call that pitifully small excuse for a bedroom. Arriving home with all the supplies and tools, he ate a quick lunch, and feeling optimisti-cally renewed, spread a tarp along the wood floor to protect the finish, then carried his claw hammer to the slats nailed to the wall. He started on the top board, wedging the two-pronged claw between the board and the wall, then used the handle of it like a lever to loosen the board. He had just about gotten the first end of it away from the wall when the sun shot through the new opening in a blinding flash. It was so bright Martin stumbled backward a few steps, rubbing his eyes with his free hand to erase the red spots from his vision.

"Holy hell!"

Approaching the wall again, Martin shielded his eyes from the glare, somewhat confused by how the sunlight was able to penetrate the outer wall. He'd checked the exterior of the bungalow several days earlier when Terrell limped into the backyard and introduced himself. Martin had recalled Terrell telling him about the Big Bang experiment, as he called it, ripping a hole through the house, but Martin found no evidence of damage to the exterior upon closer inspection. Obviously, Falco had fixed it himself or had had it fixed.

Regardless, Martin made another trip to the back of the house, the sun a pale whitish spot above the railroad tracks, barely able to burn through the low overcast sky. Confused, and a little uneasy, Martin ambled to the front of the house and went back inside. Picking up his hammer, he moved closer to the patch, to the bright glare burning through the thin space where the board hung loose from the wall. Squinting, he brought his face closer to the opening, trying to see through the gap, but the light was too intense, making him dizzy, throwing off his center of gravity. With his legs weak, he eased himself down to the floor and sat a moment trying to compose himself, holding his face in his hands. When he covered his eyes, bright swirling fireworks exploded in the dark space of his skull. It was disorienting, the sensation of spinning, like being drunk, or strapped into some insidious carnival ride.

Martin headed outside to clear his head. Across the street, Terrell was getting in his old Ford. The elderly man looked over at Martin, then pursed his lips in a half-hearted smile—or had it been a grimace? Terrell backed from the driveway and vanished up the street. Like a faulty memory from childhood, a sudden thought jumped into Martin's head. Something Terrell had tried to recount to him a few days earlier regarding Falco's experiment with the glass tank. Evidently Falco had tried to explain to Terrell the basis of the experiment. The magician hadn't drilled down into the intricate details and calculations, but related to Terrell the main concept, that the cables created an electro-magnetic field, and as the iron train passed through the magnetic field it would create the harmonic dissonance necessary to attract lightning to the highest point in the surrounding area, which was the steel rod welded to the transformer on the telephone pole. The astounding power harnessed from the lightning strike would then complete the circuit back to the tracks, while the resistance of the water would function like a capacitor as the current surged through the water in the tank, releasing the electromotive force needed to exponentially compound the pressure in the tank to the maximum pascals necessary to convert Falco's brain waves into actual matter, or antimatter, to be more exact, creating an event horizon—of sorts—of pure energy. Martin had been dumbfounded by Terrell's impossibly lucid recounting of Falco's explanation, not understanding much of anything of it himself. Terrell stood like a post, eyes glazed over. Martin had been about to shake the odd man, when Terrell appeared to snap out of his trance, as if he'd been hypnotized. He continued his story, telling Martin that Falco had smirked, a wicked glint to his eye, adjusting the electrode-studded headgear crucial to the success of the experiment. Terrell never could be sure if Falco was pulling his leg, spewing out a bunch of mumbo jumbo until Terrell just turned away and went back home. Martin had no idea either; he didn't know anything about any of that stuff. Falco certainly seemed mercurial, and perhaps even filled with madness; the entire explanation to Martin's ears sounded absurd, but then so did particle accelerators and cliff diving.

Still confounded by Terrell's first-hand account of Falco's exploits, Martin stood another minute by his rusty mailbox, sizing up the barren, forgotten street (like a marker for the end of civilization) remembering the beautiful home he and Noreen had lived in all those years, the comfort and warmth, the pleasant neighborhood, the tidy green lawns. Glancing back at the bungalow, at the crappy asphalt shingle siding, the cracked sidewalks sprouted with bindweed, the field behind the house overgrown with nutsedge, dandelions and thistle, the smell of sizzling tar and creosote from the railroad tracks, Martin felt hollow, no longer able to feel the bottom of his stomach, as if every organ in his body had evaporated. The sensation of nothingness so unsettling, Martin believed he'd made a fatal miscalculation buying this crappy little shack.

Chapter Four

Martin decided to wait until dark. Maybe the light coming through the slats, wherever it was coming from, wouldn't be so bright. Some trickster portion of his brain had him convinced the anomaly was merely sunlight, the product of some weird refraction issuing from under the eaves, reflecting off the foil-covered moisture barrier of the insulation. And he was happy to comply with that unsound reasoning.

After finishing dinner and washing the dishes, he went to his car for his sunglasses, coming back into the house feeling kind of stupid. What did he need sunglasses for? But he did need them, the light as glaring as it had been earlier that afternoon. He used the hammer to pull the boards off, prying up one end, then the other, dazzling light pouring through the opening. Squinting beneath his sunglasses, he continued down the wall, removing boards, the entire room brighter than the inside of a 200-watt bulb. Martin recalled Terrell telling him about Falco's house, how some nights it looked like a UFO taking off, light shooting out all the windows. *It must look like that now,* Martin thought, trying to wrangle the last board off the wall. A second later, holding the last slat of old wood in his hand, Martin found himself staring into… nothingness—an impossibly radiant nothingness.

The essence of the blinding white space was boundless, palpable, a sensation unlike anything Martin had ever experienced. Standing in the luminous shimmering glow, Martin felt a disruptive current sizzling along his flesh, vibrating every cell of his body, a gleaming formless void, the absence of all thought, the emptied mind—*PURE POTENTIAL!* Anything. Anything Martin could possibly think, imagine, desire, he knew would manifest. He wasn't sure *how* he knew; he just did. And a moment later, there it was, the desire he had carried with him for almost fifteen years, to be able to speak with Noreen one last time before she passed, but not the comatose Noreen he recalled, lifeless and unmoving in her hospital bed. No, this was an alert Noreen. Martin could barely trust his eyes, his good fortune. An impossible second chance. He'd be able to see her smile one last time, hold her hand, kiss her lips, feel her warmth; get to live the moment stolen from him so many years ago.

Chapter Five

Kenny visited Martin during spring break, scanning the interior of Martin's new bungalow, commenting on every picture, letting his eyes crawl along the books stacked on the wooden shelf unit, obviously taking it all in slowly, as there was so little to actually see in the constricted space. Martin had done a good job utilizing every square inch, bringing only what he needed from his previous life, buying new, small and compact when necessary. The futon in the living room was actually quite nice; Martin had fallen asleep on it many times while watching television, unable to sleep some nights in his bedroom. Kenny told his dad that it was cool, that he liked the *intimacy* of the place, which Martin knew meant "cramped."

Martin laughed and said it was probably smaller than Kenny's dorm room, and Kenny told him he wasn't living in the dorm anymore, that he and some teammates had rented a house. Kenny was working at a high-end restaurant, making good tips six nights a week as a valet, doing some web work on the side, reminding Martin he had told him all that on the phone call at Christmas, when he had decided to stay in New Jersey for the holidays, that he had met a woman and they were getting on pretty well. Martin remembered the conversation now, so distracted with the house and all the repairs it had slipped his mind.

Entering the tiny room that shared the wall with the bathroom, Kenny asked, "What are you planning to do with this?"

Martin's breath caught for a second, a swell of dread mingled with exhilaration filling the empty hole in his chest. "I don't know, maybe some kind of… you know, *anything room.*"

"Anything room?" Kenny said, chortling a little.

"Yeah, you know, it can be *anything* I want it to be, right…" Martin said, picturing Noreen, how lovely she'd been when he'd seen her yesterday, how much he was missing her in that moment, especially standing here with his son, who was now a man. Martin's heart was breaking all over again. He wondered if Kenny missed her too, but didn't want to ask. It would be too hard. Martin was on the edge of tears as it was.

"Yeah, sure, why not…" Kenny said, ambling toward the back of the room, where the damaged wall had been covered over with wooden planks when Martin bought the house. It was now a plain wooden door, stained and varnished to match the other doors in the house.

"I'm thinking maybe a drafting table over there," Martin said to his son, pointing to the blank wall on Kenny's right, trying to distract him away from the door. "Maybe next to it just a small taboret with some of those skinny drawers, you know, for my pencils and X-acto knives, kneaded erasers, pushpins and whatnot." Martin paused a moment, watching his son ease closer toward the door. "Maybe a comfortable desk chair. And an easel on the opposite wall. A small one, of course. Should fit, don't you think?"

"They don't have you on computers at Petro, Dad?" Kenny asked, standing next to the lone door, reaching out to grab the knob.

"Yeah, of course they do, but sometimes I like going old-school, you know. Tracing pads, markers, Rapidograph pens…"

"You still have your Koh-I-Noors?"

"Are you kidding? I'll never get rid of those. I love those things. Hell, I still have a full set of Prismacolor pencils in the original case. Nothing will ever replace that stuff, not for me…"

Kenny chuckled, nodding and smiling toward his dad. "Good for you. Last of the great Luddites!" he said, gripping the doorknob, rattling it, the door obviously locked. "Where does this go?"

"Just a small closet," Martin said. "Keeping it for art supplies. Not much good for anything else. I'm thinking of painting again, keep canvases and stuff in there, you know, oil paints and such." Martin hated lying to his son.

"Good to hear you're getting back to your painting." Kenny released the doorknob and walked over to his father. "Ready to order pizza?"

Martin led his son from the room. "Tell me about this girl you're seeing, Anna, right? Is it serious?" Martin gave the door at the back wall one last glance before he reached over to flick off the wall switch, the room falling into darkness.

Chapter Six

A summer wedding. That's what Anna wanted, Kenny told Martin over the phone. Martin asked if they were going to wait until she graduated college and Kenny said no, that she only had one more year and they would stay in Jersey until she finished. Just after graduation, Kenny had landed a nice job at a marketing firm as an IT specialist, writing software and programs, designing websites for the firm and their clients, making decent money for someone just out of college. "Anna was able to quit her job to concentrate on school full time," Kenny told his dad on the phone. "We've got a tiny apartment, but we love it. About the size of your house." Kenny chuckled, then said, "Not really, probably about half that size." Kenny laughed and sounded so happy.

Martin smiled, happy for his son.

"So, can you make it up here in June?" Kenny said, a bit sheepishly, as if bracing for rejection. "You know, for the wedding!"

"Of course!" Martin would take time off from work, that it would be fun to get away for a few days. That wasn't really true but Martin wasn't about to miss his son's wedding.

"I wish mom could be here," Kenny added, letting the words hang there on the line, as if he planned to say more but couldn't. Tears had already formed at the rims of Martin's eyes. He gently brushed them away with a finger, his ribs so tight he felt he was being crushed from the inside. Noreen would love it, but there was no way, and Martin felt selfish and horrible for his deception, especially knowing what it would mean to Kenny to have her at his wedding, what it would mean to both of them. Just then Janelle stuck her head in the door of Martin's office.

"Just a second, Kenny, okay?" Martin placed his palm over the receiver. "Hey, how are you? You look beautiful as ever. Are we meeting with you guys today?"

"No, I was just over here talking with Bennet and thought I'd pop in to say hello," she said, smiling. "We still on for dinner tonight?"

"Of course. Want me to pick you up?"

"Naw, I'll meet you there. No sense you driving all the way out to my house then back down here, right."

"I don't mind. Aren't you staying at the office this evening? I can pick you up there."

"No, actually I have to leave a bit early today to go home. Beth needs some help with her homework and I've been gone so much lately—"

"We can do it another night," Martin said, almost wishing they would reschedule. He wasn't feeling up to an evening out.

Janelle mouthed the word, No, then smiled, blowing him a kiss as she left. He smiled after her, watching her legs scissor past the glass walls of his office in her high heels and tight skirt. She gave him one last smile as she looked over before disappearing down the hall.

"Hey, Kenny, sorry about that," Martin said, pulling the receiver back to his ear. "Brand manager of one of our biggest clients stuck her head in."

"Do you need to go?"

"No, I'm good. Tell me more about the wedding, where you're planning to have it."

Martin was glad Kenny had found someone. Kenny hadn't dated much in high school, so vexed by one unattainable girl, yet never able to get his mind off her. Vickie something or other. Martin couldn't remember her last name. He'd never met the girl but Kenny never stopped talking about her. "Just ask her out," Martin had told him. "What's the worst that could happen?" But Kenny insisted she was out of his league, and by the time he'd worked up the courage, she was dating someone else. And for the rest of high school, that's how it went, Kenny's cycle of fear and courage corresponding exactly with Vickie's cycle of being unattached and being in a relationship. She'd broken Kenny's heart and he'd never even kissed her, or held her hand, or went on a date. They barely talked, hardly knew each other, even though she attended most of the games, and he was the starting tight end on the football team. Martin always wondered if Noreen had still been around at that point if it would have made a difference, if her presence in Kenny's life might have given him more self-assurance in matters of the heart.

Martin had yet to tell Kenny about Janelle, that they had been dating for a couple of months. Martin wasn't sure if it was serious or not and wasn't sure he wanted to bring her into the equation. Plus, she was a bit younger, a few years, and with a daughter of her own, Beth, from a previous marriage. It seemed complicated, more so than Martin wanted in his life, even though he and Janelle enjoyed each other's company, going out to dinner, to movies, Martin spending the night at her home in West County when Beth spent the weekend with her father. Then getting to know Beth on Sundays after her father dropped her off at the house. She was the around the same age as Kenny had been when his mother was killed. Maybe a bit older. How odd, Martin thought, but didn't want to make anything too cosmically significant of it. A coincidence at best. Maybe not even that, just, well, nothing.

Janelle refused to stay at the bungalow. She had spent several nights and one weekend there, unable to sleep well with all the creepy noises, the weird neighbors, the trains flying by like spaceships at fifty miles an hour, the smell of hot creosote coming off the tracks, birds banging into the glass at the front windows, breaking their necks, falling dead on the concrete porch (it had only been two birds, but freaked her out just the same, as if it had been an entire Hitchcockian flock).

Martin had actually been relieved she didn't want to stay over anymore. It was uncomfortable having her amongst his things, physically standing in his secret life; totally unaware he even had one. The Anything room. Janelle had asked him only once about the tiny space, the plain wooden door at the back wall. When she approached it, Martin's biology responded with a sudden prickly sweat, soaking the armpits of his shirt. Martin's breath had caught, picturing Noreen just beyond that door, or some inexplicable version of her, washed in brilliant light, smiling with the same warmth he'd known and loved. It was impossible. He knew that, but the reality of her existence, whatever it was, couldn't be argued. Martin finally managed to wrestle out a few words to Janelle, explaining that the door led to nothing more than a small closet. Janelle had spun toward him, her eyes narrowed, accepting quickly the premise he'd put forth, as if she intuited his lie but didn't want to know more.

It was a constant, though unintentional, deception that made Martin sick with guilt and confusion. It didn't feel right, stringing her along, yet Janelle provided the only normalcy to his life, a steady reminder of sanity, providing the necessary guard rails of conventional existence. He felt he needed that, a proper balance to his strange new life with Noreen, the correct temperature to keep him somewhere between simmering and boiling over.

However, it wasn't the Anything room that bothered Janelle, or the curious door. It was the trains. Janelle hated them, and couldn't understand how Martin could live so close to railroad tracks. But Martin loved the way the earth quaked, the way the house trembled and floors squeaked, the way the sidewalks and streets cracked ever so slightly when the massive locomotives rumbled by, as if these leviathans from the industrial age still maintained a mystifying relationship to the raw, dark iron buried deep in the earth, ore communicating with ore, an ancient bond that couldn't be broken by man's ingenuity, or his ability to mine, smelt and forge this precious metal into new and alien forms. The memory remained, in the heart of the iron itself, magnetic, an invisible, indivisible force. Martin felt it. Falco must have felt it too, the magic of the place, the sheer power of motion, the barren expanse in some kind of charged, kinetic flux. Precariously balanced, as if it could all fly apart at any instant. The only thing holding this desolate, frenzied scrap of world in check, it seemed, was the lattice work of asphalt and concrete. And the tonnage of cold steel rail spiked to half-buried, oil-soaked deadmen.

Chapter Seven

F*antabulist*. Falco must have invented the word. At first Martin thought it meant tightrope walker, but that was a *funambulist*. Or maybe Falco had thought of himself a *fabulist*—a liar, inventor of elaborate dishonest tales. No, Falco must have just liked the word, feeling no real description of his wizardry existed. Actually, what Martin knew of Falco, (which was very little, in fact) led him to regard this *fantabulist* as more of an alchemist than a magician, a shaman of sorcery and the black arts.

Before Terrell died a month or so earlier, he'd told Martin about Berlina Miller, the elderly woman up the street who swore she saw Falco flying out over the field one night. "That old gal about lost her mind," Terrell had said, sweeping his arm toward the field. "Berlina claimed Falco was flying around like a daggone crow, just soaring and gliding. Next day she listed her place for sale. Course, places round here don't sell very well and all, so she was kind of stuck, like the rest of us..."

Martin could never explain Falco to Janelle. What Martin had learned about the reclusive magician from his neighbors, well, it went beyond normal eccentricity, bleeding into the otherworldly and bizarre, far too strange for a wealthy suburban soccer mom with an ex-husband (a dentist with a sweet tooth for young dental assistants), a twelve-year-old daughter and a shiny new Beemer in a garage filled with lawn equipment, hedge trimmers and swimming pool accessories. And Martin could never tell her about the Anything room, its secrets too mind-bending for almost anyone, including himself. He endeavored to make concessions to the rational side of his brain, offering up bribes of a sort, and practiced reassuring himself that he wasn't crazy. He vowed to monitor and regulate the pulse of his mental stability on a daily basis by reading the newspaper, watching ridiculous sitcoms on television, and spending absolutely normal evenings with Janelle at her very normal and traditional home, loading the dishwasher, helping Beth with school projects; the predictable marrow of a perfectly lucid and sensible life.

Though the tension at times—the dissonance between the two realities—was stretching him thin, hounding him to make a decision one way or the other. "Choose the life you want and stick with it," the voice at the back of Martin's mind would whisper when he was sitting in a dark theater with Janelle, or driving home from one of Beth's soccer games.

Chapter Eight

The wedding was off. Kenny was crying when he called Martin. It was difficult to understand his son, but what Martin could glean between outbursts of sobbing followed by silence, was that Kenny's lovely fiancée had engaged in a little fling with one of her professors, and though she'd told Kenny the affair was over, and promised it would never happen again, not a week later Kenny happened to catch her kissing the elderly academic in a coffee shop a few blocks from the university.

There was little Martin could offer in the way of consolation, but they talked on and off over the next few months. Kenny found a new apartment, one that didn't make him feel like hanging himself every time he got home from work. He made it a point to go out with friends, and had started freelancing websites for people he knew, and small business owners who couldn't afford the big marketing firms. Kenny joined a co-ed ultimate frisbee group and played at a park near his apartment complex, going out for food and beer afterward. All in all, he was bouncing back wonderfully. With Kenny more sound of mind and heart, Martin told him about Janelle, how they'd met, about her daughter, Beth.

"Did you think you couldn't tell me about her, Dad?" Kenny said

"Why would you say that?"

"Because you waited like... seven months to tell me..."

Kenny was right. Martin had put it off. Not so much for Kenny's sake as his own, never sure where he wanted his relationship with Janelle to go. (If you could call it that? But what else could you call it. Martin had never seen himself getting this involved with anyone again, ever.)

Several times Martin had come close to ending it, especially when Janelle wanted to spend more time together. She'd even proposed that he move in with her, *on a trial basis,* she was quick to point out. That would never work. Martin wasn't about to abandon the bungalow. Couldn't see himself not spending time with Noreen, holding her hand, hugging her, kissing her.

Eventually Janelle quit Cheffield Foods to work for a chain of local banks as branch manager, wanting to avoid any undue conflict between The Petro Agency and her previous employer, Cheffield. There had been rumblings from her higher ups at Cheffield, and Martin had tried to convince her that it wasn't necessary for her to quit her job, that he would ask Bennet to make him art director on another account. She wouldn't hear of it, telling him she was ready to move on anyway. Regardless, the sacrifice Janelle had made for their *relationship,* which Martin had never asked for, had left him feeling a bit indebted and off kilter, as if it were now up to him to move the ball forward, so to speak. He wasn't ready for it.

"Is it serious?' Kenny asked. "Am I going to have a little stepsister soon?"

Prickles of heat marched up Martin's back. Implied or not, there was obviously an expectation for Martin to act. What was he supposed to do? Ask Janelle to marry him? No, no, that was never going to happen.

"I guess it's serious," Martin finally said. "I don't think it's adding-more-members-to-the-Moffett-clan serious, but, you know…"

"Jeez, Dad, such a romantic. Is that how you see it?"

Martin exhaled, shaking his head back and forth. "I—" Then, silence. Martin had nothing else to offer, to add, he wasn't sure himself about anything… well, maybe one thing…

"Dad… Mom would want you to move on with your life."

"I have!" Martin shouted, trying to cool the embers in his chest, wanting to add, "And you have no idea what your mother would want! You can't possibly know! I do!" but said nothing, quickly changing the subject to ultimate frisbee, asking if it was anything like football. Kenny chuckled. "Not really," he said, probably recalling how physical football had been, a sport his son had excelled at.

Martin was relieved Kenny had laughed; feeling bad for his outburst, and so ready to move on from the subject of Janelle and marriage.

Chapter Nine

Falco's gateway. What could Martin say about it? It was, well, impossible, for one, and extraordinary in the most unfathomable, *extraordinary* way! The day Martin pulled off the last of the boards, and stood in the ethereal luminescence of the opening, he had slowly lowered his sunglasses, his eyes no longer burning from the bright formless light, transfixed. After several minutes, maybe even longer as time seemed to have no purchase anymore, Martin started feeling a peculiar, numbing tingle seep into his body, like warm oil, followed by an image forming before his eyes several feet away, vague at first, slowly gaining cohesion and detail until he recognized the room, the flowers and plants along the window sill, the blinds partly open, the tubes and IVs seemingly growing out from the figure in the hospital bed. Cautiously, Martin had stepped forward, expecting full well to fall through the vacuous space to be lost forever in light, but his foot landed on solid floor, then his other foot, until he was fully in the hospital room, standing next to the bed, looking down at Noreen, her face peaceful, distant. All the anguish of her coma and eventual death came rushing back, a torrent of pain and hurt like lightning shooting through his veins. He shuddered, feeling weak and sick to his stomach, until she opened her eyes.

"Martin! It's so good to see you." She sat up, using the control to raise the bed, the hum filling the room, matching the buzzing behind his eyes. She'd reached her hand out to him, and when he matched his palm to hers and held it tight, he had expected to feel the cold sting of death against his skin, but her flesh was warm and soft and she squeezed his hand. Noreen eased him closer, drawing him near enough to lean up and kiss him, saying, "I love you so much."

Martin visited her hundreds of times since that night, Noreen always waking from her coma as soon as he stepped into the room. And never once had he tired or become frustrated with their short visits, even knowing she would die that night after he left. The next visit she would wake up again, and they would sit and talk, or just sit and hold each other. Martin would tell her about Kenny, how he came to hate the Catholic grade school, but loved public high school, about his football scholarship to Rutgers, his fiancée who cheated on him, filling her in on everything she had missed. Eventually Martin and Noreen tested the boundaries of this alternative world by venturing out of her room to stroll the hallway, growing bolder over time, her dressing in jeans and a top to go for a walk around the hospital grounds. They were not bound by walls or barriers; they visited coffee shops near the hospital, or sat at a pizza joint, or watched the sun slowly dip toward the skyline of St. Louis, always returning before dark. They were never sure what would happen if they were away from the hospital when night descended on the city. One time, Martin, recalling Terrell's story about Falco and Mitzi, rented a stretch limo and toured downtown St. Louis, stopped for an afternoon Cardinal baseball game with hot dogs and beer, then parked on the landing to watch the Mississippi River drift by. Martin hated leaving her in that hospital room each night, walking back into his drab little bungalow and locking the door to the *Anything* room, but they would learn of no other way. As remarkable as Falco's gateway was, it came with rules and provisos.

Chapter Ten

Two years later Kenny met the perfect woman. They were getting married, a small plain affair, justice of the peace and witnesses, like a Vegas event without the slot machines and craps tables. Elaine had no real family to speak of, had been married before, no kids, but Martin was invited. Elaine had told Kenny she would love to meet his dad and Kenny had called to give Martin the news. Martin couldn't have been happier for his son, and told him he would attend, probably bring Janelle if that was okay. They, Martin and Janelle, had discussed getting married themselves, though each time they did Martin had to run back to his bungalow and hunker down, wrapping his small home around him like a security blanket. Some nights he'd drag his sleeping bag out to the backyard and bundle himself like a burrito, seated in the green and yellow lawn chair he'd bought at Walmart, thinking about the *Anything* room. About Noreen, the taste of her still on his lips.

When fog drifted across the field, a passing train would thunder through the vacant world like a shadowy, deafening wrath, its cycloptic eye burning a narrow swath of fire through the underworld, the ground shaking beneath the bare soles of his feet. A moment later it was gone, the world restored, bland again, uninteresting.

Martin and Janelle drove her BMW to the airport, Janelle behind the wheel, Martin in the passenger seat worrying the ink off his airline ticket folder, anxious about being gone for three days. Janelle took the ticket at the entrance to the short-term parking lot at Lambert and found a spot several minutes later.

"You going to be all right?" Janelle asked Martin as she pulled their suitcases from the trunk.

"What do you mean?" Martin said, his fist unconsciously crumpling his airline ticket.

"That…" Janelle said, eyeing the mangled ticket folder in his hand. "Are you afraid of flying?"

He said he wasn't, then jerked the handle out of his suitcase and started rolling it toward the terminal, unable to get his mind off his bungalow, caught in the strange ether between reality and fantasy. Janelle hurried to catch up, rolling her bag behind her, her heels clacking across the pavement.

They arrived in Newark and rented a car. It was less than a twenty-minute trip to the hotel. Kenny had offered to pick them up at the airport, but both Janelle and Martin wanted the freedom of their own transportation. After checking into the Radisson and changing clothes, they met up with Kenny and his fiancée, Elaine, at a restaurant Kenny had told them about. The Viking—steaks, seafood and a full bar, a nice restaurant with valet parking and a no-tie policy. After the introductions and hugs, they had cocktails and looked over the menus. Kenny informed them that the event had grown somewhat since they last spoke.

"We're going to have a short church ceremony, and a small reception at a local pub. Just some friends from work," Kenny said. Elaine added, "We both caught hell for trying to *elope*… that's what everyone at the office accused us of!"

Martin didn't care one way or the other, his mind was still in St. Louis. Janelle said she didn't know they worked together at the same marketing firm, and Elaine was quick to point out that they hadn't when they met, but one thing led to another, Kenny's boss offered her a job, and that was that.

"Kenny and I discussed it to death," Elaine pointed out, smiling over at Kenny to affirm their solidarity on the subject. "We have very different jobs, so there's never any real conflicts." Elaine went on to say that she was in sales and was usually gone from the office most of the day. "We hardly see one another until we get home at night," Kenny added, further proving the decision was sound. Martin sipped his highball and tried to stay focused, but his mind refused to stay moored to the evening.

About the time the discussion waned, the food arrived. While they ate, Janelle mostly talked about working at the bank, same headaches as working at Cheffield, problems always arising from employee drama and in-house clashes. "If it was just about managing the business, it would be a breeze, but it never is…"

Martin, not in a managerial position—just one of many *employees* at Petro Agency—wondered if Bennet ever saw him, Martin, as a source of annoying drama and friction. "What do you think, Dad?" Kenny asked, the question hitting Martin like a sucker punch.

Martin looked up from his plate, dazed. "What son?"

"Is in-house squabbling an issue at Petro Agency?"

Martin shrugged, unable to respond, utterly bored with the subject. He lifted his glass to his lips and sipped his drink. "Sorry, Kenny…"

After a few awkward seconds, Janelle said, "Your father is a bit distracted tonight." Janelle forced a phony smile and patted Martin's hand on the table. Then: "He's been really busy on a new account."

Martin, as well as Janelle, knew that wasn't true. Janelle didn't believe that for a second, not deep in the chamber of her chest where truth lived and self-deception had a difficult time getting air. Martin played along.

"Harley-Davidson," Martin said, wiping his mouth with his napkin. It was true they had landed the huge motorcycle account, but it wasn't distracting, not for Martin as assistant art director. Working with execs from H-D was easy and enjoyable, as they had a very clear vision of where they wanted to take the company, and so far, had been open to any ideas that accomplished their goal, or at least moved the chains. "We're rolling out a new campaign in a few weeks, just a few television spots at first, supported by print ads."

"Sounds exciting," Kenny said, attempting to be upbeat. Martin knew his son well enough to know that this small talk would put them both to sleep eventually.

"So, what's next tonight?" Martin said, as they were wrapping up dinner.

"Why don't you guys come by the apartment," Kenny said. "Elaine bought cheese cake, apple pie and ice cream. We can make some coffee and hang out."

They all agreed and walked to the parking lot after Kenny insisted on paying the bill. Martin hadn't haggled, that false dance people do; it wasn't the relationship he had with his son. They didn't play games. As far as going to the apartment, Martin wasn't really onboard, but going to Kenny's place was a better option than going back to the Radisson where Martin was sure to get an earful from Janelle about his vacant behavior. Maybe if they stayed at Kenny and Elaine's apartment late enough, Janelle would be too tired for battle when they got back to the hotel. How would this ever work as a marriage? Martin grew exhausted just thinking about it, wishing he'd been able to stay in St. Louis, wishing he were in his bungalow right now, sitting with Noreen.

Chapter Eleven

On the drive to Elaine and Kenny's apartment, Janelle talked on her mobile phone to her daughter, Beth, who was staying with Janelle's ex-husband until she and Martin returned from New Jersey. Martin drove, trying to keep up with Kenny through the fast and furious streets of Senterville content to have some time to himself, while Janelle—always several notches happier when she was speaking to her daughter—smiled and listened earnestly to her fourteen-year-old tell her about her two-week summer soccer camp and her swimming pool friends at her father's condo complex.

During the dark and quiet ride—like a familiar, but ghostly face in a dream—Terrell Brandeshire rose unexpectedly in the back of Martin's mind. He hadn't thought of Terrell in a long while. Though Martin had never met Falco or Mitzi, and had only Terrell's curious version of events, Martin now knew exactly where Falco and Mitzi were.

"Feeling any better?" Janelle asked Martin after ending her call with her daughter. Martin, still out of sorts by his recollection, glanced over at her, shifting his attention back to Kenny's taillights tangled in among the swarming red and white lights of traffic. "I feel just fine, Jan," he said, flustered with her assumption that his silence was a sign of something wrong. For some reason, Janelle saw Martin's reticence, and lack of need for constant conversation, as an indication of disappointment, or worse, secrecy, her suspicions and hovering a tiresome source of unending discussion and examination.

"You seem a million miles away," Janelle said. "What's bothering you, Martin?"

Up ahead, Kenny's right turn signal started flashing. Kenny switched lanes between cars, then switched lanes again, positioning himself to turn at the next exit. Flipping on his right turn signal, Martin checked the mirrors for an opening, then swerved into the next lane, waited for a pickup to pass, then switched lanes again, following Kenny's car up the exit ramp to the red light.

"I'd like to talk when we get back to the hotel tonight," Janelle said, her eyes reflecting the traffic.

Martin was going to say something when the light turned green, but didn't, focusing his attention on the second set of cars rounding the turn in the lane next to his. Some vehicles went straight through the light, while others, only two feet away from scraping door paint with the rental car, hurried down the main drag—speeding up, slowing down, hitting the brakes— jockeying for the lane they wanted to be in. Traffic in St. Louis was often bad, and Martin was used to it, but New Jersey traffic was a beast of a different kind, like nothing Martin had ever experienced. Soon they were racing down four clogged lanes of traffic, everyone a second away from disaster, Martin trying to keep pace with Kenny. They hurried through a glaring intersection of small businesses and restaurants—Dunkin Donuts, Burger King, Zippy Car Wash, Mobil, Shell, Starbucks—the road narrowing to two lanes as it reached into the darkness of an industrial area with huge condo and apartment complexes on the left—lots of trees and shrubs—and sprawling tree-strewn-grass-islanded corporate parks on the right, lighted concrete signs marking the entrances with graphically smart medical logos, a traffic light at each entrance, the lights all green as far as Martin could see. By now three other vehicles had wedged themselves in between Kenny and Martin. Anytime a car or truck signaled a left turn across oncoming traffic and slowed to a stop, the cars behind would race around the turning car using the gravel shoulder as another lane. It was madness, but everything moved too fast to take umbrage.

About a half-mile ahead Kenny turned on his left signal, the FedEx van in front of him also signaling a left. Martin had just turned his on when the FedEx van rabbited across the oncoming traffic lane, Kenny on his bumper squeezing in his left turn in front of a line of glaring headlights bearing down on him, the cars behind Kenny racing past on the shoulder to his right, no one slowing. Martin's heart raced as he tapped the brakes lightly about to make his left behind Kenny, catching Janelle from the corner of his eye. She was tensing, her right foot using the phantom passenger brake on her side to help slow the car. Cars roared around Martin on the shoulder to the right, spewing gravel, clouds of dust burning red in the wake of their taillights. One more set of headlights and Martin was going for his turn, the rental still creeping slowly forward. The headlights zoomed past and Martin levered the car hard to the left, feeding it gas, more headlights approaching, the front of the rental rising slightly as it shot into the safety of the condo development entrance. Janelle let out a sigh as she sank back into the seat.

Martin's breathing settled following Kenny through a maze of streets, parked cars and buildings, coming to a stop in front of a three-story condo. Kenny was out of his car, directing Martin to pull in the spot next to his Volvo.

Janelle got out and immediately went over to where Elaine was standing and the women started talking as if continuing their discussion from the restaurant. Seemingly oblivious to Martin and Kenny, the women climbed the exterior stairwell connecting the two buildings, laughing and chatting, their high heels clattering along the steel reinforced concrete steps. Kenny came over to his father, smiling and animated, and told him how glad he was that he and Janelle made the trip.

"You live on the third floor?" Martin asked, looking up at Janelle and Elaine who were nearing the top, their voices, like soft feathers, settling down to street level.

"I think the development purposely decided against elevators to discourage the elderly from buying here," Kenny said, pulling a satchel from the trunk of his Volvo, that Martin figured contained a laptop computer. Kenny slammed the trunk and walked back toward his father.

"Well, that would do it," Martin said, still looking at the stairwell.

Elaine unlocked the door at the top floor and the women disappeared inside, the door closing with a soft whoosh and click.

"You doing okay, Dad," Kenny asked, coming up and placing his hand on his father's back.

Martin rolled his head toward him. "Yeah, son, really, I'm fine."

"I know the Harley account's not bothering you," Kenny said, thoughtfully. "Work stuff never got you down."

"Just things, Kenny," Martin said, wanting to tell his son he was having difficulties of a metaphysical nature! How stupid did that sound?

"Hey, well, let's get dessert," Kenny said, leading the way toward the steps. Martin fell in behind him, Kenny climbing briskly, as if in New Jersey the tempo and harried pace of driving informed every other action. Martin didn't bother trying to keep up, content to lose a step or two at each landing. "How about that traffic?" Kenny said, twisting back without stopping.

"Yeah, I think it aged me like ten years."

At the top landing Kenny swiveled back to check his father's progress.

"I'm still here," Martin said, starting to breathe a little harder. Kenny pushed the door open and waited just inside for Martin. When Martin reached the landing he paused a moment to collect himself. "There must be a good reason you chose to live on the top floor!" Martin said, still slightly out of breath. Kenny just gave him a mischievous grin.

As soon as Martin entered the condo, he knew why—fourteen-foot vaulted ceilings with huge skylights, a stone fireplace from floor to ceiling, a bank of glass sliding doors with a view of a small city in the distance, like a blanket of stars lying in the valley below.

"Impressive," Martin said, slowly plodding across the carpeted floor. In the kitchen off the great room, Elaine and Janelle were still talking, snickering at times—like sisters long separated—the refrigerator opening and closing with that distinctive rattle of glass against glass. Janelle pulled plates down from the cabinet and arranged them on the island counter top that divided the kitchen from the great room. Elaine was pulling the cover off the cheese cake. "Who wants ice cream with apple pie... or, cheesecake, or both?"

"Nothing for me right now," Martin said, standing at the glass doors. Kenny walked over and stood next to him.

"They're getting along well, Janelle and Elaine," Kenny said. "I'm glad."

Martin asked, "Why?" without turning toward him.

"I dunno. Looks like you guys are serious." Kenny fell quiet a moment, the women talking in the kitchen, the tinkling of silverware on the countertop. "Is that the friction? Something with you and Janelle?"

"Not that simple, Kenny."

Kenny nodded, taking his eyes out to the darkness beyond the glass.

"It's ready, fellas," Elaine said, walking to the table near the sliding glass doors. As Martin turned to walk over, Kenny said, "So, can we expect a new addition to the family soon?"

Janelle, who was carrying the cheese cake to the table looked up startled. Martin stiffened, grimacing at Kenny. "I mean a new motorcycle," Kenny quickly added, realizing the implication.

Martin relaxed and stood next to a chair, waiting to learn of the seating arrangement. "Sit anywhere," Elaine said. Janelle came over and sat, motioning for Martin to sit next to her. Martin looked down at her a moment, then pulled the chair out.

"Dad rode motorcycles since he was sixteen," Kenny said, smiling as if to diffuse any residual tension in the room. "Harley going to make you a great deal?"

Janelle and Elaine seemed to ignore the conversation about Harley-Davidson, their discussion focused on children, Janelle telling her about Beth turning fourteen and morose, hoping it was just a phase, Elaine laughing, recalling to Janelle her own travails at that schizophrenic age. Martin hesitated a moment, then slid a slice of cheesecake onto his plate.

"Actually, they are," Martin said. "The marketing manager from Harley gave me the name of a dealer in St. Louis and told me to contact him when I was ready." Elaine seemed not to notice Martin's comment, while Janelle fell suddenly quiet, fidgeting in her seat.

"Are you?" Janelle finally said, Elaine falling silent, chewing a piece of pie. Kenny sipped his water. "Are you going to buy a motorcycle?" Janelle asked.

Martin regarded her blankly. "Of course," Martin said without glee. "I'm not going to pass up an opportunity like that." A heavy silence hung over the table, the hum of the refrigerator supplying the only noise in the condo.

"Who wants coffee?" Kenny said, standing up.

"Oh crap!" Elaine shouted. "I forgot all about starting the coffee!"

"I'll get it going," Kenny said. "Finish your pie."

When Janelle asked how many bedrooms the condo had, Elaine got up and told her she would give her the nickel tour. Both women left the room chatting, leaving Martin sitting at the table by himself. Kenny returned and said the coffee would only be a few minutes.

"Is the balcony door unlocked?" Martin asked.

"Yeah, it should be nice out there now. Usually gets pretty cool at night."

Martin got up and walked to the door and slid it open, then stepped onto the balcony and shut the door behind him. When Martin looked back, Kenny was gone, most likely back to the kitchen. Martin let his eyes drift over the twinkling lights far in the distance, the sound of traffic a faint, shushing noise with the occasional groan or whine of a motorcycle. Martin loved the idea of having a bike again, though he'd never been able to afford a Harley before. But where would he park it? The driveway, probably, next to the bungalow, or maybe in the backyard. He'd get a cover for it. Or not. And Janelle? Would she ride with him? Did he want her to?

"Ready for coffee, Dad?" Kenny said, poking his head out the door. Martin hadn't heard him open the glass slider.

"Sure. Sounds good," Martin said, following his son into the great room.

Elaine and Janelle were already seated at the table, Janelle had her legs crossed, sitting back relaxed, holding her coffee cup in both hands, smiling over at Elaine who was sharing something funny, her hands animating the story.

"Decaf or high octane?" Kenny asked Martin.

"I'll take the real deal," Martin said, pulling out the chair next to Janelle. When Janelle looked up at him he smiled, then sat down.

Kenny brought the coffee over as Elaine was explaining how they, she and Kenny, planned to sell the condo and buy a house.

"I have my broker's license now, so I have access to all the listings as soon as they hit the market. I'm not ready to quit my job yet, so I'm doing it on the side for a while." Elaine told her that they hoped to start a family soon and neither of them wanted their children to grow up in a condo.

"It just feels so… I don't know," Elaine said, looking over at Kenny for help. "Impersonal, maybe?" Elaine added, still fishing for the right word. "Transient, I guess." Then: "You know?"

Janelle nodded and agreed wholeheartedly, saying that Beth had loved having the backyard to play in, her own swing set and glider. "So much more privacy. And the trees and birds, not that you don't have trees and birds here," she tried to explain, laughing, "but, Beth loved watching them land in the birdbath, splashing their wings. It was so cute."

Elaine was smiling, glancing over at Kenny. Martin sat like a grim ogre, unable to enter the conversation, not because it lacked an opening, but because he had nothing to add about any of it; no opinions one way or the other on birdbaths or swing sets or raising a child in a condo or house. All the years with Kenny he had just tried to do his best, moving through each day on autopilot, hoping he didn't make a mess of his son's psyche requiring years of therapy and analysis. And even with Martin not having any real plan for parenthood, Kenny seemed to turn out okay, at least so far.

By the time Martin came present again, Janelle and Elaine had moved on to the wedding, Elaine showing Janelle a magazine with some of the dresses she had thought about buying, Janelle remarking on how lovely they were. Kenny excused himself to the bedroom to make a phone call. Martin checked his wristwatch, looking over at Janelle, downing the last of his coffee. Janelle must have sensed Martin becoming antsy, turning toward him. "Think we should get going?" she said softly, almost lip syncing the question.

"Yeah, it's late," Martin said, standing. Then: "So Elaine, how do we get back to the Radisson from here?"

"It's simple," she said. Now all of them were standing. Kenny came out of the back bedroom.

"Taking off?" Kenny said.

"Yeah," Martin said. "The Radisson?"

"Just go back out to the entrance we came in," Kenny said, Elaine watching him, nodding. "Hang a left and go about five miles. The Radisson will be on the right. Can't miss it!"

Martin hugged Elaine and kissed her cheek, then hugged Kenny, holding him close, then almost in a whisper, said, "I love you, Son."

Janelle hugged Elaine and asked if they should bring anything tomorrow. Elaine said they were good. Janelle hugged Kenny and everyone chimed their goodbyes. Kenny and Elaine stood at the open door, light from the condo illuminating the landings of the stairwell, as Janelle and Martin carefully descended the steps, holding to the railing, Martin stealing one last glance over his shoulder at his son. He hated parting from Kenny.

Chapter Twelve

At the hotel, Janelle appeared content to let everything drop—the motorcycle, the conversation she had mentioned they should have when they got back, Martin's moodiness, his silence on the drive from the condo, all infractions that would have sparked at least an hour-long discussion, possibly more. Janelle hadn't even mentioned how lovely Elaine was, which was out of character for Janelle, especially given how she and Elaine had gotten on all evening. No, Janelle said nothing from the time they left the condo.

She headed into the bathroom for a shower. Martin sped through the channels on the television, replaying the evening, hoping Kenny hadn't been upset by his sullenness and—at least bordering on—antisocial behavior. Janelle was most likely very upset about everything; maybe so angry she couldn't even begin to discuss the multitude of offenses Martin had committed. And just like that, Martin's mind was on Noreen, how they'd had their fights, disagreements, the *silent-treatment* spats, yet always came together, found some inch of common ground to plant the peace flag. Mostly his time with Noreen had been marvelous, full of wonder and fun, slopping their way through life like a couple of springer spaniel puppies, laughing and crying, holding each other when the world got too heavy for just one person. Compromise had been the cornerstone of their relationship, Martin dragging Noreen to Cardinal baseball games, and Noreen dragging Martin to

Jefferson Airplane concerts. They drove Martin's 750 Shadow to Chicago in the summer to visit the Art Institute, maybe catch a Cubs-Cardinal afternoon game, and finish off the evening at The Navy Pier gorging on junk food and riding the enormous Ferris wheel. At night they made love in a high-rise hotel overlooking Lake Michigan, then watched the tossing lights of trawlers out on the horizon. When Kenny came along they took him to the Forest Park Zoo to laugh and coo and point his chubby little finger at the zebras and orangutans, then to Grant's Farm to see the Clydesdales, then, as he got older, to Six Flags to go on the crazy rides, Martin watching from the pavement eating popcorn, Noreen sitting next to Kenny on the Highland Fling, or one of those insane roller coasters, both of them screaming like maniacs. They took turns helping Kenny with homework, Noreen on math and science, Martin on geography and English. Noreen tended a garden in the backyard of their home, while Kenny helped Martin wash and wax his 750, letting Kenny sit on the shiny black gas tank, leaning forward to grip the handlebars. People sometimes mentioned in jest about "living the dream," but Martin and Noreen actually were, and Martin believed it would never end.

The shower went off and Martin pictured Janelle standing in the tub drying herself, the curtain pulled back, her long legs sprinkled with water droplets, her lovely breasts round and soft, her chestnut hair stringy wet and shiny, hanging down her back. She was beautiful, the body of a grad student, the classic high cheekbones and full lips of a film star, the intelligence of a nuclear physicist. She deserved better than Martin, though Martin wasn't sure she understood that. Her husband had treated her badly, no doubt, a cheating, lying fool. But instead of making Janelle more resolute in her independence, her husband's disrespect and mistreatment had had the opposite effect, destroying her self-esteem and confidence. And even though Martin understood the unsavory dynamic of their relationship (Martin's and hers)— her unshakable tolerance of his disregard for her feelings— Martin was unable to alter his behavior, often taking advantage of her in the same way her husband had, not cheating on her, but ignoring her existence. He hated himself for it, but felt powerless to do anything about it. Even when attempting to be vigilant regarding his own self-awareness of their dysfunctional bond, he would unknowingly lapse into his role as tormenter and heartless bastard. She would get quiet, or go outside to read on the porch swing, or go grocery shopping. When she'd return, everything would be fine again, telling Martin about something the heroine said or did in the romance novel she was reading, or the price of avocados, or how she and Martin could help Beth improve her C to a B in history. And he cared about her, even though it hardly ever showed in his actions.

If he could tell Janelle about the *Anything* room at the bungalow, about Falco the *Fantabulist* and the inexplicable gateway he had created, Martin could stop making excuses and telling lies, could stop tiptoeing around in Janelle's heart and commit to something real, could move forward with clarity and honesty, even love, maybe.

From the sound of the buzzing in the bathroom, it was apparent that Janelle was brushing her teeth for bed. Martin thought back to his last visit with Noreen before coming to New Jersey. He had been packing and feeling horrible for leaving, but didn't want to miss Kenny's wedding. Martin had unlocked the door to the *Anything* room and stood in the light until Noreen came into view, the room solidifying, the antiseptic hospital smell drifting past him. "Martin!" She was always excited to see him, and his heart turned to helium when she smiled. Months ago, Martin had told Noreen about Janelle, and Janelle's daughter Beth, and that he and Janelle had become serious, or serious enough, but Martin still wasn't sure. He wanted to be certain Noreen knew why he wouldn't be coming to see her for a few days. He explained that he was going to New Jersey for Kenny's wedding. Noreen had smiled, sadness mingled with joy, a tear forming at the corner of her eye. "Better put it behind you now," she said, reaching out for his hand. "What are you talking about?" Martin said, holding her hand in his. "You shouldn't come here anymore, Martin." Noreen pulled his hand to her chest and held it against her heart. "You have a woman who obviously loves you. Devote yourself to her, Martin. Make a life with her. Kenny's going to want kids, and pretty soon, you're going to be a grandfather, with grandchildren to spoil, presents to buy, little ones to babysit for. You need to be focused, Martin, present in Janelle's life. Present in yours... and Kenny's. Don't miss out on one of the most important times of your life." He was about to argue with her, his heart in pieces, tears rolling down his cheeks, but he didn't want to fight. He wasn't even sure what he felt for Janelle, not exactly anyway. He enjoyed her company, and they shared intimacy and laughter on occasion, and he loved Beth, but, choosing between spending one day with Noreen, or a lifetime with Janelle, well, didn't seem like much of a contest. Noreen would win every time.

"I have to go," Martin said, unwilling to release Noreen's hand. "I'll see you when I get back."

Noreen smiled and released his hand. "Think about what I said, Martin."

"I wish you could be there," Martin said. "At Kenny's wedding. He would really love that." Noreen had smiled and seemed distant.

"I love you," Martin had told her.

"I love you, Martin," Janelle said, standing naked next to the bed. She eased in under the blankets. "Please join me... okay?"

Martin got up and undressed and switched the television off, slipping beneath the covers. Janelle pulled him close to her, her body warm and soft, and with the side of her face resting on his chest, Martin felt a warm tear trace down the path of his torso, followed by another. "I love you so much, Martin," she said, her voice muffled against his skin. Her tears were flowing now, weaving trails through his chest hair, and Martin felt something break loose inside him, static electricity running beneath his skin, a raw mix of heat and cold, vowels and consonants coalescing into words, rising in his throat like butterflies fluttering to life.

"Let's get married," Martin said. "Let's do it soon."

Chapter Thirteen

On his son's wedding day, Martin wanted to hold off announcing that he and Janelle were getting married. It was Kenny and Elaine's day, and Martin didn't want to scratch any of the sheen off his son's special event. Martin and Janelle had a nice breakfast in the hotel, acting like newlyweds themselves, smiling and holding hands across the table. Martin couldn't tell if he was genuinely happy, or just happy to have made a decision. Eventually the subject of their future came up, how each of them saw the next few years of their lives, which somehow dovetailed into the topic Martin had been waiting for; the motorcycle. He'd hoped to postpone that debate until they were back in St. Louis.

"I've never been on a motorcycle before," Janelle said, her teeth showing when she smiled, as they always did when she was pleased.

"No?" Martin said.

"It sounds exciting," Janelle said. "I can't wait." Then: "Will I need one of those black leather jackets?"

Martin laughed, more from surprise than the joke, at least he believed it was a joke. Maybe he didn't know Janelle as well as he thought. He had expected her to be set against it, listing all the dangers, quoting motorcycle death statistics from some magazine article she'd read, or refuse to have a smelly thing like that around her house.

"If you buy a black leather jacket you know what you'll become?" Martin said.

"Dangerously desirable?"

Martin laughed. "Yes, that… and a biker chick!"

"Hmmm… biker chick! I can do biker chick!"

Martin felt a stirring of arousal when the conversation swerved off in a direction he had never imagined. He finished his coffee, wiped his mouth and stood, grabbing her hand. "Come on, let's get up to the room and get dressed or we're going to be late."

"Late?" Janelle said, her brow furrowed with surprise. "We have over three hours…"

"I know!" Martin said. "Let's go."

By the time the elevator doors closed, he had her blouse almost completely undone, while she was undoing his jeans. When the doors opened, they poured out into the hallway and dashed toward the room, giggling, Janelle trying to hold her blouse together, Martin practically dragging her by the arm. Barely inside the room, they settled for the narrow hallway leading to the bedroom. Janelle moaned, her back stuck against the wallpaper, their clothes scattered along the carpet. The ironing board hanging near the entrance door shook and banged, making a racket that could probably be heard down at the check-in desk. They finished quickly, then raced toward the bed, holding each other, kissing one another beneath the blankets until Martin rebounded. They went another half-hour until they were spent, completely shot. Martin fell asleep and Janelle took a shower, waking Martin up when she came out.

"Martin," she whispered, shaking him softly by the shoulder. "This time we really will be late if we don't get a move on." He opened his eyes and pulled her naked body down on top of him, her towel falling away. She laughed, kissing his nose, his forehead, then his lips. "Your libido is obviously no longer on speaking terms with your penis," she said, taking his flaccidness in her hand.

"Who cares, we'll find something else to do," he said, tenderly kissing her breasts, sliding his tongue down her tummy.

"God yes, who cares," she moaned.

When they finished, Janelle hurried into the bathroom to put makeup on, while Martin yanked fresh clothes from the closet, rush-ing, as if trying to get everything on at once. "We are definitely getting you a black leather motorcycle jacket," he said, jogging over to zip her dress, then kissing the back of her neck. "Whether I get the motorcycle or not."

Chapter Fourteen

At the reception, after Martin finished dancing with Elaine, Kenny remarked to him that he seemed in much better spirits. "Yeah…" Martin said, then, "Elaine is a lovely person, Kenny. You are both so lucky to have one another." Martin was truly happy for his son. And was glad Kenny had noticed his better disposition, though he couldn't tell him what had brought about this miraculous transformation. But it wasn't just the sex. Martin felt a new buoyancy, a more hopeful and forward-looking vision of the future. His realization that Janelle wasn't quite as traditional as he'd originally thought (a trait he both admired in her, and detested at times; one of the strange ironies of their relationship), had sparked a new fervor in him, had roused excitement over the prospect of exploring this more playful side of her personality.

Would it last? Who could say? These were important questions, or so it seemed, but how could anyone know if what they were feeling was real, or enduring? After all, every emotion had its own gravity, its own authenticity and was absolutely *fact* when someone felt it, and convincingly so, until the emotion changed, becoming something else altogether. In a movie theater for instance, it wasn't at all unusual that a person, at some point during the movie, would forget they were watching projected images on a screen, and suddenly find themselves leaning back from an intruder, their adrenaline pumping, *feeling* actual fear and trepidation. Did that negate emotion as merely a product of fantasy? Could feelings, emotions, not be trusted as being anymore authentic or real than dazzling projected images on a white screen? Just as Martin was beginning to dig deeper into these perplexing questions, Janelle slipped up behind him and wrapped her arms around his waist, her hands resting just below his belt—sending a tingle through his lower abdomen—then kissed his neck. A luscious shiver rose up his spine. "Will you dance with me?" she whispered, her breath warm in his ear.

He turned toward her, his eyes finding hers as though they were the only ones in the room. "It all depends," he said. "You never told me what you thought." She moved in closer, pressing her breasts against him. She used her tongue to trace the dimple in his chin.

"I have no idea what you're talking about, sir."

"You don't?" He studied her expression to see if she was playing with him. "When I said we should get married... you never told me what you thought about the idea."

Janelle held his eyes. "Dance with me... and maybe I will."

They had just finished their fourth song in a row when Martin announced he was beat. They went over and sat down, Martin sipping his melty, watered-down drink. Janelle's glass was empty. "Want another?" Martin asked, touching her hand. Janelle, looking past Martin, nodded her head toward something going on behind him. Martin turned to see Kenny and Elaine standing near the bar, Elaine's gestures animated, her mouth working painfully, like she was chewing glass, Kenny's arms at his sides, mouth hanging open, the couple apparently in the middle of a nasty dispute. And by all indications, Kenny was not faring well.

"Why don't you wait a few minutes before you go for drinks," Janelle said. Even though it was natural for couples to fight—healthy, in fact; he and Noreen had had some doozies—Martin hated seeing them at each other. Mostly he felt bad for Kenny, wondering what his son had done to make Elaine so angry.

Martin checked his watch, then eased his wrist toward Janelle. "Maybe we should get going," Martin said. Janelle nodded, standing, taking her purse from the back of the chair. By now Elaine was gone and Kenny stood near the bar by himself, his tie undone, his jacket gone, his shirttail hanging out of his trousers on one side. "I'm just gonna talk to Kenny a second," Martin said. Janelle nodded and walked toward the ladies' room.

"You heading out?" Kenny said when Martin approached.

"Yeah. It really was a wonderful ceremony and all." Then: "You okay?"

Kenny nodded, tipping his glass back, finishing his drink. Martin had never seen his son drunk before, or at least not completely sober; nonetheless, he was certainly not himself. Martin had never considered that Kenny, when he was in college, was probably drunk plenty, maybe even in high school, though Martin had never caught him. And drugs. Had Kenny tried pot, or perhaps even cocaine? God-only-knew what Kenny might have tried in college, or after college, or was still trying even now, last night, or last week. And when Martin *could* imagine all the possibilities, it gripped his heart like a vice. He wanted everything to go right for Kenny, protect him from the worst life had to offer, but was that realistic? Martin hadn't protected his son from anything as far as he could tell—the kid had already lost his mother at eleven! How right could it go after that?

Kenny looked over at Martin with tears along the lower ridges of his eyes.

"Kenny, what's going on?" Martin finally said.

"It's nothing. It's stupid." Kenny glanced across the room as if he were waiting for someone. "I want to move back to St. Louis, and Elaine and I have talked about that, but... fuck, I don't know..."

"I didn't know you were thinking about moving back."

Tears started streaming down Kenny's cheeks and he stepped closer and took Martin in a hug, shuddering, sobbing in his father's arms. Martin returned the embrace, his own chest hollow, himself at the edge of tears. After a minute or two Kenny said, "I miss you so much, Dad." Martin felt his eyes water, trying to wipe them dry with his finger.

Kenny cleared his throat and pulled back from Martin. He sniffled and wiped his eyes. "We were supposed to start driving to Maine tonight, you know, the honeymoon and all..." Kenny said, still sniffling.

"You're not going?" Martin said, trying to dry his own eyes without making a big deal of it.

"We're going... just not till morning, but..." Kenny took a deep breath. "I don't know how much longer I can stand it up here. I mean, it's not like it's terrible, but jeez, Elaine has no family here. Her mother's shacking up with some painter in Paris, and her dad's dead. She has no brothers or sisters. Fuck, she doesn't even have cousins. And what do I have? The only family I've ever known is in St. Louis! And that's you!"

Martin had no idea Kenny was so miserable.

"I've been in contact with a firm that has offices near Union Station. And they are very interested. I was planning to fly out in a few weeks, but it seems pointless! Elaine had been on board when I was in conversations with these guys. Now she won't budge! She's got this fucking broker's license now and doesn't want the hassle of getting another one in St. Louis... and, damn, everything just.... Sorry. I didn't mean to drop all this on you..."

"Listen, you can drop anything on me, Kenny. I'm glad you said something. Maybe she'll come around on the honeymoon. Or maybe there's a compromise you two haven't considered yet..."

Kenny sniffed and dragged his fingertip under his eye. "You have an early flight tomorrow, don't you?" Kenny said. "Go. Get some sleep. I think it's just the alcohol's got me spooled up." Then a moment later. "If I come out in a few weeks to meet with these guys I'll stay with you if that's okay?"

"You never have to ask that, Kenny." Martin hugged him again. Even though patting each other's back to end a hug hadn't been part of their routine, they did it this time, then smirked at each other for doing it. "Okay, so, I need to find Elaine," Martin said. "Tell her goodbye."

"Come on, I'll walk you out. I saw her go outside a while ago."

"I need to find Janelle first."

"They went out together," Kenny said, leading his dad toward the doors.

On the parking lot Janelle and Elaine were immersed in conversation, or consolation, as Janelle took a step closer to Elaine and pulled her into her arms. It was obvious, even from a hundred feet away, in the dark, that Elaine was crying.

"What a night," Martin said under his breath.

Martin started walking toward them, Kenny following. When the two women noticed them coming, Elaine stepped back from Janelle and wiped her eyes. Janelle turned toward Martin with a strained smile.

The couples hugged and traded goodbyes. Janelle smiled at Kenny and Elaine, thanked them for everything, then popped open the passenger side door and slid in. Martin gave a low wave and smile as he shuffled around the car, and was just about to get in when Kenny came over and stood by the door. "Call me when you get your bike, okay?" Kenny said, then hugged Martin again. "I love you, Dad."

"I will, Son," Martin said. "I love you, too."

Chapter Fifteen

Watching his dad back out of the parking spot, Kenny felt the air go out of him. His dad guided the rental away from the reception hall, the taillights shrinking down the empty street and disappearing around the corner. Kenny was on the brink of tears again, his breath trapped in his chest. Elaine lingered a moment, then turned to go back inside without a word.

When Kenny looked over she was already gone. The night air was cool, and swollen with humidity, as though about to rain. Kenny looked up at the sky—dark milky gray, void of stars—and was seized by a terrible, paralyzing loneliness. The wedding, the vows, the dancing and music, the drinking and laughter and celebration, now all seemed as if it had happened a decade ago. Or not at all. Like some elaborate hallucination. Miserable and a little woozy from drink, Kenny sat on the concrete steps of the reception hall, a few raindrops spotting the pavement. If Elaine wouldn't agree to move to St. Louis, Kenny wasn't sure what he'd do, no longer able to imagine a life in New Jersey, the thought tightening around him like a python. Why hadn't they discussed it more, worked out the details? Why hadn't Kenny pushed for a more definitive answer, a solid decision without the gray area? How had this gone so wrong?

Kenny felt two hands on his shoulders. A soft voice said, "Come inside, baby, you're getting soaked." Kenny hadn't been aware he was even wet. He looked up at Elaine, water dripping from his eyebrows and chin, and started crying. She pulled his hand up gently to get him to his feet, then hugged and kissed him, wrapping her arms around his waist. "Let's take care of things inside," she said. "And head home."

Elaine was talking with her friends, who had agreed to handle clean-up and ferry the presents to the condo. The small group of young women were talking and laughing. Kenny stood by himself near the tables, watching like a voyeur, or a ghost. After a few moments, he started searching the chairs and tables for his tuxedo jacket, turning the last forty-eight hours over in his mind—dinner at the restaurant with his dad and Janelle, dessert at the condo, his dad alone on the balcony, gloomy, the wedding ceremony, Elaine breathtaking in her wedding gown, the reception, dancing with Elaine, her eyes sparkling, then dancing with women from work, dancing with Katherine, the account exec, how warmly she had melted into his arms, the argument with Elaine, the guilt over not being completely honest with his father.

The spat with Elaine had started over Kenny's desire to set a date for moving to St. Louis, that was true, but the part about how closely Kenny had danced with Katherine, how upset it had made Elaine, Kenny had left out. Elaine had never been overly jealous, and Kenny had never given her reason to be, but tonight was different, the innocent dance burrowing into Elaine's heart like an auger. At work, Kenny had noticed Katherine's tenderness toward him, but had no interest in her other than a friend, and even though the dance had brought just a tinge of arousal, it was nothing Kenny would ever act upon. But to Elaine, Katherine was young, beautiful, available, and had access to Kenny at the office on a regular basis.

Kenny, his mind working like an automated piece of machinery—not at all focused on finding the rental jacket—churned through myriad unrelated thoughts, conveying them forward, rolling them back, spilling them down chutes, spinning them through sorters. Suddenly he found himself back at Normandy High in St. Louis, a drunken night out with teammates, running into Vickie Kramer at a burger joint. Beer had given him the courage to walk up to her and say hello. She had smiled—he could still see that smile, her long brown hair, her smooth cheeks and pale lips—and she'd asked what he was doing. Kenny stammered and said something stupid about... he couldn't even remember, he'd been so wasted. The guys he was with had their bags of food and were leaving and Kenny had wanted to stay, and Vickie stood, waiting for him to stay, or so he imagined, and the guys yelled, jeering and merciless, "Come on, Muppet!" the nickname he hated. But his mind had been in spin cycle and he'd said something ridiculous like, "See you at school!" then turned and hustled out the door with his buddies, joking and laughing, roughhousing with one another, his heart withering with self-disgust. Even now, all these years later, the memory filled him with the oily, bitter heat of shame and remorse. He couldn't believe he still thought about her.

"Hey, Mr. Moffett. You ready to take your wife home?"

He looked over at Elaine. "Sure, as soon as I find my jacket."

"It's in the car. I found it earlier, lying under one of the tables."

Kenny shook his head, his face flushing. "Thank you, Mrs. Moffett... I hope you like that name?"

"I do," she said. "It has a certain *Lord of the Rings* feel to it!" Then: "No, really, I do love it! And I love you... so, let's hit the sack so we can start driving in the morning, get this honeymoon on the road!"

"Listen," he said, holding her wrist, the hand with her wedding ring. "I'm sorry about earlier..."

"So am I," she said, taking both his hands in hers. "And we'll talk about St. Louis some more too, okay." She gave him a peck on the lips. "I mean, how bad can it be out there?"

Kenny scoffed, rolling his eyes. "Believe me, you can't imagine."

Chapter Sixteen

During the flight back to St. Louis, Janelle talked at length about Elaine, not gossipy-lip-flapping trash, but a somber, thoughtful exploration of the young woman's self-esteem. Elaine had confided in Janelle that the reason she and Kenny had decided on the third floor condo instead of the ground floor apartment they had originally looked at—with the walkout backyard and enough grass for a picnic table, and a privacy fence for entertaining—was because Elaine had pushed for it, never explaining to Kenny that she, Elaine, hoped it would be healthy for her to climb three flights of stairs several times a day, burn off some of the belly fat and leg flab. Janelle had been quick to insist that Elaine was lovely and didn't need to burn off anything. Later, when Elaine came outside with Janelle, Elaine told her how angry she was over Kenny dancing with Katherine, a known man-eater and "slut bag," and when Elaine confronted Kenny about it, he went walleyed, and shrugged, "What am I supposed to do?" "Dance with *me!*" she'd screamed. "What do you think, you pig! It's our fucking wedding day!" Elaine had barked and stormed off.

Martin listened quietly to Janelle, the thrum of the plane as annoying as the hollow hum after a firework explodes near your ear, surprised by what Janelle had just shared about Katherine. He'd seen Kenny dancing with the lithe young woman and her silky black hair down over her shoulders, and by the close proximity of their bodies (or maybe it had been more than that, the smooth rhythm of Katherine's hips, or something implied in the way Kenny held her waist), they had appeared, at least to Martin's eyes, more than coworkers. But who knew? The younger generation, like every generation, defines the Do's and Don'ts of their era, what's permissible and what isn't. Obviously Kenny and Katherine had violated one of their generations' social mores, at least in Elaine's mind, which was, after all, the only one that really mattered.

Martin hadn't really listened closely to what Janelle was saying, grateful to have the two-hour flight consumed with talk of Elaine rather than a deep exploration into planning their wedding and setting a date. In a ridiculously impractical corner of Martin's mind, normally reserved for sitcoms and politics, he could almost convince himself that Janelle had completely forgotten he'd even asked her to marry him. When the pilot announced they were arriving in St. Louis, Martin experienced a sudden and devastating pang of guilt, his gut clenching, as if he'd made a promise he could never keep. With his chest tightening uncomfortably, Martin felt the panic-inducing sensation of suffocation, a shuddering, prickly dread. He glanced over at Janelle who was latching her tray, and putting her seat back into the upright position. His body quavered, his eyes bright and round like tiny bulbs sunk into the caves of his eye sockets.

"What's wrong with you!" Janelle said with enough alarm to grab the attention of the man sitting across the aisle. Martin couldn't speak, the dazzling light behind his eyes dissolving every thought, like a drop of water hitting salt, leaving Martin feeling disembodied, without substance, an apparition. The man leaned across the aisle toward Janelle.

"Is he okay?"

The disturbance attracted the flight attendant, who bent over the back of the seat in front of Martin. "Sir, is everything all right?" Then, looked over at Janelle. "Is he with you, ma'am?"

Janelle nodded, obviously confused and unsure what to do. "I've never seen him like this before," she finally said.

"We'll be on the ground in just a few minutes," the flight attendant said. "I'll call ahead for medical assistance." She turned and walked to the back of the cabin. By then Martin was sitting wide-eyed, his face blank, his skin like the slimy cold membrane of an oyster, his mind wired to some place beyond the corporeal world.

The sensation of floating, or walking on clouds, moving somewhere, yet not knowing where, barely a delineation between here and there, or up or down, disorienting in the sense of a physical presence, like being without arms or legs or a head, as foreign as being trapped inside one's own mind, yet familiar, the quality of a dream maybe, sleepwalking perhaps, though Martin, to the best of his recollection, had never done that. The realization suddenly morphed into a "man," who appeared as a vague silhouette in the white mist, someone Martin might possibly recognize as the man came closer, as if the figure moving toward him was a figment his mind had constructed from memory, or imagination, maybe even a personage from another time, someone Martin had seen in a play, or on television, or in a movie, or a nobody, somebody from the street, a clerk maybe, or a salesman, or a waiter from an expensive restaurant, and as the man stepped from the mist it became suddenly clear that the man *was* someone Martin could almost be certain he recognized, a magician? or an alchemist? or just possibly a mercurial fusion of the two, with a thin mustache, wavy black hair, and a tuxedo with tails and satin lapels, with a bright red lining that glowed when the man spread his arms as he was doing right now, a young man in his mid-forties with impeccable shiny shoes and creased black trousers and… yes, of course! Yes! Yes! Falco! Unmistakably! Falco the *Fantabulist!*

"Mr. Moffett? Can you hear me? Follow my finger. That's it, good. Are you feeling better now? Don't try to get up, just rest a few more minutes. You're okay, just a panic attack. Mrs. Moffett is here."

"Noreen!"

"No, it's me, Janelle, Martin. You had a little episode. But you're fine now."

"Janelle? Where am I?"

"The hospital."

"No, *where* am I, what place? What city? Is this New Jersey?"

"St. Louis, Martin. We're home in St. Louis."

"Let's give Mr. Moffett a few minutes to gather himself." Then: "Mrs. Moffett, can you join me in the hall a moment?"

"I'll be right back, Martin. Don't try to get up."

Falco was gone. The brilliant sparkling mist was gone. Gravity pushed down on Martin's body with the weight of an elephant. His lungs burned as if they had recently been in flames and put out with a fire extinguisher. The light above him made it impossible to open his eyes. He tried squinting detail into the room, into his mind, to fill the disturbing void, but there was no detail to gather, like being stuck inside a star.

Chapter Seventeen

Janelle drove back to her house and helped Martin inside. Martin, still wobbly, was bent on driving back to his bungalow that night. Janelle insisted he stay and that was that. In the morning, he woke feeling renewed and somewhat confused by the ordeal of the day before. They went to breakfast at Denny's and Janelle tried to explain what she could, telling him that the doctor had diagnosed it as a panic attack, but suggested that it would be prudent to get a CT scan, possibly even an MRI, just to be sure. Martin waved them both off and said he was fine.

When they walked out of the restaurant, Martin squinted, shielding his eyes. Janelle pulled her sunglasses from her purse and slipped them on. "Do you mind riding over to Carl's with me to pick up Beth?" Janelle said to Martin.

"I think I'd rather you drive me back to the house first so I can get my car," Martin said.

"Are you heading home?" Janelle lowered her sunglasses to peer over the rims.

"I need to check on the house." That wasn't a lie; Martin did feel the need to check on things, but mostly, he just wanted to be by himself; yet, that wasn't really the truth either—he wanted to see Noreen. How would that play if he just blurted it out? "I just need to see Noreen!" "Your dead wife?" "Yeah." "At the cemetery?" "No, in my special room reserved for anomalous events and communing with the dead." "How does that work?" "I have no idea, it just does." "Okay… well, tell her hello for me. Are you coming back out to my house for supper tonight?"

When Martin turned to walk back to the car, Janelle grabbed his arm. "Martin, please don't ignore me," she said, her brow crinkled with annoyance.

"What?" Martin said. "I'm not ignoring you…"

"Well, are you?"

Martin wasn't following her at all. "Am I *what?*" What the hell was she talking about? Now he could only gape at her, his mind ratcheting like a faulty tool, something adrift inside his chest.

"Are you coming back out to my house for supper tonight?" Janelle repeated, this time with an edge in her voice.

It was starting again, the gulf opening between them, Martin watching from his side of the canyon, Janelle shrinking away across the great divide. She must feel it, she had to, him racing away like a train behind schedule, picking up speed, never looking back. It was out of his control, this propensity for beating a hasty retreat, or so he thought, and if it wasn't, then how could he change things, how could Martin avoid the inevitable alienation he felt? In New Jersey, things between them had been amazing, the best they'd ever been, at least to his mind, but now, he couldn't wait to make a break for it, like Janelle was a maximum-security prison, and he was on death row.

"Can I decide later, after I—?" Martin said.

"Let's talk in the car," she said, digging her keys from her purse.

They rode in silence all the way to her house. Janelle turned off the engine, the car stereo falling dead in the driveway, the familiar rush of tinnitus in Martin's ears. He sat unmoving, except for his thumbs, which tussled with each other in his lap like wrestlers, until he popped the door open. "Wait," Janelle said. Then: "We need to talk."

Martin pulled the door closed and swiveled toward her. Janelle sat a long time, staring straight ahead, her face a blank card, but Martin could feel her mind sorting through all the different ways she might phrase what she wanted to say, trying out a multitude of approaches, like an actress exploring dissimilar techniques of delivering her lines, searching for just the right strategy so she didn't go off the rails in the middle of the script and lose the thread of her argument. Martin waited, taking his eyes to Janelle's immaculately trimmed, impossibly green lawn, then to her imported Bradford pear trees that conservation officials had urged Missourians to stop planting because the species was so invasive. It wasn't that Janelle was rebellious or had a disregard for authority, or didn't give a fig about the environment, she just really loved the way the normally harmless-looking little trees blossomed so suddenly in early spring—a miraculous explosion of white flowers so thick it took on the appearance of an enormous bouquet—performing its floral fireworks before any of the other trees in her yard had barely sprouted buds.

"Martin," she said, her gaze forward, as if she had cue cards taped to the garage doors, "look, I don't want to—"

"Please stop, Janelle. I don't want to spoil the speech you've been working on in your head, but please, let's just take a pause, okay... or I'm afraid we're gonna make a decision we'll both regret later." He had not wanted it to sound severe, but by Janelle's expression, that's how it must have landed. She appeared not only stunned, but ill, as if she'd bitten into something temperamental, like a raw onion, bringing tears to her eyes. Martin drew a deep breath and wasn't sure what to do with it. When he'd cut her off he'd thought he'd recognized a plan in his head, something that made sense and sounded rational, but it was nothing more than a desperate desire to buy time, stop her from saying words he didn't want to hear, not yet, at least, which would certainly undermine any attempt at moving forward. It was selfish, he knew that, to stall and make excuses and pretend he cared, which maybe he did, but he needed time to be certain. In that moment, Martin was even delusional enough to think that at some future moment in time she might even be grateful he had slammed on the brakes, trying to preserve the *status quo*, or the *fulcrum*, as Martin liked to see it, the exact point where nothing actually changes, but from where everything pivots.

"Why don't I call you later," Martin said.

"Don't bother," Janelle said, jumping from the car and slamming the door. She strode up the walk, her long legs briskly slicing the air like the confident shears of a master tailor, and disappeared inside the front entrance of her palatial home.

Martin was relieved and devastated, saved from the roasting oil and cast into the hot bubbling tar all in the same instant. Confusion and despair reigned as Martin dragged his miserable headache and his tangle of thoughts to his car and drove off.

Chapter Eighteen

The street was dark and empty when Martin turned onto Yurning Place Road, all the dull, white houses like skulls sitting in the front yards, the windows, black eye sockets flickering with the blue lightning of television sets. Martin drove slowly down the road, his dinky, pale white skull sitting at the end. Heat lightning splashed across the purple sky beyond his house. Martin hadn't planned to get home so late, but he'd needed to stop for groceries, then grabbed dinner at Ahab's bar on the Landing, where he watched the second half of the Missouri Tigers playing Auburn on the road, and drank a few beers. When the game ended, he stayed for a few more beers, thinking about Janelle, wondering if she'd tried to call him at the bungalow, if he should call her when he got home. He missed her and hated how they'd left things. A second later, he was glad it was finally over, then miserable again when he thought about how much fun they'd had in New Jersey—but was that even real, their time away, both of them out of their element, existing in a fantasy bubble free of responsibilities and work and bills and ex-husbands and teenage daughters and soccer practice? Martin tried to take a rigorous, merciless, inventory of his feelings, eventually coming away with nothing more than a headache and a thirty-five-dollar bar tab.

Martin nosed his Taurus into the driveway, then shifted into park and shut off the engine. The terrain beyond his house was black and indefinite until heat lightning burned the sky incandescent, silhouetting skeletal telephone poles, the noxious little heads of thistle overtaking the field and the arthritic hawthorns looming beyond the railroad tracks. A grizzly, depressing site, Martin thought, picturing Janelle's illuminated walkways and spot-lit trees, the green leaves glowing like neon, the lovely warm parabolas of light displayed along the exterior brick, projected by small floods hidden behind shrubs. Martin didn't even have shrubs. For just a brief second, Martin pictured the home he and Noreen had owned, but the memory passed quickly, the image part of a dusty scrapbook in his mind, a dark page from a different life.

With keys jangling from his fingers, he stepped up onto the concrete porch of the bungalow and unlocked the door. Within seconds of snapping on the living room lights, Martin knew someone had been in his house; the pillow and rumpled blanket on the futon, the dishes stacked in the drainer (he'd washed and put away everything before he'd left for New Jersey), the kitchen table stacked with *his mail! What the hell!* Someone had not only broken in, but had made themselves right at home, sleeping on his pillow, eating off his dishes, and bringing his mail! Hearing his words bounce back in his mind, he thought of himself as one of the three bears bedeviled by Goldilocks! Interrupting the strange fairy tale allusion, was a new realization about the intruders: They hadn't *broken* in, not exactly; the door had been locked when Martin got home. Then, the awfullest notion shot through him as he dashed toward the *Anything* room. What if someone came in and opened the door to the... whatever it was?—the infinite chamber of light? the luminosity room? the radiant ether of the dead?—what would they think? He checked the door; it was partially open, just an inch, not enough to trigger the brilliant light. That was the odd thing about the light in that room; it didn't possess the natural properties of light. If it became more than ninety-five percent (or thereabouts, Martin wasn't going to measure it) blocked—by any object; a door, wood slats with spaces between, even a thin white sheet!—the light extinguished. But what if someone had come in and opened the door all the way and witnessed the inexplicable luminescence? What would they think?

Martin's mind was tripping over itself trying to recall if he'd locked the door before he left for New Jersey? He couldn't remember. Had he inadvertently left it partially open? Then an even worse notion hit him: What if they (whoever *they* were), had actually entered the *light… and were still in there?* Martin stared goggle-eyed at the door for less than a second, then quickly slammed it shut, his left hand pushing against the wood, while his right hand wrestled in his pocket for his keys. He withdrew them under a nervous clatter, then locked the door. His heart thudded wildly, threatening to loosen his molars. Sweat prickled along his neck and back, his shirt sticky as contact paper.

Martin wondered which of his neighbors would be sneaky enough to get into his house while he was gone. Terrell was dead, so that left him out; well, maybe not. Berlina Miller! She was certainly nosy enough, but in her wheelchair that could be tricky getting up onto the concrete porch. Martin had thought maybe Janelle would call once she cooled off. Obviously not. Jerry Bonomo, the curious biker with the corner lot at the other end of the block? If he was stoned, and he usually was, he may have wandered in by accident.

Martin went to his bureau and checked his cash box in the top drawer—untouched—then plopped down on the bed, rubbing the patch of forehead over his left eye. Why hadn't Janelle called? He brought out his cell and started to tap her number, ending the call before the first ring. Martin got up and went back out to the car to retrieve his suitcase from the trunk. He unpacked and threw most of his clothes in the laundry hamper. He got out his phone again and started to dial, then left it on the nightstand. Taking a quick shower, he noticed someone had left the cap off the shampoo, and felt violated and uneasy, then outraged that some unknown person had been standing barefoot and naked in this very shower in the past three days! He twisted the faucet off and ripped the towel from the rack, then threw it to the floor when he realized they probably used his towel, too! "Fuck!"

By the time Martin got into his sweatpants and t-shirt for bed, he had calmed down. He had planned to see Noreen tonight, tell her about the wedding, the reception, and Elaine, how happy Kenny had been. He'd leave out the part about the squabble between the newly-weds, and what Janelle had shared about that Katherine woman who worked with Kenny. But his mind was a wreck from everything that happened over the past few days and was in no place to meet with her. Tomorrow morning would be better. He had already requested the day off before he'd left for New Jersey.

He shut off the lights and stared at the dark ceiling, his mind a whirl of impressions he couldn't control, a parade of faces and bodies and puzzles.

The phone woke him. Groggy, he fumbled in the dark for it, finally knocking it to the floor. He found it and hit the talk button.

"Hello?"

"Martin?"

"Janelle?"

They talked until four in the morning, when Janelle said she had to get some sleep. She needed to be at the bank by ten-thirty, then apologized again for calling so late. They planned to meet for lunch on Tuesday, near the bank. As Martin was placing the phone on the nightstand, he heard Janelle say, "I love you," the words sounding vague and small and a thousand miles away.

The next morning, the split-second Martin was aware he was conscious, his mind was already gnawing away on a list of people who could have been in his house—neighbors, coworkers, Bonomo's crazy biker friends, hobos walking the rails—almost as if his brain had been chewing on the problem all night while he slept. He got up, ate breakfast, and put on some nice jeans and a clean shirt, then sat on a kitchen chair and tied his sneakers. He brushed his hair in the bathroom mirror, then fixed his collar, wiped some crusty sleep-muck from the corner of his right eye, then went to the *Anything* room, his stomach in knots. There was always a twitchy, neurotic conductivity in his blood before he opened that door, one that boiled in his gut and quickly emigrated to every cell of his body, and would last until Noreen's hospital bed came clearly into view. At that point, the feeling passed. After that, Martin didn't really care what happened; he'd be with her.

He pulled his keys from his pocket, found the one he needed and inserted it, then twisted it until the door latch clicked open. Almost as if he were outside his body, observing himself do these things, every detail intensified, he watched his fingers grip the ordinary doorknob, turn it to the right, and then, with the deft touch of a safecracker, he felt the latch pull clear from the strike plate. Martin drew the door open slowly, a brilliant sheet of light expanding out until the room filled with unfathomable luminosity. Martin stood transfixed, staring, waiting as he had done hundreds of times before, and yet, the experience of watching the room materialize never ceased to astound him. And it appeared, forming vaguely at first, as if caught in a thin mist, details sharpening gradually, colors becoming more saturated, the smell of betadine and disinfectant, the sound of hardened rubber soles clicking along tile floors, the squawking calls for doctors over the PA speakers in the hallways, the subtle beep of life-monitoring machines in the room.

"Martin!" Noreen said, her eyes lidded, still trying to wake up from a long sleep, her smile weak and soft and lovely, her lips pale and dry. Martin went to her, took her hand, tears in his eyes, and kissed her on the forehead, then on the lips, detecting a hint of stale breath from the affliction of sleep. She sniffled and her tongue swept across her dry lips, unconsciously wetting them, and she took Martin's hand on top of the blanket.

"How are you today?" Martin said, pulling up the chair with his free hand, then sitting.

"Good, good," she said, her eyes losing their dullness, the blue growing more resplendent. "How long have I been out?"

"A few days," Martin said, the same lie he always told her. It didn't matter, things were going to run their course no matter what he told her, and before two in the morning, she'd be dead. Again. And he felt horrible knowing she would suffer. He had once made the mistake of staying too long, they'd been having so much fun all afternoon attending a concert in the park in Clayton, and he could see no reason not to spend the night together at a hotel nearby. This was before Martin had any understanding of the *rules* of this phenomenon. The night was a disaster, Noreen waking just after midnight, coughing up blood, hardly able to breathe, her skin clammy, her eyes bagged with dark skin, shaking uncontrollably. Martin called an ambulance and they got her to the hospital, giving her oxygen along the way to help her breathe, then got her back to her room. She was hooked to a morphine drip until she slipped back into her coma and died thirty minutes later. Martin had cried so hard the hospital staff had to sedate him. For months after that he avoided the

Anything room, refused to put her through that ordeal again, missing her and crying himself to sleep nearly every night. Eventually he convinced himself that if he used good sense and didn't get greedy, that he could see her again.

"Hey, it looks like a beautiful day outside, Martin," she said, more perky now. "Let's take a drive down to the riverfront." A little wobbly when she first climbed out of bed, she soon gained control over her limbs and got dressed, pulling on a pair of tight jeans and a soft plaid blouse with mid-length sleeves. The nurse came in and said, "Where are you off to today?" smiling, starting to make the bed.

Noreen spun from the mirror, pulling her brush down through her hair. "The riverfront!" she said, her eyes shiny and bright. "Martin's going to take me to a casino."

"Stick to the slot machines by the entrances," the nurse warned, laughing over at Martin. "Those are the ones that hit the most!"

This was all news to Martin—Noreen wanting to gamble, slot machines and roulette wheels, nurses handing out gambling advice— never having stepped foot in any casino himself. Nonetheless, it sounded like fun.

It had taken Martin a long time to acclimate to this new paradigm, the laxity of hospital regulations when it came to Noreen, her being able to come and go as she pleased, the nurses and doctors wishing her well, happy for her, always keeping her room free until she returned that night, never treating her with malice or derision if she returned late feeling ill. It was unlike anything Martin could ever imagine in the real world.

On the drive to the riverfront, Martin told Noreen about Kenny's new wife, Elaine, and how wonderful she was and how well they seemed to fit together (pushing away the images of the fight), the wedding, how beautiful it had been, the reception, the dancing and drinking. Noreen smiled from the passenger side of the seat, her hair flaming out from the opened window, her smile unmarred by time or illness. He could not have wished for a better last moment with her, Noreen fully alert, fully alive, at least for the next few hours.

They parked and got out of the car, met by the pong of fish mingled with the earthy smell of river mud and damp cobblestone, the Mississippi flowing slow and steady, like an ancient sentry, a silent, timeless witness, and periodic participant, to strife and tragedy, prosperity and triumph.

Inside the casino was mayhem, dinging and clanking, music floating down from ceiling speakers, the constant cacophony of conversation, the howls of celebration and defeat, the jangle of coins in plastic cups. Noreen's eyes grew large and shiny as silver dollars.

"Where do we start?" Noreen said with the excitement of a child at a traveling circus.

"Over there, I think," Martin said, pointing at a line of windows. They walked over and Martin exchanged a hundred-dollar bill for a small bucket of slot machine tokens. Noreen slipped the bucket off the counter and walked back toward the entrance, Martin hurrying to catch up, still trying to stuff his wallet in his pocket. By the time he caught up to her, she looked like a regular, pushing the button, barely waiting for the wheels to stop churning before she pushed the big red button again, the machine suddenly dinging and buzzing when the spindles stopped, the light above the machine flashing. She squealed as tokens flooded out from the coin tray near her lap, splashing out onto the garish, swirling red, green and gold carpeting at her feet.

"I'll get those!" Martin shouted, hastily gathering tokens and dropping them into her bucket. Noreen played on, a short while later hitting another jackpot, Martin helping with the tokens on the floor. They laughed and Noreen looked absolutely intoxicated, her head thrown back, leaning away from the machine like a taunting lover, her long thin fingers pressing the big red button, the reels spinning, dizzy and blurred, again and again, Noreen laughing each turn, like someone with three lifetimes to look forward to. Martin could not have hoped for a happier afternoon. He too was inebriated, smitten again and again, as he always was spending time with this electrifying woman.

They played at the machines, moving to new ones occasionally, for another couple of hours and when they were getting ready to leave, Noreen said she didn't want to cash in her tokens, finding an empty plastic cup on one of the machines to dump them into.

"What are you going to do with them?" Martin asked.

"Give them to Maggie," Noreen said, holding the cup with both hands, "the nurse who told us which machines to play."

Martin and Noreen went to the car, Martin discreetly checking his watch as he walked to the driver's side door. At times, he could almost believe everything was real—his car sitting in the covered hospital garage when he and Noreen went out to leave, the streets familiar, the restaurants where they were supposed to be, like an exact duplicate of the last day he'd seen Noreen alive, though she had been completely oblivious to his presence in the room. It was uncanny, how seamless it all appeared, how true to *life.*

Pulling from the casino parking, out onto cobblestone, Martin noticed a man walking past parked cars several aisles over, staring at Martin, tall and lanky, nice dresser, but Martin didn't recognize him. The man kept his eyes on Martin until he pulled from the lot. Martin picked him up in his rearview mirror and would have sworn the man smirked at him.

Noreen and Martin had dinner at Ahab's, her favorite restaurant in the city, and were having drinks when Noreen fell quiet.

"Something wrong?" Martin asked.

"You haven't mentioned Janelle this entire afternoon," she said, sipping her daiquiri. "Even when you told me about the wedding. Didn't she go with you?"

Martin didn't know what to say. "Yes, she did."

"So?"

"Look, Noreen, I don't really want to talk about this."

Noreen set down her drink and reached across the table to take Martin's hand. "Listen, Martin, I love seeing you like this. It was so much fun today, beyond my wildest dreams… but you have to think about your future. About Kenny's future. His children. Your grandchildren. Janelle. I don't want to harp, and it breaks my heart to say this, but you must move on, Martin…."

Martin's brain was stammering, justifications and excuses piling up, one atop another, all vying to be the first words out of his mouth. "I'm not ready," he said, the most honest thing he could have said. She smiled and slipped her sweater from the chair back and pulled it onto her shoulders.

"Okay, so, how about some frozen yogurt at Minelli's, then call it a night," Noreen said.

"Yeah… that sounds good," Martin said, feeling the tears forming in his chest, pushing up toward his eyes. He sniffed and got up, leaving cash in the leather wallet for the check.

Holding hands, they walked to the car, Martin opening the door for her, then going around to the other side and sliding in. Before he could turn the ignition key, Noreen reached over and grabbed his hand, pulling him to her lips, kissing him until he could almost see himself never leaving. When Noreen drew back, she smiled and reached up and touched the side of his cheek. "I'll always love you, Martin."

After yogurt, they drove back to the hospital. Martin rode up with her in the elevator, hugging each other until the doors opened on her floor. He walked with his arm around her shoulder, hers around his waist. When he helped her into bed, he smiled, the tears waiting no longer. She smiled and pulled the blankets to her waist.

"I wish I could see that door," she said, looking over at the entrance to her hospital room. To Martin's eyes, the door to the *Anything* room floated like an apparition, something else that had taken Martin time to process. Noreen, nor any of the hospital staff, could see it, even when he'd tried to point it out to her. In a minute he would walk toward it, give Noreen one last look, and be gone, the *Anything* room filled with impossible light, him standing alone in his tiny bungalow, tears streaming down his cheeks.

Chapter Nineteen

L unch with Janelle didn't go well. It wasn't a travesty, exactly, but Janelle had obviously hoped for some clarity regarding their relationship. She deserved that, Martin knew, but could offer nothing concrete, only indistinct generalities, like, "When we get married, I'd like it to be a small plain affair, you know, justice of the peace, a couple witnesses," he said.

"You mean like one of those sad affairs in someone's drab musty office?" Janelle shot back, more than a little frustrated at that point. Martin tried to assure her that he had never imagined it that way, but upon further thought, picturing it, the idea had appeal, as if the ceremony would be so trifling, lacking any real gravity or significance, Martin could almost allow himself the belief they weren't really married, more of a lark, a sham ritual satisfying her need for commitment and his need to… remain *fluid*.

In the parking lot, Martin kissed her goodbye and said they should get together for dinner in the next few days, trying to make more definite plans, feeling as if he needed to give her something more to pin her hopes on than *whens, coulds* and *shoulds*. Janelle listened half-heartedly, almost bored, one hand on her cocked hip, her skirt riding up, the slender fingers of her other hand wrapping the strap of her purse slung over her shoulder, as if poised to bolt at any second.

Late in the week they talked and agreed to get together on Sunday afternoon after Beth left to be with her father, Carl taking her to a beachside resort as part of a Dental Conference in Malibu, California. Martin hadn't told Janelle his good news, that he'd bought his new motorcycle, wanting to keep it a surprise until he rumbled up her driveway on his black and chrome Fat Boy. Martin had always seen himself with a Sportster, but while browsing the Harley showroom, the Fat Boy had *spoken* to him, and when he sat in that big black saddle, his legs straddling the chrome, arms outstretched gripping the handlebars, a million miles of road spreading out before his eyes, he was hooked. Michael Turner, the account exec from Harley-Davidson Martin was working with, had given him the name of the dealer to see about his new bike. "Robbie will treat you right," Turner had told Martin. And he had. Robbie, the Harley dealer, had told Martin they'd have to order his Fat Boy with the extras Martin wanted, but not to worry, they'd put a rush on it and he should have it in a week or so. "That's a great bike," Robbie had told him. "You're gonna love it!"

Martin couldn't wait to tell Noreen, though he wasn't sure that was a great idea, since she would never get to ride on it with him. What was the point in telling her? It just felt right to. At times like this, when Martin thought about Noreen, he wondered if she ever noticed how much older he was now, while she hadn't aged a day. If she had noticed the gray at his temples, it must not have mattered to her. Feeling a bit woozy, Martin brought his attention back to the dark road, the beers he'd had earlier still sloshing through his gut.

From a half-mile away, it was clear Geronimo was having another biker bash, his corner lot lit up like the *Grand Opening* of a new Ford dealership. There were no balloons or streamers or Batman type search lights, but motorcycles clogged the neighborhood, driving across lawns, headlights shining through trees and shrubs like grounded UFOs, guys doing lazy donuts in the middle of the road—leg outstretched, pivoting on one boot—to see how low they could get to the pavement without dumping their bikes. Biker chicks strolled around in sleeveless leather vests unzipped to their navels with nothing underneath, wearing jeans tight enough to smother atoms.

Geronimo (the moniker Jerry Bonomo got from his biker buddies), had worked as a pipefitter at Granite City Steel until a millwright inadvertently kicked an enormous crescent wrench off a suspended metal catwalk, cracking Bonomo right on the crown of his skull, requiring thirty stitches, and a year of follow-up visits checking for brain damage. He'd been out cold for two days, taking nearly six months to recover, and plagued by dizzy spells ever since. Bonomo took a small fraction of his workman's comp settlement and paid cash for a brand-new Sierra-red Harley Road King Classic with black leather saddle bags and lots of chrome, and then, for kicks, took a job dealing black-jack at one of the river boat casinos on the Landing.

Martin slowed his car to make the left onto his street, being careful not to hit anyone staggering past, then had to stop a quarter-mile from his house, waiting for two bikers to finish their drag race. The bikers skidded to a stop ten feet before crashing through the front of Martin's bungalow at the end of the block. Berlina Miller sat in her wheelchair watching from her front porch, her face grim as an Edvard Munch painting, her phone clutched in her hand. It wouldn't be long before the police showed up, which would only encourage the wild bunch to move their party to the field behind Martin's bungalow. Other neighbors, ones Martin had never met, stood cross-armed and severe in the shadow of their porches, like dark zombies, the windows of their houses flickering with the eerie blue glow of television sets. A few stood with arms akimbo, like superheroes, in their front yards, staring through squinty eyes, or hunched over, scribbling down license plate numbers.

When the drag race ended, Martin eased his Ford Taurus down the block, creeping along to avoid any surprise encounters with drunken bikers, then pulled up his driveway and shut off the engine. He set the emergency brake, an old habit (the ground was perfectly flat), then got out and slammed his door. A new drag race was in progress, the husky bikes screaming down the street directly at him, smoke pouring from the rear tires. Martin double-stepped it onto his concrete porch, hurrying to unlock his front door. The first biker to reach Martin's front walk screeched his brakes, the front fork digging in, the rear tire rising off the ground. A couple seconds later, the other biker did the same. Both bikers, now in Martin's front yard, eased forward, still seated, their legs "walking" out to the sides, as if *swimming* the motorcycles forward under a minimum of throttle to execute the wide turns through the blotchy grass. They pointed their bikes back toward

Geronimo's corner lot and thundered away, the porch shaking. A few bones in Martin's chest still vibrated.

The *Renagades* were harmless, mostly, not even a real motorcycle gang exactly. Most of these guys were from the suburbs, nine-to-fivers with white-collar jobs, not dangerous like criminals, but definitely reckless when they were drunk or coked-up. And most of the women strutting around half-naked were wives, probably prepared a three-bean casserole for supper earlier that evening, then lined up a babysitter, painted on some makeup, and slipped the silver-studded leather vests off the hangars in their walk-in closets. Martin didn't care. For these folks, all this raucous hoopla—the leather clothes, the hell-rattling Harleys, the gang patches—was an experiment in freedom. *Knock yourself out!* was Martin's attitude toward the whole deal. Hell, in a week or so, when he got his own Harley, Martin might join them, get a black leather jacket engraved with the gang emblem, join them on poker runs, even drag race down Yurning Place Road on Saturday nights giving his neighbors the finger.

With his key in the front door, Martin was temporarily surprised the living room lights were on, then remembered he'd left them on so neighbors would think he was at home when he wasn't, discourage snoopy visitors. Martin opened the door, then closed it behind him, shutting out the biker Olympics, noticing, quite disturbingly, movement from the edge of his vision. But not just movement, a person, a man, standing with his back to Martin at the sink, apparently washing dishes. Martin took a step back, a cold snake of panic slithering up his spine.

"Who are you!" Martin yelped, holding his front door key toward the intruder like a tiny little knife.

"You must be Martin Moffett," the stranger said, turning from the sink.

At first, the stranger's features didn't register in Martin's mind, but soon took on familiarity, like someone Martin may have seen in a magazine at one time, or a television personality that Martin had never met but knew vicariously from a movie or TV show. Then, just as quickly as Martin had thought he recognized the man, the recognition vanished, like smoke, like magic.

"Benjamin," the man said, wiping his hands with the dishtowel to dry them, walking toward Martin. "Benjamin Falco." The tall man shot his hand out toward Martin, and Martin, with great caution, took it like a hot lever, reluctantly closing his fingers around the man's palm to shake it.

After the introductions, and Falco's offer of supper, Martin, still a bit stupefied by his unexpected visitor, sat at the kitchen table, while Falco scooped spaghetti from the sauce pan onto a fresh plate, then placed it in front of him. After grabbing a clean fork and butter knife from the dish drainer, Falco set them down in front of Martin and asked if he wanted anything to drink. Martin said, "Water," feeling like a guest in his own home. About then, red and blue flashing lights splashed through the kitchen and living room windows.

"Looks like they're breaking up Geronimo's little soirée," Falco said, setting a glass of water down in front of Martin. Falco scraped the other chair out from the table and sat across from him, watching Martin take a bite of spaghetti.

"Good, right? Secret recipe!" Falco said, smiling, his eyes lidded, his dark, wavy hair ruffled, as if he'd been sleeping on it all day. Falco looked nothing at all how Martin had pictured him. Falco was tall, and solid as a bar of steel, but his hair was not movie star lush—though maybe it had been at some time in the past—streaked with gray at the ears, with just a hint of a bald spot showing on the back nine. But with those cheekbones and dark eyebrows and full lips, and eyes that sparked like blue lightning, he was Hollywood handsome, a heartbreaker at any gathering.

Martin nodded, taking another bite of pasta. "It is good," Martin said. "So, are you staying the night?"

"Only if you'll have me, Sport," Falco said, jumping up from the table to light a cigarette. He drew hard and blew swirling smoke toward the ceiling light from the little opening at the corner of his mouth. "You the one that nailed those boards over the portal?"

"The portal?" Martin said.

"What would you call it?" Falco said, leaning against the kitchen counter, flicking an ash into the sink.

Just then, a rumble, like rolling thunder, started down the street, then moved steadily toward the bungalow, growing louder, like a tornado, shaking the window glass as it passed the house with the steady roar of a locomotive, lasting almost a full five minutes before ending up behind the house and falling silent. That's when the shouting and hooting started and a huge blaze flared in the field behind Martin's house, light flickering across Martin's kitchen walls. Falco leaned toward the small kitchen window, the edge of his face rimmed with orange light from the enormous bonfire. Falco shook his head. "They'll be partying until four in the morning if they don't kill someone before then."

Martin knew Falco was right. They'd drink and play music and dance, some of the women taking off their tops when it wasn't too cold, the men hollering for more like a strip joint, then everyone laughing and rushing toward the tracks when a train came through so they could hurl empty beer bottles at the passing train to watch them shatter against the coal cars.

"Terrell must have nailed those boards up," Martin said, ignoring the interruption in the conversation.

"Terrell!" Falco said with mock disgust, smirking, rolling his eyes as he took another drag on the cigarette. "He was a piece of work." A second later, with the muffled sound of shouting and cheering coming from the vacant field behind the bungalow, Falco came back over and sat down, holding his cigarette out to the side, down below the table to keep the smoke away from their faces. "Did you install the door?" Falco asked, his brows dipping toward his nose like a hawk.

Martin could only nod sheepishly, as if he'd done something wrong. Falco nodded back, maybe approvingly, or maybe with contempt, it was impossible to tell by the fixed and somewhat grave expression on the man's face. Martin felt slippage in his stomach, some organ or muscle twitching, drifting out of alignment.

After several minutes of silence, Martin was first to speak. "So, that stuff you told Terrell about how the water tank and lightning and the train created some kind of electrical, magnetic convergence and... was that true?" Martin said, recalling not what Terrell had actually told him, but what it had sounded like to Martin's ears—a jumble of important sounding terms. Falco started laughing, then coughing, jumping up to put out the cigarette in the sink.

"That's what he said?" Falco blurted out when he could finally speak, then started laughing again, quickly putting out his open palm as if to stop Martin from answering. "Terrell... dense as a car battery! You couldn't explain *snow* to Terrell if he lived in Alaska!"

"That wasn't what happened?" Martin asked, with reticence in his voice, scratching the whiskers on his chin.

Falco's features hardened, his smile gone, turning toward Martin with a threatening new edge to his appearance. "Terrell saw what he wanted to see... with his limited imagination..." Then, after a brief staring contest with Martin (that Martin was just about to concede), Falco said, softening, and genuinely contrite, "I did feel bad about his leg, though."

Falco came over and pulled a glass from the drainer and stuck it under the faucet and filled it with water. "For a shithole in the middle of nowhere," Falco said, taking a long drink from the glass. "Pretty damn good water."

Martin nodded, himself surprised when he'd first looked at the place, half expecting sewage to flow from the faucets. About then the bikers out back started whooping and shouting. Falco fixed his eyes in their direction, as if he had x-ray vision and could see through walls. That's when they both turned to the distant rumble. Falco looked up at the clock. "Two-thirty-seven," Falco said, "that'll be the ten-fifty-eight out of Perryville! Come on." Falco finished his water, then placed the glass in the sink. "We're not gonna get any sleep tonight with that racket," Falco added. "Let's break up that little shindig."

Martin, fairly certain Falco was a madman, knew trying to roust that bunch was suicide. "That may not be the best idea," Martin said.

Falco started for the front door. "You know those clowns aren't an actual motorcycle gang, right?" Falco said, looking back to make sure Martin was following. Falco opened the front door and stepped out onto the porch. "They're like Borg, you know," Falco said, looking over the couple making out on Martin's porch.

"Beautiful evening," Falco said, walking past them. The couple glanced over at Falco, then tilted their heads back to watch Martin walk by. Martin smiled down at them and kept moving. "Like Borg, I was saying, you know, walking around mechanically, bumping into shit like the Energizer Bunny, that whole 'Resistance is futile,' or so they like to believe." Falco looked back at Martin, walking toward the bonfire. "But they're idiots!" Falco continued, not really caring if anyone heard him. When Martin caught up to him he could hear Falco better.

"Have you looked at the back of their jackets?" Falco said. "They misspelled *Renegades*, for chrissakes! With a fucking 'a.' They're weekend warriors. Monday morning, they'll all be back at work, lying to customers, squeezing their secretary's tit behind closed doors, sucking up to the boss. That motorcycle is the only thing keeping the suffocating hands of desperation off their throats."

By now the bikers were getting up with empty beer bottles to pelt the oncoming train, which was still several miles off, but closing fast.

"That you Falco?" someone sitting near the bonfire said.

"Hi, Jerry," Falco said, glancing over without stopping, walking past the bikers toward the railroad tracks. He stopped a short distance away, the light of the train coming toward them like a distant meteor. Falco looked over at Martin. "Ever save anyone's life, Martin?" Falco said. Before Martin could answer, Falco added, "You'll get your chance tonight."

Falco walked out to the tracks, stepped carefully over the closest rail and stood in the middle of a railroad tie, centered between the rails, facing the train. Martin walked closer, protesting, but Falco seemed not to hear. Bikers standing near the tracks down the line— ready to pitch bottles at the train—migrated back toward Falco and Martin. Others sitting around the bonfire got up, brushed off the seat of their jeans and came closer to the two men.

"Have you ever considered your body, Martin," Falco said, glancing in Martin's direction, then taking his eyes back to the train. "Your lungs for instance, they keep on pulling in air, letting it out, whether you're aware of it or not. And your heart, Martin, just keeps beating, pumping blood though your veins, nourishing every cell in your body while you sit on the couch brain dead watching some inane sitcom. Your digestive system, works at turning whatever garbage you dump into it into usable fuel for your muscles and tendons." Falco looked over at Martin, his eyes reflecting a strange light. Bikers were gathered around Martin, looking at Falco, standing still as telephone poles, beer bottles dangling by the neck from some of their hands.

"Your organs, Martin," Falco continued, "your spleen, your liver, churning through the toxins you've put into your body, breaking them down and washing them from your system while you ogle women in miniskirts at the grocery store. Your hair and fingernails growing with no help from you, and cuts and bruises healing miraculously while you pick your nose at a stoplight, healing over so perfectly that most of the time you can't even remember the wounds."

The train was closer now, a few hundred yards, blowing its whistle, the shrill din cutting the night. Bikers and their women shifted their eyes furtively between Falco and the train, the beady-eyed light of the moving monolith burning brighter, larger and more menacing, hurtling down the tracks toward them. "Your birth, Martin, have you even considered that?" Falco said, his eyes fixed on the approaching train. "Your birth was completely orchestrated without one bit of input from you, or anyone else, your little nest of cells growing into arms and legs and a head and a brain, then becoming a little boy, then a youngster, then a young man, and you had no part in the process whatsoever, your mind focused on playing with friends, looking at girls, doing homework, learning to drive, getting a job, all the while your body is creating everything you'll need to perform in the world."

Falco paused a moment, the train closing fast, less than a hundred yards now, the whistle screaming frantically, over and over, the ground at their feet vibrating, the light from the train shimmering off the rails in the distance. Martin could hear low mutters and grumblings of concern and disbelief from bikers standing nearby, their shadowy bodies becoming animated, fidgeting. Martin himself felt the dread building. "So, answer me this, Martin, and save my life."

A second later, Falco said, "If our bodies are able to maintain themselves without our help or input, autonomously, other than providing food and water, then what does that make us?" Martin stared at Falco with headlight eyes, the train speeding closer, the whistle a long pleading cry for help followed by a string of urgent blasts. Falco said, "Come on, Martin, what does that make us? What does that make me? What does it make you? And Jerry over there, what does it make him? And that fella," Falco said, nodding toward the guy next to Martin.

"Dwayne," the man said nervously, looking at Martin, then back to Falco. "My name's Dwayne."

"Yeah. Dwayne. What does that make Dwayne, Martin? Come on now, we're running out of time!" Martin felt himself going rigid, like some fast-acting rigor mortis, an unnamed turbulence rising inside him. By now the ground beneath his feet was quaking, the enormous, black locomotive hurtling through the night like a dark city block, growing ever bigger, racing forward, pushing ahead of it the stale, humid air from Perryville and every town in between, shaking the world, the headlamp glaring off the front of Falco's shirt, the oscillating ditch light burning along the eyes and faces of onlookers, the crowd yelling, screaming for Martin to answer him, "Say something, Moffett!" People crowded in closer. Someone shook Martin by the shoulder, another shouting in his ear, the train whistle eating into Martin's head like a giant hungry beetle, the heat of lava rising all around him, the thunder inside Martin's chest rattling his ribs. Moffett! Say something! What are you waiting for! Moffett! Martin! Answer him! Quick! The train closing, Falco nearly erased by the sheer brightness of the locomotive's beam flashing maniacally back and forth, Falco's face blanched white, his mouth a black irregular hole screaming into the train, *What does that make us, Martin!* and Martin, shocked by the hammering, electrical charge of adrenaline, tried to think. What did it *make us* that our bodies did everything for us and we didn't have to do a thing? *What does that make us? What does that make us?* followed by the craziest answer, but Martin was out of time, Falco was out of time, and Martin just screamed it out, *"LAZY?"* and the train charged past in a great rush of heat and tar, dragging the acrid stench of burning oil, the metal growling and bellowing like the end of the world, the steel wheels sparking against the shiny burnished rails, drowning out the collective screams of the crowd, people holding their mouths, falling back, staggering, stumbling through the smoke, Falco gone, their horror and trauma swallowed by the guttural roar of the speeding locomotive, the train finally passing, heading back into the seamless dark, sucking with it all the sound from the universe, leaving behind the clack clack clack clack clack clack clack clack clack clack clack of steel wheels sounding over a seam a half-mile away, the mechanical din of a thousand generators fading quickly, the train no more than a shadow now, shrinking away into darkness, no sound or fury, the ground still, the air cold and soundless as deep space, the weeds near the tracks barely swaying, then stillness.

Stillness.

Unable to speak, unable to move, everyone stood gobsmacked and flabbergasted, staring into nothingness.

"Pure consciousness..." Falco said from behind the crowd. Everyone spun toward the odd man, no less shocked or stunned (or maybe even more so) than they had been only seconds earlier. No one spoke, gaping wide-eyed, frightened, trembling.

Falco walked up to Martin.

"It makes us pure consciousness, Martin. That's all that's left when you remove the body from the equation," Falco said, taking Martin's arm and leading him away from the congregation, back toward the house. Some of the bikers climbed on their motorcycles, started the engines and drove off. Others kicked dirt onto the bonfire with their boots, while others urinated on it, or poured beer on it, trying to put out the last remaining flames. As Martin and Falco passed dazed bikers shuffling back to their machines, Falco wished everyone a good evening, told the men and women to have safe trips home, telling them to be careful. Before Martin and Falco reached the bungalow, most of the gang was gone, the last of them firing up the big engines, rumbling to the street, exhausts booming out boisterous escapes.

At the porch, Falco said, "Don't you see, Martin, we, you and me," then pointing out toward the last departing *Renagades*, "them, all of us, are beings of pure consciousness, riding in our *space*-ship bodies through the material world, our essence as different from the organic intelligence of our cells and molecules as water is from fire."

Martin—his *intelligent cells* (as Falco called them) still attempting to realign themselves into a coherent order—could only gape at Falco, stunned, trying to comprehend what he, Martin, had just witnessed at the railroad tracks, the train clearly running right over, or through, Falco. That was beyond any *magic trick,* leaving Martin with no part of his brain suitable for storing such a demented illusion. Was it all wizardry? Merely theater, legerdemain? Martin shifted his attention to the field, to the smoke rising from the flickering bed of brilliant orange cinders where the bonfire had been, the motorcycle tracks, deep-cut ruts, crisscrossing the ground, the sidewalk next to Martin's bungalow drawn with wide, muddy tread marks. The bikers had obviously been real. The train had been real, Martin was almost certain. Yet when it was all gone, the bikers, the train, the bonfire, it was difficult to be sure if any of it had ever been real.

"I tried to explain all this to Terrell, once," Falco said, moving around Martin to the front door, "until the light flared out behind his eyes." Martin knew the feeling, following Falco into the house, easing the door closed behind them. Martin's legs felt weak, yet, in the same moment, dense and heavy as lead pipes. Falco turned toward Martin— who stood dumb as a post in the middle of the living room—and said, "You want the futon or the bed?"

Chapter Twenty

In the morning Falco was gone. On the kitchen table was a note: "You can lock the portal door. I had a key made. The leftover spaghetti is in the Tupperware container with the blue lid. Oh, help yourself to the garlic bread on the plate covered with aluminum foil. See you soon. Falco."

"Are we roommates now?" Martin said to the note, then crumpled it in his fist and tossed it in the trash. Martin went to the bathroom for a shower and noticed that the towels, which had been in the hamper ready for him to take to the laundromat, now sat on the shelf in the narrow closet next to the tub, washed, folded and stacked. Falco must have done it.

Martin showered, picturing Falco picking the lock on the portal door, standing somewhere on the *other side*—maybe a dark alley, or Mitzi's apartment, or a sandwich shop—people walking by wondering what the hell Falco was doing, working at some invisible door (invisible to passersby), Falco looking like a street mime. "Luckily, it was easy to pick," Falco had told Martin when Martin had asked how he'd gotten into the house. Now getting in would be easy, Falco with his own key. Martin wasn't sure if he was comfortable with that madman having easy access to his bungalow, but felt strangely indebted to him; if not for the portal, Martin wouldn't be able to see Noreen.

Martin headed out, locking the front door behind him, giving the field a departing glance, the beer bottles, the smashed weeds from all the bike traffic, the image of Falco, face to face with the train—a snapshot fixed in Martin's mind—Falco absolutely still, leaning away from the monster, his figure small and trifling against the shadowy iron leviathan.

The drive to Janelle's house was pleasant, though Martin had only been able to carve out a few moments for himself to think about what he'd say to her, the remainder of his thoughts tangled up with Falco's antics and theories, especially his ideas concerning consciousness, going on and on as they had been getting ready for bed the night before. "*Choice*, Martin," Falco yelled from the living room, Martin in the bathroom brushing his teeth. "*Choice* is our superpower! Do you understand that?" Martin hadn't understood, but also hadn't cared, so tired from the long, wearisome day, afraid he'd fall asleep at the bathroom sink and swallow his toothbrush. Finding his eyes in the mirror of the medicine cabinet, Martin had stared at himself staring back, wondering which one was real—the one he could feel, or the one he could see—Falco's voice bellowing from the other room. "When you realize that your body is essentially autonomous, and doesn't depend on you for much, you're left with your pure consciousness and its purpose in the world. And what is that purpose? *Choice!* Can you hear me, Martin? Choice! We, you and me, and everybody in the world, that's what we do: Choose! This or that, up or down, black or white, hate or acceptance, love or fear! That is the sole responsibility, the *soul* function, of our pure consciousness, right! Sounds simplistic, but it really isn't when you dig deeper, realize that all through your life that's what you've been doing every second of every day. It's actually pretty mind-boggling." Falco had finished with an unmistakable satisfaction in his voice. Then: "Martin?" Falco continued, walking toward the bedroom, his socked-feet clumping on the hollow floor. Martin pulled the blankets up over his head, rolled to his side and pretended to be asleep, forgetting he hadn't turned off the overhead light. "Damn it," he whispered to himself. Falco stuck his head in, smiled, then flipped the switch off. "Goodnight, Sport."

Pulling into Janelle's driveway, Martin was still wrestling with how much to tell her about the previous evening, the motorcycle gang, Falco, the train—none of it! "What the hell's wrong with you!" Martin said to the dashboard, admonishing himself, pushing the shifter to park. But it was funny about the *Renagades,* and Janelle would appreciate the story, the beautifully embroidered emblem, the size of a medium-sized pizza, sewn on the backs of their black leather jackets. MISSOURI, curving along the top of the circle, RENAGADES, curving along the bottom, with a maniacal, crazed eagle bursting from the center, claws opened, ready for the kill. The problem was they spelled Renegades with an "A" where the second "E" should have been, Martin had never noticed it before, until Falco pointed it out, and Martin had checked out a few of the bikers last night. How could no one have caught that mistake, or maybe they did and said, "Fuck it! We're *Renagades,* and we'll spell it whatever the fuck way we want!"

Smiling and distracted, Martin got out of the car and strolled up the pristine walk toward Janelle's front door. "Martin! Over here!" Martin turned to see Janelle wearing shorts and a tank top, her hair pulled back with a scrunchie, her gardening gloves dirt-stained and worn. She put down her spade and came over.

"Are you early?" she said.

He came closer and pulled her to him, kissing her on the lips. He loved how she looked in a tight sweater, miniskirt and high heels, but something about her in her gardening attire—a smudge of dirt on her cheek, her arms bare and soiled, dried mud on her knees, her fatigued socks drooping down her ankles and resting over her shoes—proved to be an instant turn-on, as if she needed rescuing from whatever beast she'd been trying to conquer. She laughed nervously, pulling away from him, smiling, her eyebrows dipping in confusion toward the bridge of her nose.

"I'm cruddy, Martin," she said, almost embarrassed, crossing her right arm over her chest, her left arm resting across her abdomen. "Let me get a shower first," she added, then gave her legs a cursory inventory, as if scribbling mental notes on how she appeared to Martin.

"I'll help you with that," Martin said, slipping his right hand around her waist to pull her closer. She gently, but quickly, levered his hand away and gave it back to him, probably picturing the mud that would be running down off her body along the shower floor.

"No," she said. "You go make yourself comfortable on the kitchen patio, and I'll get myself together." She turned quickly to make sure

Martin understood he would not be helping in the bathroom, then glanced back at him when she got to the front door. "Cold beer in the fridge," she said. "I won't be long."

Waiting for Janelle to come outside, sipping the iced tea he'd poured himself from the pitcher on the kitchen counter, Martin sat at her patio table listening to birds chirping and chittering from the trees in her backyard, realizing how few inhabited the area around Yurning Place, at least that he ever heard. Maybe they had all killed themselves against Martin's window panes after he moved in. Actually, not much wildlife in the neighborhood, unless he counted the *Renagades*. And of course, Falco. Maybe the strangeness of the place discouraged animals and birds from making it their home. Or maybe it was something far more nefarious, that most living creatures, with the exception of humans, could sense and avoid. Falco rose up, quite unexpectedly, from the center of Martin's mind with the unsettling burden of a premonition, Martin wondering where the odd man had gone when he left the bungalow. Perhaps back to Mitzi on the *other side* (as Martin was beginning to think of it), or maybe to run errands in the real world, though the note the magician had left made it sound as if his vanishing act was more long term.

"Okay, so…" Janelle said, stepping from the French doors off the kitchen wearing a custard and cranberry fall dress that swayed and bounced against her tanned legs, her cork platform sandals clapping along the flagstone patio, looking like a model from the Fall edition of *Fashion Fold*. "Sorry about before," she added, coming over to kiss him. "I lost track of the time."

She sat across from him. "This for me?" she said, touching the glass of iced tea Martin had poured for her. "Thanks." She took a drink, then set it down, apparently feeling as nervous as Martin about this conversation. If this didn't go well, the way forward, they both knew, was going to be more than dubious.

First they talked about Beth, if she was looking forward to her time with her father in Malibu, Janelle telling Martin about shopping for two hours trying to find her a bathing suit that Beth liked and Janelle could live with. "She tried on one… her ass was practically hanging out…" Janelle said, rolling her eyes. "And she didn't see anything wrong with that."

Martin listened, uninterested, trying not to picture Beth's ass at all, hanging out or not, the young girl having morphed into a woman over the past few months. Janelle, out of character (and not hiding her irritation), told Martin about her ex, Carl, and his new, bright red BMW Z8 convertible. "That thing cost over a $100,000! Can you fucking believe that?" Janelle picked up her tea and chugged the last of it as if it contained alcohol, the ice cubes tinkling as she set the glass down a bit firmly, as if she didn't trust gravity in that moment. "That's some message to send our daughter, right?" she added, when Martin didn't respond.

"*Our* daughter?"

"You know what I mean!" Janelle's eyes were fiery slits, not to be trifled with, the skin of her chin tight, shiny.

Martin was struggling with what *message* Janelle found so disturbing about a $100,000 automobile. Janelle was no stranger to wealth, having grown up around money, and Beth, well, she was no stranger to it either. What was Martin missing? Was it considered vulgar and extravagant to blow a 100k on a car? Were there unwritten rules and bylaws around affluence outlining the proper etiquette for spending as opposed to investing? As far as Martin knew, that little Beemer Z8, unlike most cars, would be worth a lot of money in the future if Carl took care of it and didn't spin the wheels on the odometer like a slot machine. A classic, no doubt, and in excellent condition, twenty years from now, could bring twice its sticker price. But that couldn't be it. Martin was baffled, until he saw Janelle's lower lip quaver almost imperceptibly, a sign that tears, a lot of them, would soon appear. A moment later, they streamed down Janelle's smooth cheeks, her eyes varnished with rage, staring at nothing, fixated on some situation she felt powerless to change.

"What's really going on, Janelle?" Martin said, perfectly still, not making the mistake again of trying to comfort her by touching her hand.

Janelle shuddered, putting her hands to her face, shaking her head. "Fucking, Carl! That fucking bastard," she said, glowering at Martin like he was to blame for whatever Carl had done. "He's carrying a gun on his belt now! A pistol! A black pistol in a black holster! Some young men yelled at him coming out of his office a couple weeks ago, and now he's carrying a gun! His office is in Chesterfield, for fuck's sake! What the hell does he need a gun for!"

Martin was about to cut in, but knew this was a time for listening, not reciting statistics on the uptick in crime in affluent areas of St. Louis.

"What is my daughter supposed to think about that? That shooting someone is how you problem-solve?" Janelle wiped her eyes, sniffed a few times, then said, "You get divorced, and you think that will resolve so many issues, but you forget that it only gets the asshole out of *your* life, not your daughter's!" A pause, then: "I don't want Carl in her life. I don't want her to associate with people like him. I don't know how I could ever have married such a piece of shit! When we divorced, I guess I should have used a gun instead of a lawyer! Right? That's the answer now! Shoot whoever is in your fucking way!" At this point, Janelle was shaking all over, her hands sitting on the table, her fingers tightly wound into fists.

After a few minutes, she calmed down, her fingers unfurling, the blood coming back to her knuckles. She rocked her head gently from side to side, as if addressing every possible solution with one continuous *no*. "What am I gonna do, Martin? I don't want her anywhere near him... ever again..."

Martin cleared his throat. "He's her father, Jan," Martin finally said. "But he's only half the equation, less than half." Then: "Don't discount your influence. And the gun... Beth is sharp, she's no dummy. She'll see how ridiculous the gun is, maybe even be embarrassed by it. Only an idiot wouldn't be. That's not who Beth is... because it's not who you are." Martin waited, not sure how his words would land. Janelle looked over at him and sighed, still shaking her head.

"There's more to it than that, Martin," Janelle said, her eyes reddening again. "I'm afraid for Beth. You don't know Carl the way I do. He's ruled by fear. He walks cocky, with his polished white smile and his air of superiority, but in truth, he's still the frightened little boy whose father raged and beat him with a strap..."

Love or fear; the words crept into Martin's thoughts with the stealth of a thief. Janelle was still speaking, but Martin was no longer listening. *Love or fear.* Is that what Falco had said the night before when Martin was tucked beneath the blankets pretending to be asleep? Was that the choice; *love* or *fear?* The words seemed mismatched somehow, not quite opposites, or so it felt to Martin. Wasn't it *love* or *hate?*

"...It's like anyone who upsets Carl in the least is suddenly his father, and Carl lashes out. He gets crazed. My therapist told me that certain triggers probably throw Carl into a *complex.* She said being in a complex is like being possessed, and you can't trust a thought in your head! How fucking frightening is that? And now Carl has a fucking gun on his hip!" She paused, then: "But Carl refuses to get help! He won't see a therapist, or anyone who could help him... and I'm just afraid Beth..." Janelle shut her eyes and started shaking her head, trying to drive out some unthinkable horror from behind her eyes, and Martin could do nothing but watch.

"Janelle," he said softly after nearly a minute.

Janelle slid her eyes open, looking past him at first, then bringing her eyes level with his. She sniffled, then wiped her nose with her knuckle.

"What would you do?" Janelle finally asked, clearing the tears off her cheeks.

"Give it time," Martin said, unsure if that was the best advice. Being a single parent without a living spouse, he'd not had to deal with mixed-messages or crazy exes. Kenny, no matter how myopic it might have been, was only shown one side of things. Martin's side. Right or wrong, damaging or healthy, who could say. "I know you're scared, but Beth's going to be okay. I'm sure of it. And as far as the gun, wait till Beth gets home next week. I think she'll surprise you. She's not going to fall for that macho, tough guy bullshit..."

Janelle sighed and forced a weak smile. "That's not why you came out here today, to listen to my problems," Janelle said, her eyes still red. "You want something to eat?"

They went inside and Janelle cut up a big salad, while Martin made sandwiches. They took the food to the living room floor, leaning against huge cushions Janelle had bought for just this kind of casual dining, and ate by the sliding glass doors that looked out on the pool. When they finished lunch, they started kissing, then undressing each other, eventually making love on the carpet. They held each other for a long while without speaking. Janelle broke the silence. "Will getting married ruin this?"

"If by *this*, you mean the potato chips stuck to the cheeks of my ass..." Martin said, lifting onto one elbow and twisting his body. Janelle burst out laughing, one hand over her mouth, pulling Martin toward her to peek over his waist, then brushing away the potato chip crumbs. Still laughing, they laid back down, Martin on his back, Janelle on her side, her head on his shoulder, tucked against his chest, and eventually fell asleep.

For the rest of the week, Martin slept at Janelle's house, driving home from his office at lunch to check on the bungalow. It seemed Falco had not returned. On Friday, Martin dug the last of his mail from the mailbox, mostly junk and fast-food coupons, and threw it on the front seat of his car. Robbie, from the Harley dealership had called on Thursday and left a message saying Martin's bike was in. "It's sweet, Mr. Moffett! You're gonna love it!" Martin couldn't wait to go get it, but he still wanted it to be a surprise to Janelle, so he had to figure out a way to get his Fat Boy without her finding out.

Martin was about to head back to work when he decided to visit Noreen. He hadn't seen her all week. He unlocked the door in the *Anything* room and waited in the brilliant glow until her hospital room appeared.

"Martin!" she said, opening her eyes.

"Hey." He came over to sit next to her bed. "You look really good today." He leaned in and kissed her on the lips. Over the past several days Janelle and he had talked about marriage—where they would live, about their jobs, if they should find a home together, Beth's school, how Martin felt about getting rid of his bungalow—and had finally set a date, six months from now. Martin planned to tell Noreen about the wedding, knowing it would make her happy, but also knowing Noreen would urge him to put their life behind him, Noreen's and his, and commit fully to his new life with Janelle and her daughter.

It was to be a simple wedding, close relatives only, in a church, with a small reception at a restaurant near Janelle's home. They weren't even sure about a honeymoon, with Beth and all, Janelle not wanting to leave her with Carl any more than necessary. In lieu of planning a honeymoon, they decided to just imagine all the places they might like to go together. Martin had always thought about going to Thailand, visiting Bangkok, spending time on the beaches, while Janelle wanted Paris, and Venice, her eyes lighting up when Martin mentioned gondolas, and Martin agreed, adding, that if they were going to Europe, they should plan on the Greek isles, especially Santorini, Martin telling her about pictures he'd seen, the white villas built into the mountainside, and Janelle sipped her wine and when she mentioned she just had to visit Ireland, the color had drained from Martin's face. *Ireland.* Noreen's great grandfather had emigrated from Kilkenny, the Flanders clan, and Noreen had always dreamed of seeing the castles, visiting St. Canice's Cathedral.

When Noreen noticed the sour look on Martin's face she asked if something was wrong with his cheesecake. She and Martin had walked the two blocks from the hospital to Dresser's Bakery. The day was cool and sunny and the walk had been pleasant, though Martin was distracted the entire time, his mind on the wedding, on the imaginary travelogue of honeymoon locations he and Janelle had been contemplating.

Martin forked another bite of his white chocolate raspberry cheesecake and slipped it past his lips. "No, it's fabulous," Martin said, smiling at Noreen, feeling horrible that his mind had drifted to Janelle. It didn't bother him, though, when the current flowed the other way and he was unable to be present with Janelle, his thoughts consumed with Noreen.

"Here, taste this," Noreen said, her face radiant, smiling, easing her fork with a bite of cheesecake toward Martin's mouth.

Martin grimaced. "Chocolate peanut butter?" Martin said. Then: "Em, I don't think so."

Noreen laughed and performed a quick mid-air loop with her fork, landing the cheesecake in her own mouth. "Your loss!"

Martin sat eating, not talking, still distracted.

"Hey, what's with you today? Everything okay?" Noreen said.

Martin was crushed, the guilt opening in his chest, a torturous swelling. "Yes, of course... I'm sorry."

"Nothing to be sorry about. I just want you to be happy."

He looked at her, reaching out to place his hand on hers. "As long as I can look into those beautiful green eyes, I'm happy!" And he was, but the guilt persisted, heating up, churning the cheesecake in his gut.

"Noreen," he said. "Are you disappointed we never made it to Kilkenny?"

Her curious smirk turned into a broad smile. "Not at all, Martin," she said, turning her hand over to grip his in her palm. "I couldn't have imagined a better life than the one I shared with you." She reached across the small round table and wiped a tear from his eye. "There is nothing to be sad about," she said, chuckling a little. "We'll always have *Mehlville!*"

Mehlville, the suburb of St. Louis where they'd bought their house, where Kenny grew up, a beautiful neighborhood near the city, with Grant's Farm, parks, and great schools. Martin met her eyes with his, wanting to tell her about the wedding. "Do you miss me when I'm not here?" he said, not sure where the question came from.

Noreen dropped her eyes, smiling. "The truth is, Martin, I have no sensation when you're not here, at least any I can remember. It's like sleeping without dreaming. Until I wake up, it's just… I mean, I don't even know how to explain it… it's as if I don't even exist, if that makes any sense…"

"You're not in pain, you're not suffering?"

"Of course not." Then, a moment later: "We should get back."

"Do you remember what we did last week?" Martin said, needing to understand how she processed his visits.

"Um… last week?" she said, her eyes unfocused, as if disoriented. Then: "I remember yesterday, going to the casino and playing the slot machines."

"I didn't mean to upset you," Martin said, standing up, wishing he hadn't confused her. It seemed that she processed each of his visits in a daily consecutive order, no matter how much time passed in between.

"I'm not upset." Noreen laughed a little. "You have to stop worrying. I love you so much! You couldn't upset me."

After Martin left her hospital room, he eased the door closed over the portal and locked it, a curious tingling beneath his skin. He stared at the door for at least twenty seconds, then walked to the front of the bungalow, pulled the door open, then locked it behind him. The tingling was still present, but outside, in the cool breeze, the sensation was less intense. The sun over the field glowed like a bright smudge through the thin cover of clouds, the day a strange, silvery gray.

Chapter Twenty-One

At the end of the block, Martin stopped at Geronimo's house on the corner. Geronimo was home and said he'd be glad to ride over to the Harley dealership and help him get his bike, then bring the car back and park it in Martin's driveway.

"A brand-new Fat Boy," Geronimo said, lighting a joint. "That's some fine bike. You'll have to become a Renegade!"

On the drive to the dealership, Geronimo started asking Martin about Falco, how he knew the magician, where he'd been the past few years, working up to the real questions he wanted to ask. "What the hell was that the other night?" Geronimo said, drawing on his joint, offering it to Martin.

Martin refused, telling him he had no idea. Geronimo asked if Falco had explained how he pulled off that crazy illusion, swearing it looked like the train went right through him. Martin only listened, hoping the drive to the dealership wasn't much longer. "I guess that was Falco who stayed at your place when you were in New Jersey for you son's wedding," Geronimo said. "I saw somebody down there, but hell, I didn't know who it was. It's been... I don't even remember how many years since I seen Falco last. Long time. Shame about that pretty assistant of his. She was a knockout, that one."

Martin was about to ask why Geronimo hadn't called the police when he saw someone in Martin's house, but then decided against it.

What would be the point? Three blocks away, the Harley-Dealership marquee rose above the fast-food signs. Martin pulled into the parking lot, shut off the motor and handed Geronimo the key to his Taurus. "I have a spare, so you can just lock it in the car under the front mat and I'll get it tomorrow." Geronimo took the key and finished his joint, dropping it on the pavement and crushing the roach under the heel of his boot.

Martin thanked him and started walking toward the front doors when he noticed Geronimo following. "Anything wrong?" Martin asked.

"Naw, just thought I'd get a look at that new bike!"

"Sure, sure, Jerry, come on in."

Robbie walked over as soon as he saw Martin come through the door, then showed him to the bike. Martin sat on it, brought it upright off the kickstand, his legs out to the sides. Geronimo walked around it, inspecting every cubic centimeter. When Martin went over with Robbie to finish up the paperwork and get the helmets and leather jackets he'd bought, Geronimo sat on the bike, like it was his own. Robbie thanked Martin, shaking his hand, then opened both front doors of the dealership. Robbie came back over and rolled the big bike from the showroom into the parking lot. Geronimo stood around with his hands in the back pockets of his jeans, as if waiting for some kind of show to begin. Robbie showed Martin where everything was— shifter, throttle, brakes, switches— then handed him the keys.

"You call me if you have any problems," Robbie said.

Martin inserted the key into the ignition and pushed the starter. The engine fired immediately, the low rumble oozing up through the seat into his bloodstream. Geronimo stood a moment, just nodding, smiling, then started clapping slowly.

"That's one helluva piece of machinery," he said to Martin, giving him the thumbs up. "I'll make sure your car gets back to the house." Geronimo patted Martin on the back like they'd been friends since high school. Martin nodded and mouthed thanks back to Geronimo, then tightened the chin strap on his helmet, pulled from the parking lot out onto the busy four-lane street, and headed for the entrance ramp onto Highway 55.

Martin drove all the way to North St. Louis, then out on the highway to West County, filled with the inimitable, lofty peace of riding a motorcycle, his thoughts swept away, the wind rushing past his face. The sun was low over the trees when Martin pulled into Janelle's driveway, much later than he had planned to arrive. He knocked on her front door. When she opened it, her eyes went first to his black leather jacket, then to the helmet dangling from his hand by the strap, then to the glistening new Fat Boy sitting behind her BMW.

"Oh my God, Martin," she squealed. "I had no idea it would be that big!"

She hurried past him, Martin following, and she couldn't keep her hands off the shiny surfaces, running her fingers down the tank, across the black leather seat, then touching the second helmet strapped to the side. She looked down at the black saddlebags, walking around the bike to take it all in, the chrome shimmering in the pink-tinged, early evening light.

"Let's go for a ride!" she said.

"You'll need this, then," Martin said, pulling a black leather jacket from the side saddlebag. She wound her arms into the sleeves and pulled it down in front, checking the zippers at the pockets, the chrome snaps on the chest and sleeves, her face resplendent. Martin could feel Janelle bubbling over, jubilant, and for a moment it turned him gloomy, as if it should've been Noreen trying on the jacket, overflowing with joy and delight. Noreen had hoped Martin would get another motorcycle, like the one he'd had when they met, the one he got rid of a few years after Kenny was born, so worried something was going to happen to him and he would no longer be around to see his son grow up.

Janelle pulled Martin into an embrace and kissed him on the lips. "Let me go change into jeans," she said, beaming, her arms still wrapped around him.

"When does Beth get home?" Martin asked.

"Not till tomorrow evening. What have you got in mind, Easy Rider?"

"Dinner, a midnight drive across the Mississippi River bridge toward Edwardsville, a twelve pack of beer, and a nice little out-of-the-way motel."

She kissed him again. "That's sounds wonderful! I'll get our tooth-brushes and—"

"No, just leave that stuff. We'll buy what we need on the road!"

"*On the road!*" Then: "I love how that sounds… like *renegades!*"

Martin laughed to himself.

Janelle wasted no time changing, then locking the house, coming across the lawn with nothing but a small purse swinging from her shoulder. She fiddled with the helmet a moment, trying to figure out how to work the strap, eventually pulling it on over her hair. She looked at Martin and puckered a kiss at him, then tightened the strap under her chin and threw her right leg over the seat. When Martin climbed on, Janelle wound her arms around his waist and pulled her body tight against his. Martin hadn't even started the engine and already he was ecstatic, a warm buzz running up his spine, down his legs, out to his fingertips. They rumbled from the neighborhood, Janelle holding him tighter as he turned onto Manchester Road, but not from fear; he could tell she was into it!

Hitting all green lights at the intersections, Martin was soon on Interstate 270 headed for Edwardsville, Janelle resting her helmet against his back, her hands winding up inside his jacket, the warmth of her flesh bleeding through his shirt onto his belly. "This could work," Martin whispered to himself, smiling to the highway stretching out like an infinite possibility. "I think we could really be happy, Janelle and I…" For the first time since they'd set the wedding date, Martin was truly at ease, thrilled at the thought of spending the remainder of his life with this lovely, playful, intelligent woman and her daughter, until the idea of having Carl in his life cast a dark pall over his enthusiasm.

Chapter Twenty-Two

The wedding had been a simple affair in the backyard of Janelle's home, under the pavilion beyond the swimming pool. Janelle had wanted to have the wedding in the St. Louis Wedding Chapel, but that's where Martin and Noreen had been married years ago, so that was out. There were nice venues in North St. Louis, and St. Charles, but all of them farther than Martin and Janelle had wanted anyone to have to drive. So the backyard it was. Janelle's friend from the bank, Leanna Weiland, a woman legally ordained to perform wedding ceremonies, married them. Kenny had stood as Martin's best man, and Beth as maid of honor.

After the ceremony, Kenny walked over to Martin and hugged him again. "I'm so happy for you, Dad," Kenny said, truly delighted for his father. Kenny had always felt that his father had given up so much to raise him on his own. Kenny was glad to see his father so happy.

"Hey, where's Elaine? Is she doing okay?"

"Oh yeah, she's fine," Kenny said, remembering that he and Elaine had discussed the possibility of her not coming. She was five months pregnant and having some difficulty, nothing that was threatening to the baby, but uncomfortable for the mother, nausea and back pain. "She'll be along any second."

Elaine walked up and hugged Martin, kissing him on the cheek.

"We can stay at a hotel, Martin," she said. "I understand you guys are honeymooning at home!"

Martin smiled at her. "No, this is perfect, you staying with us. Gives Beth a chance to know you both better."

That was odd, for Kenny, as odd as it must be for Beth, them being step-siblings, if that's what one called it. Both Kenny and Beth had grown up as only children, not that any grand bonding would occur, given the gap in their ages.

"You feeling any better?" Martin said to Elaine.

"Yeah, not nearly as dizzy. I think it was the flight, you know, the turbulence." She looked at Kenny. "Right? It was rough, wasn't it?"

Kenny nodded. "Yeah, crazy rough!" he said, trying to hold himself together, his heart jumping with a strange lightness, his stomach fluttery. When his dad had called several months earlier to tell them about the wedding, Kenny had imagined, during the visit, seeing old friends in St. Louis, mostly classmates from high school, people he hadn't seen since leaving for Rutgers. One night, while Elaine was going over new listings on her computer, he'd gotten out his high school yearbook, flipping through the pages, telling himself he was just figuring out who he might like to see, coming quickly to Vickie Kramer's photo. He had no idea why he'd been thinking about her so much over the past few months. Not like every day, but often enough to be distracting at work, and at home. A couple of times he'd even told himself what harm could come from just calling her, quickly putting down his office phone before dialing all the numbers.

Kenny already felt guilty just getting Vickie's contact information from an old classmate, Russell Brever, Russ, who worked in the front office of the Enterprise Center, home to the St. Louis Blues. Russ knew everyone from high school, kept up with careers, and career changes, relocations away from St. Louis, even deaths, though there had only been a couple. Russ worked on the reunion committee for their graduating class, and put out a yearly newsletter to keep folks updated. Kenny had never signed up for the newsletter, which in hindsight, would have been smart. Russ mailed him one, with a complete listing for everyone in the class—name, address, phone number.

"When do I get to see this new bike?" Kenny said, wanting to usher his mind into new territory.

Janelle walked up and hooked her arm through Martin's, then asked Elaine if she was feeling better. "I'm fine," Elaine said, nodding. Janelle shifted her eyes toward Kenny. "Do you know how to drive a motorcycle?"

Kenny laughed. "Naw, dad's motorcycle days were before my time."

"Martin will have to give you a ride later," Janelle said. "I never thought I'd like being on one, but… we're having fun on it."

"So, Dad, did you sell the bungalow?" Kenny said, noticing the look Janelle gave his father, waiting for Martin's answer as if she also didn't know.

Martin cleared his throat. "Well, I was going to put it on the market, then, Jerry Bonomo, a neighbor up the road from my place, said he had a biker friend who wanted to rent it from me."

Janelle said nothing, just stared at Martin, holding a faint smile on her solemn face.

"A biker?" Kenny said, imagining the worst; wild parties, parking their motorcycles in the living room, degreasing the carburetors and engines in the bathroom tub, weekend-long orgies, bit by bit ripping the place to shreds.

"Yeah, well, these guys aren't like Hell's Angels or anything," Martin said, shifting his eyes momentarily toward Janelle, then back to Kenny. "They're more like a… a co-ed softball team with Harleys."

By the sour look on Janelle's face, Kenny wasn't sure she believed that. Or maybe it was something else bothering her. Either way, Kenny was sorry he'd brought it up.

With her arm still wrapped through Martin's, Janelle turned toward him and said, "Let's get dinner put out. Will you help me in the kitchen?"

"I'll help," Elaine said, eager to do something.

"Martin can help," Janelle said. "You should rest."

"We'll both help, right Martin?" Elaine said, smiling over at Kenny before heading toward the sliding glass doors at the back of the house. Martin and Janelle followed and soon disappeared inside. Kenny stood back, watching them, feeling like odd-man-out for not having gone, too, Vickie Kramer suddenly bright in his thoughts, or maybe she was never gone, just sitting in the dark, waiting.

When they'd spoken on the phone, at first, when Kenny told her his name, Vickie hesitated, as if she hadn't remembered who he was. Kenny had waited, then said, "Kenny Moffett, you know, from the football team," as if that detail should jog her memory. "Jeez, Kenny, I know who the fuck you are." Her gruff manner had put Kenny off, sorry he had called, not sure why she was being so cross. "Sorry, Kenny, you just caught me at a bad time. Where are you? Still in Jersey?" They talked a while, Vickie explaining how she'd married Tommy Roiter from the wrestling team. "You remember him?" Vickie said. Kenny did, and had always hated him. Roiter was a bully and even though Kenny had been quite a bit bigger, Roiter was still able to push him around. To Roiter, size didn't matter; you had to be meaner, thumb tacks and gasoline flowing through your veins, or you didn't stand a chance. Roiter would have been perfect for the military, and would have become a Marine if not for some problem with his feet. They fought once, Kenny and Roiter, a short bout, Kenny going down hard after Roiter caught him under the jaw. Roiter probably only joined the wrestling team because the high school didn't offer boxing. Roiter sparred at a real gym, boxing guys ten years older than he was, probably happy to give, as well as receive, beatings. Kenny wasn't sure if Vickie ever heard about the fight. It had been at some burger joint on a Saturday night, Kenny with a few friends, Roiter by himself as always. Sometimes Roiter would drive around with some slut he'd picked up in the city, but mostly he went solo. Kenny was flabbergasted Vickie had married the loser. "How about you," Vickie had said. "You married?" Kenny had told her he was, that he had a baby on the way. They talked about high school for a while, then Vickie said she had to go. "If you're ever in St. Louis," she'd told him over the phone, "give me a call. I'd love to see you."

It was a few weeks after that when Martin called and told Kenny about the wedding, wanting Kenny to be his Best Man if Kenny could swing the time off from work. "Of course, I'm going to be there!" Kenny had said. "I'll quit if they won't give me the time off!" His dad had laughed, then told Kenny how much he appreciated it, and couldn't wait to see him. "We need to get together more often than just for weddings!" Martin had said, joking. "Or we're both going to have to get married a lot more often!" When he'd hung up with his dad, he phoned Vickie, told her when he'd be in St. Louis, and asked if she'd like to get together for coffee or something. She told him it wouldn't be possible, then started crying before she disconnected the call. A month later she'd phoned him at work, apologized, and said she'd love to see him. They'd only spoken once since then, but made plans to meet at Bokas Coffee Haus near Washington University. He was supposed to meet her around ten-thirty in the morning. Now he wasn't so sure. At the time, he thought it was nothing, just meeting up with an old class-mate, but he'd never told Elaine about it, knowing she wouldn't be keen on the idea.

"What are you up to?" Martin said, walking up behind him. "You look like you just got caught stealing cookies."

Kenny laughed, smiling. "Hey, let's have a look at that bike."

"I think we're getting ready to eat," Martin said. "We'll look at the bike later, okay."

Kenny followed him in, noticing Elaine standing in the food line. He smiled at her and she motioned for him to come over, that she was saving him a spot. Walking toward her, his stomach in his chest, Kenny wasn't sure he could eat and carry on this ruse at the same time. Maybe he should call it off, but then, he pictured Vickie, how she'd looked in high school, how she smelled, the way she moved, and he had to at least see her, then he'd be heading back to New Jersey. End of story.

Chapter Twenty-Three

A few mornings later, Elaine was in the kitchen when Kenny came out of the bathroom. "You look nice," she said. "Meeting up with your friends?" Kenny nodded, heading to the coffee maker to pour himself a cup. "I'm sorry I can't go, Kenny. Are you angry?"

"Come on, don't be ridiculous," Kenny said. "They're just some classmates." Elaine had told him before they flew out to St. Louis that she wasn't sure she was up to meeting a bunch of new people. "I don't know," she'd said. "I'm just so run down lately. I don't have the energy. I hope you don't mind." He'd been relieved, of course, but he had already decided that if Elaine had insisted, he'd plan to take her with him. Let her meet Vickie. Then it would all be above board. What difference would it make; it wasn't like Kenny planned to have some great love affair with someone he hadn't seen since high school, someone who had never even noticed him.

Strolling in wearing his bathrobe and looking scruffy, Martin proceeded to the coffee maker behind Kenny. "Here, Pop," Kenny said, getting his dad a cup and filling it from the carafe. "Thanks, Son," Martin said, ambling to the kitchen table to sit down. "You heading out?" Martin said, noticing how Kenny was dressed.

"Yeah, meeting some friends from high school," he said, trying to pretend to himself it wasn't a lie. Maybe the words weren't a huge lie, but the deception they were covering certainly was.

"Anybody see Janelle this morning?" Martin asked, sipping his coffee.

"She went to the grocery store," Elaine said, unloading the dishwasher from the night before.

"Let me get those," Martin said, starting to get up.

"Stay where you are. This isn't a big deal."

Kenny checked his watch, then downed the rest of his coffee. "Gotta go." Kenny went over to hold Elaine from behind, kissing her on the cheek. She spun in his arms and pushed up on her toes, kissing him on the lips. "Have fun," she said. "See you later. I think we're gonna try to hit a movie tonight." She looked in Martin's direction. He nodded. "Maybe dinner out."

Beth came in and opened the refrigerator door, then poured herself some orange juice. "You going somewhere New Big Brother?" Beth smirked, trying out their new names for each other.

"Yes, New Little Sister," Kenny said, making his eyes big. "Are you going to the movies with us tonight?"

"Only if I get to help choose the picture! I'm not gonna sit through one of those *As Good As It Gets* deals!" Beth said, dropping a couple of pieces of bread in the toaster, then turned toward Martin sitting at the table. "You want toast, Marty?" Beth said. That's what they agreed she would call him. Marty. Martin shook his head.

"Okay, I'll see you all later," Kenny said, making sure he had the keys to his dad's Taurus. Then: "Thanks again for the loaner." Martin smiled and winked at Kenny.

In the driveway, Janelle was just coming home from the store with several bags of groceries. "Leaving us?" Janelle said.

"Meeting some friends. Here, let me give you a hand with those." Janelle swung a couple of the heavier ones into Kenny's arms, then grabbed the smaller ones and carried them in. Kenny placed them on the kitchen table, then said goodbye to everyone again. As he left the kitchen, they all said goodbye again, but this time in unison, laughing about something.

Standing in the driveway, Kenny wasn't sure he could feel much worse. He hadn't done the final tally yet, but he was pretty sure he'd lied at least once to everyone he cared about this morning.

~

The drive to Bokas Coffee Haus took longer than Kenny had expected. He almost hoped Vickie had grown tired of waiting for him and left; then, at least, he could drive back to his dad's house with a shred of dignity. After parking the car, he came down the sidewalk, a passel of outdoor tables ahead, many with people talking or reading, wondering if he'd even recognize her. "Kenny!"

He swiveled toward one of the tables and saw her. His heart dropped. She was as beautiful as he remembered from high school, more beautiful, not even sure how that was possible. "Vickie," he said, sitting down opposite her. "I wasn't sure if you'd wait. Sorry to be so late."

"Did you get lost?"

"No, just miscalculated the distance, I think."

"You want coffee?"

Kenny really didn't, but that had been the reason for meeting.

"I don't either," she said, standing up, wearing black leggings, heavy black boots and a tank top with a blue jean jacket over it. "Let's walk, okay."

"You look amazing," Kenny said, letting her lead the way. They crossed Skinker and walked down the sidewalk bordering Forest Park. They were quiet for a long time, Kenny wanting to say something but his mind was spinning. Even though she said she wasn't going to bring her husband, Roiter, Kenny had been nervous she would. A few minutes later Vickie cut onto the grass and found a place to sit by a tree. It was already more intimate than Kenny had wanted it to get. Sitting at a table outside a very public coffee shop was easy to explain; this wasn't.

"You okay with this?" Vickie asked, pulling her knees to her chest.

"Yeah, sure, beautiful day for being out here."

He met her eyes, trying not to stare at her lips, red and moist. "Why did you call me after all these years, Kenny?"

Those lips were working now, more mesmerizing than ever. Now he knew she wasn't going to bother catching up on old times. "I don't know… I was going through the year book when I found out I was coming to St. Louis for my dad's wedding, and—"

"You happened to come across my picture?"

Kenny nodded. "Yeah, and I thought—"

"This isn't a good start, Kenny. Why did you call me?"

Kenny sighed, running his fingers through his hair. He had forgotten this about Vickie, her directness, her ability to dismantle him with a question, with a look. Elaine was everywhere in his head, at their apartment, in the kitchen at his dad's house, in the bed last night kissing him, at her computer browsing listings, sighing, sipping juice on Janelle's patio. He scratched his ear.

"I don't know," he said. "I've been thinking about you so much, and I have no idea why."

She turned toward him and put her hand on his forearm. "Why didn't you ask me out in high school? Jesus, I gave you every possible opportunity, and you just... ignored me..."

"I didn't ignore you, Vickie...! Jeez, I was nuts about you, but you were always with someone, or... I don't know... the time never seemed right."

She scoffed, shaking her head. "And now is? You're married, a kid on the way. I'm married to a lunatic that will kill me if I even mention spending time apart to figure things out. How is this the right time, Kenny?"

Kenny sucked in a deep breath, swirling around on some dizzying carnival ride. This was discussion for married couples, people who've been together for years, maybe hitting a rough patch and trying to work things out. He hadn't seen Vickie since high school, hadn't talked in months—they didn't really even know each other—and they were breaking things down in ways he and Elaine still couldn't. He wanted to leave, wishing he had never bothered contacting her. "It isn't the right time, Vickie. It never has been," he said, getting up to leave.

"Don't leave, Kenny," she said without moving. "I have never loved anyone but you, and if you leave now, without figuring this out, you will never have another moment's peace for the rest of your life. You will always wonder, What if? Always... just the way you were when you called me... the way I've been doing for years..."

He stopped, his insides upside down, his legs wobbly, his hands like ice. His head rocked side to side, as if a vertebra had come loose in his neck. Turning toward her, unable to look into her eyes, he went back over and sat down next to her. After a few minutes, he said, "This is impossible."

She leaned forward, resting her forehead on her folded arms, then twisted her head to look at him. "So many times I wanted to ask you out," she said, sighing. "I felt like a fool, too embarrassed you'd turn me down, but now, thinking back, I was just stupid, so stupid not to have chanced it." She watched him until he turned his head, his eyes meeting hers. "I knew what I wanted, and sure," she continued, "it may never have worked out, but this, you calling me after all those years, me married to that fucking ape... this is torture, Kenny, and I don't know what to do."

"Can't you leave him?" Kenny said.

"I did once," she said, "and he nearly put me in the hospital." She let her eyes drift down to the grass. "You know how he is." After a pause, she added, "Actually you don't... he's way worse than you could imagine."

They sat in silence for a long time, the sound of traffic whooshing past, the occasional car horn, the grumble of a bus accelerating up Skinker. Cyclists rode by wearing helmets and brightly colored skin-tight garb, their skinny tires spinning out a low, shushing sound, like breath. Birds chattered in the trees while squirrels scampered sound-lessly along the grass.

"When you left for Rutgers, I thought I was going to die," she said. "I thought about taking a bus to come visit you, but I was too much of a coward. Still am."

Tears came down her cheeks, not in great rivers, but one, then another, falling without sound onto her folded arms.

"I'm going to leave him, though," she said, staring at the grass. "In the next few weeks. I'm going to move in with a girlfriend from work. I've talked with a policeman friend of mine and he said he'd help anyway he can... I'm going to get a restraining order..."

Kenny looked over at her, unsure how to say what he was dread-ing, then said it anyway. "Not for me, I hope."

She looked over, smiling. "No, of course not," she said. "But you calling me woke me up from some cryogenic freeze. I know I can't live like this anymore." She fell quiet again, staring at her boots. "But in a way, I wish I were doing it for you... because I know it's going to be tough. But if you were the prize, that I got to be with you... it would make it so much easier." She looked away, her face coloring, flushing pink.

After a few minutes, she said, "I'm so thankful you called, Kenny." She reached over and touched the side of his face, letting her fingers trace the smooth skin of his cheek. "It is so wonderful seeing you again." She leaned toward him and gently brought her lips to his, holding the kiss briefly. "I better get going," she said, getting to her feet.

He pushed himself up and looked out at the traffic rushing past, feeling as though he were trapped in some kind of bubble, a void floating through, yet outside, the real world.

On the walk back to the coffee shop, they talked about regular things, Kenny telling her about his dad's wedding, and his stepsister, Beth, the pet names they have for each other, "I call her New Little Sister and she calls me New Big Brother," then about Janelle, his step-mother, how wonderful she is. Vickie told Kenny about the flower shop she and her best friend, Amy, bought together not far from Bokas Coffee Haus, over on Delmar, explaining that Roiter doesn't know she's part owner, only that she works for Amy.

"You know Amy, right? Amy Gelden?"

Kenny said he did, remembering how they were the prettiest two girls in school, with Vickie edging her out in a close race. Vickie said she worked two jobs to come up with her half, waitressing every day, tending bar on weekends and a few nights a week, hiding her tips from Roiter.

"It isn't that Roiter doesn't have a job, he does," she told Kenny. "A pretty good one, in fact, he just doesn't know how to stop spending when it comes to money." Vickie told him that she and Amy did weddings and birthday parties, and funerals were big, that they even sold flowers to the local grocery stores.

"It's called, *Floral & Party*," Vickie said.

Kenny said, "That sounds like—"

"Yeah, Laurel and Hardy," Vickie said, laughing. "We wanted it to be fun, and it's probably lame, but now it's caught on, so, you know, whatever..." Vickie smiled, then: "Amy, she's so creative, and I've got a pretty good head for business. Plus, I rock on the computer, maintaining our website, writing a bit of code to make it easier for people to order online, stuff like that. So, we make a good team."

"You write code?" Kenny said, chuckling. "That's what I do all day long, that and trouble shoot the computer systems."

"Well, don't confuse what you do with what I'm doing," Vickie said, rolling her eyes and laughing. "If you saw how I write code you'd... I don't know... but it isn't pretty. I barely know enough to get by... the good thing is, if I mess up, there's nobody around to rag on me. Amy has no idea because she is clueless on the computer. Plus, I have a friend I can call if I get in real trouble..."

More people were sitting outside the coffee shop when they returned, some waiting in line to get in, part of the lunch crowd arriving. Vickie asked if he wanted a coffee before he left.

"No, I better get going," Kenny said.

"You know I met your dad once," she said. "At one of your football games. I was with some guy, I don't even remember who, and your dad was sitting right next to me. I mean, I didn't know he was your dad until he started cheering every time you had the ball. He'd stand up yelling, 'Go, Kenny! Go! Go! Go, Kenny!' At one point I turned to him and said, 'Mr. Moffett?' and he said, 'Yes,' and I swear to God, Kenny, I was just about to say, 'I'm in love with your son!' But I didn't. I chickened out and told him you and I went to school together. But I knew everything about you then, how your mom had died from that car accident, how your dad raised you all on his own. And I knew your dad had to be a pretty special guy because... because of how you turned out." She looked away for a moment, then met Kenny's eyes.

"You take care of yourself," she said. "And I wish you infinite happiness with your new baby."

Kenny could feel the tears coming as she walked away. She stopped, and looked back at him. "Class reunion coming up in a couple of years," she said. "Maybe I'll have my shit together by then." She waved, then crossed the street and disappeared between a line of parked cars.

Chapter Twenty-Four

B y the look of the pillowed gray sky, snow seemed inevitable. Overnight the temperatures had dropped almost thirty degrees; winter in St. Louis finally waking up. Martin and Janelle had planned to take a motorcycle ride by themselves, but when the weather turned, Martin decided to head to the bungalow; he hadn't been in over a week, too busy at work to get away at lunch to check on things, or to see Noreen. He tried to visit her at least three times a week, but with only his lunch hour available, the visits were short and frustrating, at least for him. No sooner would he and Noreen go somewhere, than Martin had to get back to work. Noreen didn't seem to notice, as if she had no concept of time, or didn't care, just happy to spend every moment with Martin.

Martin, putting on his jeans and shirt to leave, asked Janelle if she wanted to take a drive down with him, knowing she would pass. She wanted nothing to do with the place, often wondering out loud why he didn't just sell it. "What is it with you and that... place?"

Martin told her he collected nice rent on the bungalow, which was a lie. And since they managed their own personal finances, having separate accounts for the house and expenses, she had no way of knowing.

Martin was walking toward the door off the kitchen, which led to the garage, when he passed Janelle sitting at the kitchen island reading a recipe book. He stopped and kissed her on the neck, then asked one more time if she wanted to go with him. "No, thanks," she said, turning enough to kiss him. "Will you be late?"

"Not unless I get stranded by snow!"

When her face fell, he quickly said he was joking, then gave her a kiss on the nose.

"I'll go," Beth said, sitting at the other end of the island working in a notebook.

Martin's breath caught. Janelle looked over at Beth, then at Martin, and Martin was certain Janelle would put the kibosh on the idea. He waited, but Janelle took her eyes back to her recipe book, browsing the appetizing photos of colorful cooked meals hot from the oven.

"Sure, if you want," he said.

"Just give me a sec!" Beth said excitedly, bolting from the kitchen, still in her pajamas, as if driving to the bungalow was the best thing she could imagine doing with her Saturday. Beth had never seen it, and only knew of Martin's other residence through the quarrels he and her mother had about the curious *shack,* as Janelle called it when she was perturbed. Janelle had asked him to put it on the market before the holidays, and maybe it would be gone by spring. Martin had said he'd think about it, but was pretty sure he had another *renter.*

Martin waited for Beth, knowing he'd not be able to see Noreen, but couldn't merely change his mind about going. Too suspicious. Maybe the snow would grow into a blizzard and he'd have to turn around and come back home. After all, what was the point of going if he couldn't see Noreen. Beth returned after about ten minutes, wearing skinny jeans with knee-high boots, a sweater that fit her snuggly at the chest, eye make-up and lipstick, her puffy jacket unzipped, her long hair brushed down to her shoulders and no hat.

"You going to be warm enough in that?" Martin asked, not sure what to say; she'd left the kitchen a scrawny fourteen-year-old and came back a college coed.

"Your Taurus doesn't have heat?" Beth said, a bit sarcastic it seemed to Martin, but her true meaning was hard for him to read. Janelle chuckled, never bringing her eyes up from the book.

"Okay, let's roll," Martin said.

"Have fun you two!" Janelle said, still smiling.

When they got on the highway, Martin glanced over at Beth,

wondering why girls in junior high already looked like women. The first time Beth had friends over, Martin was shocked to see these girls so fully developed.

"Everything okay?" Beth said, looking down at her clothes, then back to Martin when she'd seen him look over.

"Just fine," he said, taking his eyes back to the road, a few snowflakes streaking toward the windshield. At times, the sun would peek out for just a moment, causing the flakes to sparkle like holiday decorations tumbling from the dark gray sky, until the sun tucked back behind the clouds, the flakes once again dull and frozen.

Riding in silence, the radio playing music Beth had tuned to, Martin struggled with his disappointment over Beth coming along. He was glad to have the one-on-one with Janelle's daughter, they didn't do it that much, but Martin's time was so accounted for now that he was married, it felt a bit suffocating.

"I really like Kenny," Beth said, as if she'd just seen his picture on a billboard, the suddenness of her comment catching Martin off guard.

Martin cleared his throat, forming words in his head, none of them an adequate response to her statement.

"Boys at school are so foolish," Beth said, apparently wanting to open a discussion Martin wasn't sure he wanted to be part of. Martin knew what she was talking about, boys trying desperately to feel adequate around the girls, yet still holding onto the most childish and vulgar notions about sexuality and their own bodies. It was hard for them to come off as anything other than clowns, walking around like a jumble of spare parts, giggling and laughing at the dumbest stuff.

"It was nice being around Kenny," she said. "He's mature, you know, but not stuffy like most adults. He was fun!"

Oh, brother. Martin wasn't sure what to say to her. Did she have a crush on his son? It had been two months since the wedding and Martin couldn't help but wonder what kind of impulses this young girl was entertaining, but it felt like an issue to discuss with her mother. Had this been the reason she was so keen to ride along into the city?

"Do you think Kenny will ever move back to St. Louis?" she said, swiveling her head toward Martin for just a moment before taking her eyes back out the windshield. "He told me he was looking at companies downtown to submit his resume. He must be very talented at what he does, some kind of software engineer or something. It sounds fascinating..." Beth laughed like an adult here. "Though I have no idea what that means. But anything to do with computers would surely be looking toward the future."

"What did you think about Elaine?" Martin quickly interjected.

"She's nice," Beth said, looking out the side window toward the trees in a park they were passing. "Kenny was explaining how the future of medicine would be forever changed by computer technology." She smiled, her eyes sparkly and assured, as if someone had shared the secret of the universe with her. Then: "Because of AI..." she paused, probably replaying the explanation his son had given her, trying to recall the meaning.

"Artificial Intelligence?" Martin offered.

"No, that's not it..." Then, an instant later: "*Advanced Intelligence!* Yes, that at some point in the future, that, through AI, it would be possible for people who are ill or hurt to enter a beautiful facility, with paintings and sculpture and wonderful music, completely void of doctors and nurses and medical staff, and walk into one of a thousand chambers, no waiting, which would scan your body from head to toe. You wouldn't even have to undress. And then, the computer would read your DNA, and greet you personally, like, 'Good afternoon, Marty. So good to see you again. I see you're having a bit of a problem with your aorta. Don't worry, nothing serious. We'll get you fixed up pronto.' And then you'd stand around while the machine would do whatever necessary, probably some kind of ultrasound and electrical impulses to eradicate the problem, realigning cells and tissue, repairing the damage flawlessly, and super-fast. All using non-" she paused again, her face a puzzle trying to recall the term. "*Non-invasive* techniques! In a short time, with no hospital stay, you'd be on your way! No charge! It would all be free!"

Beth sat across from Martin beaming, a million light years away, on some planet where marrying your stepbrother was not only encouraged, but preferred, especially when there was a ten-year age difference! "Kenny is so smart!" she said, her lips parted as if in the thralls of some phantom kiss, thrilled, proud to be included in an adult world of ideas and visions. "He even had a name for the facility: *Flanders Medical Assistance Center.*"

Flanders? Noreen's maiden name. Martin could imagine where Kenny's inspiration had sprung from, seeing his own mother rotting away in her hospital room, the medical staff incapable of doing anything but keeping her vital signs beeping, waiting for a miracle, knowing science had failed them again, no longer able to offer solutions. It had made Martin furious, and it obviously caused Kenny more pain than Martin had ever imagined, the boy's spirits seemingly undiminished upon seeing his mother's unmoving body, her unblinking eyes. Nevertheless, Martin should have known better, gotten Kenny help, but Martin had been so wrecked himself he could barely maintain his own sanity.

After twenty minutes—Beth filling the time with questions about Kenny's childhood, and growing up without a mother—Martin turned onto Yurning Place Road and drove to the end of the street.

"We're here!" Martin announced, grateful to see an end to the discussion.

"Wow, it really is kind of a crap hole," Beth said, popping her door open. She walked around the car, looking toward the field behind the house, then up the block. The gray sky, the absence of leaves and greenery, painted the place gloomier and more desperate than it usually was. Martin stood next to her, then walked toward the front door. Beth followed, paying special attention to the ground beneath her boots, stepping carefully to avoid the mud slicks.

When Martin opened the front door, he was shocked to see Falco sleeping on the unopened futon. Before he could shoo Beth away, she was standing next to him, her eyes wide, her mouth open. Martin walked over to him, and shook him gently by the shoulder. Falco stirred, but didn't wake up, his face crushed against the futon cushions.

"Do you mind waiting in the car a second, Beth," Martin said, not believing this was happening. He could already hear the discussion when Janelle heard about this.

After Beth turned and walked out, Martin went over and shut the front door, then returned to the futon. "Falco! Hey, wake up!"

Falco turned toward Martin, smacking his lips, his tongue

attempting to remove the film from his mouth, his eyes still closed, his face bruised and cut. "Jesus, what happened to you?" Martin said.

Falco managed to open his eyes to slits. "Hey, Sport! How you been?"

"What happened, Falco?"

Falco tried to sit up, wincing and grabbing his ribs. Martin reached out to help Falco get himself upright. "Ah, that's better," Falco said, smiling, smacking his lips again, coming back to the world slowly. He cleared his throat several times, wincing in pain. "I need to get to the bathroom," Falco said.

"Just a second," Martin said. "I want to get my step-daughter to help me move you, okay?"

Falco nodded.

Martin rushed out to the car, the snow coming heavier now, and checked for Beth but she wasn't around. Panicked, he took his eyes up the street, maybe she was walking, then out to the field, a man standing with her near the railroad tracks. "For fuck's sake!" Martin said, jogging toward the field. A moment later he saw the pizza-sized emblem on the man's black jacket, *RENAGADES*, and hurried toward them, calling Beth's name. Beth turned toward Martin, smiling, then swiveled her head, still laughing, back toward the scraggly long-haired biker who was wearing black leather pants, his behemoth tricked-out Harley parked a few feet away.

"Beth!" Martin called, high-stepping through the weeds, Beth acting as though she couldn't hear him. "Beth!" All at once, as if out of thin air, a huge, black locomotive appeared, roaring through the field it looked like to Martin, shaking the earth, Beth and the biker laughing, their mouths dark open holes, watching the train race by. Beth raised her arms above her head, doing some kind of celebratory dance or something, her puffy jacket riding up her back, the biker checking out the ass of her skin-tight jeans.

"Beth!" Martin screamed, trying to get her attention over the rumble of the train. She threw her head back, laughing, her hair sucking sideways in the current of the locomotive, the biker throwing his arms up now, cheering stupidly at nothing, both of them like escapees from the loony bin.

Martin was jogging toward them when Beth scribbled something on a piece of paper and handed it to the biker. Martin reached them before the biker could stick it in his pocket.

"She's fourteen, Terrence," Martin said, snatching the scrap of paper from his hand.

"Yeah," Terrence said, "and the *Renagades* are just a co-ed softball team."

Martin groaned and ushered Beth back toward the house.

"Tarantula is kind of cute," Beth said, looking over at Martin.

"*Tarantula!* Jeez," Martin said, grumbling to himself. "Before you start thinking you met an honest-to-God outlaw, know this: His name is Terrence Potter, and he's a concessioner down at Busch Stadium, hawking peanuts and foam rubber fingers! He belongs to a union, for chrissakes! That's how much of a non-conformist *Tarantula* is."

Beth was laughing, following Martin back to the house. About to go in, Martin spun toward her, panicked and angry. "How could you give him your phone number, Beth! He's like forty years old!"

Still smiling about the encounter, Beth said, "Yeah, like I'm going to give my phone number to a guy who calls himself *Tarantula!* It was my gynecologist's number."

"Oh, brother! Come on," Martin said, hurrying through the front door. "Beth, this is Mr. Falco, Falco, Beth. Grab under his left arm and help me get him to the bathroom. Be careful, he may have broken ribs."

Slowly, Falco pushing with his legs, they got him to his feet and into the bathroom. "I got it from here," Falco said, closing the door. Martin and Beth went back to the living room to wait for him. "Want something to drink, water…?"

Beth shook her head and sat down on the futon. "You know what Tarantula said to me when I told him Renegades was spelled wrong?" Beth said to Martin.

Martin looked at her, then toward the hallway, trying to hear if Falco was okay. "No, what?"

"He said, 'I don't care if it's spelt wrong, I don't have to look at it.'" Beth scoffed, letting her eyes rove the tiny space. She got up and started to walk from the room to give herself a tour of the bungalow. Martin jumped up and caught her just as she was entering the *Anything* room, relieved the door to the portal was shut. She flipped the light switch on, then looked back at Martin, then back to the empty space. Flipping the light switch off, she went into his bedroom across the hall. Martin walked back to the living room and looked around. Everything was pretty much the way he'd left it last time he'd dropped by. He sat down at the kitchen table, wondering what had happened to Falco. Beth came back in and sat on the Futon. She looked over at him, then at the tiny television set, her eyes rising toward the rinky-dink air conditioner in the small window. "You lived here?"

Martin nodded. The bathroom was very quiet and Martin was getting concerned. He got up and moved partway down the hall, waiting near the bathroom door to see if he could hear Falco. Nothing. Martin heard Beth rummaging through the kitchen cabinets above the counters, then the drawers, pulling the cabinet doors beneath the sink open, letting them slam shut.

"Falco...? Are you okay?" Martin said almost in a whisper, moving closer to the door. Nothing. He put his palm on the door knob and tried to twist it. Locked. "Falco?" he said again, a little louder. Beth was quiet in the living room and Martin wasn't sure what she was up to. He walked out and Beth was sitting at the kitchen table going through Martin's mail, reading where the letters had come from. "We'll be going soon, Sweetie," Martin said.

She looked up from the mail. "No rush, Marty."

Even though he'd agreed to her calling him *Marty*, he wasn't sure he'd ever get used to it. He leaned back toward the hallway, about to say something when the door burst open, and Falco walked out a new man, standing upright, his hair combed, his shirt tucked in, his pants oddly wrinkle free.

"So, let me meet this little beauty you brought with you today, Martin," Falco said, walking past him to the kitchen. Falco turned his head, his eyes meeting Beth's at the table. Beth put the mail down, her eyes fixed.

"That's pretty remarkable," she said flatly, clearly unimpressed, and a bit suspicious.

"Falco the *Fantabulist!*" Falco said, holding his hand toward Beth. When she gave him hers, he bent at the waist and kissed the back of it gently, holding it as if it was to be his. "I'm a magician!"

"I'll say," Beth said, waiting for her hand back. Falco smiled and released it, letting her slender fingers slip through his. "What's a *fantabulist?"*

"One who does fantastic, fabulous things!"

That was it? Martin thought. That's what it meant? Fantastic and fabulous jammed together like a peanut butter and jelly sandwich?

"If I decide to go back on the road..." Falco said, his eyes sizzling with blue fire, meeting Beth's. "I'm going to need a beautiful assistant!"

"I'm fourteen."

"You won't be forever," Falco said, unfazed by that little detail, spinning toward Martin. "What do you think?"

"About what exactly?"

"About the future of our wretched existence when faced with such inexplicable beauty! How can vile and lowly beasts such as ourselves possibly cohabit the same plane with creatures as lovely as this?"

"Okay..." Beth said, standing up, smirking. "Marty, I think it's time to go."

"Falco, you going to be all right?" Martin said.

"Golden," Falco said to Martin, then, looking over at Beth, said, "Can I have a private moment with Marty before you leave?"

"Sure. Nice meeting you." Then: "I'll be in the car with the doors locked, Marty."

Before she could leave, Falco brought his hand out from behind his back and handed her a perfect live, white rose. She took it and smirked. "You're one strange dude," she said. Falco waited until she closed the front door, then turned briskly toward Martin. "We have to talk, Martin," Falco said, suddenly gloomy, worried.

"Can it wait?"

"How long?"

"Monday would be best. Can it wait until then?"

Falco nodded, looking at the floor.

"You sure it can wait?" Martin said. "I could try to get—"

"No, Monday's good."

"Need food or anything?"

Falco shook his head. Martin went to the drawer and found a pen and a scrap of paper and scrawled something, then handed it to Falco. "This is my phone number. If you have any—"

"Thanks, *Marty*," Falco said, smirking. "I'll be fine till Monday."

Martin was nodding, looking at Falco, needing to ask him something. "Is it the portal? Is something wrong with the portal?"

"No, it's fine." Then a moment later, trying to force a smile: "Monday."

Martin smiled, patted Falco on the upper arm, then went out the door, pulling it shut behind him. Snow was coming harder now. Beth had the car running, exhaust billowing out the tailpipe, the music so loud Martin could hear it from the porch. He looked up the street, then out to the barren, muddy field, the gray sky so low overhead if seemed as if he could reach up and touch it, the stench of the railroad tracks mingling with the sterile, steely smell of winter. Martin threw himself into the front seat of the car, the heater blowing air like a furnace, shaking his head side to side trying to slow the tumbling thoughts, and shut the door.

They were soon on the highway, the snow a smear beyond the windshield, the wipers slapping across the glass as the gray day crawled toward night.

"You have some interesting friends down there," Beth said. The comment came in the midst of a numbing silence, Martin concentrating on the road, lost in the thump of the wipers.

"Not really friends, Beth," Martin said, trying to dispel any illusions, not only for her sake, but his own, knowing all of this *information* was going straight back to Janelle when they got home. Janelle had met the *Renagades* one time when she and Martin had joined them on a biker day trip to Hannibal, so she was familiar with the group. But she knew nothing of Falco, and Martin wasn't sure how he was going to handle that. He'd already told Janelle that his renter had moved out (though there had never been one), and had told her there were new prospects, but nothing certain. At the end of all these discussions, Janelle would offer her most persistent solution: "Sell the place. You don't need it anymore." To which Martin would reply, "If I get stranded downtown by weather, I could spend the night." Which she would quickly counter with, "Or you could get a hotel room."

"Do you carry a gun, Marty?" Beth said into the new darkness filling the Taurus. Visibility was less than fifty feet now, the headlights burning white smudges on the wall of blowing snow. Oh, Jesus, not now, Martin thought, his fingers like talons wrapping the steering wheel, the car feeling airborne for a second or two slipping on the snowy wet pavement.

"No, Beth," Martin said. "I don't care for guns."

Beth sat perfectly still across from Martin. Like a mannequin; eerie how quiet she could be, never clearing her throat, her breathing soundless, not even the occasional sniff or cough. He thought she needed a bell attached to her jacket, something to remind him she was there.

"My dad carries a gun… in plain sight… on his hip. It's small, like a child's toy, black, in a black leather holster." Martin thought he heard her laugh a little, or scoff, maybe. Then she said: "Everyone can see it. *Carl* doesn't realize how people look at us in stores and stuff. It's creepy."

Beth was quiet a long time as Martin maneuvered in traffic, the snow lighter now, visibility improving. Red taillights burned along the slick pavement, reflecting quivering red snakes, occasionally glowing brighter with alarm when the driver hit his brakes.

"Do you ever think you need a gun when you go down to that house of yours?" Beth said, turning her head toward him, impossible to read her expression in the dark.

"Just because people are poor, it doesn't make them criminals," Martin said, the tires slipping just a split second before catching, an unnerving feeling of being out of control.

"That woman that got killed at the mall a few months ago," Beth said. Then, after a pause: "*Carl* said the man who killed her was poor, and stole her purse and jewelry."

Since Martin and Janelle married, and Martin was spending much more time with Beth, he had noticed something about her, that she would often refer to her father as *Carl* when she didn't completely agree with him. Maybe it was her way of distancing herself from his beliefs, while still grappling with his ideas on life. Martin shook his head. "No, Beth, the man didn't kill her because he was poor. He killed her because that's how he *chose* to deal with his problem. It's a choice, Beth. There are plenty of poor people who would never kill someone for their money or jewelry."

Beth fell quiet, resuming her zombie status on the passenger side of the car. They were only ten minutes from the house now, and Martin hoped for a quiet interlude to figure out how to explain the events of the afternoon to Janelle.

A few minutes later Beth said, "Is he really a magician, that Falco character?"

"Yeah, I guess so," Martin said turning onto the country road, which was delightfully free of snow. The county must have salted.

"I think he was faking those injuries," Beth said, "then came out of the bathroom like he magically healed himself." She turned her head toward him, then forward again. "It was a nice illusion. Had me going for a few seconds."

Martin cleared his throat and guided the car into the subdivision.

"Why was he at your house?" Beth said, looking out the side window.

"He's just staying for a while, until he gets back on his feet."

Beth shot her head around. From the edge of his vision, Martin could tell she was scowling at him. He swung his eyes toward her. "What?" he said.

"If you don't want to tell me, just say so, but don't lie to me."

Martin felt horrible, shooting glances in her direction, then back to the subdivision street. Cars in driveways were dusted with a thin layer of snow, almost like powder, along the roofs, trunks and hoods, the yards like brown toast sprinkled with sugar.

"I'm sorry. You're right," he said. Then: "I can't tell you, okay."

She said nothing, her eyes tracing the slow curve of the cul-de-sac until Martin pulled into Janelle's driveway. The garage door lifted when he hit the button, both of them watching the wide door rattle up along the ceiling of the garage, the light in the garage coming on automatically. When the door stopped, Martin nosed the Taurus into his spot, then shifted the car into park and shut off the engine. In the harsh glow of the singular garage light, Beth turned toward him. "Thanks for taking me," she said, "It was fun." She picked up the rose off the seat and got out, walking toward the door leading to the kitchen.

Martin followed, closing the door behind him. Janelle was seated at the kitchen island, as if she had spent her entire day there without moving. She looked up, meeting Beth's eyes first, then Martin's, trying to mine information on how the afternoon might have gone, then said, "The adventurers return!" Janelle smiled at Martin, then looked over at

Beth. "That's a beautiful flower. Where did you get that?" Janelle asked her daughter.

Beth held it up to her nose and sniffed, then let her mother sniff it. "Um," Janelle said smiling.

"A man down in the city was selling them at one of the stoplights," Beth said, bringing the flower back to her nose. "Marty bought me one. Isn't that sweet?"

"That *is* sweet," Janelle said, smiling over at Martin. "Dinner in about an hour."

"Okay," Beth said, walking from the kitchen. "I'll be in my room. Just holler."

Janelle brought her eyes to Martin, and Martin gave her a stupid grin. "So…" Janelle started to say, then stopped, waiting for Martin to fill in the blanks.

"Everything was fine," he said. "It was fun." He was still wondering why Beth had chosen to tell her mother the flower vendor story, surprised by the girl's allegiances, and her apparent respect for Martin's privacy, and secrets. Even so, the lie had thrown Martin out of alignment, his mind scrambling to figure out the fourteen-year-old's angle. Did this constitute some kind of tacit quid pro quo, one Beth would exploit later. Martin had fully expected to do battle with Janelle over the bungalow, followed by a lengthy discussion of Tarantula and her daughter, and of course, Falco the *Fantabulist*, which Martin had yet to concoct an adequate story for, but Beth's tactical maneuver had saved him from all that. Even so, it left him feeling more indentured than free, and standing, quite awkwardly, on shaky ground.

Chapter Twenty-Five

Already feeling late, Martin hurried back to his office after his last meeting, past his secretary's desk, noticing the bouquet of flowers in the glass vase. Laverne, his secretary, was gone, probably in the restroom down the hall, so Martin peeked at the card. *Love, Harvey.* Laverne's husband of thirty-two years. Martin studied the card a second longer, making note of the florist, deciding he, Martin, might need a peace offering to Janelle when he got home this evening, already certain it was going to be a late night. Laverne returned a moment later.

"Aren't they beautiful?" she said to Martin, her head cocked to the side, her smile stretching from coast to coast. They were, but to Martin, it looked as though Harvey was trying too hard, the bouquet too elaborate and big to be just a spontaneous declaration of affection. Maybe Harvey was compensating for some trespass he was ashamed of.

"Anniversary? Birthday?" Martin said.

"No, none of that," she said, her eyes dreamy, now more convinced than ever of Harvey's incorruptible love for her. She touched a few of the buds, then sat down at her desk. After grabbing his briefcase, Martin walked back out and told Laverne he was leaving for the day.

"Are you expecting any calls I should contact you about?" she said, meeting Martin's eyes, stealing furtive glances at her flowers.

"No." He hurried toward the elevators. "Tell Harvey hello for me."

As the elevator doors were closing, Martin saw Laverne bending toward her flowers again, as if the bouquet was the sun, and she was a tender rose herself.

Martin hadn't told Falco what time he'd arrive, only said it would be around noon. It was already after one, Martin's meeting with Harley-Davidson running much longer than he'd expected, and for whatever reason, Martin was worried, not liking Falco's bizarre demeanor Saturday afternoon. Falco had seemed desperate, more unhinged than usual.

With the threat of snow gone, and the sun restored to its proper throne in the sky, droves of people were out and about, gridlock at every intersection. "Jeez," Martin said, switching channels on the radio, playing back the previous day, Super Bowl Sunday, not the game, so much—Martin unable to even remember who won—but Beth's warmth and unexpected yearning for camaraderie, or so it seemed to Martin. He thought she hated football, and yet spent the evening lying at the opposite end of the couch, wrapped in an Afghan, her double-socked-feet in Martin's lap. Even though Beth seemed bored at times, she surprised Martin with questions about some formation players rushed to get into, or why the players kept switching in and out on certain downs, or why the officials threw a flag. Martin was able to answer all of them, having spent years watching Kenny's team, helping his son learn the plays, going over strategies. Janelle sat on the other side of Martin, leaning against him, sometimes rubbing her daughter's feet. At one point Beth said, "Which of those guys on offense is playing the position my New Big Brother played in college?" The question caught Martin off guard, considering the discussion he and Beth had had about Kenny the previous afternoon. Janelle tilted up toward Martin, waiting for the answer as well, her palm resting on his chest. "Number 84, the tight end, the one lined up on the outside," Martin said. Beth had seemed satisfied, with no further discussion about Kenny, to Martin's relief. Janelle knew nothing about that conversation or anything else Martin and Beth had talked about on the drive down or back from the bungalow. And he had no plans to tell her, not even about Beth's questions about Carl. Putting Martin's discomfort over Beth's interest in Kenny aside, the evening, overall, had been fun, snacking on pizza and chips and m&m's throughout the game, then making love to Janelle later that night after Beth went to bed.

It took almost thirty minutes to get to the bungalow, and by now, the sky had clouded over again, a fine mist drifting across the seemingly deserted neighborhood. Martin parked and went inside, and not seeing Falco, called out to him. When he didn't answer, Martin went into the bedroom, the bed unmade, a towel on the floor, then noticed something outside the back window. There, all alone, squatting out near the railroad tracks, was Falco, no coat or hat, just staring across the tracks, lying in wait like Jesse James to ambush the 4:17 from Carbondale. Martin went outside and started walking through the field, calling to Falco when he got close so he didn't spook him. Falco got up slowly, unwinding, as if unscrewing his body from the earth, to face Martin.

"Hey, Sport, I thought you forgot about me!"

"Aren't you freezing out here?" Martin called to him.

"Feels good. That bungalow's like a furnace."

Martin had always felt it was drafty, but warm enough most of the time.

Falco watched him approach for a second, then turned back toward the fields beyond the tracks. Martin came up beside him, feeling a strained affinity for the eccentric man. Several miles beyond the field and the thicket of trees, flowed the Mississippi River, and on certain days, when the wind blew from the east it would carry the odor of dead fish and river mud.

"Your step-daughter is a delight," Falco said, without turning toward Martin.

"Yeah, she is."

Falco, without presaging his statement in any way, said, "The universe is dynamic, in a constant state of flux, just like our bodies, cells dying, cells dividing, replicating. Nothing stays the same, and yet, nothing changes. The paradox of existence, I suppose. The price we pay for our fleeting drama here on earth."

Martin didn't bother trying to respond. It was obvious Falco was headed somewhere, but Martin would wait until he revealed his agenda. Falco eased his head around toward Martin. "Was that your daughter I saw you with some time ago, coming out of the casino? The red-haired girl in the parking lot? Absolutely beautiful!"

Martin was confused until he remembered Noreen and playing the slot machines, then recalled the man he'd seen skulking around between parked cars. "That was you, then?" Martin said. "That was my wife. Noreen."

"Your wife? How long has she been dead?"

Falco sounded surprised, but Noreen hadn't aged a minute, while Martin had grayed and grown pudgier, so maybe she could have looked like his daughter. "Over fourteen years."

At this, Falco's eyes grew as big and shiny as flying saucers. "Fourteen years? How? How is that possible?"

Martin shook his head. "I don't know what you mean."

"Do you still see her? Is she still in love with you?" The always composed Falco now appeared on the brink of destruction, animated and forlorn, confused and edgy.

Martin tried to explain the situation, how he would come into her hospital room, and they'd spend the day doing something, then he'd leave. Then the next time he'd visit her, they would do something different, or just walk the hospital halls, or get a cab to drive them to a mall. Martin then explained the downside, how, that night, after he left her to come back to the bungalow, she would die. He could never stay past a certain time or it was too horrible to see.

As if by magic, the gloom lifted from Falco's face, his features alive, radiating a new and luminous glow. "Oh my God, that's the answer!" he said, rushing back to the bungalow.

Martin started running after him. "Where are you going?" Martin yelled.

"Inside!" Falco shouted back without turning around. "I'm freezing my ass off out here."

In the living room, Falco paced, patting warmth into his arms, his eyes wide and far too bright, like light bulbs in their last seconds of life. "It's genius!" Falco said. "How did you figure that out?" Then: "No, don't answer that. I don't want to be disappointed if your answer is stupid!"

Martin was at a loss for what Falco was going on about; Martin

hadn't figured anything out as far as he could tell. "I don't understand," he finally said.

Falco came over and plopped down on the futon, his expression
gloomy again. "Does Noreen suffer? Does she have to go through the
whole process every time you visit her, the process of dying?"

"She told me she feels nothing?" Martin said.

"Does she remember you each time?"

"Of course… she just, well, she doesn't really know how long it is
between visits," Martin said. "Like, if I visited her today, she would
think the last time I saw her was yesterday, even though it's been over
a week."

"Fascinating," Falco said, squeezing his chin between his thumb
and forefinger. "I never thought to picture Mitzi the morning before
she was killed. I always wanted to try to change the outcome, and I
did, but…"

"I don't understand, Falco."

Falco thought a moment, hesitant about what he was about to
share. "Martin, you probably don't know this, but you could have
Noreen back at any point in her life, like, say for instance, your
wedding day. Or the day you met. All you'd have to do is picture her
on that day, fix her in your mind, and… presto!"

Instantly, as if on command, Martin was back in Forest Park where
he'd asked Noreen to marry him. He'd had the ring with him, in his
pocket, but hadn't planned to ask her until they had dinner that night on
The Hill. They'd been walking past the birdhouse at the zoo and talking
about something, and then she stopped and looked in at the birds, then
said something about the flamingos, like… "My mom had flamingos in
our front yard when I was a kid. She loved those goofy things." And
Martin had said, "Wow, how did she keep them from flying away?" And
Noreen looked over at him, and said, "You're kidding right?" And
Martin said, "Oh, um, I didn't know flamingos couldn't fly." That's
when Noreen burst out laughing, bent over double, grabbing Martin's
shirt as if she couldn't balance on her own, laughing so hard. When she
finally stopped, she straightened and met Martin's eyes. He'd been dead
serious and didn't get what was so funny. "Plastic flamingos, Martin,"
Noreen said. "She had plastic flamingos." And Martin, so embarrassed,

sweating under his shirt and not knowing what to say, blurted out, "Will you marry me?" Noreen, with a look of confusion, fixed her eyes on him, and said, "Now I don't get it." He reached in his pocket, pulled out the ring and opened the box. She smiled, then said, "On one condition… we have to have two plastic flamingos at our wedding." And they did, up on the alter with them, held in place by the best man and maid of honor. The wedding ended up flamingo-themed, everything pink; tuxes and dresses, all the flowers, everything, but they never told anyone why.

"There's a caveat, Martin," Falco said, explaining to Martin, that whatever day he chose to be with Noreen again, he could not expect their lives to follow the same trajectory as it originally had. Everything could, and would, start changing from that day forward. "Noreen could fall out of love with you. She could end up hating you one day and fall in love with someone else, like some big trombone player who beats the hell out of you and leaves you in an alley for dead!"

"Is that what happened?" Martin said.

Falco looked down at the floor. "I've been trying to get Mitzi back in my life for so long, choosing different times in our lives, happy, amazing times, and they all go to shit!"

"You don't have to choose the same day each time?"

"No, but don't expect the same level of emotion you've been used to," Falco said, then paused to ponder something. "Like unconditional love. Most people think they want unconditional love from their partner without ever stopping to consider how that would feel. Unconditional, Martin, is love without emotion, a deep abiding appreciation without ego, without lust or even desire, almost passionless… cold by the way we measure romantic love." Falco gave his eyes to Martin for just a moment, then took them far away. "It's almost as if no overwhelming emotions exist in the portal, no sorrow, no fear or anger, no attachment to anything…"

Martin had to think on the incongruities, suddenly cast back to the night Beth had come down to the bungalow with him, when they found Falco hurt and battered. "But the guy who beat you up, the trumpet player, wasn't that aggression, anger?" Martin said, hoping he hadn't missed some subtlety he'd be ostracized for.

Falco smirked, then huffed, as if he'd just realized something. "That's the thing that was so weird… that musician wasn't angry when he gave me the beating of my life. He wasn't anything, no emotion, no rage, like he'd been ordained to beat the hell out of me." Falco sat completely still, then added: "Mitzi changed over time. Every time. The more time I was with her, the more she drifted away, not out of anger or hate, but… some kind of entropy. A slow, almost unnoticeable, inexplicable decay." Falco turned to Martin, his eyes a few watts brighter. "The only reason you haven't experienced that is because Noreen dies the night you leave, and everything starts over from the hospital room the next time you visit," Falco said, renewed, reborn. "And it's genius!"

"I don't get it."

"It's not like starting over each time. Noreen is already in love with you and she knows it. You get to spend the entire day together, do what you both want, enjoy each other's company… it's perfect…"

"But then she dies…"

"How is that any different than what you have with Janelle? You spend the day with Janelle, and go to sleep at night, then wake up the next day and spend it with her again. The only difference is you don't get to sleep with Noreen. But the upside is, you can spend each day with her if you choose, or spend one or two a week with her, and the rest with Janelle. Best of both worlds… if you play it smart."

"But what you're saying is, if I wanted, I could choose a time in Noreen's life when we were already in love, but long before she was killed in the car accident, and stay in the portal, spend every day, and every night, with Noreen, just like I did before she died! A regular, normal life! Is that right?"

"Tap the brakes, Sport," Falco said, putting out his palm toward Martin. "There's no guarantee Noreen will continue to love you the way she did before. Trust me on this, Marty. Mitzi has broken my heart at least a half a dozen times already, and this new guy she's with, the trombone player, he practically killed me."

"But—"

"No 'buts,' Sport. And no guarantees. You could lose Noreen, and Janelle, and that lovely stepdaughter you had down here the other day. Everything! Tread lightly, my friend."

Martin fell quiet, contemplating everything Falco had said, but the notion of being with Noreen again, going to bed with her each night, waking up with her in the morning… sharing their lives together the way they once had… it was hard to imagine them falling out of love no matter what happened…

Falco walked to the refrigerator and pulled out a beer, bringing one over to Martin. They sat at the kitchen table without talking. Martin looked at the clock on the stove, then met Falco's eyes. Just then the glass in the windows started rattling, the floor trembled, the table started shaking until the entire house shuddered, seeming on the verge of coming off its foundation, the 2:06 from Perryville (running a few minutes ahead of schedule) rumbling by.

"It's almost five o'clock," Martin said. "I need to get going." He knocked back the beer and stood up.

"I'm going to stay a couple of days if that's okay," Falco said.

"What are you gonna do, you know, about Mitzi?"

"Don't know, Sport."

"Will I see you again?"

"Count on it."

They hugged and Martin went out to the car. When he drove past Geronimo's house, Geronimo was on the front porch. He waved and Martin waved back. Martin wanted to stop at the florist, the ones who had delivered Harvey's flower bouquet to Laverne, to pick up flowers for Janelle. Janelle, the Super Bowl yesterday, lounging together on the sofa, her absently caressing his chest while she watched the game, making love when they went to bed. But mostly what Martin was remembering, were all the *remarkable* unremarkable moments in between, the subtle glances, the passing touch, the kiss on the ear lobe, the pat on the ass, her laugh, the way her eyes sparkled when she was upset, the way a single tear could betray the emotion she was trying to bury. Why was he even considering what Falco had told him, imagining a life with Noreen again? A full life, not just a day! And in the same moment, his mind simultaneously tracking two separate scenarios, he imagined his life without Janelle, without Beth, but most of all, without Kenny, and it filled him with dread.

Chapter Twenty-Six

I t was Thursday. Martin sat at his desk, looking out through the glass wall of his office at Laverne, her flowers as fresh and bright as if someone had just delivered them. The flowers Martin had brought Janelle on Monday had gone over well, Janelle neither suspicious of Martin's intent—which in reality there was nothing to be suspicious of —nor reacting as if his unexpected gesture was some outlandish over-statement of his affection. He could never be sure when it came to flowers, how much was too much or too little, and had trusted the florist's suggestion of a simple bouquet. It was pretty, but Martin had no idea what kind of flowers they were.

The truth was, Martin was never certain of anything. Even with graphic design, he felt out of sorts, as though he was always one botched job away from living under a bridge. To coworkers, and prob-ably even Janelle, and possibly even to Beth, Martin came off as self-assured, but in reality, Martin never fully understood anything completely, a part of his mind always unhinged, chasing unmapped mercurial goals, or in pursuit of truths so elusive even he didn't know what they were. Somewhere deep in his chest—the discomfort present since childhood as far as he could remember—loomed a vague, insol-uble problem, one that left him always discombobulated, at the edge of anxiety, and if he could just figure out that one thing, whatever it was, his world would come into perfect focus. When Martin and Noreen started to date, the deeply entombed conundrum in his chest disappeared, remaining at bay for all those years, and he felt nearly complete, until she died, when it suddenly returned. Noreen provided some intangible commodity that Martin needed, like air, and wasn't sure Janelle could satisfy that requirement. If anyone could.

Along came Falco, who seemed to be a gatekeeper of sorts, a special being with the answers to everything, and just being around the peculiar man transformed Martin. Calmed him and made it seem that everything would become clear given enough time. Martin had hoped to get back to the bungalow before now—meetings and responsibilities had chained him to the office—because he needed to talk with Falco again, get clarity on a few points Martin had thought were clear, but had grown foggy over the past few days. He finished what he was doing on the computer and put it to sleep.

He shut off the light and walked past Laverne, stopping briefly to wish her a pleasant evening. It was only one o'clock, but he planned to take the rest of the afternoon off.

"Not coming back?" Laverne said, not with an accusatory tone, but needing to know how she should handle inquiries.

"Yes, need to see a client," he said, the lie attempting to dissipate the prickly guilt tingling beneath his skin. But his self-reproach was unwarranted; he was a creative director now and answered to no one but the owner of the agency, Bennet Petro, who trusted Martin to get the job done, even if he never showed up for work.

The drive to the bungalow was filled with mental machinations, mostly about the portal, Noreen, Janelle and Beth, Kenny, Falco's assertions about the *other side*, or whatever the hell it was, and that was the problem; Martin had no idea what it was! Of course, Noreen was dead in this reality of Janelle and Kenny and Petro Agency and Beth and the *Renagades*. Yet, on the other side of the portal, where Noreen spoke Martin's name with warmth and desire and laughed and held his hand and kissed his lips; what was that?

Pulling into the bungalow driveway, Martin hadn't even come to a complete stop and was already searching for clues that Falco might be inside. The day was chilly and had started to cloud over before Martin jumped from the Taurus. He was about to head for the concrete porch when he spied something out in the field near the railroad tracks, someone sitting in a lawn chair, Martin's lawn chair, facing the tracks. It had to be Falco.

Martin grabbed another lawn chair from the back of the house, then hurried through the field, the ground soft where the snow had melted over the past day or so. When Martin got closer to Falco, he spoke in hushed tones as not to startle the man. Falco said hello to Martin without ever turning around.

"Can I sit with you?" Martin said.

Falco nodded, his fingers steepled in front of his chest, his eyes planted out beyond the fields and trees, fixed on some unknowable spot near the edge of the universe.

After several minutes of silence, Falco spoke, his body unmoving. "Hardly ever am I stumped, Sport. But the past few days have been a challenge even for my resources."

"Your resources?" Martin said, believing Falco wanted to talk, yet not wanting to pry.

After a pause, where it seemed Falco was trying to weave together an explanation Martin would understand, he finally said, "While the intellect stumbles around in convoluted paradigms of creation and evolution, and the more mundane matters of miracle cures, special diets and the national debt, my intuition opens thresholds to possibilities science will never be able to cross, blinded by its own self-limiting network of observable facts."

Here Falco paused again, as if replaying his own words back in his head. Falco could take as long as he needed, Martin figured; Martin had no idea what any of that meant, and wasn't even sure he knew what *intuition* actually was. Did anyone?

"But my subconscious mind has failed me!" Falco stated, forlorn, his voice filled with concern. "I have met the insoluble problem, and, at this moment have nowhere to turn."

Before Martin could delve deeper into Falco's situation, Falco explained to Martin that he—as Martin had done with Noreen—had gone to Mitzi on the day of her death to spend those final hours with her in bliss and happiness, but had, like Martin, stayed too long, having to relive Mitzi's horrible death in hopes of changing the outcome.

"But her death hadn't come by the same means!" Falco, said,

distraught. "She was killed by a single assailant with a gun!" Falco explained that the next time, they left the Glass Menagerie, the night-club they'd been partying at, earlier in the evening, only for Mitzi to be struck by an out-of-control delivery truck that ran up on the sidewalk. Once again, the very night before, he tried the portal with Mitzi one last time, waiting until much later to leave the speakeasy, only to have Mitzi meet her end in such horrendous fashion Falco couldn't even bring himself to recount it. "It's hopeless." Falco finally said, slipping down into the lawn chair, his fingers once again steepled in front of his chest. Martin had only known the man a short while, but had never seen him hopeless, and certainly not defeated.

Martin wanted to ask questions, needing answers, but wasn't sure if this was the best time to start making inquiries. But then, when would be the best time?

"What is it exactly, Falco? The *portal*... what is it? Is everyone dead? Is it like heaven...?" Then a moment later: "Or hell?"

Falco looked at Martin for the first time since Martin sat down, wearing a look of incredulity that made Martin cower inside. Was the question that insipid?

"I figured you for a pretty sharp guy, Sport," Falco said, his eyes narrowed to slits, like razor blades aimed at the center of Martin's face. "Heaven and hell? Really?" Falco said. "Okay, so you may be a bit dull after all. Listen, heaven and hell are constructs of religious domination. What better way to control the multitudes, the unwashed, if you will, than to create an all-powerful god with a nasty disposition and a zeal for retribution, then add in an eternal punishment beyond all human comprehension, like being burned alive until the end of time, and what have you got? The keys to the asylum, Sport!"

Martin recoiled back into his chair, wishing he could have gotten Falco's dissertation on tape so he could replay it until he actually understood it. Which also may take until the end of time.

"Humans were never meant to live in cages built of facts, statistical probabilities and scientific studies, most of which have a shelf life of ten years at best," Falco said, as if preaching to the weeds. "But we've lost our ability to truly imagine the unimaginable. We've misplaced the magic that is absolute and unconditional in the universe. It's all around, everywhere, if you know how to tap into it."

Falco stood up abruptly and for a moment Martin thought he might leave him sitting alone. It was then the ground began to shake beneath Martin's shoes. A moment later a huge diesel train rumbled up the tracks from Illinois, but Martin didn't know which train this was. Falco, like metal shavings to a magnet, slid forward toward the tracks, as if on a sheet of air. Martin wasn't even sure he'd seen Falco's legs move. When the man was within a few feet of the speeding train, his lawn chair churned over slowly, like a feather, tumbling along the weeds caught in the current of the massive machine. Martin sat forward, his legs cocked, ready to grab Falco if he moved any closer to the steel behemoth. A second later, the end of the train whooshed past, grumbling away, and Falco turned without a word and walked back toward the house. Martin got up and retrieved the lawn chair that had been tangled in the locomotive breath, then gathered up his chair and carried them both back to the house.

Falco was seated at the kitchen table with an opened beer in front of him, another beer sitting opened by the empty seat across the table. Martin sat down and sipped the beer, looking over at Falco. Falco's eyes met his. "Tell me about your family, Sport."

"What do you want to know?" Martin said, putting his beer down, a bit uncomfortable with Falco's new demeanor.

Falco gave him a half-smile, arms folded on the table, his face relaxed, no longer the mask of a madman. "Everything! Tell me how you met Noreen, if you had children with her, how she died, and your new wife, Janelle, and her lovely daughter Beth..." Then, a moment later: "And don't leave anything out... we've got plenty of beer."

Chapter Twenty-Seven

K enny phoned Vickie from New Jersey. She picked up on the third ring. *"Floral & Party,"* she said. They talked between customers, Vickie telling him that Amy had the day off so it was just her manning everything, including the phone. Kenny offered to call back at a better time, but she refused, as long as he didn't mind the interruptions. They had spoken one other time, a few weeks after he returned to New Jersey, helping her with some code snippets on her website, teaching her about *classes*, that by creating classes for the different product groups they offered, it would streamline the website and make it easier when she added new merchandise or services, keeping styles consistent throughout the site. Though she was taking night courses in CSS, she appreciated the accelerated help, as the instructor was taking his time getting to the *cool stuff*, marching the students through a litany of good coding practices. Kenny told her it was better to learn solid methods than some slapdash shortcuts to instant gratification, which were always more costly in the long run, at least in time and aggravation.

"Well, I really appreciate everything you've done," Vickie said. "We've been learning about *classes* at school, but until you showed me on my website how they worked, I didn't really understand the advantage of using them. It's not like I'm looking to a career in coding."

"I know, but it makes life easier knowing that stuff," Kenny said, loving her voice over the phone. "How are things with Roiter?"

"Amazing! He's out of the picture. When we spoke last, I was so angry the bastard wouldn't give me a divorce. But when I told him I had filed a complaint with Liam McCormack, the cop—you remember him from high school, right…?"

Kenny didn't, but it had been a huge graduating class. There were kids he probably passed in the hall all the time and never met.

"Anyway, Roiter found out about the report, but he still didn't care, until McCormack and Buddy Aherns—"

"The *Bulldozer!* Is he a cop now, too?"

"Yeah, that's right, you played with Buddy. Yeah, so you know how big he is, right? And in his uniform with the bullet proof vest and all that, he's like scary big, twice the size of Schwarzenegger! And McCormack's pretty big too. Anyway, they paid Roiter a visit, and things went more smoothly after that."

"Did Roiter get part of your business?" Kenny asked, knowing how successful Vickie and Amy have been.

"No, the business is all in Amy's name. I'm hourly and part time, which amounts to next to nothing. In a year we're going to change things over, and then we'll be equal partners, once all this divorce business is fully in the rearview mirror."

"I'm really glad for you, Vickie!" Kenny said, wishing they didn't live almost a thousand miles apart.

Vickie started helping a customer, then had to take another phone call. Kenny worked at his computer while she had him on hold, but his mind was on Elaine, and the baby, which was only weeks away. What was that going to be like? Elaine was already experiencing changes in her biology, feeling rundown much of the time, causing her to cut back on her hours. She had gained a bit of weight, which put her in a foul mood, though it didn't matter to Kenny, but he'd quickly learned not to mention that to her. "Not everything is about you, Kenny!" she shot back, standing in front of the mirror, disgusted.

When Vickie came back on the line, she started telling Kenny about his dad coming into the store a couple weeks earlier. "He was so cute," she said. "He said he needed flowers for his wife, but nothing so extravagant it would set off alarms like he'd done something wrong, but nothing so feeble to make her think he didn't care! It was funny."

"Did he recognize you?"

"For a second I thought he did, like he was going to say something, but then… no, not really, I guess. I recognized him as soon as he walked through the door. He hasn't changed all that much."

Another customer came in, then a few more, the tiny bell on the door ringing like crazy. "Man, I am really getting busy here," Vickie said. "I'm sorry, Kenny. I need to go."

"Of course, so, if you run into any problems with the website or anything, just—"

"Will you be back in St. Louis anytime soon?" she said in a quiet voice, as if she had her hand covering the phone somewhat.

"Not that I know of. The baby's coming soon, and I'm not sure how much traveling we'll be doing after that."

A long silence followed and Kenny could hear customers in the background, but didn't hear Vickie speaking with them. "Hello?" Kenny said.

"I'm here," Vickie said, sniffling. She cleared her throat quietly, then said, "It's so great to hear your voice. Thanks for calling, and all the help…" Then: "Bye." And the line went dead.

A few hours later Martin called and asked how he was doing. Kenny told him fine, busy at work, and filled him in on Elaine and the expected due date, which hadn't changed, but Kenny didn't know what to say to his dad, still feeling a wicked emptiness in his gut after hanging up with Vickie. Was he that guy, the one who cheats on his pregnant wife? Kenny felt horrible and talking to his dad only made the guilt worse, more repulsive, sour heat rising into his esophagus. For a moment he thought he could throw up.

Martin talked about Janelle wanting to fly out to New Jersey when the baby was born, and that Martin wasn't sure if he could make it, but Beth might even come, though she had school, so Janelle would have to pull her out and Kenny was suddenly overwhelmed, picturing the women at their condo, Elaine with her moods, and how Elaine would respond to the idea of Janelle and Beth flying out, and the baby crying and fussing and his dad droned on about this and that and not really much of anything of interest and Kenny was mortified with his own impatience with his father and wanted to tell him about Vickie, and that the flower shop he'd gone into a couple of weeks back to buy flowers for Janelle was owned by Vickie, and that he, Martin, had met her years ago in the bleachers at one of Kenny's high school football games and that Vickie had wanted to tell Martin right then and there that she was in love with his son, but had been too afraid, though it didn't matter now, because she was still in love with his son, and his son was still in love with her.

"Don't let it overwhelm you, Son," Martin said. "A new baby sounds like a lot, but you'll see, things go much smoother than you can imagine. And Janelle will be a godsend for Elaine. Cooking. Taking care of the baby so Elaine can rest. Changing diapers. You'll see."

Kenny knew his dad was trying to help, but the more he talked the deeper Kenny fell into despair, the walls coming down, the oxygen being sucked from the room. Saucer-sized puddles of sweat soaked the armpits of his shirt, the odor of his own perspiration wafting up under his nose. He wiped tiny beads of sweat from his brow and told his dad he had to get going or he'd be late for a meeting.

"I love you, Son," Martin said. "I'll be in touch soon!"

"Me too, Dad," Kenny said, relieved to be off the phone, unable to fend off the crushing loneliness in his chest.

Chapter Twenty-Eight

The baby arrived exactly when the doctor had predicted, due mostly to the miracle of modern medicine and induced labor. Kenny and Elaine named their new son, Michael, and Janelle, as Martin had predicted, was a great help with the baby and meals and taking care of things at the condo, while Elaine and Kenny acclimated to their new life.

Martin joined them after a few days, spending time with Janelle while Elaine breastfed Michael and worked around the house and got back on her feet, feeling much better and stronger since the birth. Beth had wanted to come but Janelle, to Beth's great disappointment, refused to pull her out of school. "It's only a few days," Beth argued. And Janelle countered with, "That's right, and kind of pointless to disrupt the routine." Beth had been upset and huffed off, spending much of her time in her room until Janelle left for New Jersey. Beth had begged to stay with Martin until he flew out to join her, but Janelle insisted Beth stay with her father, that Martin was far too busy at work to keep up with a fourteen-year-old. Martin had been thankful for Janelle's decision and at the same time a bit hurt by it; Janelle obviously didn't see Martin as a suitable father figure for her daughter, but then neither did Martin, or maybe it was something else altogether; Janelle not feeling that the responsibility for watching Beth should fall to him. Either way, he relished the time alone at Janelle's house (even though Janelle repeatedly reminded him that it was now his house, too. A difficult pill to swallow, never feeling right-at-home.

Martin had been playing over and over everything Falco had told him the last time they were together at the bungalow a few months earlier, about how Falco, shortly after the portal had been forged, had chosen the point in time when he'd first met Mitzi at one of his magic shows in Minneapolis. She'd been in the audience and his assistant at the time had taken ill quite suddenly. After having an usher roust the blonde in the fifth row from her seat, Falco had waited back stage for her to be brought to him. When she entered his dressing room, Falco jumped up and thrust a sparkly red dress into her hands and asked if she could fit into it. She'd held it up by the spaghetti straps and looked it over. "Sure," she said, her smile more sparkling than the dress. Falco sent the usher away and escorted the young woman to the four-panel changing screen where she could pour herself into the dress while he explained what she'd be doing for him. When she finished, she stepped out from behind the screen and gave her back to Falco, who couldn't stop staring at her lush, creamy skin. "Zip please," she'd said, then asked where the shoes were. "Shoes!" Falco shouted to the dully painted room, arms out in appeasement, running in circles, trying to remember where the damn shoes were. The woman went over to the large lighted makeup mirror and found them on the floor beneath the table, then wiggled her feet into them. Falco had been about ready to tell her she needed a splash of makeup, then realized she was perfect. Absolutely perfect! "You're an utterly stunning creature," he said, his hands holding to her upper arms, admiring her as if he had created her himself. "You all set?" Falco said a moment later. She nodded, and in her high-heels, stood almost as tall as Falco. It took every ounce of Falco's self-control not to take her into his arms and kiss her lovely full lips. Escorting her from the dressing room, Falco was telling her where she needed to be when the curtains opened, and how she should keep her eyes on the audience ninety-five-percent of the time. "Only glance at me occasionally, and with great self-assurance, as if nothing could possibly go wrong!" Falco said, hurrying her to the left side of the stage. "Ready?" he said, the music rising. "Yes!" she said. "What's your name?" he asked, edging backward across the stage away from her in order to burst out and hit his spot. "Joan!" she said in a high whisper, Falco halfway across the stage. Falco paused, his eyes boring into hers. "Mitzi! Your name is Mitzi!" The young girl smiled her approval, nodding yes, and the curtain rose to thundering applause.

"Absolutely perfect," Falco had said sitting at Martin's kitchen table at the bungalow. "That's why I chose that moment to find her again, the beginning of everything, because I wanted to relive every possible second we'd shared right up until the day she was..." Falco had broken off, his voice faltering, his eyes refusing the tears.

"What happened?" Martin had asked Falco, imagining his life with Noreen, and how he'd do anything for the chance to relive every second with her again, too, if he could. My God, he thought, nearly in tears himself, so giddy over the prospect, his body juddering with electricity.

"It was amazing for so many years, Marty, everything just as I remembered it from the first time, but even better, every color and sound and sensation more intense, if you can imagine that! But then..." Falco paused, his eyes flickering like a movie projector, trying to map out the exact moment when things went wrong, his beer poised in his hand just above the table. An instant later, Falco snapped back. "Then, it just... I don't know... Mitzi lost interest in our lives. In me," Falco said, setting the can down gently, like it was a stick of dynamite. "It was more devastating than the night she actually got killed in the physical world. I know that sounds horrible, but the night she was taken from me by thugs, she'd still been crazy in love with me, the kind that never dies. But this, her just drifting away from me like dust, sometimes looking at me with disgust, or worse, with indifference. It tore out my heart."

Martin, even entertaining the possibility that Noreen could ever look upon him with cool indifference, felt like he had an explosive detonating in his chest. It stole his breath. Falco explained that he'd gone back in through the portal at a different time in their lives together, shortly after they had talked about getting married. "That was a wonderful time," Falco had told Martin. "We were living in Chicago, but headed for Las Vegas. Talk about magic!" Falco told Martin how after only a month, Falco had been in such demand he'd had to hire an agent to handle bookings. "Money was rolling in and Mitzi and I were living the dream! Jeez it was incredible! So, I decided to go back through the portal at that precise time, when Mitzi and I were moving into our high-rise condo right on The Vegas Strip." Falco told Martin that about two years after arriving in Vegas, in the portal reality, that Mitzi felt the grind was becoming too much, all the shows, every night of the week, and wanted to slow down, move back to Chicago. "That didn't happen originally with Mitzi. She was nuts for Vegas in the real world, and no amount of work dampened her spirit, both of us partying till dawn every night, buying artwork for our condo, new cars, doing lines with big stars. It was a rush, and she'd loved every stoned-out hung-over moment of it! Both of us did! But that changed in the portal-reality." Eventually Mitzi moved out of Vegas, telling Falco she needed space, changed her name back to Joan, and finally ended up marrying Falco's manager. They'd moved back to Minneapolis and bought a house, and started doing auto, boat and RV shows all over the Midwest. Falco followed her around for years, trying to convince her to come back to him, but when she got pregnant, he gave up and came back through the portal, hoping to hatch a better plan.

"In the real world, our lives were so perfect, that no alternative existence could possibly compare," Falco had told Martin, going to the fridge for another beer, bringing back two and setting one in front of Martin. "The universe seemed to be regurgitating every flawed version of our lives so I'd grow tired of trying. But I couldn't give up on what Mitzi and I had," Falco had recounted trial after trial to Martin, all starting off wonderfully, all ending like a bad dream, Falco always the recipient of a shattered heart and broken spirit.

"When you told me how you managed to spend all that time with Noreen by choosing the day of her death, I couldn't believe my good fortune," Falco had told Martin that evening, grinning, more at ease under the influence of lots of beer. Then he turned glum, recalling how those attempts had gone. It was futile.

"What will you do?" Martin had asked, Falco appearing despondent at that point.

Falco sighed, finishing his beer and tossing the empty toward the corner trash container, the can bouncing off the kitchen cabinet and spinning across the floor, hitting the far wall. "Sorry, Sport. I'll clean that up," Falco, said, his elbows on the table, his forehead dropping into his palms.

"I better get going," Martin had said that night, knowing he wanted to pick up flowers for Janelle. Falco walked outside with Martin and waited in the driveway until Martin pulled his car out. Martin had just started down the street when Falco turned and walked into the field behind the house, Martin wondering if he was going to be okay.

The memory of that night was still fresh, even two months later, as Martin pulled up the driveway of the bungalow. The neighborhood was dark, as it almost always was. The lights in the bungalow were off, and Martin figured Falco was gone, maybe for good. It was possible Falco entered the portal to try another approach with Mitzi, or something far worse, Martin trying to push away the disturbing thought that maybe Falco, feeling defeated and without prospects, had walked out to the tracks the last night Martin had seen him, and stood still, waiting to come face to face with the 4:12 from Carbondale.

Martin closed the door of the Taurus and went up on the concrete porch and unlocked his front door. Flipping on the living room light, he first checked the futon to make sure Falco wasn't asleep, though it was still early in the evening. Martin walked to the kitchen and checked the dish drainer. Empty. Then the fridge, empty, except for condiments and a new twelve pack of beer. Martin went to the bedroom, the bed made. The bathroom, towels neatly folded in the closet, a fresh one with washcloth hanging on the bar, like a small hotel room. The little indented rectangle on the porcelain bathroom sink held a fresh bar of soap.

Martin took off his jacket and set it on the bed, then walked to the *Anything* room. He couldn't remember the last time he'd been here. Contemplating what he was about to do set off a flurry of butterflies in his gut. He exhaled roughly, his left hand over his mouth, staring at the portal door. He eased closer and jiggled the handle. It was locked. Martin withdrew his keys and found the correct one, then inserted it in the tumbler.

"You have to be very clear, Martin," he told himself, as if he needed a pep talk to get things rolling. He pictured Noreen standing outside the Midtown Credit Union. They planned to meet at lunch and apply for the loan on the house they'd found in Mehlville. After weeks of deliberation, trying to see around the impossible corners of life to know if they were making the right decision, they were ready to move forward. They had saved enough for a down payment, and had decided to both take a long lunch from work and meet at the credit union. In his mind, he could see her standing out front as clear as day, her red hair catching sunlight, her yellow dress swaying like a freshly dried sheet in the breeze, her white purse slung over her shoulder. She was smiling, as she always did, as if life had vowed to bring her nothing but happiness.

With her firmly in his mind, Martin pulled the door open, light flooding the room. He waited, the bright fog beginning to clear, the street corner coming into focus, the sign on the credit union, traffic rushing by, a car horn, a bus rumbling through the traffic light, the smell of exhaust, a couple with a dog in the crosswalk. At the entrance to the credit union stood a woman in a yellow dress, smiling, and every function of Martin's body stopped, held in stasis, as if he had turned to stone. Less than fifty yards away, she waited, in high heels, her lips painted a pale red, her fingernails painted to match, her green eyes a-sparkle with sunlight, every detail so sharp and clear he felt he was viewing her from five feet away. How could it be? All he had to do was cross the street, guide himself up the sidewalk, take her in his arms and kiss her, then walk inside to speak to the loan officer. And they would start their life again. And yet, his stomach was inside out and twisted sideways. His life as he knew it now would end. He may never see Kenny again, or Janelle, or even Beth, never get to watch his new grandson, Michael, grow up. Martin was supposed to drive to Lambert in the morning, fly to New Jersey to spend a few days with Kenny and Elaine, hold Michael in his arms, then return home with Janelle. What would happen when he didn't show up?

Noreen, across the street waiting in the shade of the credit union portico, glanced at her watch, then said hello to a man entering the building, then took her eyes out to the street. She looked so vibrant and alive and healthy and Martin ached to hold her. Could he live a double life, part time with Noreen, the other with Janelle and Beth? Men did it. He'd heard accounts in the news, but grew weary just thinking of the familial gymnastics of pulling off such a feat, the logistics alone overwhelming. But isn't that what he'd been doing? *No, not at all!* He told himself. *Nothing of the kind!* Nevertheless, his knees grew wobbly and frail. He wasn't ready for this, that much was obvious. He backed up slowly, tears pressing up from his chest and rolling down his cheeks, Noreen smiling, full of anticipation and hope, picturing her life with Martin in their new home, waiting with her wonderful news until after they'd signed the papers. "I'm pregnant, Martin!" she would tell him. "Let's skip work today and go somewhere expensive and celebrate!"

Martin backed away and slowly slid the door back into the jamb, the rays of lights compressing thinner and thinner until the *Anything* room fell dark. He padded through the living room, flipping off the light switch, then locking the front door behind him. Out beyond the field, soundless lightning flashed above the railroad tracks, like cannon fire too far away to hear, bursting across the sky, flaring out a moment later as if the phantom battle had ended.

Martin walked to his Taurus and started the engine, sitting a long time before switching on the headlights, then backed down the driveway, trying to remember where Janelle had told him to look for his suitcase.

Chapter Twenty-Nine

A couple of months before Beth's fifteenth birthday, Janelle and Martin decided to take a motorcycle trip while Beth was at her father's house for the weekend. They were going to follow the original Route 66 all the way to Tulsa, stay for the night, see the sights, then head back home the next day. It would be about a six- to seven-hour journey each way. Martin hoped to drive the entire Route 66 someday, starting in Chicago and going all the way to the west coast.

They headed out early that morning, planning to stop around Rolla or Lebanon for lunch, depending on the time. The day started a bit chilly, but was growing more pleasant with every mile, the trip giving Martin lots of time to wrestle with his guilt, Janelle on the back, holding around his waist, the road noise making it nearly impossible to converse. On several occasions over the past year, Martin had only gotten as far as his first attempt, watching Noreen from across the street, ultimately ruling against the decision to take it further, then leaving the portal. Until a month ago, when he'd worked up the courage to cross the street, Noreen ribbing him about being late for their meeting with the loan officer, then laughing and throwing her arms around him to kiss him. "Come on, Mr. Moffett, let's go buy a house!" They'd gone in and sat down across from Mr. Denton as he explained the terms of the loan in more specific language so they would understand completely how it worked. They looked over the papers, Martin especially struck by his own occupation, *Owner of Phoenix Design Group*, a dream of his since attending Washington University for his bachelor's in art. He read down the paper, the details stating that he had three employees, as well as the net earnings of the company. It was doing well, very well. He then paid extremely close attention to the address of the company, as it was his only way of knowing where it was. Already, this alternate version of his life was both fascinating and troubling, as he had never owned his own company, but had always aspired to; it was as if the portal was capable of fulfilling any and all unfilled dreams. They signed the papers and walked outside, Martin waiting for Noreen to announce the good news and propose playing hooky from work that afternoon to celebrate her pregnancy, but she only asked how Martin felt about being a home-owner, and was sorry they hadn't planned to take the rest of the day off to celebrate their new home.

That was the beginning of a new life, or more exactly, a parallel life, one that required Martin to make up a story for Janelle about how Bennet Petro had opened an office in Chicago, and that Martin would be traveling to Chi-town on a fairly regular basis, a few days a week. Janelle hated the idea, but the discussion only lasted through dinner that first night, Janelle occasionally bringing it up when he packed to leave. It was a horrible and theatrically silly ruse, Martin pretending to think about what clothes he needed to pack, telling Janelle how much he'd miss her, that this wouldn't be forever, explaining to her, "It's temporary, until Bennet can get things running smoothly," then driving from the neighborhood, almost convinced himself of the lie, that he was leaving on a six-hour drive to Chicago, though secretly giddy for the relatively short drive to the bungalow, where he'd be reunited with Noreen.

When Janelle's fingernails dug into Martin's sides—the signal to stop—he pulled his Harley into the rest area and parked near the restrooms. Janelle got off and lifted her helmet from her head, then shook out her hair, smiling. "Gorgeous day!" she said. "This was a great idea!" Then, looking over at Martin, said, "What should I do with this?"

Martin took her helmet and locked it to the motorcycle. Following Janelle into the building, he went to a huge map on the wall showing

Route 66 in a bold red line, cutting south-westward across Missouri, but his mind was on Falco's warning. It's unpredictable, he'd told Martin, Martin recalling all the failed attempts Falco had gone through with Mitzi. Martin had only been at it for a month and already could see changes, like the first two hours, Noreen not saying anything about being pregnant, because she wasn't. Then little changes at home with Noreen, nothing big or alarming, but small idiosyncrasies, the way she brushed her teeth, always using mouthwash as soon as she finished. Not this Noreen; she brushed, flossed and only occasionally used mouthwash. But other things were off, such as this Noreen loving avocados, his original Noreen not so much. Another unsettling aspect to this life with Noreen now, was that Time seemed to have no purchase in this new reality. Martin could be gone for four days, at home with Janelle, and Noreen would treat his return as if she'd seen him that morning when he'd left for work. Martin was still trying to grasp the rules of this new paradigm (it seemed different than Falco's experience), but it felt to Martin as though Noreen knew he had a second life, but never brought it up or alluded to it. Martin couldn't even say why he felt that way. Maybe this was a cosmically inferior rendition of their lives together, as Falco had told him to expect if Martin decided to move forward. Yet even with the inconsistencies, Noreen's love for him was never in question, which made it all worthwhile, except for the deception concerning Janelle. After Martin had told Falco all about his family, Kenny, Janelle, Beth, and Noreen, of course, and how she'd died, Falco had been quick to point out that Martin had a good thing with Janelle and her daughter, and there was Kenny to think about. "Don't mess that up, Sport! It doesn't come along that often!" And that was true, Janelle and her daughter were an amazing find, but Noreen was the missing piece of his heart, the lungs in his chest, the air he breathed.

"Is that it?" Janelle said, walking up behind him. He spun toward her, shocked to see he was in a rest area, Janelle standing two feet away, the image of Noreen before his eyes melting slowly. "You okay, Martin?"

"Yeah, good, I just have to hit the bathroom first." He hurried away, turning once to see her studying the big map on the wall before she walked to the counter to peruse the folded brochures in the rack.

When he came out of the restroom, she was nowhere in the building. A moment later he spotted her through the entrance doors, standing outside talking on her phone, her expression anguished, her features tortured. Martin pushed through the doors to catch the end of her conversation; her face like chalk as she disconnected the call. When her gaze met his, it seemed she was falling from some great height, the fear in her red swollen eyes pouring down her cheeks. Before Martin could speak, she said, "We have to go back now!"

It took a little over two hours to get back to her home, Martin pressing the speed limit all the way back to St. Louis. Before they left the rest area, Janelle, hurrying to the motorcycle, spoke in broken phrases, sobbing helplessly into the words, Martin only able to deduce from the fractured explanation that Beth was in the hospital, and something about a shooting.

When Martin pulled beneath the portico of the hospital emergency entrance and stopped the motorcycle, Janelle shot from the bike wrenching off the helmet, then handed it to Martin and rushed away through the automatic doors. After he parked the motorcycle, Martin hurried the helmet off his head and locked both to the bike, then scrambled across the parking to find Janelle inside.

She was seated on the bed, holding Beth to her chest, Beth looking like a zombie, her red, watery eyes frozen open. When Martin walked over, Janelle gazed up, shaking her head, her eyes scalded red and soggy. The nurse in the hallway had told Martin that Beth was in shock, but that she should be fine. Martin and Janelle would find out later when they spoke to police, that Beth and her father, Carl, had been at the grocery store that morning, pushing their cart down the cereal aisle, when a stranger, apparently noticing the gun strapped to Carl's belt, came up to Carl and Beth and started drilling Carl on why he would come into a grocery store wearing a gun. The way the policewoman told it, the stranger, who was shopping with his eleven-year-old daughter, had admonished Carl for carrying a firearm and setting an unsavory precedent for the two young girls, Beth and the stranger's daughter, as well as any other children in the store, the lesson to the children being that the only way to cope with disagreement was through deadly force.

"We have the CCTV footage from the store, but it is still under review," the police officer said. "According to eye witness accounts, the stranger, Dr. Nevins, approached Dr. Drake just talking, his arms at his sides so as not to threaten or provoke alarm. He did move rather close to Dr. Drake, according to the report."

"How close?" Martin asked, stunned, looking at Janelle, who was ashen, her features blank.

"Maybe two feet," the police officer said. Martin nodded, unable to compute the distance logically, was that too close? Was it okay to shoot someone if they came within two feet? Martin, after a few moments of tugging the information through his head, finally, said, "What happened?"

"According to the report," the officer said. "Dr. Drake withdrew his weapon and fired four shots into Dr. Nevins' chest, then walked over and fired one last time into Dr. Nevins' forehead." Martin must have been glowering at the policewoman like an owl, unable to register the scene fully, about to ask the dumbest question, *Is Nevins dead?* when he caught himself and pushed the inquiry away.

"We have Dr. Drake in custody," the policewoman said. "We'll contact you if we need to interview Beth further." At this, the police-woman just stared, no more words.

The police had also told them that Dr. Geoffrey Nevins had been a sociology professor at Weldon University, and that Nevins' daughter, Naomi Nevins, nor anyone else in the store at the time, had been injured during the encounter.

While Janelle sat with Beth at the hospital, Martin drove the motor-cycle home, returning with Janelle's BMW, hoping to bring Beth home. The doctors told them that she should spend at least one night so they could observe how she handled the medication. Janelle had argued with the doctors about staying all night with her daughter, but the doctors assured it was best if she didn't. "Beth should be more alert by morning," the doctor said. "Let's give her time, okay."

That evening, at home, a dark foreboding spread over everything, as if the furniture and rooms were merely props in some surreal and twisted stage production of their lives. Janelle was in the bedroom, crying, not twenty feet away, but to Martin's ears it sounded as though the wailing issued from the other side of the planet, like they were both caught in a dream they were unable to awaken from.

Part Two

Chapter Thirty

M ichael was two, and Elaine was pregnant with their second child. Kenny, had dropped the subject of moving to St. Louis almost a year earlier when it appeared futile to push it further with Elaine. Elaine was still working, but just like with Michael, she was exhausted most of the time, though able to keep off the weight. The doctor had told her she was doing a great job, but not to starve herself, that it could be bad for the baby. She assured him that she was eating plenty, and exercising regularly, but still felt tired much of the time.

Kenny had mentioned to her about his upcoming ten-year high school reunion around the third month of her pregnancy, and she had responded favorably, saying that it sounded like fun and that she couldn't wait to meet all his old girlfriends. He assured her she'd be disappointed if that was the only reason she was going. But over the past several weeks, she'd said she was too fatigued to travel that far, plus, what would they do with Michael. "What are you talking about? We'll take him with us!" Kenny had said. "Janelle would love to watch Michael for a few days!" Elaine had given him a pained look, reminding Kenny of the issues his dad and Janelle were facing with Beth since the shooting. "You're right," Kenny had said, recalling the conversation he had with his dad a few months earlier. "The psychiatrist has her on Prozac, but she's still struggling," Martin had told him. "You wouldn't even recognize her, Kenny. She's lost so much weight she looks anorexic, but doctors assured us she isn't." Kenny asked if she was bulimic, but Martin said no, as far as they could tell. They had never caught her binging or throwing up. "Janelle wants to take her to a trauma specialist from St. Louis University, who has a private practice in the Central West End, but she's not accepting any new patients. Janelle keeps sending her letters, trying to enlist some sympathy, but no luck so far," Martin said, clearly exasperated. "It's been almost two years since the shooting." Kenny had asked how she was doing in school. Struggling, Martin had told him, adding she had missed a lot, especially right after it happened, and was so listless she could barely focus. "The shrink is going to try her on lithium for a while. Maybe that will help. Janelle's already on lithium, just to get through the day. She's lost a lot of weight too, and hasn't been herself since the… fuck! What a mess!"

Kenny planned to call his dad that evening to let him know he was flying to St. Louis for his class reunion in a couple of months, and figured his dad would want him to stay with them, but that made no sense. Not with the problems they were having with Beth. It would be ridiculous. Kenny hoped to at least see his dad and everyone when he visited, but he wasn't going to force it. He had offered any help he could, but his dad had thanked him and told him there was nothing he could do.

What was the point of going to the reunion anyway? He hadn't bought his airline ticket yet, and with Elaine feeling so rundown, he could hardly feel good about leaving Michael alone with her. Why was he going? Vickie Kramer? He hadn't spoken to her in over eighteen months and wasn't even sure if she'd attend, and even if she did, then what?

Within a half-hour Kenny's office phone rang. "Kenny Moffett," Kenny answered.

"Kenny. Dad. Catch you at a bad time?"

"No, actually, I was going to call you later this evening."

"What's up?" his dad asked, concerned.

"Just to chat."

"Well… you want to just talk later?"

"No, I'm not busy," Kenny said, knowing he had a deadline to meet, but his mind wasn't on coding. The first thing he asked was how

Beth was doing. Martin said they were trying the lithium, and they had seen some improvement, until the trial started. "The prosecution subpoenaed Beth to testify," Martin said.

"Against her own father? I didn't think they could do that!"

"What do I know about the law," Martin said. "But she's a mess again. And Janelle is writing letters, and appealing to Beth's doctors and psychiatrist to write letters, telling the court it would be damaging for her to appear. Janelle has a lawyer petitioning the court, but... I mean, fuck! What more proof does the prosecution need, for fuck's sake! They have Carl on CCTV shooting this poor bastard in cold blood. Beth will have to sit through that footage if they force her to testify. Can you imagine the effect that will have on her?"

Kenny knew nothing about any of it either, but couldn't imagine having to sit in that courtroom watching her dad kill this guy over and over in front of strangers, much less anyone else, especially since Beth probably had not been able to stop the real-life footage from playing in her head as it was. Obviously, the drugs weren't helping much with that.

Martin had asked how work was going, how Michael was doing, Kenny telling him work was the same, but Michael was turning into a handful, jabbering away about everything, pretending to read his books to Elaine. "Of course, he's not really reading, but his memory is pretty amazing!" Kenny said.

"How's Elaine?" Martin asked.

"Okay," Kenny said, wishing she'd come around on moving to St. Louis. He missed his dad, and phone calls didn't always cut it. When Kenny left for Rutgers, he had never imagined staying in New Jersey, but here he was, not liking it any more than he had before. "I was thinking about flying out to St. Louis for my high school reunion in a few months," Kenny said, testing the waters for his dad's opinion on the subject. "But with Elaine and—"

"She and Michael will come with you, won't they?" Martin said, interrupting.

"Yeah, no, I don't think so... I'm not even sure I'm coming now. It feels wrong to leave Michael with her alone, while I'm off at—"

"Bring them, Kenny! Janelle and I would love to see you all! She talks about wanting to see Michael, Elaine and you, but doesn't feel comfortable leaving the city with everything that's going on."

"Of course, but it seems like such an imposition for us to come, you know… And Elaine isn't sure she wants to travel right now…"

"It might even do Beth some good! She used to talk about you a lot… I think she really missed having you around…"

"Really? I didn't think I made that much of an impression on her."

"You did, Son. I'll clear it with Janelle tonight, make sure she's up to it, but talk with Elaine. It would be so great to see you, and Michael, before he starts driving!"

"Well, I'll see, but phone me right away if Janelle thinks it's a bad idea. It's a lot, you know… company with everything going on…"

"Let us decide that, okay! You just get Elaine on board! I'll talk to you in a few days. I love you, Kenny."

"I love you, too. Bye."

Kenny felt the same profound sadness, the same hollow void every time he hung up with his father. He tried to focus on his work, the reunion suddenly a possibility again.

Later that night, after Michael was in bed, he brought up the trip with Elaine. She asked how Beth was doing and he told her about the trial, the meds. "It's pretty messed up," he said, then shared what his dad had said about them all coming out for Kenny's reunion.

Elaine sipped her ice water and sat back in the chair, her hand resting on her stomach. "I don't know, Kenny," she said after a short time. "I know your dad would love to see you, but man, that stuff with Beth and the trial has got to be taking its toll on them. I can't imagine Janelle would be in any place for company, especially a two-year-old bouncing off the walls."

While they were talking, Kenny's phone rang. "Hello."

"It's Dad, Kenny. Janelle would love for you all to come. She can't wait to see Michael. It's the most I've seen her smile in a very long time. I'll let you go. Hit me back with some dates when you get things finalized. This will be great, really! Love you, Son!"

Kenny disconnected the call and set the phone down on the end table.

"Your dad?" Elaine said.

"Yeah, Janelle is really stoked about us coming," Kenny said.

Elaine ran her palm back and forth along the side of her neck, looking into the space beyond Kenny. "I guess I could take some time off," she said, stretching her neck to loosen a kink. "How long would we stay?" she asked, meeting Kenny's eyes.

"I don't know, maybe five days. What do you think? The reunion is Friday and Saturday. We could fly out on Thursday, and fly back Tuesday morning, get home around five or six that evening. How does that sound?"

"Sounds like Michael will be off the charts by then…"

"Who knows, maybe he travels well."

"Travels well? A two-year-old who can't sit still for thirty seconds?"

"We could overnight him by FedEx!"

Elaine laughed half-heartedly, most likely, like Kenny, unable to fully release the image of her son running up and down the center of the airplane, screaming and shouting, and doing his crazy rolling, floppy somersaults, then hugging everyone in the aisle seats.

"We don't have to decide tonight," Kenny said. "How about I run you a hot bath and rub your feet while you soak and sip your icy-cold raspberry LaCroix?"

"Like last time?" she smirked, chuckling cynically. "My bath-slash-foot-rub-icy-cold-LaCroix lasted about three minutes until you were in the tub, all over me, slopping water across the bathroom floor."

Kenny laughed, narrowing his eyes on her. "That was a one-off," he said. "I'm a different man now than I was back then!"

"Really? That was last week!"

"I'm a Zen master of self-control now."

"Okay, *Obi-Wan Kenobi*, but you can't start rubbing my feet until I've finished my LaCroix. Do we have a deal?"

"Whatever you say. Let me get that bath going!"

Chapter Thirty-One

When they entered the hotel ballroom, Kenny was struck by how many of his high school classmates had attended. Elaine even remarked on how large his graduating class must have been. "I think we had fifteen students in mine!" Elaine said, joking, but Kenny missed her comment, looking at the temporary stage toward the far end of the auditorium, the band playing, lights splashing across people on the makeshift dance floor, formed by a circle of festively decorated tables marking the perimeter, a banner draped from the ceiling.

"What?" he said, his eyes bouncing from person to person, everything a blur of bodies so far. He looked around trying to find a table for them to sit, when someone ran up and yelled, "Muppet! You made it!" Kenny jerked toward the voice. Devan Strand from the football team. "We've got a couple tables," Strand said, pointing toward the far corner. Slowly, as if someone was pulling focus on the scene, faces became familiar.

"This is my wife, Elaine," Kenny said to Strand, letting his eyes rove the shadowy profiles in the dim light. Strand shook her hand and led them around the edge of the dance floor to the tables.

Players jumped up and welcomed him, turning to Elaine, introducing themselves, their wives or girlfriends, shaking Kenny's hand, or patting him on the back, firing questions about where Kenny and Elaine were living, if they were still in Jersey, how many kids, where they both worked, on and on, and Kenny remembered why he had wanted to avoid the celebration; they hadn't been there five minutes and he was already on overload. Elaine, with her arm looped through his, squeezed his wrist and whispered, "Just hang in there, it'll settle down soon."

Many of his ex-teammates were still calling him *Muppet*, the moniker he'd always hated. He hoped he wouldn't have to listen to it all evening. The reminiscing had started, guys from his team recalling games they'd won, then ones they'd lost, Kenny wishing he could sit at a different table, not really enjoying the rehash. Peter Macklin asked Kenny about Rutgers, about his football scholarship, Kenny explaining that after the first year, he pretty much rode the pine. Only a handful of guys from the high school football team had managed to play college ball, none of them making it to the NFL. "It's a long shot, for sure!" Macklin said, as if to mitigate some unspoken disappointment of Kenny's, but mostly to ease his own. Macklin had been a promising candidate as a high school linebacker, but the competition in college had been severe. Now Macklin sold insurance.

When Elaine stood up and asked Kenny to dance, he jumped at the chance to get away from the table, even though he wasn't much of a dancer. He held her without talking, moving his feet in little circles to Whitney Houston's, *I Will Always Love You*. When the song ended, they walked to the bar, Kenny remembering how their son had reacted to Beth the day before when they'd arrived at his dad and Janelle's house, Beth with dark half-moons beneath her eyes, her hair cut short and a bit scraggly and multi-colored, her clothes baggie and ill-fitting. Kenny, holding Michael's hand, had walked him over to Beth and said, "This is your Aunt Beth." Michael had looked up at Kenny, then let go of his hand and went over and hugged Beth's legs and said, "I love you." Beth squatted down, her eyes filling with tears, and hugged Michael close to her. "I love you, too," she said. A moment later Michael kissed her on the lips, then wiped one of her tears. "Are you sad?" Michael said. "No," Beth said, "Just really happy to meet you."

Kenny mentioned it to Elaine as they sipped their Cokes.

"I saw you talking to your dad last night," Elaine said. "Did he say how she's doing?"

"He talked a little about it. Did Janelle?"

Elaine looked away, then brought her eyes back to Kenny. "She's really worried," Elaine said. "Beth's not responding well to the new drug. It's not like she's having an adverse reaction or anything, but Janelle said it doesn't seem to be helping."

"How so?"

"Beth's really obsessed with morbid imagery and music. She sketches really bizarre stuff in her notebooks…"

"Did you see any of the drawings?"

"Yeah… fucking weird."

Kenny took his eyes back to the dance floor. Elaine set her glass down on a table and said she had to find the ladies' room.

"I saw one near the entrance, where we came in," Kenny said. "I'll wait here for you."

Kenny watched Elaine weave her way through the throngs, a group of people near Kenny laughing and talking, but he only recognized one of them, a girl he'd been in math class with the last year.

"Kenny!" someone said. He turned. Vickie was standing before him in a sleek, silvery dress. "I didn't think you'd make it," she said.

"God, you look fabulous!" He set his glass on the bar next to Elaine's.

"Is your wife with you?"

"Yeah, she just went to find the restroom. How's your flower business going?"

"Great…" she said, looking around behind her. "Amy's here somewhere…" Vickie started waving her arms at a young woman walking by. "Amy, come here!" Vickie shouted over the music, then turned to Kenny when Amy started over toward them. "Do you remember her now," Vickie said to Kenny.

Kenny shook his head.

"Amy, this is Kenny!"

"Hi," she said, reaching out to shake his hand. "I can't thank you enough for all the help you gave us on the website. Vickie did an amazing job on that!" Amy turned toward Vickie and gave her a peck on the cheek, smiling, then hugged her. A moment later, Amy turned a bit gloomy.

"I just saw Roiter come in," she whispered to Vickie. Kenny heard and looked over at Vickie, the color draining from her face. Vickie tugged at her dress with her thumb and finger, near her ribs, unaware she was doing it, then brought her eyes to Kenny, trying to force a smile. Amy touched Vickie's arm.

"You okay, Sweetie," Amy said. Vickie's head was on a swivel, a tiny flame of fear flickering in her eyes. She scratched the back of her neck, then brought her eyes to Amy, tears beginning to form along the lower rims. Kenny had thought things with Roiter had gone fairly well, but maybe she hadn't told him everything. About then, a tall young man came toward them. He had a lopsided smile, a husky build and buzz-cut hair the color and look of sprinkled paprika on his pale scalp.

"Liam!" Vickie said, visibly relieved. She hugged him. "Kenny, this is Liam McCormack. Did you two know each other in high school?"

McCormick shook Kenny's hand. "Tight end, right?" Liam said. "You and Aherns played together. He's around here somewhere."

"Yeah," Kenny said. "But I don't think you and I ever met." Kenny shouldn't have been jealous, and crushed, but he was, watching McCormick slide his arm around Vickie's waist.

"I don't think so," McCormick said. "Aherns talks about you from time to time, reliving his glory days on the offensive line."

Kenny should have been happy for Vickie, McCormick able to protect her against that lunatic, Roiter, especially with the help of Buddy *Bulldozer* Aherns, but Kenny felt like he'd been benched in a game he shouldn't even be playing. Amy drifted away when she saw someone she recognized, but not before holding Vickie's hand, letting Vickie's fingers slide through hers, giving her a knowing, supportive smile.

"I just need to borrow Vickie a minute, Muppet," McCormack said with a straight face, then broke up, chuckling apologetically: "Sorry, Aherns told me to call you that."

Even though it was a joke, and McCormick seemed like a good guy, it was embarrassing to be called Muppet in front of Vickie. As McCormick and Vickie walked a few feet away, Kenny sighed, sipping his Pepsi, wondering where Elaine had gotten to, and trying, though not very hard, to give Vickie and McCormick space. Even so, he couldn't help noticing that Vickie was trembling as McCormick spoke to her. When McCormick finished, he smiled, holding her bare upper arms. A moment later, he turned away and walked into the crowd. Vickie drifted back over. Kenny cleared his throat.

"I guess you heard," Vickie said, her eyes tinged red.

Kenny nodded. "McCormick seems like a good guy. I don't think he'll let anything happen to you."

Vickie scoffed, unable to keep her eyes still, as if she were on sentry duty. "Yeah, unfortunately, I don't think his wife's going to care much for him always trying to protect me." Vickie spun around, bringing her eyes to Kenny's. "McCormack and I aren't... you know... nothing like that, Kenny."

"I didn't think you—"

"Yes you did. I saw your face drop when he put his arm around me."

Kenny could feel himself redden, searching for Elaine's face in the crowd, wanting to leave the reunion, get back to Michael at Janelle and his father's home, back to New Jersey. Why did he come? He shouldn't be feeling any shame or embarrassment, or any competition with McCormack, or Roiter, or concerns for these people who weren't even satellites circling his world, whose drama should not become his, whose decisions should not impact his well-being, but they were, and it was maddening. His knees felt wispy, his gyro off-kilter. He wanted Vickie to walk away, but she lingered, frightened as a tiny creature in a world of meat eaters, and he wanted to hold her, wanted to drop the pretense, the formalities, and feel her flesh against his, hating her the entire time for coming over to say hello.

"Kenny, I'm sorry," Vickie said. "This sucks, meeting here like this, like we're nothing but old classmates." She was about to take his hands in hers, then pulled them down to her sides, nervously smoothing out the sparkly dress material over her hips.

"Bet you thought I was kidnapped," Elaine said to Kenny, walking up behind Vickie. Then, to Vickie: "Hi, I'm Kenny's wife, Elaine."

"Hi, Vickie Kramer," she said, smiling, shaking Elaine's hand. "So nice to meet you."

"I knew if I came tonight I'd get to meet some of Kenny's old flames from high school!" Elaine said, lightly, smiling over at Kenny.

"No," Vickie said, "I wasn't one of them... but not for lack of trying!"

Both women laughed, Elaine looking over at Kenny. Kenny looked at his watch, then downed the rest of his Pepsi, suddenly unhinged by the silence spreading between the three of them.

"What do you do?" Elaine asked.

Vickie explained about her and Amy's flower shop, how they'd been dreaming about the business since high school, then told Elaine the name. "It's kind of goofy, I know…"

"No, it's great! I love it," Elaine said, sincerely excited. "If we get a chance, I'd love to drive down and see it." She turned toward Kenny. "Maybe tomorrow, huh?" Then, back to Vickie: "Do you have a card?"

Vickie reached into her little foil bag and brought one out, handing it to Elaine, who handed it to Kenny. "Do you know where that is?" she asked him.

"Yeah," he said.

"I hope you make it down," Vickie said. "Well, it was really great seeing you, Kenny." Then: "And so nice meeting you, Elaine."

Vickie smiled and turned away, walking toward a small crowd of young women that Amy was talking to.

"Wouldn't even give her a chance, huh?" Elaine said to Kenny.

"I don't know what you're talking about," Kenny said.

"Hey, you okay?" Elaine said, putting her hand on his arm.

"Let's just go," he said. "I don't feel so good."

They walked to the car, Kenny trying to avoid interacting with people he recognized, turning toward Elaine, Elaine telling him why it took so long to get back from the restroom. Buddy *Bulldog* Aherns had come up to her, introduced himself, said he knew she was Kenny's wife, then asked her to dance. "He was a really good dancer," she said.

Other people came up and interrupted Kenny and Elaine's conversation, asking if he was leaving, if he was coming to the luau at the Glenwood Hills Country Club tomorrow night. Kenny smiled and said he wasn't sure, but that they had to get going. Kenny's mind was a network of misfiring connections, muddled and knotted and angry, his chest hot, his stomach coming to a boil. About then a short but stout clean-shaven man walked up in a three-piece suit and spoke Kenny's name, calling him Moffett.

"You don't remember me, do you?" the man said, holding his hand out to shake, his eyes shifting between Kenny and Elaine. "Roiter. Tommy Roiter."

Kenny introduced Elaine and they talked a short while, Roiter telling Kenny he worked for Edward Jones, investment counselor, handing Kenny his card, told him if he needed any help with anything to give him a call.

"If you just want advice, that's fine," Roiter added, then smiled at Elaine. "You don't have to open an account with me."

It was hard for Kenny to fit this dapperly dressed, smooth-spoken executive type into the brawler, wife-beater persona Kenny had wrapped Roiter in. Roiter was getting ready to leave, saying it was nice to see Kenny again, then asked if he'd seen Vickie. "She's wearing a sparkly silver dress," Roiter said, not bothering to mention they had been married, were divorced, and that Vickie had a restraining order against him.

Elaine looked at Kenny, puzzled, most likely wondering why Kenny didn't say anything right away. After a moment, Kenny said, "Yeah, we were talking with her a while ago, but I'm not sure where she is." Roiter walked away, back toward the hotel and Kenny figured he hadn't given up on finding Vickie.

In the parking lot, Kenny, so unsettled, led them to the wrong car, then missed his turn getting back on the highway, taking him miles out of the way by the time he noticed. Elaine sat quietly in the dark, adjusting the air conditioner to drive the humidity out. She had no idea they'd been lost, and Kenny was angry about that, that she seemed to take no interest in St. Louis, didn't raise her eyes to the passing buildings or skyscrapers, or inquire about the highway signs showing exits for parks and landmarks, had no interest in seeing the Arch, or Busch Stadium, or taking Michael to the Forest Park Zoo. But then Kenny wasn't sure he was even interested in returning to St. Louis anymore, ready to abandon the crazy illusion he'd nurtured for so long that his life would be better in this city than any other. What an odd notion, his life would be *better?* Until he played his own words back, Kenny hadn't been aware that he felt his life wasn't as good as it could be.

"Do you know if Vickie's flower shop is near the zoo?" Elaine asked, as if she'd been monitoring his thoughts. Kenny, pretending not to hear, reached over to turn up the news when it came on the radio.

Chapter Thirty-Two

Saturday morning, everyone sitting around the breakfast table making plans, Elaine announced that she, Kenny and Michael were going to the zoo, and that anyone who was so inclined, was welcome to join. "The zoo!" Michael said, making bright eyes over at Beth who was seated next to him.

"Giraffes, and elephants, and tigers!" Janelle said to Michael, seated on his other side.

Michael growled, scrunching his face into a ferocious mask, his hands out like claws. Janelle got up and came back with a wet dishcloth and started wiping off Michael's face and hands.

"You have to have clean paws, though," she said.

"Why?" Michael asked, "Do I get to pet the tiger?"

"Well, I would love to, but I have to go downtown," Martin said, finishing his coffee.

"To the bungalow?" Kenny asked, topping off his coffee.

"No, I sold that," Martin said, then got up and carried his plate and utensils to the dishwasher.

"I was so glad," Janelle said, lifting Michael from his highchair. "He didn't need that old place anymore."

"Janelle's right, especially with all the traveling I'm doing now," Martin said, removing other plates from the table to load into the dishwasher. Martin explained that he was going to Chicago a few days every week, helping Petro get the agency up and running. Kenny recalled his dad mentioning the new Chicago branch, and the travel responsibilities, but he'd never said anything about selling the bungalow. While his dad was talking, Kenny overheard Beth ask Elaine if she could go with them to the zoo. Elaine said, "Of course, if it's cool with your mom."

Beth said, "Mom?" Janelle was listening and gave Beth a pained look, Michael attacking Janelle's legs like a harmless tiger, growling, then hugging her and telling her he loved her. "I love you too, little tiger," she said down to Michael, then looked up at Beth. "You have Dr. Reichert at five o'clock. Will you be back in time?"

"I imagine we'll be back by two, three at the latest," Elaine said, "Or Michael will be a monster..." At that, Michael roared loud enough to make Janelle cringe.

"Inside voice, noisy little tiger," Elaine said, squinting over at Michael, smiling.

Kenny watched Beth's expression lighten when Janelle said it was okay. Beth gave Kenny a vague smile as she got up from the table to take her dishes to the dishwasher, then said she was going to her bedroom to change. "I hope she doesn't become... contentious..." Janelle said to Elaine after Beth left. "She has mood swings..."

Kenny overheard and said, "We'll be fine. Really."

Martin was in the shower when Kenny took Michael out to Janelle's BMW and strapped him into the toddler seat they'd brought from home. Janelle had offered to buy one, whatever brand and type that Elaine and Kenny were comfortable with, so it would always be at the house when they came to visit. Elaine had thanked her, but said they needed it for the plane anyway.

On the drive to Forest Park, Elaine asked Kenny about Vickie's flower shop, if they should stop before the zoo, or after. "I want to get Janelle a nice arrangement," Elaine said, glancing back at Michael over her shoulder. Michael didn't notice, too busy reading a book to Beth.

"Probably be better on the way back," Kenny said, "so the flowers aren't sitting in a hot car for hours."

By noon, the heat at the zoo was nearly unbearable, so they went inside the Lakeside Café for lunch, Michael talking nonstop about the monkeys. Beth was quiet, but pleasant, and amazingly patient, much of the time managing Michael, holding his hand, explaining this and that, Michael with a million questions. "Why do those pink birds only have one leg, Ant Beff?" "They're flamingos, Michael, and they stand on one leg even though they have two," Beth said, Michael immediately showing her how he could stand on one leg.

They walked around the zoo for a while longer after lunch, until Michael wanted ice cream, popcorn, a Coke; anything anyone walking by was eating or drinking, Michael wanted. "Time to go," Kenny said, picking Michael up to carry him on his shoulders to the parking lot.

By the time they got to the car, Michael was asleep. Elaine secured him in the toddler seat and asked Beth if she wanted to ride up front with Kenny. "Sure," Beth said, sliding into the front seat and fastening her seatbelt.

"We still doing the flower shop?" Kenny asked, not really wanting Elaine and Vickie to be in the same place again, hoping Vickie and Amy didn't mention anything about him helping Vickie with the website. As far as Elaine knew, he'd had no contact with Vickie since high school, and didn't want to spend half the night well into the early hours trying to explain to Elaine why he had never mentioned anything about Vickie before.

"Of course," Elaine said.

It took less than ten minutes to find the shop. "I can wait in the car with Michael," Kenny said, hoping to take the coward's way out. "That way we don't have to wake him."

"He'll be fine," said Elaine, unbuckling the straps. Michael stirred, rubbing his eyes, his eyelids fluttering, trying to stay open.

"I'll take him," Beth said, coming around to the other side of the car. She picked him up and kissed his plump cheek. Still half asleep, he wound his skinny arms around her neck and set his head next to hers. Elaine was already through the front door of *Floral & Party* when Kenny rushed up to hold the door for Beth and Michael, a tiny brass bell dinging near the top of the doorjamb announcing their arrival.

The shop was small, thick with the fragrance of blooms and blossoms, colorful explosions of flowers displayed in cases, on tables and counters, while metallic balloons, printed with cheery well-wishing salutations, floated high in the air above everything, inviting attention to the charming old pressed-tin ceiling, which glimmered and gave back vague, reflections of splashy color and movement. Amy was helping another customer when Vickie looked up from the counter. Her eyes seemed to fall on Elaine first, quizzical, as if maybe she recognized the face, then fixed on Kenny for a few seconds. She smiled, hurrying out from behind the counter, saying hello to Kenny, then to Elaine.

"So good to see you again," Vickie said, her eyes finding Beth and Michael for a second, giving them a soft casual smile, before bringing her attention back to Elaine.

"Your shop is amazing!" Elaine said, gushing, gently touching the vases, running a finger along the petals of flowers.

"This is Beth," said Kenny, "my step-sister... and our son, Michael."

Vickie took Beth's free hand and shook it, telling her it was nice to meet her, then took her attention to Michael, peeking around Beth to get a better look, then brought her eyes back to Kenny, and with the faintest of sound, practically just mouthing the words, she said, "He's adorable..."

That was it—Vickie had now met everyone in his life who was dear to him, with the exception of Janelle—and Kenny felt exposed, and silly, as if the once illicit affair he'd imagined with Vickie was now nothing more than the ridiculous fantasy of a timorous IT computer guy, married, with one child and one on the way. He wanted to crawl back out to the car, slump down in the seat with the motor running, the windows rolled up, and vanish as a pale fog filled the interior. Whatever image, or illusion, Vickie had held of him to this point was now gone; he was a family guy.

Kenny tried to look interested in the flowers, then walked to a shelving unit with gifts, glass trinkets and what-not, Beth and Michael milling around nearby, while Vickie suggested an array of flowers that might make a nice bouquet for Janelle. He could hear them talking, and laughing, and felt his anger at Elaine rising, as if she, his own wife, were somehow sabotaging his chances with Vickie! It was absurd! The whole notion was insanity, and Kenny felt himself slipping off a steep ledge, heat prickling up his neck (maybe he was breaking out in hives?), his embarrassment over his stupid invention, imagining himself and Vickie together, romantically! It caught in his throat like a big clump of dirt. Then felt even more disgraced looking over at his beautiful son, asleep in Beth's arms.

He closed his eyes, hoping to vanquish the shame, destroy his delusions, when he felt the touch of a soft hand on his wrist. "Are you okay?" Beth whispered, as if not to wake Michael. Kenny gasped, not realizing he'd been holding his breath, trying to restore the slightest shred of dignity, something inside him still in flames, still falling as if it might never hit bottom. He felt dizzy, looking for a place to sit.

"I'm fine," he said. "I think it's the smell of all the flowers."

About then, Vickie and Elaine walked past, Vickie showing her a line of vases, explaining that they had just gotten them in. He heard Elaine comment on how beautiful they were, but Kenny's head was buzzing, unable to take his eyes off Vickie, how the hair piled up at the back of her head, held in place with a shiny, red clip, revealing her slender white neck. How her shoulders sloped away gently, the two skinny straps of her dress falling naturally into the dips of her shoulders, then rounded perfectly into her arms, the cut of the dress in back displaying the perfect pale flesh between her shoulder blades. As she moved her arms, showing Elaine different vases, the tendons just beneath the skin stretched and relaxed, twitched, and receded. Kenny was mesmerized, falling into a trance until he felt eyes on him, observing him the way he was studying Vickie. He turned to see Beth's eyes coming at him, not alarmed or concerned, but inquisitive, searching and gentle.

"Maybe we should go outside," Beth said quietly, "if the smell is still getting to you?"

Kenny nodded, turning to walk out when Vickie said something to him.

"What?" he said.

"You looked like you were leaving, and I was just wondering if you and Elaine were coming to the luau tonight?" Vickie looked over at Elaine and smiled, then back to Kenny. "It'll probably be lame, but..."

"We weren't sure," Kenny said, just wanting to leave, upset with Vickie now, as if she had colluded with Elaine in some bizarre way, and spoiled everything, and in the second that followed, Kenny was suddenly enraged at himself for being so childish and idiotic, berating himself for feeling the emotions he was feeling, a subtle quaking starting in his knees, his stomach tightening, constricting, a battle raging inside him, between the wild horses running loose in his chest, and holding the calm, stable veneer, of an adult.

Vickie gave him a pained smile, then brightened when she turned to Elaine, showing her to the counter and the cash register. Amy came up and took the vase, and the list of flower selections, to the back to finalize the arrangement. Vickie and Elaine continued talking at the counter, like old college roommates, as Kenny and Beth walked out onto the sunny sidewalk, traffic rushing by, the familiar sounds of car horns and police sirens in the distance.

Kenny was filled with guilt, and couldn't even face Beth, who stood casually by, rocking Michael in her arms. "You're really good with kids," Kenny finally said, trying to restore himself to adulthood, only glancing at Beth's eyes for a second, certain his face would betray his own betrayal, before shifting his attention back out to the busy four-lane street.

Feeling a bit calmer, Kenny checked his watch, then turned to Beth. "Is Dr. Reichert far from the house?" Kenny said, concerned about the time. It was almost three and traffic would start backing up.

"Only about ten minutes," Beth said. "It'll be fine." Kenny waited a moment, then took Michael from Beth's arms, figuring to get a jump on things by fastening Michael into the car seat. Michael fussed a bit when Kenny took him, but then fell back to sleep once he was in his seat. Kenny got in the driver's side, and told Beth she could sit up front with him.

"Elaine won't mind?" Beth said.

Kenny shook his head. "She prefers to sit in back with Michael."

Elaine came out a few minutes later and slid into the backseat, setting the arrangement between her and Michael. "I hope I didn't take too long, Beth," Elaine said. "I know you have an appointment this afternoon."

"It's fine," she said, turning her head slightly toward the backseat when she spoke, then brought her eyes to the front.

When they were on the highway, everyone mostly quiet to that point, Michael woke and quietly pretended to read about monkeys. Elaine said, "What's wrong with you, Kenny? Why were you so rude to Vickie and Amy? You didn't even say goodbye when you walked out."

Kenny put on his right turn signal to change lanes, checking the mirror, quietly cursing the pickup truck riding his bumper. Upset, not only with the traffic, but the entire visit to the flower shop, trying out different versions of the past hour in his head, seeing if one might have gone better, or worse, than another, his impulses enemy to his own better judgement. Kenny felt Beth looking at him, as if he owed Elaine an answer.

"My mom's gonna love the flowers you bought," Beth said, turning in the front seat to look at the floral arrangement. "She loves getting flowers."

"Well, you'll be no stranger to getting flowers, Beth, as long as chivalry isn't completely dead by the time you start dating," Elaine said. "You're not dating yet, are you?"

Beth shook her head, then smiled as if it were a lovely thought, someone buying her flowers, though she didn't really believe it.

The car fell silent again, and Michael started asking Elaine questions about the zoo—Why do the elephants make that loud noise? Who watches the animals at night? What keeps the tigers from getting out of their pen? —until he tired of the questions, and announced that his belly hurt, that he was really, really hungry. Elaine assured him they'd be home soon and gave him his book and asked him to read it to her.

By the time they pulled in the driveway, Michael was asleep again. Kenny shut off the engine and told Elaine he'd grab Michael so she could carry the flowers. Beth got out and went up the front walk to the house and opened the door for Elaine, waiting for Kenny to come up with Michael. "I hope you're not going to be late," Kenny said.

"We've got plenty of time," Beth said. "I'm going like this."

Kenny took Michael to the bathroom, then came back announcing that he had a very hungry little boy in his arms. Janelle was still praising the flowers, thanking Elaine, then Kenny when he came to the kitchen, almost happy, or sad—Kenny couldn't tell—to the point of tears. While Kenny was fixing Michael in the high chair, he asked where his dad was. For a moment it looked as if Janelle couldn't speak, her eyes filling with tears, which she quickly wiped away, then gave him a weird, fractured smile.

"He said he might be late tonight," Janelle said, reciting the words though not believing them for a second. "Something about the new Chicago office. A conference call, I think. Some kind of problem."

Janelle sniffed and rubbed her hands together, then looked at the flowers again, her smile turning real, and relaxed, before taking her eyes to the clock. "Oh boy," she said. Then yelled toward the back bedrooms, "Beth, we need to leave in fifteen minutes!" Turning to Kenny, she said, "Sorry, are you okay for supper? Everything's in the fridge from last night. We won't be too long."

Elaine assured her they were fine and apologized for being late.

"No, no, you were fine. It's just me, I get anxious. I've just got to get myself together…" Janelle said and hurried toward her bedroom.

Kenny was heating up leftovers when Janelle and Beth came from the back, Beth in a jacket, Janelle with her purse over her shoulder, looking for her keys. "Oh, here," Kenny said, digging in his pocket.

She took them, smiled, and told them they wouldn't be too late. "Martin should be back before us," Janelle said, with a sudden worried look. "Don't you have some kind of reunion thing again tonight? What will you do with Michael?"

"It's later," Elaine said, "I'm not even sure we're going."

After Janelle and Beth left, it was just the three of them, and Kenny needed to figure out what he was doing about this luau. "Are you serious about not going?" Kenny asked Elaine, fixing Michael's plate, Michael not waiting for him to finish before digging his fork into the peas. Elaine frowned, pouring juice into a small plastic cup for Michael.

"It was fun last night and all," Elaine said. "But, you know, when it's not your own reunion, I don't know…"

"That's fine," Kenny said, sitting down with his plate next to Michael. "We don't have to go." Kenny felt both relief and disappointment, his stomach churning over and over, first with anticipation, then with dread, the source of both emotions exactly the same; what if Vickie comes to the luau and, at some point, they ended up together, alone?

"No, you should go, Kenny," Elaine said. "These things don't come around that often… well, they do, I guess, but you never know if you'll be able to go to the next one… No, you should go. Have fun. And whatever you do, if you see Vickie and Amy, apologize for being such a zombie today! And have fun with your football buddies! You'll have more fun if I'm not hanging around…"

Kenny felt the air rush out of him, the thought of Vickie nog being at the luau, no one to provide guardrails, imagining the dark green fairways at the country club, the wooded hazards, the calm-surfaced lakes, the lighted, bubbling fountains, the alcohol, maybe drugs, the cool night air, chilled inhibitions, frenzied anticipation, the sizzle of hormones and rushing blood, moist warm flesh on flesh. Kenny sucked in a desperate gulp of air and looked over at Elaine to see if she was monitoring his meltdown, his heart whamming in his chest; this was the worst idea ever! Elaine smiled over at him, then glanced at Michael, and went back to her supper. Rivulets of sweat flowed from his armpits, down over his ribs.

After supper, Kenny excused himself to take a shower, still wrestling with what to do. When he came out of the bathroom wearing jeans and a shirt, still in bare feet, he heard his dad in the kitchen talking to Elaine. "Hey," Martin said when Kenny came down the hall. He hugged Kenny, then asked about the reunion. Kenny shrugged, still conflicted over opening a door that would never go shut again, and said to Martin he wasn't sure if he was going, explaining that Elaine was staying home tonight.

"Elaine's not going?" Martin said. "Well… you should go, Kenny! You came all the way out here for this reunion!"

If Elaine and Martin knew Kenny's heart, they wouldn't be so lavish with their encouragement. Kenny was a fraud, but worse, a cheat and a liar. Even knowing that, he wanted to go, felt compelled to walk the rim of the volcano, gaze down into the flames, feel the forbidden heat of long buried lust and love. Michael ran up and grabbed Kenny's legs, extended his arms to be lifted. Kenny brought him up and Michael immediately turned toward Martin and started babbling about monkeys and one-legged pink birds and a fat *nosorus* with a big horn on his nose! Martin listened and eventually took Michael in his arms so Kenny could finish getting dressed. Kenny hadn't planned to leave for another hour or so, but appreciated the time to himself.

Martin and Michael were sitting on the living room floor, putting together the puzzle Michael had gotten at the zoo, when Kenny came out of the bedroom. Michael was naming each animal as Martin put it into place. When the puzzle was finished, Michael dumped out the pieces, yelling, "The aminals are scaping!" to which Elaine hurried to calm him down.

"Not so loud, sweetie." Michael's eyes got big, and he gave her a toothy grin, then looked back at Martin, handing him the wooden elephant, trying out his loud, trumpeting screech.

"Michael!" Elaine said.

Kenny walked over and hugged Elaine, a Judas move without the silver, his compulsion running roughshod over his conscience, his conscience putting up one hell of a fight, clawing at the inside of his chest, stomping on his gut.

"Be careful," Elaine whispered, briefly kissing him on the lips. "And please, if you drink too much, or *smoke* too much, call a cab. Just be careful, okay, I don't want to raise Elephant Man over there by myself!" Again, the loud, trumpeting screech, Martin laughing, Michael raising his arm like an elephant trunk.

"Not too late to change your mind about going," Kenny said, almost hoping she would, curious why she'd become teary-eyed.

"No... go, have fun. Really. I love you!" She wiped her right eye casually, as if it was just an itch.

"I love you, too," Kenny said, the words echoing a little falsely in his head, expecting them to burn his tongue like acid. Kenny said goodbye to his dad, then hugged and kissed Michael, who wouldn't stop wiggling in his arms, trying to get back to the floor, to the puzzle and his grandfather. "Be good, little man!" Kenny said, setting Michael down, then almost hugged Elaine again, delaying his departure another moment, allowing for a new resolve to intervene, vanquish this stupid, foolhardy venture.

In the driveway, Kenny, heading to his father's Taurus, passed Janelle and Beth coming back from the doctor's office. Janelle told Kenny to have fun, and went inside. Beth walked up the driveway slowly, and even in the dim light of the street lamp, Kenny could see she'd been crying. Beth sniffed, and wiped the back of her hand under her nose. "You leaving for your reunion?" she said.

Kenny nodded. "You okay?"

"As good as can be expected, I guess," she said, laughing a little, swiping her lower lip up over her upper to remove tears, then stared into his eyes as if trying to tell him something.

"Have a really good time tonight, Kenny! Really. I mean that," she said. "The future is never how we imagine it." At that, she stepped forward and hugged him close, then spun away and rushed up the driveway to the house, pausing a moment at the door, looking at him, silhouetted in the narrow bar of light before closing the door a moment later.

Kenny held his eyes on the front entrance, rewinding Beth's words back through his head, as if she knew what was going on. But how could she? Even Elaine seemed to have no inkling about what he was struggling with, or how he felt about Vickie. And what did Beth mean; *the future is never how we imagine it?*

Chapter Thirty-Three

He'd been at the country club for over an hour and a half. Some of the football cheerleaders, and a few other girls from the graduating class, including one guy who was pretty wasted, had just finished a hula dance competition, the mock award ceremony still going on, the guy, tipsy and about to fall off the stage, was still in the running for the trophy made from coconuts. Kenny, with buddies from the team, was seated at a large outdoor round table, under suspended strung white lights. A few new teammates who couldn't make it the night before had shown up tonight, while a few others were missing.

At the hotel ballroom the previous evening, everyone was excited to see one another, find out what people had been doing since graduation, share and re-share stories that had been shared so many times they were threadbare, but mostly to see how people had fared in the real world, how fat or bald or worn the storytellers themselves had become. Tonight though, conversation revolved mostly around classmates, students who'd had high ideals in school, planned on becoming captains of industry and ended up captain of their son's baseball team, or daughter's soccer league, pushing paper under the buzz of fluorescent lighting. And aspiring authors who ended up writing copy for the company annual reports. Tonight was, in a word, about gossip, the lifeblood of any reunion.

Kenny, for the most part, sat uninterested, nursing his fifth beer, occasionally sending his eyes out to scout the mob, hoping to glimpse Vickie, but she hadn't shown. Neither had Amy. He was checking his watch again, when someone to his right asked about the Tate girl, and whatever happened to her. "I don't remember a Tate girl," Kenny said.

"Sure you do, Muppet. Kerri Tate, or Gerri Tate, maybe? You dated her for like three months! The blonde with the great legs? She always wore those tight skirts! You don't remember her?"

Kenny shook his head, the memory returning slowly, or maybe it wasn't a memory at all, but a mirage created from the description, picturing a tall blonde with long legs and a pinched waist. What was the point anyway? Obviously, Kerri or Gerri, or maybe even Sherri, Tate wasn't at the reunion, so what did it matter if Kenny remembered her or not. It was all fairly inane, this obsession with the past, trying to breathe new life into it, if one bothered to give it much thought.

After a while, Kenny got up and walked around, hitting the bar for one last beer, listening to the band cover some great songs, *Hungry Like a Wolf, We're Not Gonna Take It, Purple Rain*. A commotion rose out on the parking lot, red and blue lights flashing, like an ambulance, or the police. Several people moved toward the disturbance, curious what was going on. Kenny didn't care—and most of the others didn't either —finding a spot near one of the fountains, where a few couples were dancing. He sat on the stone ledge, drinking his beer, grateful to have the choice about Vickie made for him. All evening, especially on the drive over, he'd been fretting this night. When he got here, he figured the decision was made, that whatever happened, happened, and he would flow with the current of the evening, no matter where it carried him, or how deep the water got. But now he was just tired and ready to go home. Tipping his beer back, he was headed toward the bar to drop off the empty bottle when someone grabbed his arm.

"Kenny." When he spun around, he had expected to see Vickie, but it wasn't.

"Amy!" he said, surprised and lifted, the night suddenly springing new life. "Is Vickie with you?" That's when Kenny noticed how distressed she looked, dark circles beneath her eyes, or maybe it was just the weak outdoor lighting making her appear gaunt and dismal.

"Everything all right?" Kenny said.

Amy brought her eyes up and said, "Not really. Vickie's in the parking lot. The police just left. Roiter was waiting for her when we drove up. What a dick! He started harassing her, saying she lied about her stake in our flower shop. He said he was taking her to court to sue her for his share of *Floral & Hardy!* There's no way to prove it, but that asshole will drag her through hell."

"I don't understand," Kenny said. "If he can't prove it, how can he win?"

Amy scoffed, her eyes narrowed. "Roiter doesn't care about winning, only making her miserable! Roiter makes a ton of money, and he knows Vickie and I are still struggling. We're doing okay, and business is getting better every month, but we can't weather some big drawn-out fucking lawsuit. And that bastard knows it!" She paused to gather herself. "If he can't have her, then he's gonna make sure her life's a living hell."

Kenny was quiet, still wondering about Vickie. "Was she hurt? Is she okay?"

"Yeah, she's fine, a little shook up. He pushed her a little, and got a little handsy. He was drunk. I called the police as soon as I saw him, but it took about ten minutes for them to get here. Anyway, they arrested him, but he didn't give a shit. Roiter's a fucking animal, not afraid of anything. Cops are dragging him away in cuffs and he just laughs, yelling that pretty soon he's gonna have to learn how to arrange flowers!"

"I'm sorry all that went down," Kenny said. "Did Vickie go home?"

Amy turned to face Kenny with a strange look in her eyes. "She wanted me to find you. She's in the parking lot waiting for you."

Kenny nodded, his heart starting to gallop, not sure what to say.

"Kenny," Amy said, her expression cloudy, troubled. "It's none of my business what you two do, but you have a lovely wife, and a beautiful son, and Vickie has a freight train full of setbacks and drama. Don't get me wrong, she's my best friend in the world, closer to me than my own sister, and I love her to pieces and will do anything for her, but she doesn't need extra crap or new disasters in her life..." Then, after a moment: "And from where I'm standing, all I can see for both of you is a world of heartbreak..."

Kenny rubbed his ear, then his neck, everything inside him

tumbling, slipping, his legs growing weak, failing. He knew it was true, but hearing it from someone else made it all too real.

"I appreciate everything you've done for us, Kenny!" Amy said, her eyes softer, damp, reflecting the tiny white lights strung above them. "I really do, but go home, go back to New Jersey and take your son to the park, and buy your beautiful wife dinner and flowers, and grow old and stupid and fat together."

Kenny took in a long breath, the evening in free fall. He felt light-headed, unhinged, the sensation of weightlessness making him woozy, and a bit ill. "Thanks," he finally brought out after what seemed like ten minutes. "Good luck with everything." Amy stepped forward and hugged him for the length of a breath, then turned and walked away.

Leaving by the side entrance—it was closer to where he'd parked the car—Kenny thought about something Vickie had told him walking back from the park that day when they'd met under the guise of having coffee. "You know how memories are?" Vickie had said to him, tugging at his arm to make him stop walking. "You hear a song, or detect a certain scent, and it instantly brings up a memory." She had looked at him with eyes sad and on the edge of tears, begging to be understood and taken seriously. "That's how it felt the first time I met you at school," she continued, "hearing your voice, maybe, or seeing your face, it was like… I didn't *meet you* so much as *remember you*, you know, like I already *knew* who you were somehow, before we even met… and it was like… I don't know, like I was just waiting for you to come back into my life… like, *expecting* you. I know that must sound corny…" Even now, under the pull of the memory, Kenny was embarrassed that he had not reacted in any way, as if he were a condemned man, his hands tied behind his back, the noose draped around his neck, ready to swing from the gallows, and was getting news that may have saved his life, but came too late to make a difference.

And now, like a thief, or a coward, was walking out on his chance again, leaving without even talking to her, even though it was the proper thing to do. Amy's words lingered in his chest—*a world of heartbreak*—like the terrifying, claustrophobic feeling of hiding in a dark closet waiting for an armed intruder to leave your house.

The fresh night air heartened Kenny as he hurried out the side exit, his leather-soled shoes slapping loudly on the concrete steps. Heat rose from the parking lot asphalt with the smell of oil and tar. The yellow lines painted on the pavement surface—illuminated by the bright sodium-vapor parking lot lights—glowed with the intensity of neon. A hundred feet from his car, slowing his pace, he couldn't help but run his eyes over every roof, hood and fender, the reflections coming back like slivered glass, hoping to glimpse Vickie, and at the same time, hoping he wouldn't. With his car less than twenty feet away, Kenny pressed the unlock button, the lights flashed with the alarm chirp, and he stood at the door and opened it slowly, swiveling his head back and forth, his eyes finding nothing and no one in the dark. He cleared his throat and something happened, the night, and the unmoving cars, the odors and reflections and heat, took on the vague, ephemeral quality of a memory, or the recollection of a dream, and the sensation of falling through space returned. Kenny gripped the edge of the door with both hands to steady himself, then tossed himself into the seat, gulping at air, quickly pulling the door shut.

Vacuum-sealed inside the car, the interior dark, the only sound the hush of blood running through his veins, Kenny was alone, safe, mesmerized by his rapidly ticking heart, a tiny frightened bird trapped in his chest. He sat a moment, letting the roar in his brain subside, everything too fluid, too uncertain, calming his mind, making the world solid again. Should he call a cab? But he didn't feel drunk, exactly, but something wasn't right, as if he had gone out of his body and had yet to return.

He started the engine and cranked up the radio. Rock and roll blared from the speakers. David Lee Roth, *Might as well jump. Go ahead and jump.* He checked the rearview mirror and backed out slowly, the skin of his arms shredding under a Van Halen guitar solo, dashboard lights jouncing to the pounding in his head. Easing the car up the aisle, he finally remembered to turn on the headlights, the sudden brightness bringing a welcome clarity to the shadow-drenched lot. The fog in his head had just started to clear when his beams flashed off a woman in a short red dress, bent at the waist, resting her elbows on the trunk of a car, her face cupped in her hands. It was Vickie, and she was crying. She glanced briefly over her shoulder back at Kenny's car, her eyes as big as moons in Kenny's mind, then returned her tear-ravaged face back to the cradle of her palms. There was no way she could have seen who was driving, and Kenny rolled past her, continuing down the hill to the concrete-pillared exit of the country club. At the open gates, he signaled for a right turn, then tapped the brakes long enough to see a clearing in the traffic. Within seconds of joining the busy street, he swerved into a lane to his liking, blending seamlessly with all the other faceless drivers rushing through the hectic city night.

Might as well jump.

Go ahead and jump.

It could have happened that way, Kenny continuing past Vickie down the hill toward the ornamental iron and stone country club entrance, merging perfectly, safely, into traffic, and in Kenny's mind that is what happened, and in some protected quadrant of Kenny's brain he was still driving home in Saturday night traffic, even though Vickie—straddling him in his dad's Taurus, which was now sitting in a dark corner of the parking lot, engine off, windows down, the driver's side seat back as far as if would go, the top of Vickie's dress pulled down to her waist, her bra God-only-knew-where, the bottom of her dress bunched up to her thighs—moved and moaned in his lap, her white knees pressing into the upholstery on either side of him, her pale slender fingers wrapping his neck, his pants to his knees, his lips and tongue exploring her breasts.

The lights had flared when he hit the brakes, causing Vickie to turn toward the brilliant red blaze. In his rearview mirror he saw her straighten, then wipe her eyes, yet still confused as he backed up toward her. When Kenny's finger hit the button, the passenger side window slid down smoothly, with the faintest hum, and Vickie walked closer, curious but apprehensive. It was impossible for her to know the car. Standing back a few feet, she lowered her head sideways, dipping her bare shoulders, focusing her eyes to see who was driving, then: "Oh my God, Kenny! I didn't think you came tonight!" Without hesitation, she had thrown herself into the car, and without thinking, leaned across the seat into him, kissing him hard on the mouth, her hands guiding his neck, her fingers plowing his hair, touching his ear until she realized what she'd done and jerked away. "Oh! Kenny! I am so sorry! I just... oh, God..."

Without a word, Kenny had eased away and drove to the spot near the edge of a stand of trees where the parking lot lights couldn't reach.

He had noticed it when he arrived, and for a split second, had imagined them sitting alone in the dark.

When they stopped near the trees and Kenny shut off the engine, they had talked a long while, well actually, maybe only fifteen or twenty minutes, though it felt much longer to Kenny, the faint smell of Vickie's perfume filling his head, the warmth of her lips lingering on his. He only wanted to kiss her again, watching her lips move in the dim light as she tried explaining about Roiter, Kenny telling her that Amy had filled him in. Things turned quiet. She scooted closer, her hand coming to his face, her fingers caressing his cheek.

When they finished, Vickie leaned forward, resting her head on Kenny's shoulder, gently kissing his neck, her arms around him. "I love you," she whispered. "I always have." Kenny held her close, could feel her heart beating, or so it seemed, his fingers splayed across her naked back, transfixed by a calm he had never felt before in his life. It was what he always imagined it would be like, loving someone, though it had never been that way, not even with Elaine. It went beyond caring, beyond enjoying another's company, or the giddy feeling that often fades, more even than sharing important moments together, or suffering in each other's arms, or laughing together. This was nearly inexplicable; this sensation of everything in the world lining up, finally, making sense in ways you always hoped it could, suddenly, and implausibly, every detail falling into some logical order, every cell in your body alive. "I love you, too," Kenny said, and for now, it was enough.

There would be days and weeks and months, maybe even years, ahead for regret, and lying, and crushing guilt, and arguments and tears, but tonight Kenny would take Vickie for ice cream, then a drive to the landing, park the car on the cobblestones to watch the tugs push a dozen barges against the current up the Mississippi, the lonely searchlight swinging across the muddy water from one bank to the other. In the distance, across the river in Illinois, glowed the peculiar, alien orange lights and smoke stacks of Granite City, like a mirage reflecting in the dark shiny water. Leaving the landing, they drove to a Denny's and had breakfast at two in the morning, the sheen beginning to wear off for Kenny, the dense universe of excuses and remorse displacing the lightness and magnificence of the past few hours.

"You okay, Kenny?" Vickie asked, reaching across the table to take his hand. He smiled, squeezing hers, a genuine display of affection, wanting her to know how happy he was, yet trying to imagine a resolution that didn't leave him feeling greedy and selfish, or cause pain for those he loved.

"I should get going," Kenny said, a sadness he hadn't anticipated rushing through him, making him falter.

Vickie nodded, still holding his hand. "I hope you're not sorry," she said. "I'm not." Then: "I know it was only one night, not even that, really, but I have that to hold onto now, instead of always just imagining it. I will never forget your smell, how your lips feel, how I felt when you held me..." She released his hand and took money out of her purse. "I'll get this," she said. "Why don't you go. You have a long drive. Amy will pick me up here. I called her when I went to the restroom."

"No, I should drive you..." he started to say, then realized she was right. There was no way to say goodbye that wasn't going to make this hurt any less. She stood with the check and her money in her hand. They walked to the register together. After she paid, she followed him outside, then kissed him on the lips, tears flowing down her cheeks. When she pulled back from him, she dropped her arms to her sides, her features rose-colored and pained, collapsing down on themselves, her lips trembling as if she were about to speak, but she turned and hurried back into the restaurant, pushing through the glass doors, the first one coming closed as she pushed through the second. With both of them falling shut, she shot one glance his way and disappeared past the register.

Chapter Thirty-Four

Sunday morning, Kenny slept in. When he got up, the house was quiet. He walked into the living room, checked the kitchen, then saw someone sitting outside by the pool. Beth was in one of the loungers, reading a paperback, wearing baggy shorts, and a long sleeve shirt, unbuttoned, a T-shirt underneath. "Hey," Kenny said, "Where is everybody?"

"They all went to Saint Jude's Church to pray for us," Beth said, raising her sunglasses. "The patron saint of desperate cases and lost causes."

"What?" Kenny said, laughing skittishly, unsure what to make of Beth's comment. "Church? Really?"

Beth chuckled, putting her sunglasses down, then taking her attention back to her book. "They went for donuts. They're bringing some back."

Kenny drifted over to the chair near Beth, shielding his eyes, sitting with his back to the sun, facing her. "Are you a lost cause, or just a desperate case?" Kenny said, trying to make light of her comment, but still uneasy, like someone dangling from a cliff by their fingertips.

"The jury's still out," she said, suddenly gloomy. She sat forward, holding her finger in the book to mark her place, then removing her sunglasses with her other hand. "How did last night go?" she said, shielding her eyes from the sun when she looked over at Kenny. "Did you have fun?"

Fun? Kenny wasn't sure what it was, but wouldn't label it *fun*. The police, Roiter, Vickie in the parking lot crying, then in the front seat straddling him... "It was okay," Kenny said, the freight of the previous evening still sitting in his chest. He'd yet to face Elaine, and was glad no one was home. A bit hungover, he was just about to go inside and make toast, not sure his stomach was going to wait for donuts, when Beth stopped him cold.

"Are you in love with that Vickie woman, the one from the flower shop?"

Kenny spun back toward her with his best impression of incredulity, about to set her straight, but what would be the point? She knew. He wasn't sure how, but she knew. He nodded, then said, "Since high school."

Beth was quiet for a bit, then said, "That's a long time. How long did you go out with her in high school?"

Kenny scoffed and shook his head. "We didn't, that was the problem." He brought his eyes to Beth's. "We never dated in high school. I was in love with her, but we never connected. A few years ago, I found out she felt the same... but I never knew. All that time... wasted..."

They both sat without talking, Kenny watching the pool, a narrow ripple on the surface near the diving board where fresh water rushed in.

"Did you see her last night?" Beth said, sitting forward, shifting her body so her face was out of the sun.

"You are direct," Kenny said, shaking his head.

"Sorry," Beth said, letting her head drop forward.

"She was there," Kenny said, grateful to have someone to talk to about it. "So, does that make me a desperate case, or a lost cause?"

Beth thought about it for a few seconds. "You could be both..." she said with a straight face.

Kenny dropped his head into his hands, and sat staring at some ants on the concrete near his feet, watching them march in single file, well almost single file, a few of them hearing a different beat, apparently. After nearly a minute, he cocked his head toward Beth. "Do you have your driver's license yet?" Kenny asked Beth.

Beth laughed. "Wow, that is not even trying to be a segue!"

"Yeah, I'm too exhausted for anything else. I don't even know why I asked..."

"Well, since you did, the answer is, no. I turned seventeen a few months ago, but my mom still wants me to wait, you know, with the drugs I'm taking and all. At least that's her excuse. But I don't care," Beth said, rocking back a little, kicking her bare feet out, off the side of it, one, then the other, as if slowly walking on air.

"How are you doing, you know, with everything?" Kenny asked, not sure if the question was insensitive.

"Well, if by *everything* you mean my dad killing a harmless man in front of me in a crowded grocery store, then, as good as can be expected, I suppose," she said, her feet suddenly still. "I just wish he had killed me too..."

"You don't mean that!" Kenny said, upset and shocked.

"In a way, he did kill me that day," she said, her face devoid of color, emotion. "In a month or two, when my father's trial begins, I'll have to sit in a courtroom full of strangers, and tell what happened that day, tell everyone how ashamed I am of what he did, how ashamed I am of myself for not speaking up, and watch my father's face as I help send him to prison for the rest of his life. It would have been easier if he had just shot me too."

Kenny started to speak, but had no words, had no idea what to offer her.

"Two things play over and over in my head," Beth continued. "Two things that have not faded one bit since that day?" Tears filled her eyes, but held suspended, as if she'd willed away gravity, forbidden the tears to run down her cheeks, her face fixed with the hardness of stone. "First, my dad's expression when he was shooting that man..." Beth was staring off into space, the image of her father etched onto her retinas, following her everywhere. "He looked deranged, smirking with some kind of sick satisfaction, as if he had just rid the world of the most heinous monster." Beth shook her head back and forth, gently, as if trying to erase the image in her mind. "It took him almost five seconds to realize what he'd done. He dropped the gun and looked over at me, trembling, his eyes like empty red holes, his face contorted in this weird way, terrified. He was so pitiful... so frightened... he peed his pants like a small child. Nothing I could do..."

Beth sat a long while, studying the hedgerow at the far end of the backyard, then said, "The second thing, far worse than the first, was Mr. Nevins' eleven-year-old daughter, Naomi, screaming, unable to stop, unable to move, watching her father fall to the floor of the grocery store, all those ridiculous cartoons on the cereal boxes watching, smiling and happy. Naomi fell to her knees, bent at the waist like someone had punched her in the stomach, leaning forward, her eyes like rivers, drool hanging from her quivering mouth like a rabid dog, her body shaking so hard she couldn't get her breath." Beth breathed in deeply, quietly. "And I did nothing. I stood there, that poor little girl staring at her father, his shirt covered in blood, more blood spreading along the floor around his head..."

Still Beth did not cry, her eyes like cups, holding big pink tears, her face pale and lifeless. After a moment, she scoffed, then said, "I was the biggest weakling, standing by, secretly rooting for Mr. Nevins in the goddamn cereal aisle. He was trying to talk sense into my dad, telling my own father everything I secretly hated about that stupid gun. How ridiculous and cowardly *Carl* looked, walking into that store like Wyatt *fucking* Earp or something. As if someone had put him in charge of law and order. How embarrassed I was, how insane... and for what? Then poor Mr. Nevins, saying everything I was too chickenshit to say to my own father... and because I was too chicken, Naomi grows up without a dad... it all comes down to choices... lousy fucking choices..."

Kenny wanted to hold Beth, wanted to console her, tell her it wasn't her fault, that there was nothing she could have done, blah blah blah, but she'd heard it all before, and had gotten this far without his bullshit help, not that he could have given her anything of substance anyway. After several minutes, Beth turned her head toward the glass sliding doors that led from the patio into the living room. "They're home. Finally," she said. "I'm starving."

Kenny could hear the muffled conversation inside, like foreign agents, or strangers at a bus terminal, the buzzing inside his head making it impossible to move, or maybe it was something else holding him, keeping him from trying to stand, from joining the others. Beth got up and was about to go in, then turned back to Kenny.

"The first time I met you," she said, smiling. "I had the worst crush on you! It lasted a long time, but I got over it, and I'm glad I did, because I love you better as a brother." Then, after a pause: "And I really like Elaine a lot, so don't take this the wrong way, Kenny, but I hope you're able to figure things out with Vickie, one way or the other. I don't pretend to know what you're going through, but I love you, and want you to be happy…"

Beth opened the glass sliding door and went in, pulling it almost completely shut behind her, but not quite, asking about the donuts, if they bought any bear claws, or chocolate eclairs, the voices packed in cotton, or far away, yet somehow so clear to Kenny's ears. He thought he heard her joking with Michael, making fun of the chocolate ring around his mouth, and could almost see the ring himself, everyone laughing, talking, as if under water, Elaine asking if Kenny was still asleep, Martin telling them how Kenny used to sleep until one in the afternoon, common family interaction, funny anecdotes and stories, normal everyday life, or so it seemed on the surface, but maybe that was the only place *normal* actually existed, just a very thin layer on the surface, and you had to be satisfied with that, because that *shell* of normal was all you ever got. A minute later, Elaine pulled the slider open farther and leaned out through the space, holding to the handle. "Hey, we've got gourmet donuts in here, bub, but I can't guarantee how long they'll last!" Kenny forced a smile, and got up, feeling torn over his own drama, over the events at the luau, trying to imagine how Beth, with all she'd been through, all she was yet to go through, was holding everything together.

Chapter Thirty-Five

On the plane, Kenny was still sad over telling his dad goodbye at the airport, unsure when he'd see him again. Or maybe it wasn't just about the teary farewells, and more about Vickie, the few hours they spent together Saturday night, trying to cram all the dating they'd missed in high school into three hours and forty-five minutes. Because of school, Beth hadn't been able to come to the airport either to see them off, and he was sad about that, too, and wished he had returned to St. Louis after college, but then he wouldn't have met Elaine, and he wouldn't have Michael. He glanced down at the top of Michael's head, Michael playing with his zoo puzzle in his toddler seat, the decaled wooden puzzle pieces sitting on the tray Kenny had lowered down for him. Just then, Michael tilted his eyes up at Kenny and held a wooden tiger piece over the edge of the tray, smiled at Kenny, then dropped it to the floor.

"Aminal scaped the zoo!" Michael shouted, smiling, pleased with himself. Kenny leaned over, until his head was almost on Michael's tray, then stretched his arm down between the seats, feeling around on the floor until he found it, bringing the wooden tiger up and holding it in front of Michael.

"If one more animal escapes from the zoo, little buddy," Kenny said, "the zoo will be closed down until further notice. Got it?"

Michael gave him a stern look, his face puckered, then extended his first finger out and placed his fist on the tip of his nose, as if to make his nose look longer, pointing it at Kenny. It was his newest trick since the zoo, and they knew he was mimicking a rhinoceros, which Michael had thought was really scary, but the gesture had an obscene quality to it they weren't wild about. However, they thought the best way to get him to stop was not to make a big deal out of it.

Elaine laughed, looking over at Kenny. Kenny smiled at her. "Yeah, that should help to discourage him," Kenny said, trying to be light, feeling horrible about what had happened with Vickie Saturday night, and yet, the image of her, her scent, her breath, the moist softness of her lips, the feel of her flesh, were permanent impressions now, but it was much more than a laundry list of sensations; the attraction seemed unknowable to the brain, something intangible that prowled his mind, crept along his skin, haunting and sensual and addictive, as it had been all through high school, and ever since, and he wondered if he'd see her again.

"Can you put her behind you now?" Elaine asked, no longer smiling.

"What?" Kenny said, unsure what her question had to do with Michael.

"Vickie. Can you put her behind you now?" Elaine said again.

Kenny felt loopy, as if he still hadn't heard her correctly, feeling as though he'd been kicked in the chest, and trying to act as if he hadn't. Had Beth said something to Elaine about what they'd talked about by the pool? How could she? Then Kenny remembered back to what Elaine had said Saturday evening when he was getting ready to leave for the reunion, telling him to be careful, drinking and drugs, that she didn't want to raise Michael by herself. He had thought she was referring only to him driving drunk or stoned, but she'd had tears in her eyes, which had seemed odd at the time. She sensed something was up before he'd even left for the country club.

"After Beth went to bed last night…" Elaine said, explaining how she, Martin and Janelle had been talking about Janelle's husband, Carl, and how the prosecution was going for second degree murder, and that Carl's defense team was pleading self-defense. Janelle was still trying to block Beth from having to testify, but it wasn't going well and she feared Beth would have no choice but to show up in court. Elaine paused a moment, clearing her throat. "Anyway, the conversation went to your reunion, and I joked that I didn't get to meet any of your old girlfriends from high school," Elaine said. "Your dad said there were only a couple. Then he seemed to recall one girl you were crazy about, someone named Nikki, or Vickie, he couldn't remember." Elaine stopped, shaking her head, her eyes closed, suddenly sad, unable to continue right away. After a few moments, then: "Things started falling into place, the reunion Friday night, how quiet you were around Vickie and her friend Amy, which was not like you. Then at the flower shop the next day, how rude and weird you were, which really made me curious, and a little suspicious, but I kept telling myself I was just being paranoid. Until your dad talked about some girl named Vickie... and, wow... my heart dropped into my stomach... Are you still in love with her?" Then, two seconds later: "Is it reciprocal?"

"It's not like that," Kenny said, tears beginning to squeeze from Elaine's eyes. Elaine sniffed, her eyes shrinking back into redness. She reached into her purse for a Kleenex as the flight attendant rolled the cart down the aisle taking drink orders. Elaine cleared her throat again and put the tissue to her eyes, dabbing one, then the other.

The flight attendant asked what they would like to drink. Kenny was on the aisle seat, and knew Elaine would want water. He asked for a Coke, bottled water and juice for Michael, who was asleep now. Kenny put his tray down and set the drinks on it, handing Elaine her bottle of water. She took it without looking at him, her shoulders shuddering, her face turned to the window to hide her tears. When the flight attendant moved down the aisle helping other passengers, Elaine turned back to Kenny, more composed, calmer. "I'm sorry," she said. "I jumped to conclusions. I guess I was feeling out of place around your friends, especially Vickie, even before your dad said anything." Then, after taking a drink from her water bottle: "She really is quite striking. And pleasant. Someone I could be friends with. I think that's why it threw me so much."

"Please don't be sorry," Kenny said. "I just feel bad that you were so uncomfortable."

The conversation stopped, but hadn't really ended.

Michael woke up a half hour before they landed and Kenny hurried to get him changed before they touched down. Once they had their luggage, Elaine waited with Michael outside the terminal for Kenny to bring the car around.

That evening, they refrained from discussing Vickie further until Michael was down for the evening. Elaine never inferred, not in any way Kenny could detect, that he had cheated on her, but Elaine was interested to know more about his relationship to Vickie in high school, and what it was now, if anything. Kenny didn't know what to say, wanting to explain that all through high school he'd had a terrible crush on her, but that they never even dated. He'd tried to ask her out on several occasions, never able to work up the courage. "She was like one of the most beautiful, most popular, smartest girls in school. It wasn't meant for me to be with her. It just wasn't. So, at the reunion, it really felt weird. Then again at the flower shop. Of course I still had feelings for her. I mean, I didn't know that I would, but then... well," Kenny was going to say, but it all sounded so ridiculous when he played it through his head, the disclosure awkward and juvenile, trying to transcribe his feelings into words, so he just lied: "It's nothing. I mean, it was in high school for sure, but she never felt that way about me. I was kind of surprised she even remembered me." The only thing Kenny was sure of, is that he needed more time. Time for *what* he wasn't sure; to figure things out, maybe, or enough time to forget about Vickie, or perhaps, enough to work up the courage to leave Elaine... "No!" the word came back so forcefully inside his head it startled him. Obviously, ending his marriage was not an option, and yet, the true nature of his need for time was at best, elusive, but mostly, just confusing; how could more time change the way this was going to end?

Elaine wasn't completely convinced by his deception, he could see that, and this ordeal was far from over, but for the immediate future— or maybe she was as fatigued as he was and just wanted to sleep— Elaine seemed willing to go along with his half-truths, if it meant finding some peace. And maybe she figured that if Vickie was a thousand miles away, that maybe this thing, whatever it was, would suffocate and wither away. Kenny wasn't so sure. Being with Vickie brought him a serenity he'd never imagined in his life, silenced all the demons, aligned the tumblers in his brain, everything clicking into place, bringing the universe into focus, and for the first time in his life, everything made sense. How could that just die? Why would he want it to?

Several days went by, Elaine and Kenny not avoiding one another, but not going out of their way to converse or watch television together, or just sit on the deck and read quietly in each other's company. It was workable, though not enjoyable. Numerous times at work Kenny had dialed Vickie and hung up before her phone rang, then returned home in the evenings feeling like a stranger, an outlier, stiff and mechanical. Elaine was pleasant, conversing about their day over dinner, maybe more herself than he could discern through the many filters of his guilt. He wanted to believe things were returning to normal between them, though he felt at times she was just hiding her true emotions. Or maybe it was the reflection of his own treachery, his own furtive desires, he was reading in her face.

On Saturday, while Kenny was in the backyard trimming the weeds along the slatted wooden privacy fence, Elaine brought him out an iced tea. "Can we talk a minute?" Elaine said, handing him the glass.

"Thanks," he said, gulping it, then wiping the sweat from his forehead. "You want to sit on the patio?" It was nice finally having their own home, though it required much more upkeep than the condo ever had, but it was worth it, for the privacy alone. They'd felt it was a good move to purchase it after Michael was born, providing him a safe place to play and roam. And Michael loved it, his swing set, a sandbox, and lots of green grass to romp, run and fall down. Kenny thought all the boy needed now was a dog, one he could wrestle with and sit on, tug its ears and tail, chase each other around the yard, though Kenny wasn't ready for the added responsibility.

Elaine and Kenny sat opposite each other, Elaine setting the baby monitor on the table between them. They only used it now when they were outside, or in the garage working, when Michael was asleep. Elaine was quiet, glancing at the monitor, then at the French doors that led into the dining room.

"Look," she finally said. "I know you made it sound like nothing happened between you and Vickie, but, I'm sorry, I just don't believe you, okay? I'm not calling you a liar, exactly, but I think there are things you're not telling me."

Kenny was about to dispute her claim, holding to the lifeline of mendacity, but Elaine held out her hand, squelching his attempt before he could get the words out.

"I know you don't go in much for therapy," she said, "but look, we both have abandonment issues, right? Your mom left you when you were eleven. My dad when I was five, and my mom, I'm not sure she was ever there except physically. So, I don't have any illusions about love, okay, at least the made-for-TV kind. But I think what we have is wonderful, and worth saving, and—"

She stopped, her eyes fixed with new concern, maybe noticing him growing gloomier. Kenny couldn't speak, trying to understand Elaine's explanation. Was that what he was doing with Vickie, trying to get something from her he'd lost at eleven? What would that even be? He didn't understand. Was that what Elaine was saying? "I think what we have is great, too," he said, his hands trembling, cupping his fingers around his iced tea glass to steady them. "Are you questioning our marriage? That's how it sounds to me! *Worth saving?*" Deep into the minefield now, Kenny knew he had to step carefully, needed to answer from the point of view that nothing had happened, or would happen, weigh his every response before he brought it out, but trying to construct the nuance of his deception became overwhelming, taxing enough to nearly force a confession.

"I'm just saying that when it comes to relationships, we, you and me, are vulnerable," she said. "We don't have all the necessary software to guard against false readings, like most people."

"Is that what Maggie told you?" Kenny said, remembering when he and Elaine started talking about getting married, and Elaine insisted they meet her therapist, Maggie. He did, and it was fine, but Maggie had teased out a prognosis pretty quickly over the course of that initial session, that Kenny had abandonment issues, just like Elaine. Maggie had asked about his mother, his girlfriends in school, his relationship with his father. Maggie was nice enough, but Kenny wasn't wild about connecting every dot of his life back to his mother's death, like one of those detective shows on television where they have the big board with photos pinned all over the place, and bright colored yarn criss-crossing between them to understand how the suspects and victims were interrelated.

"Kenny, I just want us to be able to communicate, okay," Elaine said. "That's all. And if you still have feelings for this woman, I think we need to look at that. Or you need to explore those feelings with a therapist or something, someone you can trust…"

"Will you just believe me if I tell you everything's fine?" he said, desperate to get back to the safety of the dandelions lining the property, the whine of the gas-powered weed eater loud enough to choke out every thought, pleasing or otherwise, and indulge the uncomplicated pleasure of smelling freshly-mown grass.

She laughed, but her good-nature was freighted with sadness and cynicism. "If you could hear yourself, and see your face right now," she said, "you'd know, as well as I do, that everything is far from being fine." She stood up, holding him with her stormy eyes, then shifted her attention to the lawn, to Michael's yellow and blue swing set, a tear escaping down her cheek. Kenny was knotted up inside, everything slipping off center, unable to parse what she was telling him. Elaine's chin was trembling now, a breath away from emotional failure. She picked up the baby monitor, then leaned over and kissed Kenny on the cheek, a kiss of dubious intent, before disappearing through the French doors into the house.

Chapter Thirty-Six

The weekend came and went, with an uneventful cloudy Sunday night ushering in a wet and gloomy Monday morning. Martin had decided to take the day off, as he was going out of town that afternoon, gone until the following weekend, back to Chicago, the lie becoming harder and harder to fortify. Bennet Petro, the owner of Petro Agency, had doubts regarding Martin's effectiveness on the Harley-Davidson account. Evidently, grumblings had surfaced from the motorcycle giant about costly tasks falling through those proverbial cracks, mishaps and missed details, scheduling issues for actors and film crews to produce a series of on location commercials along the Mississippi River up near Hannibal, Missouri. The agency had had to absorb the costs to preserve the account. Martin knew he'd fucked up, absent from the agency too much to handle things properly on the account, but almost didn't care anymore. He was spending most of his time with Noreen now, at least three to four days a week, redirecting the hard and rewarding work away from Petro Agency and driving it into his own design firm, Phoenix Design Group, in Noreen's reality. Their life together, his and Noreen's, was almost the way he remembered it before she'd died, except for owning his own design firm, and Kenny, of course—in this new life it was just Martin and Noreen; Kenny had never been born. But Martin made a point of staying in touch with his son whenever he was back at Janelle's house (Martin still couldn't think of her house as his, Janelle accusing him of not being invested in their lives together), calling his son, talking sometimes for an hour or two.

Martin would make some calls to his contacts at Harley-Davidson from home, set things in motion, then pass the details onto his new assistant, Zoe, before leaving for Chicago in the afternoon, telling Janelle that that would put him in the Windy City around six o'clock that evening. The agency had a condo for him to use, one normally reserved for out-of-town clients needing a place to stay. Of course, none of that was true since Petro Agency didn't have an office in Chicago.

Janelle had taken the day off to work on getting Beth out of testifying, though she was making little progress. After lunch, she would watch Martin back down the driveway, waving and smiling like the loving wife she was, while Martin, waving and smiling like the phony scoundrel he was, feeling guilty, yes, but unable to help himself, would be thinking about the forty-five-minute drive to the bungalow, and how his heart would lift when he opened the door to the portal, luminous shadowless light washing over him, his and Noreen's beautiful home gradually coming into focus. Noreen would be in their home, maybe in the bedroom, showering for work. Sometimes they'd make love before she got dressed and headed to the office. Or maybe they'd play hooky and spend the afternoon at Lone Elk Park watching the wild buffalo that had been transplanted from who-knew-where, then drive to Applebee's, with all the windows down, for one of those grilled oriental chicken salads she loved. And all of this, his time with Noreen, trying to lead two lives, as amazing as it was, would all be infinitely less stressful if Martin were independently wealthy and didn't have to work in either reality.

"Hey, you have a minute before you leave?" Janelle asked Martin. Martin was seated at the kitchen island going over actress headshots for an upcoming commercial. She had just come in from their bedroom after speaking on the phone with Barry Levitz, her lawyer. Martin knew she was still trying to get Beth out of testifying at her own father's trial. Janelle sat down and pulled a few of the headshots toward her, studied them for a second, then looked over at Martin with tears in her eyes. "Barry can't do it, can't get the judge to stop Beth's court appearance, can't get the prosecution to listen…" Janelle said, her head slowly shifting back and forth in disbelief. "Beth's gonna have to testify."

There was nothing for Martin to say. He thought it was unfair, but what was the point of tossing gasoline on Janelle's already out-of-control fire?

"Did you tell Carl yet?" Martin asked. Janelle glowered at Martin with such loathing he recoiled, playing his question over in his head, trying to figure out what he'd said that was so wrong. Over the past several months, Carl phoned at least four times a week, and on occasion, several times in one day, wanting to know how it was going with Beth and the subpoena. He and Janelle would talk for up to two hours now and again, Janelle trying to console Carl, Carl mostly inconsolable. At times Martin could hear Carl wailing on the phone and he, Martin, would have to leave the room, go for a walk around the block, or wax his motorcycle in the garage. Carl, not being much of a flight risk, had been out on bail since the arraignment (where he'd pleaded not guilty) on a million-dollar bond, which Martin was fairly certain Janelle had helped finance, though he knew better than to ask. Carl, trying to do something with his time other than sit around and brood, had tried to keep his high-end dentistry practice alive, but too many people had heard about the shooting and were having their expensive crowns installed elsewhere. Now Carl had countless hours to think about his fate, often needing a shoulder to sob on, and Janelle didn't mind volunteering.

"Why do you have to bring up Carl?" Janelle said, her face flushed. "Does it bother you that we talk on the phone? There's nothing going on, Martin, if that's what you think. He's just in a very bad place right now." Then: "He's Beth's father!"

Martin said nothing, nodding, giving her his empathetic face, the one that said, "I'm sorry, Of course, I understand. Yes, by all means, Carl's her father. It's nice Carl has someone to turn to…" By this time Janelle was no longer looking at Martin, staring out into space as if she were in the house alone, seated with her back straight, her face blank, like someone in shock, or drugged.

After gathering up the 8 x 10 glossies scattered across the kitchen island, Martin stuffed the actresses into his leather satchel and zipped it closed. He went to the bedroom to get his suitcase and laptop, coming out with the keys to his Taurus jangling from his hand. Janelle's head tilted back, her gaze coming up to meet his.

"Are you leaving already?" she said, glancing at her watch, then the clock on the wall as if maybe her timepiece was wrong. "It's a little after eleven! We haven't had lunch yet."

"I have to stop at the agency downtown before I head to Chicago," he said, part of the lie being true, the detail about stopping at Petro. "I'm just gonna grab lunch on the road."

Janelle rubbed the sides of her nostrils with her thumb and forefinger, new tears forming. "I'm sorry about what I said before," she told him, standing up and walking over to him. She pulled him close, so close their noses almost touched, then drew him nearer, pressing her lips to his, easing her body against him, her tongue exploring the inside of his mouth. "Do you have to leave right this minute?" she whispered, her hands going to his belt, unbuckling it, then undoing his trousers, letting them fall to the kitchen floor. Her right hand went into his boxers, her tongue tracing the tender skin along the outside of his cheek. Martin set his leather briefcase and laptop on the kitchen island, then started undoing Janelle's blouse, and was unfastening her bra and slipping it off her arms, when her phone rang.

"Don't answer it," Martin said, leaning down to kiss her breast. She drew back gently, her eyes sad, her mouth tortured into a frown.

"It might be Barry," she said, pulling her blouse off the floor and wrapping herself into the sleeves, as if she needed to cover herself before she could talk to her lawyer. Martin fixed his trousers and carried his things out to the car, then came back to see if Janelle was off the phone. She was still talking, but it was Carl, not Barry. Martin shook his head and walked over, mouthing, "I have to go." She looked up, pleading with her eyes for him to wait, then said into the phone, "Carl, give me one second, okay?"

When she set the phone down, Martin could hear Carl sniffling. "I'm sorry, Martin. I really am. Will I be able to reach you on your mobile in Chicago this time?"

"It's really tough, Janelle," he said, trying to sound believable, but his mobile phone didn't ring in Noreen's reality. There was no way for Janelle to reach him unless he had come out to spend a little time at

Petro Agency, which he did sometimes for a few hours in the afternoons so Bennet would at least see him in his office occasionally. "I'm in meetings all day. It's just crazy." Then, seeing her face fall, Martin said, "I'll try to call you one evening, okay?"

She sniffled and pulled him close. Then, still holding him around the waist, drew back her head to look at him. "I love you," she said, giving him a broken smile.

"Me to," he said. "I'll be back before you know it."

Martin, hurrying from the kitchen, heard Janelle state rather flatly to Carl on the phone, "I'm back," as Martin fled into the garage, hitting the door opener. When the garage door rattled up along its silver tracks, Martin backed out, not waiting for the door to stop. The sun was trying to poke through the dingy gray clouds, a few sprinkles hitting the windshield. After Martin tapped the switch to close the garage door, he glanced toward the front of the house, surprised to see Janelle standing in the opened door, the phone to her ear, her blouse still mostly open, fastened near the middle by one button, smiling at Martin with her hand raised, unmoving, a forlorn goodbye. He smiled back, waved, then backed down the driveway and sped away down the block.

Feeling like he was running late, Martin didn't bother with lunch. Maybe he and Noreen would grab some food together, maybe tacos at that place she loved, *Olé Guacamole*, but he had to stop at Petro Agency first, to consult with his assistant, Zoe.

Getting off the elevator, Martin said hello to Laverne, who wished him a good morning, then handed him a note with people he needed to call back.

"Are these from this morning?" Martin asked, getting edgy, not wanting to get bogged down with a bunch of phone calls.

"Two of them," she said, looking over the top of her glasses, poking the note with her pink fingernail to show him which two, "But the other is from Friday. After you left."

Martin knew all three, only one of them a client. The other two were persistent printing salesmen who Martin had no intention of calling back. "Thanks, Laverne... can you reach Zoe for me, have her meet me here when she's free?"

Laverne smiled and nodded, punching the buttons on the phone as

Martin went into his office to call Michael Turner at Harley-Davidson. Turner's secretary answered, telling Martin that Mr. Turner wouldn't be back until around two o'clock. Martin checked his watch, knowing he planned to be with Noreen by then, and told Michael's secretary that he'd call back around two-thirty and hung up.

Zoe came in, young, tall and fresh from college, with short, tousled blonde hair, like David Bowie, and a bachelor's in film and design.

"Hey, Zoe," Martin said, fishing the headshots out of his soft leather briefcase. "I picked out a couple here," Martin said, still looking at the glossy photos, then finally up at the young woman. "Have a seat." Why she was still standing? he wondered. When she sat, she pushed her glasses up on the bridge of her nose, Martin finally noticing her sour expression. She was attractive in an all-business sort of way, narrow face, large eyes, or maybe it was the glasses creating the illusion, magnifying her eyes. "Everything okay?" Martin asked.

"Have you spoken with Mr. Petro yet?" she said, with a sheepish hesitance incongruous with her flinty persona, tugging at her ear, the bracelets on her thin wrist clanking together. Something was off. Martin held her gaze a moment longer and saw the slightest strain at the corners of her eyes.

"What's up, Zoe? What happened?"

She gave him an unhappy smile, then straightened her back, as if steeling herself, her narrow features squeezed more than normal. "They're letting you go," she finally said. "I'm sorry. I wasn't supposed to say anything, but... I'm so sorry, Mr. Moffett."

Fired! Was that possible, after more than twenty-five years, that Bennet, who had known Noreen and attended her funeral, had been at Kenny's high school graduation, had even offered Kenny a job if he ever returned to St. Louis after college, had spoken to Martin about a possible partnership, had fired him! Martin looked at Zoe wondering if she'd gotten it wrong, had misunderstood Bennet, somehow. "How did you hear that?" Martin finally asked her.

She cleared her throat a couple of times, almost silent, nervous little grunts. "Mr. Petro said I'd be taking the lead on the Harley-Davidson account..." she said. "I asked what you would be doing, and he said, 'Finding employment elsewhere.'"

This disclosure opened Zoe's floodgates, her shoulders beginning to quake. Martin got up and closed the door to his office, Laverne craning around to see what all the commotion was about. Zoe was young, Petro Agency her first real job in advertising, and she and Martin had only worked together a few months, but Martin could understand why Bennet gave her the account; she had fresh ideas, a work ethic of someone three times her age, and enough energy to power a small city. Martin should have felt worse about the news, but oddly, once the initial sensation of falling through a trapdoor faded, a pleasant lightness filled him; everything would be simpler now; as long as he never told Janelle he'd been fired.

"It's not your fault, Zoe," Martin said, already beginning to clean out his desk, shoving stuff into his leather case. "To tell the truth, I've been distracted lately. And you're doing a fantastic job!" This didn't seem to help, Zoe looking up at him through her glasses.

"But I don't know—"

"You know all you need to know, Zoe. Trust me, and what you don't know you'll learn as you go. Harley loves you, they love your ideas, and honestly, you know more about this business than you realize."

Martin stood up and grabbed a few things from his shelves, then decided he should see Bennet before asking Laverne if she could find him a box for the last of his stuff. Zoe stood up and walked over to Martin, and gave him a stiff hug, that he returned half-heartedly—he wasn't a hugger—and told her once again she was going to do great. "Truth is, Zoe, you've been carrying me for a while, now!"

She smiled at him. "I can't thank you enough for all I've learned from you," she said, her face brightening, like an eager sky trying to dissipate a storm.

"Well, that's great, really," Martin said, rushing to leave. He wanted to cut his meeting with Bennet short; ardent apologies, sincere regrets, optimistically reminding each other that things happen for a reason, and shake on the promise to remain friends. Sure. "I just hope you didn't pick up any of my slacker tendencies!" Martin added. "And if you need anything, just reach out to me, Zoe. You have my number."

Martin smiled at her, then walked to Laverne's desk and asked if she could find him a box about yay big, holding his hands out to demonstrate the size. Laverne asked what was going on, and Martin said he was being canned, saying that he had to get to Bennet's office for the final nail, and that it's been great working with her. Zoe walked past, smiling sadly at Martin, touching his hand, heading down the hall to her office. Laverne's face turned glum, crushed; she'd been with him for over fifteen years. "It won't be the same without you, Mr. Moffett," she said, sincerely.

"It'll be better, Laverne," he said. "Trust me!" Then: "I'll be back for the rest of my stuff in a few minutes... if you can find me a box?"

"Absolutely," she said, getting up from her desk, heading for the storeroom.

Martin was glad she wasn't making a big deal about it. He scurried for Petro's office, avoiding eye contact with anyone who might want to stop and talk. Petro's secretary spoke to Mr. Petro on the intercom and Bennet told him to come right in. It was just as expected, apologies, regrets, Bennet almost teary at one point, as if he'd acted rashly firing Martin, saying words to that effect. Martin worried Bennet was about to recant the dismissal, reminding Bennet that he, Martin, had been very distracted of late, and he understood and wished Bennet and the agency all the best of luck, then beat a hasty retreat from Bennet's office, leaving his prior boss a bit pale, contemplative, as if Bennet was pondering if he'd acted impulsively in the turmoil of his anger over Martin's slapdash performance of late. Or maybe he was thinking it was unconscionable to fire someone after twenty-five years of service with nothing more than a severance check. None of it mattered to Martin. He wasn't looking back and finished cleaning out his office, waving and smiling at a now teary Laverne, the box under his arm.

In less than twenty minutes, if traffic cooperated, Martin would be at the bungalow, already doing some banking and calculating in his head during the drive. He and Janelle had agreed to pool some of their money, a thousand a month, a kind of slush fund for groceries and utilities and incidentals, and the rest of their individual expenses would come out of their own accounts. It was a great deal for him, as Janelle had paid off her mortgage years ago, and Martin had managed to pay off his mortgage on the bungalow, allowing him to bank much of his paycheck from Petro Agency, building up quite a nice savings, investing some in mutual funds. If he didn't earn a buck over the next two years, he could still easily afford the grand a month to Janelle, plus his other expenses, and that was if he wanted to keep things as they were, fueling these parallel lives. But instead, if he chose to live in Noreen's reality full-time, with The Phoenix Group doing extremely well financially, as well as creatively, and Noreen's university tenure, he would... "Oh my God!" ...be living his most creative, unencumbered dream! He cranked up the radio and started singing along, effulgent, and nearly insane with giddy fervor, the only dampening component; never seeing Beth and Janelle again. "One day at a time!" he reminded himself. And this one, so far, was fantastic...

Chapter Thirty-Seven

The only thing flowing effortlessly in Kenny's life was work, and without the constant tug of regret and longing. No matter how many times he assured himself that things between Elaine and him were getting better, he couldn't deny being bogged down by thoughts of Vickie. He ached, physically ached, thinking of her, the few hours they'd spent together, every detail etched on an indelible slate in his mind, kept in the mosque his brain had erected in Vickie's honor, replete with photos, perfect audio recordings of her voice, 3D simulations of her expressions, a looping video of her naked torso writhing on his lap in his father's Taurus, her laugh, the smell of her hair, the taste of her skin. It was maddening.

Kenny managed to focus on work, grateful for the mind-centering aspects of coding and software, almost like a drug now, and Kenny was addicted, spending long hours at the office, cleaning up projects that had been sitting for weeks, even months, new ones arriving daily, to his great relief. The extra hours were perfect, serving a purpose now, anything to keep him from the constant lie of his home life, the anguish of pretending around Elaine, putting on the pleasant face while plodding around the house with an active volcano in his gut.

Vickie and Kenny had managed for these past few weeks since the reunion, not to contact one another, Kenny wondering if it was as diffi-cult for her as it was for him. He could only hope it was; the possibility that it wasn't crushed his soul. Had she moved on? Had she ever really been onboard to begin with? The doubts piling up like storm clouds the size of mountains. These feelings should have started fading by now, he thought, charging chin-first into the next assignment; the brief intervals between projects unbearable, his mind launching heart-churning uncertainties into the target-rich environment of his chest.

He had just come back with coffee when his phone rang. "Hello, Kenny Moffett."

After a long silence, a woman spoke, her voice tentative. "Kenny?" Then: "It's Vickie."

Kenny, falling back into his chair, the strength leaving his legs, spilled some of his coffee down his shirt. "Vickie!" He wanted to say everything he was feeling, but the words were tripping over one another in a mad rush to get out of his brain, leaving a tricky, protracted silence between them.

"I hope this is okay," she said. "I know it's selfish to call you like this... but... I had to hear your voice..." She sounded as if she were crying.

Of course it was okay! More than okay! Kenny all at once jittery with excitement and disbelief, silencing the stupid sentiment before it leaped from his lips, trying to quell the nervous chatter in his brain. "No, it's actually really great to hear from you," he said, trying to remain low key, checking his enthusiasm at the door. Sure, hearing her voice was miraculous, but he was already sensing the crushing void he'd feel when the call ended. What then? How could he put poor Mr. Dumpty back together again?

"I have wanted to call you so many times since the reunion—" she said, breaking off abruptly, as if needing to censor herself. The silence that followed had the empty, suffocating quality of a vacuum. Kenny was going to say the same thing, about to finally speak again when Vickie said, "How have you been?"

He shook his head, the pressure building, pressing in on his ribs. "So messed up!" he finally blurted out, releasing some of the tension in his stomach. "I have been crazy since that night, missing you so much it hurts!" He bolted up from his chair to close his office door, then hurried back to his desk, sitting, spinning toward his windows, the office buildings of the Newark skyline catching the yellow, late afternoon sun, the slick surface of the Hudson River patched and scuffed with swirling currents and simmering eddies.

They talked freely now, as if a wall had been ripped down, Kenny turning in his seat occasionally, seeing fellow employees leaving for the day, some shooting him a brief wave as they walked past his office, others engaged in conversation, Kenny smiling at nothing, his breathing spacious, unfettered, Vickie's voice floating like a soothing melody in his head.

It seemed that only seconds had passed before the lights of the city sparkled against the black sky like a new, radiant world, one Kenny had never seen before. The conversation had begun to wind down, both of them comfortable with the periodic intervals of silence, Vickie usually the one to initiate a new turn in their chat. During one such interlude of quiet, Kenny, feeling pangs of longing, said, "I'd give anything if I could hold you right now…"

What followed was a tense and unexpected silence. Had he said something he shouldn't have? In that moment, Kenny tapped some keys on his computer to close the documents on his screen, unsure why Vickie hadn't responded. He was about to ask if she was still on the line, thinking they'd been disconnected, when Vickie said, "Did you mean it?"

"Mean what?" Kenny said, not understanding her question, hoping he hadn't upset her in some way.

"Did you mean it… about giving anything if you could hold me right now?"

"Absolutely!" he said without hesitation, trying to make clear how he felt about her.

Another empty space, this one so charged Kenny felt a tingle rising up his legs.

"I'm here, Kenny. In Newark. At the Charter House Inn."

The plumbing in Kenny's chest suddenly failed, everything stalled, his mind stumbling. "In Newark? Newark, New Jersey?" he said, grappling with the implausibility of this likelihood, trying to picture her at the Charter House Inn, right here in Newark? That hotel was less than a fifteen-minute walk from his office building. "Are you serious?"

"I'm here for a floral trade show," she said.

"A trade show? How long will you—" he said.

"It doesn't matter." Then: "Room 507. I can see the Hudson from my balcony…"

"I'll be right over. Just give me a few minutes."

"Have you eaten?"

"No, but I'm—"

"I'll order room service…"

"Okay, fifteen minutes or so…" Kenny said. When the phone clicked, and went dead, something shifted, and the city, the night sky, the traffic on the street below took on the flimsy characteristics of projected images on a screen, more illusion than solid. Kenny tried to draw back from the alarming sensation of whirling, his legs no longer under him, and he was now barely a wisp of air, vaporous. He closed his eyes, or they were already closed, something spilling out inside him, draining away, a dizzying mechanism spinning out of control. He gripped the desk with both hands, popped open his eyes, and his breathing began to pace itself again, returning to normal. The office chair squeaked, and bounced a little, when he shot up to grab his jacket. Kenny considered getting his car from the parking garage and driving over, but he needed the walk, the fresh air, time to figure out exactly what it was he was doing.

On his way to the hotel, he phoned Elaine to let her know he'd be late. The call went to voicemail. "Not sure when I'll be home. Walking out to grab some dinner right now. Tell Michael goodnight for me." Then, before her phone disconnected, he added: "I love you." He clicked his phone off and stuck it in his jacket pocket. *I love you?* The words were clunky pieces of wood coming from his mouth. The cool night air, the earthy pong of the Hudson mingled with the oil-smoke odor of exhaust, the metallic sounds of traffic over the murmur of pedestrians, all calming reminders of a solid, ordered world, a place with reliable gravity and observable rules, rotating on an unfailing axis as old as the universe itself. Sensing a new alignment to things codified him, lent him stability, though it clarified nothing in his ravaged mind, just made it so he could walk without swaying, the trembling in his legs gone.

The Charter House, old but dignified, and the way he remembered it, expensive. Vickie had said she was here for some kind of floral trade show, but he knew florists didn't make that much money. How could she afford it? He went in through the antique revolving doors, and walked to the elevator, and pushed the button for the fifth floor. He found the room and knocked, and heard someone running across the floor. When the door flew open, Vickie launched herself at him, kissing him hard on the lips, throwing her arms around him, walking backward dragging him into the room, kicking the door shut with her bare foot. Still moving, they stumbled into the food cart, rattling the dishes and metal lids. Vickie slammed it aside with her hip, dragging him toward the bed, Kenny caught in the current of her fierce greeting. Finally, the tide ceased, and Kenny could catch his breath. Vickie drew back just enough to look into his eyes.

"I'm so glad you came," she said, her eyes damp, elated. "I didn't know if you would."

"I was shocked when you said you were—"

"I lied," she said, "about the floral trade show. I came to see you." Then, as if not to seem so pitiful: "But I'm going to look for some gift ideas for the shop."

Vickie, wearing a white bathrobe monogrammed with an elegant *CH*, pulled him toward a table with two chairs as she told him of the plans she and Amy had for their business. "We have this idea to carry everything and anything related to flowers. Paintings, etchings, earrings, necklaces, pottery with a floral theme…"

With Kenny seated, she went back to the hotel cart and pushed it near the table, setting the dishes, glasses and silverware in the center between them, then continued: "…mostly by local St. Louis artists, like art students at Washington U, and arts and crafts people. And other things we can find, you know…?" She sat down and put her dinner napkin in her lap, removing the metal cloche covering her meal, "… like towels and washcloths, and decorator soaps, but not the ordinary kind you find at discount stores, but unique soaps, that you'd feel good about giving as gifts. We may even make them ourselves, with an actual flower or two in them. I've already started researching how to do it. Then we'd have dried flower displays, like those ones in glass decanters… Just everything we can think of!"

Kenny was energized by her enthusiasm, his life as a programmer-software geek paling by comparison. Vickie was still talking about her and Amy's plans when Kenny's attention flagged, now thinking about his own life. Working on his CIS Degree, Kenny was fascinated learning not only the latest software and techniques, but how to use technology to achieve certain goals. He was equally enthralled with his programming courses, like learning any new language, the excitement of acquiring skills that would last him a lifetime. However, what he hadn't counted on was how quickly, once these ends were reached, the work would become mechanical and mindless. At times there were challenges, but mostly, he was expected to color inside the lines.

"I'm sorry," Vickie said, her cheeks reddening slightly. "I've been blathering on like a meth addict. How's your dinner? I hope the Charter House Gourmet Burger was okay. It's not too cold, is it?"

"It's delicious," Kenny said, unable to remember when he'd had a better burger; this was more like an expensive, tender steak on a bun. Vickie asked him what he'd been up to since the reunion, the discussion bending toward their few hours together, the riverfront, making love in his father's Taurus. Vickie became quiet, looking over at Kenny, an odd sheen to her eyes. Without a word, she stood up at the table and unfastened her robe, letting it fall from her shoulders. Naked, she came around to Kenny's side of the table, behind him, bringing her face next to his, kissing his neck, biting his ear, unbuttoning his shirt, running her hands down his chest, to his waist, unbuckling his belt. In a moment her right hand was under the waistband of his boxers. Kenny leaned back in the chair, moaning.

After indicating with her body that she wanted Kenny to turn his chair out from the table, he eased it around toward her. Removing his pants and boxers, Vickie turned her back toward him and lowered herself onto his lap, his hands instinctively wrapping her from behind, cupping her breasts. Bent at the waist, she rocked back and forth, almost a circular motion, and Kenny was gone in seconds. She continued moving for a while longer, then raised up and sat back down facing him. "I love you so much, Kenny," she said. "I regret that we wasted our time in high school, that we weren't together all those years." Then, a few tears dropping: "That we're not together now..." A new hush filled the room. "Will you hold me on the bed?"

They slid in beneath the comforter, under the cool sheets, and clung to one another, Vickie nestling into the cave of his arms and shoulders, tangling her legs in his, as if trying to crawl inside him somehow. After several minutes, Kenny said in a low voice, that he felt the same. "I wish we had figured this out over a decade ago…" A murky, deeper sadness than he'd ever known—not even after his mother had died, at least that he could recall—expanded in his chest with the persistence of a predatory organism.

They fell asleep in each other's arms, Kenny waking first, checking his watch, surprised Elaine had not tried to call. Vickie stirred next to him, rolling over, away from him, then scooted backward, tucking up against his body. Kenny wrapped his arms around her and whispered in her ear. "I've got to go, Vickie."

She turned over to face him. "You can't spend the night?" She shook her head and grimaced. "Sorry," she said. "That was stupid."

He smiled, and slipped out from under the blankets, and found his clothes on the floor. She sat up against the headboard. "Can you join me for breakfast?" she said, pulling the sheet up over her chest. "They have amazing room service in the morning. Waffles and pancakes, enormous strawberries with Greek yogurt, the most incredible French toast…"

"How long have you been here?" Kenny said, curious, pulling up his pants.

"I had two breakfasts," she said. "Early this morning, then again before they stopped serving breakfast."

Kenny laughed, buttoning his shirt. "How long are you staying?"

"I leave day after tomorrow," she said. "Can you spend the day with me?"

Kenny wasn't sure that was a good idea, already uncomfortable with why Elaine hadn't called. Any time he worked late, she would usually phone, sometimes put Michael on to say goodnight. He found his jacket on the chair by the desk, not remembering how it ended up there.

"You could help me find some cool stuff for the store," she said, getting out of bed and coming over to the table to get her robe. Kenny grabbed her and pulled her to him before she could put it on.

"I wish I could spend the night," he said. Then, after a few seconds: "I wish I could spend every night."

She got up on her toes and kissed him, pressing against his body. "Spend tomorrow with me. It'll be fun."

"I'll take you to Kernstown. They have a lot of cool shops."

"What time can you be here? I'll have breakfast waiting!"

"Is seven-thirty too early?"

"In that case, I'll have this waiting for you…" sweeping her hands slowly downward, bringing his attention to her body, "…and when I'm finished with you, we'll order breakfast together."

Kenny chuckled, holding her, running his hands along her slender waist, to her luscious hips. "Sounds like a plan. I'll be here at seven-thirty."

They kissed again, then Kenny drew back and turned to leave, Vickie escorting him to the door, naked. She blew him a kiss, her eyes soft, maybe sad, he couldn't tell, as she slid the door closed. The sudden void in the hotel hallway stole his breath. He had not expected to feel so emptied, so crushingly alone, and fought the urge to knock on her door. He turned and went down the hall to the elevator, looking back to see if she'd come running after him, in her robe, her bare feet splashing along the dark green and lavender carpet, and plead with him to stay. If she did, he'd already decided he would, whatever the cost. And the cost would be great.

The elevator dinged, the doors opened, and he waited a couple of seconds, scanning the empty hallway, then ambled into the space, the doors closing. Exiting the hotel, he walked down the busy sidewalk, the sudden din of traffic both exhilarating and numbing. Before he knew it, he was in the parking garage of his office building, starting his car, and then, as if losing some strange bout with time, was pulling into his driveway, then inside reading a note on the kitchen table.

Kenny, Michael and I are going to spend the night at JoAnn's apartment. I needed some time. I'll try to call you tomorrow. Michael misses you. Elaine.

With so much unspoken angst in Elaine's note Kenny didn't know how to begin to decode it all. Everything Elaine had wanted to convey she did through the power of omission. *I needed some time* was about the only straight forward thing, other than their names, in the note.

For the shortest possible second Kenny considered going back to Charter House and knocking on door 507, spending the night with

Vickie, the ache in his chest nearly unbearable, but decided against it, a decision he would regret for the rest of his life.

Chapter Thirty-Eight

M artin slept in. Noreen was already in the kitchen making breakfast when he walked in wearing his robe. He slid up behind her and kissed the back of her neck.

"I couldn't send you off without a proper meal," Noreen said, bright and cheerful as a pure blue sky. There were no questions about where he was off to, or when he'd return. It was the strangest aspect of Noreen's reality; things were taken at face value, no questions asked. It was almost too perfect, too civilized to be healthy, Martin thought. There was no reason to lie. If he told her he was leaving on Friday, she smiled and said she loved him and walked him to the front door, kissing him before he left, never a question as to when he'd return. Maybe it was like he imagined a dog's world to be, no urgency, or real sense of the passage of time. When Martin did return, it was as if he'd never left, no anger or tears about where he'd been, or what he'd been doing. And yet there was nothing odd at all about the time they spent together, and he could easily imagine living out the rest of his life with Noreen in this unusual paradigm.

He hated the thought of leaving her, but he'd told Janelle he'd be back sometime Friday late afternoon, that they'd go see a movie together. He'd spoken to her on the phone two times since he'd been gone, leaving Noreen's reality to step back into the bungalow and phone Janelle. They talked about Beth, and the trial, her latest conversation with her ex-husband, Carl, how they'd met for lunch one after-noon and what a mess he'd been, dark bags under his eyes, gaunt and bony with a sickly greenish cast to his skin. "He didn't look healthy," Janelle had said, genuinely concerned.

With breakfast finished, Martin and Noreen said their goodbyes, hugging, kissing, Martin waving as he headed for the front door. If he allowed himself, he could almost believe all of this was real, that he was just leaving for work, and would return that evening, possibly exhilarated about a new design project he'd landed, or maybe frus-trated with the constant stream of client changes, no different than if he were still working at Petro Agency. He gave Noreen one last smile, receiving a warm smile in return, and a peck on the cheek, then walked outside, the ghostly door to the bungalow floating there across the street. Taking his eyes to the immediate neighbors' houses, Martin always wondered if anyone could see the strange apparition, but it seemed that even if someone stood near it, the door right beside them, it was still invisible to their eyes.

Martin approached it, glanced back across the street at his and Noreen's house, then twisted the knob, walked through the shim-mering light and closed the bungalow door behind him. Returning was always a letdown, like air escaping a balloon, the real world deflated by comparison, flat and colorless, at least for the first hour or so. Martin stood staring at the door, asking himself why he'd left at all, and had just started turning away when someone called his name.

"Sport? Is that you?" Falco appeared in the doorway to the *Anything* room, bare-chested, wide white bandages circling his abdomen, a tinge of pink the size of a fist bleeding through in one area.

"You okay?" Martin asked, following Falco back into the living room. Falco sat down at the kitchen table, an opened beer in front of him, and lit a cigarette, blowing smoke toward the ceiling fan. Martin noticed that Falco had opened the kitchen window to let out the smoke, then sat down across from him. "When did we get that fan?" Martin asked. He liked the feel of the breeze circulating out the stale air, or maybe it was the stagnation he felt inside beginning to seep away.

"I put that in a few days ago," Falco said, sucking on the cigarette, blowing the smoke toward the window, as if it might actually go out.

"It's nice, huh? Should have done it years ago." Then he sat a moment, staring at Martin, until Martin felt a shiver of unease sidle though him.

"What?" Martin finally said.

"How're things working with Noreen, Sport?"

Martin scrunched up his bottom lip, as if thinking on the question, but he knew the answer. "Couldn't be better."

Falco took another long drag on the cigarette, forming a tiny vent at the corner of his mouth to release the smoke, never taking his dark eyes off Martin. "You need to be careful, Sport. That's not Disney World through that door in there."

Martin was uncomfortable, fidgeting in his chair, checking his watch. "Are you going to be around for a few days?" Martin finally said, steering the mood in a different direction. Falco finished his beer and got up to get a new one, asking if Martin wanted one. "No, I have to get moving. Janelle and I are going to a movie tonight."

"Good for you," Falco said, popping the top on the beer can, some foam spilling over the side. "This is the world that matters."

Martin could only nod, unsure how to respond to Falco's peculiar, negative demeanor, figuring it had something to do with the bandages around his waist. "What happened?" Martin said, nodding toward Falco's apparent injury.

Falco took a long pull from the can, then set it down near the ashtray, snuffing out the butt. "Mitzi, happened," Falco said flatly. "She tried to kill me."

Martin felt his eyes narrow, like an involuntary response to Falco's disclosure, a thousand questions wheeling inside his head.

"A butcher knife," Falco said. "We were in her kitchen, laughing, talking, me getting ready to leave. I've only been going on the day of her death, like you were doing with Noreen, and it had been working great... at least for a while, until things started getting weird, little things, like glitches in her normal behavior. I noticed subtle clues, like in her expression, maybe a fleeting tic she'd never had before, you know, a muscle under her eye would jump, like she was some kind of android on the fritz.

"Then, last night, we're having a wonderful time and I'm getting ready to leave, like I said, and she comes over smiling and loving and WHAM! jams that huge knife into my gut." Then, as if Falco were rewinding the memory to take another look, still in disbelief about what happened next, said, "She stood there smiling, watching the blood run out of me. Then she says, 'You want a band-aid or something?'

"I lost it! 'A band-aid,' I screamed. 'Are you serious?' Then I got out of there," Falco said, gently twisting his head back and forth, his eyes unfocused, cloudy as a storm, unable to shake the event from his head. The two men sat in silence, the fan beating the air above their heads. After several minutes, Martin, reviewing the past four days with Noreen, was trying to pick up on clues, things out of the ordinary; but everything about Noreen's world was out of the ordinary; how would he even notice. Falco took another drink, then got up slowly, grimacing from the pain, unable to straighten completely, and went into the bathroom. When he returned, he reached into the fridge and brought out a plastic container, then grabbed a pot and twisted the gas burner on, dumping the contents of the bowl into the pot. "Plenty for both of us, Sport, if you're hungry…"

"Did you go to the hospital?" Martin asked.

"Yeah… Mitzi drove me! Isn't that something? Can't explain it other than to say she's crazy…" With his back to Martin, Falco stood at the stove, stirring his meal.

"What will you do now?"

Falco spun his head back toward Martin. "Going back on the road, see if anyone's interested in magic anymore."

The spark had gone out of Falco. It was hard to believe that a man who'd been brilliant enough to open this *portal*, or whatever it was, was giving it all up, ready to reenter the world of the mundane, where novels and movies with subject matter dealing with *portals* of any kind, were often regarded as ridiculous, illogical, and a waste of time; what did any of that have to do with the real world?

Martin was no different, refusing to suffer through films or *literature* (if you could even call it that), based on farcical romps about time travel and UFOs and alternate realities. Even dreams, which topped the list of the most ordinary, extraordinary human experiences, could easily be explained by eating pizza too late at night, or too many highballs during dinner, or watching a silly wolfman movie just before bed! All chemicals, psychologists said, panicky chemicals in the brain churning out those wild images and scenarios! That's all dreams were. The world was what it appeared to be, nothing more, nothing less, its predictability proven time and time again, statistically accurate down to the human cell, the molecule, the *atom!* Everything was known, written in books, indisputable, perfectly portrayed through thousands, if not millions, of scientific tomes gathering dust in libraries and universities across the world. Once scientists split the atom, mapped the human genome, discovered through rigorous exploration and conjecture the source of all life on the planet, and *hell!* for that matter, teased out, through mind-bending mathematical gymnastics, how the entire universe came into being millions (or billions?) of years ago! what was left to wander about? Was there really any doubt about the essence of reality?

Martin was a solid believer in science, what could be seen and felt, and yet, for some reason, had no issue with the idea of Noreen's *reality*, as if he'd found a safe, quiet place in his mind to store such anomalies and ludicrous eventualities without them impinging on his daily life. The way he figured it, the existence, if you could even call it that, of Noreen, in the portal, could all be a figment of Martin's imagination— as real as a dream image, with smell and taste, color and dimension— and in no way negated science, or its findings. And, Martin knew, if scientists were allowed to study Falco's portal, they would find that the actual source of the phenomenon—breaking it down, measuring it, dissecting it—the portal, with its scintillating, lustrous light, was rooted in the oldest trick in the magician's tool box; the phenomenon, if that was the word for it, was conditioned on the time-honored, elab-orately dazzling *illusion!* So what? Even that in no way dampened Martin's enthusiasm for Falco's dizzying achievement. Didn't Eastern mystics believe everything was illusion anyway? Another concept Martin never could bend his brain around. And as far as Noreen, he wasn't about to toss over his time with her just because he didn't believe it was possible!

"I need to get going," Martin said, standing, the food Falco was heating, whatever it was, smelled good, awakening Martin's own appetite.

Falco turned stiffly from the stove, careful not to twist his torso. "I'm going to hang out here at the bungalow for a while if that's okay with you, Martin," Falco said, his eyes horribly sadder, and puffier, than Martin had ever seen them before.

"Sure, sure, whatever you need to do," Martin said, feeling like Falco needed a hug or something, but Martin wasn't going to be the one. "Do you need help changing your dressing or anything?"

Falco, head angled down toward the stove, continued stirring the pot, his back to Martin. "I'm fine. Just be careful, Sport. Don't let it eat away your life…"

Martin eased away, slowly at first, from the kitchen table, as if not to disturb Falco's meditation on stirring, keeping his eyes on the failing magician, mechanically taking himself toward the front door, glancing one last time at Falco, who stood at the stove—his neck stiff, his shoulders slumped oddly, one hand twisting the serving spoon around the pot—like a damaged robot.

Chapter Thirty-Nine

The next morning, Kenny left for the Charter House Inn at seven-thirty in the morning. In the shower earlier, he'd thought it unusual that he'd gotten no call from Elaine, and equally strange, that his calls went straight to her voicemail. Even Elaine going to her friend's apartment, the very same night that Vickie called from the hotel, smacked, in his mind, of some convoluted conspiracy, as if Elaine wanted Kenny to get Vickie *out of his system!* Wasn't that the way she'd put it? As best he could remember. Or at least the sentiment she had intended. Maybe she'd planned the little junket to JoAnn's so she'd be absent, leaving Kenny free to gad about unencumbered, figuring that if he could just see how wrong Vickie was for him, he'd get past her, past his silly high school crush. Was it nothing more than that, a childish fantasy he'd never outgrown?

As promised, Vickie was naked and waiting when he arrived. A short time later they ordered breakfast. She was bubbly, all smiles, chattering on about her and Amy's floral business, then about her and Kenny's previous evening together, finally asking if there'd been any problems with Elaine when he'd gotten home.

"No," he said, not wanting to tell Vickie she hadn't even been home, that he hadn't talked with her. "She's used to me working late."

"I guess working all night is out of the question?" Vickie said, trying to make a joke out of wanting him to spend the night with her, but Kenny could tell she was disappointed, glimpsing the momentary sadness that passed over her features like a shadow. How different would the trajectory of Kenny's life be now if he'd known in high school how much she cared for him. It saddened him, not that he didn't appreciate the life he had with Elaine, and especially with Michael, but when would the "What ifs?" stop?

When they finished eating, Kenny drove Vickie to Kernstown and they walked the shops, Kenny with one eye on the people around them, on the street, always wondering if they'd run into someone he knew. Not only Elaine's friends, but anyone from work as well. Kenny had called in that morning and left word that he wouldn't be coming in today. It wouldn't be great if someone from the office saw him hanging out with some beautiful young woman.

Vickie had purchased some floral themed objects she found interesting, asking for Kenny's input on other items, if he thought they'd be a fit for *Floral & Party*. He tried to be helpful and present, but was unable to focus, being so exposed in public, the guilt consuming him, the fear of being caught making it worse. He wished he'd driven farther from his office, maybe into Manhattan, or up to Stamford, or even down to Toms River. Kernstown was just too close to home.

Around one in the afternoon, Vickie announced she was hungry. "Let's eat!" she said. "I'm buying!"

"I know some cool places in Toms River," he said, hoping the idea sounded good to her; his stomach was balled up. He wasn't sure he could eat.

"How far is that?" she asked, smiling, her face alive with the anticipation of a child.

"Little over an hour."

"Okay... let's pop into that bakery and find something for the road."

They snacked on cinnamon rolls driving the Garden State Parkway, Kenny explaining about the Toms River boardwalk, the amusement park, and some other spots he thought Vickie might be interested in.

"This place is on the ocean?" Vickie said, even more thrilled with their adventure. "This sounds so fun!" Then, a moment later, biting into another baked good they'd bought at the bakery, her mouth full.

"I thought it might have been on some smelly river like the Mississippi, you know, like St. Louis!"

They were approaching a tollbooth and Kenny lifted the compartment lid between the seats. "Can you grab a couple of bucks out of that tray?" Kenny asked her.

Vickie picked up the dollar bill and sifted through the change to find four quarters. Kenny took the money from her, and was the third car in line to the booth.

"You have got to try this caramel apple crumb bar," she said, holding it up to his lips. The car in front of him pulled forward, him easing up behind, opening his mouth for the crumb bar. He bit down and chewed, pulling up to the booth and handing the woman the money. They got the green light and pulled away, Kenny merging quickly into traffic, still chewing the bar.

"We should have bought more of those, right?" Vickie said, waiting for him to respond, watching his jaw working.

"Chewy!" he finally brought out.

"Yeah," she said, slipping the last of the treat past her lips. "It's almost worth the cavities!" She dug the other one out of the bag and asked if he wanted more.

"No, that should do until my next dentist appointment."

Vickie got quiet, letting her eyes rove out the windows, her face radiant with the afternoon sun. Kenny knew nothing was wrong, or at least thought there wasn't, not completely comfortable reading her mood. "You any good with a hatchet?" he finally said, wanting to see her smile. When she did, it was like a light switch flicking on.

"What?" she said, giving him a curious look.

"Are you any good with a hatchet?" he repeated, trying to hold a straight face.

"Why, are we going to have to kill our lunch in Toms River?"

"No," Kenny said, wondering how she came to such a bizarre conclusion. "I'll take you to Bury the Hatchet. It's an axe throwing place. It's actually kind of fun."

"Axe throwing. That sounds like a skill that could come in handy, especially with Roiter around!"

This was the first she'd mentioned her ex since calling him the night before. "He still bothering you?" Kenny asked, not wanting to sound like a protective boyfriend. Roiter was out of Kenny's league in the brawl department, and had proved that in their two-minute fight in high school.

"It's just this ridiculous lawsuit," she said, sullen. "Right before I left to come out here, we got a letter from his lawyer." Vickie was shaking her head, her eyes distant. Kenny didn't want to pursue it further, never enjoying Roiter as the centerpiece of his and Vickie's discussions. In her world, though, Roiter was a reality she couldn't just ignore, and Kenny wished he could do something to help her.

"I could hack into his email account… if he has one…!" Kenny tried for the joke, Vickie giving him a weak chuckle, her gaze traveling out toward the edge of the universe.

"You don't have to feel responsible for me," she said after a long silence. "I shouldn't have joked about Roiter and the axe throwing…"

"I don't feel responsible, but I wish there was something I could do to help, that's all. You'd feel the same if I was having some kind of problem…" Kenny wasn't sure that was true, and felt stupid saying it.

"That's not true… your problems are your problems, Muppet…" she said.

Muppet? She had never called him by that stupid nickname, and was trying to mount a response when she stretched across the seat and kissed him.

"I'm messing with you, Kenny. It's sweet you want to help, really it is, but I don't want you to make Roiter your problem, okay?" Then, a few moments later. "And you're right, if you had a *Roiter* in your life, I'd want to help you too."

They both laughed at how that sounded, having a *Roiter* in your life, as if it were a boil, or some other heinous growth.

"Yeah, now that I think of it," Kenny said. "We might actually see a *Roiter* at Insectropolis!"

"Where?" Vickie said laughing. "What?"

"The Bugseum of New Jersey. We have it all here in the Garden State!"

"Jeez, a museum of bugs!"

After Kenny found a parking spot, they strolled the boardwalk, Vickie taking Kenny's hand in hers. Sensing his reluctance to hold hands in public, she released it and smiled up at him. After lunch they walked the shops, Vickie finding a few trinkets, but most of the items were ocean related. They left the boardwalk and took their shoes off to walk the beach, carrying them in their hands, the ocean surging in and out, as if the world were breathing. Kenny hadn't planned on this day turning so romantic, but it was. Vickie's dress rustled in the breeze coming off the water, her hair flagging out behind her. Away from everyone else, finally alone, Vickie stopped and brought her eyes to Kenny's.

"I don't want this to ever end," she said, kissing him before he could respond to her comment, as if she didn't want to spoil the moment with the logistics and impossibilities of the real world. She pulled him against her, her tongue slipping inside his mouth, holding him gently around his neck. Kenny's head was spinning, images coming from the backroom of his mind, recalling watching her in the high school hallway, seeing her in the bleachers at football games, wanting her so bad it was like a virus, then Forest Park several years ago when they'd met for the first time since high school, how hostile she'd been at first, wanting to know why he'd contacted her after all those years. The reunion, wishing he had danced with her, then the front seat of his dad's Taurus, feeling her bare skin against his for the first time, and last night, holding each other in her hotel room bed, having breakfast this morning, driving to Toms River, now barefoot on the beach, gulls wheeling and crying out over the rushing breakers.

"Axe throwing and bugs sound fascinating," Vickie said, drawing away just enough to see his face. "But I want you. And if we don't head back to my hotel room right now, I may take you right here on this beach."

A couple approached, their Irish setter running up, hopping near Vickie, looking for attention. "Jenny!" the woman called to the dog.

Vickie reached out to pet the dog's head with both hands. "Oh, aren't you just so sweet!" Vickie said to the dog, then looked up at Kenny, and said, "Not a dog person?"

Kenny screwed up his lips. "Not really."

"Well, that's okay, isn't it, Jenny?" Vickie said to the dog's muzzle, the dog seemingly unsure if it was okay, prancing, her tongue hanging out, panting, looking up at Kenny with sheepish eyes.

When the woman called her dog again the animal kicked up a little sand with its hasty retreat.

"How old is she?" Vickie asked.

"Three," the woman said. "Still a big baby!"

"She's beautiful," Vickie said, then looked over at Kenny. "Hotel now, okay?"

Kenny nodded. They raced up to the boardwalk, Vickie winning the first leg of the impromptu competition, followed by putting on their shoes, Vickie fastening the straps on her wedge platform sandals, Kenny tying his sneakers, Vickie undoing one of Kenny's laces before dashing off toward the parking lot before he could retaliate. She was waiting for him at the car, or so she thought. He walked toward her, then veered off sharply, shouting that the one she was standing by wasn't his. "You rat," she said, laughing, hurtling toward him, wrapping him in her arms, kissing him. He unlocked the doors and they jumped in.

"One for the road?" she said, easing over the console toward him. "A little something to tide us over till we get back?"

A family walked through the parking lot, the kids shouting and running between the cars, bumping into Kenny's Mazda. Vickie burst out laughing, sliding back over to her seat. She reached into the bakery bag, coming out with the other caramel apple crumb bar.

"I'll make do with this," she said, taking a bite, then holding it out to Kenny. Kenny took a bite, then pulled out of the parking spot and pointed his car toward the exit. Vickie dug into the change console and brought out money for the toll station. "We're ready now," she said.

The afternoon had transformed into evening by the time they pulled into the hotel parking lot. They played in the elevator after the elderly couple got out on the second floor, Vickie pulling out Kenny's shirttail and running her hand up under it to his chest, Kenny finding her breast with his right hand. When the elevator doors opened, they rushed from the elevator, the momentum of their desire carrying them to the room, Vickie opening the door quickly, Kenny pushing it closed, undressing each other on the way to the bed.

After making love they drifted off in each other's arms, Vickie asleep with her back wedged against Kenny's chest. Kenny had dozed off, but woke after a short while, feeling an odd and pervasive contentment, like finding the serenity of balance between himself and the world. Making love with Vickie wasn't necessarily more profound than anything he'd ever experienced, but lying in bed, just holding her, was. Being with her in this way, after all the hormonal gymnastics and chemical collisions had faded to the background, when the urgency and rush of anticipation fell silent, a subtler, more powerful, enduring connection surfaced, a link to this woman that was so natural it was hard to believe he'd never felt anything like it before. Except when Michael was born. Loving Vickie felt as natural and immutable as loving his own son. He had no idea what he was supposed to do with those feelings.

"Hey, Moffett," Vickie whispered, nestling closer to him. "Are you awake?"

He kissed her ear, then her neck. "I'm gonna have to go soon," he said. She went limp in his arms, as if the life had drained out of her, but she said nothing, as still now as a corpse.

A new hush filled the hotel room, the quiet now so absolute that small street sounds floated like wraiths through the dark space, then someone talking in the next room, or maybe they were in the hallway. A door banged, then more voices, strangers outside their door, or next door, moving luggage in, perhaps, or out. On the street below, a car horn shrieked out an aggrieved, steady cry for justice. When the television came on in the room next to theirs, the sound burrowed through, muffled, distorted, like aliens trapped inside the walls. Vickie got up and went into the bathroom.

Kenny sighed, not wanting to leave, but knowing he had to. He sat up and dragged his legs off the edge of the bed, his bare feet resting on the soft carpet. Looking toward the bathroom, he wondered if she was going to take a shower, if she was upset, then figured she was. Pulling himself up, he went to the floor near the room entrance and started gathering up clothes, sorting them out as he went, hers on his right arm, his on his left. He set her clothes on one corner of the bed, his on the other, and started dressing.

"Hey, you're not going to have dinner before you go?" she said, coming out of the bathroom in her white hotel robe, and by her red eyes, it was obvious she'd been crying.

"It's almost eight o'clock, Vickie," he said, on the edge of tears himself. "I wish I could…" He fastened his belt, then sat on the edge of the bed to pull on his socks. Vickie came over and sat next to him, resting her head on his shoulder.

After a few moments, she said, "I'm leaving in the morning." Then, another pause, shorter this time: "I don't want to… I don't want to ever leave." Kenny turned and brought his eyes to hers which were welling again.

"I've never felt anything like this before," she said, wiping a tear from her eye. "And it's not about the sex, which is great, okay, but it's about how I feel afterwards, or when we're just hanging out together, like today at Toms River, or when we were holding each other before… I can't even explain it… it's like perfect, like symbiosis…" Then, frowning: "I'm not making sense, I know…"

"No, you are," Kenny said, and was about to tell her he felt the same, but couldn't. Somehow it didn't feel right, and at the same time, felt righter than anything ever had. He bent down to tie his laces. When he finished, he stood up and lifted his jacket off the floor, then wound himself methodically into the sleeves, trying to dress as slowly as possible, drawing out these last few minutes.

"I want to see you again," Vickie said, standing in front of him now, her fingers fiddling with his collar as if she were working on a floral arrangement. "Can we plan something?"

A sickly dread washed up inside him, like decaying remains on a Jersey shore. An uncomfortable current crackled in his chest. He needed time to think, and Elaine was giving him time, lots of time. That's when he realized that the note Elaine had left him about staying at JoAnn's had been from *five days ago*. Five days ago! How was that possible that he had blocked that out, had been expecting her to call him, had been confused why she wasn't picking up when he called, or returning his messages? From some furtive chamber of his mind, it was all moving toward him now, the fight they'd had after the long, painful silences, the congenial but bloodless conversations they'd been having until she finally said they needed space. Space! Not only did Kenny have time, but now he had *space*. Elaine leaving had not been part of some elaborate plot to throw Kenny and Vickie together, give him a chance to get over her. How could he, even for a second, have considered such a ridiculous possibility? It was insane. A low vibration started in his chest, nudging him off center, and he had to sit. He felt for the bed behind him, his fingers finding a wrinkle in the spread, then sat as his legs gave out.

"Kenny!" Vickie cried. "Are you all right?" She sat down beside him, feeling his head, then his neck. "You're white as a sheet!"

He wasn't all right, that much he knew; the cunning forgetfulness his mind had employed after his mother's death as a young boy had returned. How could he have blocked out Elaine leaving? Every night he came home from work and read her note as if for the first time, always surprised, but never overly worried or concerned. She just needed time, like him, to sort things out. Though now he realized he hadn't spoken to Elaine in almost a week. Or had it been longer than that? Just then, a memory, as if urgently needed in that moment, rose from the past, and he was eleven again, sitting at the kitchen table eating Cheerios with milk before school, his father making him hot cocoa, sipping coffee waiting for the milk to get hot, preparing a sandwich for Kenny's lunch. Gathering up the sandwich, a bag of potato chips and box of raisins, his father packed everything into Kenny's tin lunchbox, then shut the lid and placed it next to his books on the table. His father's movements were stiff, his eyes blank, his face gray as driftwood from lack of sleep. A moment later Kenny's father left the kitchen to finish getting ready for work in the bathroom and Kenny could hear him sobbing, brushing his teeth. The reality of Kenny's mother's death at the time seemed as mutable to this boy of eleven as the changing of a blue sky—at times stacked with enormous white clouds, at other times completely erased, as if they had never existed in the first place. The concept of her being gone was too abstract to process, so for Kenny, she wasn't gone, not in the way she was for his father, who grieved and wailed and dragged himself through each and every day with the torpor and malaise of a dying elephant.

"I have to go," Kenny said to Vickie, a juddery discomfort shifting through his cells. He felt nauseous, uncertain about his faculties, if they would become unreliable. Testing the resolve of his own machinery, he stood, a liquid sensation rising and falling inside him, as if he were made of oil. The feeling unhinged him, causing him to lurch, his head aching under the troublesome tide.

Vickie steadied him, gently easing him back to the bed until he was seated again, then laid him back, supporting him. When he was prone, his legs hanging over the edge, she rushed to the bathroom, coming back with a cold washcloth that she placed on his forehead. She undid his shoes and pulled them off, letting each one fall to the floor with a thud, then crawled up and sat next to him on the bed.

As Vickie massaged his shoulders, the room started to return, moving slowly back toward him, as if returning from a long distance, fitting itself around him, becoming more solid, the walls and ceiling aligning, subordinate once again to the unfailing principles of geometry. When his eyes came open, he saw Vickie's mouth pulled almost to a frown. Her eyes, though wet, seemed to smile down at him.

"Hey, you're back," she said, her lips bending to a smile. His body still swayed, like an aftershock, at least that's how it felt, his body becoming gelatin. Grasping the washcloth in his palm, he sat up and looked over at her.

"Do you mind if I spend the night?" he said, feeling like a visitor from another country, everything around him foreign, unmoored from anything remotely familiar.

Vickie smiled, then leaned over to kiss him. "Nothing would make me happier."

She suggested dinner, and asked if he wanted to look over the hotel kitchen menu. Whatever sounded good to her would work for him and he asked if they had any more robes like the one she was wearing. After ordering dinner, she called to the front desk and one of the staff brought one to the room. Kenny changed, then the two of them sat on the bed watching television, Kenny's mind on Elaine. After about ten minutes, Kenny finally said, "Elaine and I are separated."

"Separated!" Vickie was surprised, but seemingly not upset that Kenny had apparently lied. It was all coming back to him, gradually, tediously, with the pacing of a long novel, the details of the past two weeks revealing themselves with disarming clarity. The despair Kenny had hoped to avoid through his involuntary denial (involuntary in that he hadn't purposely tried to trick himself into believing everything was okay between them), was bearing down with the weight of a thousand disappointments, dragging him toward a sheer, dark cliff. His body shuddered under soundless weeping, and Vickie, without speaking or trying to console him, scooted closer, reaching over to rest her palm on his thigh.

After the food came, and they ate, they soaked in a hot bath together, scrubbing each other's backs, then went to bed. Vickie had told him she would try to postpone her flight and see if she could get a later departure time, or move her flight to the following day. Kenny had told her to leave it as it was, that he would need to get back to work in the morning anyway, that he was glad to have this one extra night in her arms.

With Vickie asleep, wrapped in his embrace, the hotel room dark as a moonless night, Kenny remembered that he was supposed to be looking for a place to live for a while, an apartment or one-room flat, so Elaine and Michael could return to the house, and some semblance of normalcy, Michael, at least, back in his own room. The realization struck him like a sharp stick in the heart, that he and Elaine were indeed, separated, and for several seconds he couldn't breathe. The guilt kicked in moments later; how could he be so callous, totally forgetting to look for a place to live so Elaine and Michael could go back home? There was much to do in the morning. After taking Vickie to the airport, he would need to find an apartment, try to contact Elaine to apologize for procrastinating on his new living quarters, maybe see if they could meet for lunch and talk, then call his therapist, make an appointment to explain that he was zoning out again, retreating back into the vague yet comfortable world of denial.

Chapter Forty

Martin had been back at Janelle's home for a couple of weeks, planning his trip to Noreen's world, preparing himself to live there on a regular basis. It was terrible timing, with the trial starting in a couple of weeks, and Beth—even against Janelle's best efforts—unable to avoid testifying against her own father. It just so happened—according to some research Janelle's lawyer had conducted on the judge in Carl's case—that this particular judge was not happy with the lax attitude toward Missouri's conceal and carry laws, which were hardly laws at all, and was determined to make an example of Carl by compelling Beth to testify. It wasn't that he wanted to punish her. Regardless, that would be the effect of his actions. He wanted to make it clear to those who wished to take the law into their own hands just how adversely it affected the lives of their loved ones. Janelle could only think about Beth, the horrible impact Carl's actions had already leveled on her daughter's life. Even in the face of persistent setbacks, and a judge fixed on using Beth to bring about a harsher justice, Janelle was unwilling to give up on convincing him of the long-term and deleterious effects it would have on her daughter. Janelle didn't know that as fact, but Beth's therapist felt it could be damaging, yet tried to assure Janelle that Beth was resilient, plenty strong enough to weather such an ordeal. *So what!* Janelle felt ardently that Beth shouldn't have to *weather* any of this, making it very clear she thought it was unconscionable to make a seventeen-year-old stand up against her father, possibly have a hand in sending him to prison. Nevertheless, even with Janelle and Beth's worlds in turmoil, Martin figured there was no time that would be better than any other. This would be difficult no matter what.

However, there was the problem of Kenny. Martin wasn't willing to turn his back on his son, no matter what. He figured he could meet with Kenny from time to time, take a respite from Noreen's world, fly out to New Jersey for a couple of days to catch up with him, get in a visit with his grandson, Michael. The thought boosted his resolve, that he wasn't giving up everything to live in Noreen's world, whatever her world was. Falco's words still bothered him, though, reverberating from some little speaker in the back of his mind, that Noreen's world *was not to be trusted*. Falco had become so disillusioned with Mitzi's world, he was leaving it, and her, behind. Forever. Just the thought of leaving Noreen, now that he had her back, left a gaping, sucking hole at the center of his chest.

He had not told Janelle about losing his job at Petro Agency. What would be the point? Every morning he left for work, as he'd always done, then spent the day planning things, or dropping in on Noreen, telling her about his plans of being with her full time. He'd return home in the evening to have dinner with Janelle and hear about how the pre-trial drama was going. Most nights Beth joined them, then spent the remainder of the evening alone in her room. Occasionally, if she liked the movie they were watching, she'd curl up on the couch in a thick blanket and watch without comment, quiet as a sculpture. There was no doubt, Martin was going to miss them both, and hoped the trial wouldn't be too rough on Beth, or her mother. The idea of not being there for their ordeal, especially for Beth, made him feel criminal, a pathetic, soulless fiend.

Sitting outside Starbucks, sipping his latte, Martin pulled out his phone to call Kenny. They hadn't talked in weeks, maybe a month or more, Martin trying to recall when he and Elaine had visited with Michael for the reunion. Kenny picked up on the fourth ring and gave Martin a flat, standard greeting.

"Kenny! It's Dad!"

"Hey, Dad, how are you?"

"Good! How are you? Is this a bad time?"

"No... I can talk. You in Chicago?"

The question was like a knife to the heart; a painful reminder he had lied to his son, along with everyone else. And now, unless he ignored telling Kenny anything at all, he would have to lie to his son again about what he was preparing to do.

"No, I'm in St. Louis. How's Michael? And Elaine?" Martin veered the conversation away from work, waiting for Kenny to respond, thinking maybe he'd heard Kenny sigh when he asked about his family. Then, after a long pause, Martin thought he heard Kenny sobbing. "Kenny?"

Kenny sniffled, and cleared his throat. "Yeah, Dad, I'm here." He sniffed again, then another long pause.

"Hey, what's going on, Son?" Martin said, urgency focusing his attention now, his concentration tunneling away from his own spectacle.

"We're separated," Kenny finally said after a few moments.

"Separated! You and Elaine!" Martin blurted out, wishing he could call the words back, or at least the force with which he'd spoken them. "What happened?" he then asked, calmer, dialing back the shock a few decibels.

Kenny paused to gather himself, then started explaining about the reunion, and Vickie, asking Martin if he remembered Kenny talking about her in high school, about how he and Vickie had met a couple of years ago, before the reunion, at a coffee shop in the Central West End, and spent a few hours together. "There was no sex or anything like that," Kenny was quick to add, then, "We just talked," pausing a moment before continuing on with his story, Martin listening, his heart slowly sinking into his stomach; he wanted nothing but good things for Kenny, as any father would want for his son, or at any rate, imagined any father would want, becoming distracted, projecting out Kenny's future into the next few months, years, wondering if he and Elaine would be able to work through their difficulties, and Michael, and the new baby!

"We spent the last two days together, Vickie and me," Kenny said, sobbing again, telling his dad to wait a second while he got up to close his office door.

Martin waited, his thoughts spinning like a frenzied flock of seagulls, screeching out an ungodly racket inside his skull. Was Kenny in St. Louis? How could he spend two days with Vickie? Was she the young woman who owned the flower shop? High school was over years ago, how could they still be connected after all this time?

"I don't understand," Martin said when Kenny came back on the phone, trying not to sound judgmental, but there was no mistaking the edge in his voice. When only silence returned, Martin felt horrible that Kenny had apparently picked up on his critical tone. He hadn't meant it to be; after all, who was he to condemn anyone for infidelity. Martin had managed to convince himself that since Noreen was for all practical purposes, *dead,* or at least, not of *this* world any longer, that seeing her in Falco's peculiar paradigm didn't really constitute adultery, at least in the conventional sense. It was a fiction Martin could live with, one that allowed him to sleep at night, and make love to Janelle without the burden of remorse, almost as if being with Noreen now was like watching himself in a foreign film.

"She was here," Kenny said, responding to Martin's confusion over how they, Kenny and Vickie, could possibly have gotten together. "Vickie flew up to New Jersey…"

"Did you ask her to?" Martin said, hearing his own question too late to realize how cruel and meaningless it was, yet, Martin couldn't deny that he felt Kenny was screwing up his life. When Kenny stammered a bit trying to answer, Martin quickly added an apology, saying, "I'm sorry, Kenny. That was stupid…" Then, after a moment: "Are you in love with her?"

Martin waited through the long silence, hoping the answer was no.

"Yes," Kenny said. "I've never *not* been in love with her. Since high school…"

Something collapsed in Martin, rebuttals stampeding through his brain. That's crazy! He wanted to tell his son. You must be mistaken; nobody could carry a torch for someone that long, for someone he barely knew in high school! Martin wanted to further make clear that Kenny and Vickie had been kids back then, and could not possibly have forged the kind of enduring love Martin held for Noreen! It wasn't possible! *And you're willing to throw away everything for a woman you barely know?* Martin wanted to scream sense into his son, wanted to

262

jerk him back from the edge of this very precarious ledge, away from a mistake so irreparable and devastating that it could destroy his life, and adversely affect Michael's as well! The imagined consequences were unbearable to Martin, rendering him speechless.

"Dad?" Kenny said after a long quiet spell. "Are you there?"

Martin cleared his throat, his words a tangle of barbed wire in his mouth. "Does Elaine know you're in love with this woman?"

"It's Vickie, Dad. Her name is Vickie. And no, I never told Elaine I was in love with her. I never told her much at all, but Elaine took my silence as guilt, and she was right to do that..."

"Where is she now?"

"Elaine? Back in the house with Michael. I moved to a small apartment about ten minutes from them."

Martin couldn't stop shaking his head, watching the traffic speed by, listening to the drone of tires on pavement, the rumble of exhaust, the occasional siren or car horn. What a mess, Martin thought, blaming himself for his son's predicament. Martin couldn't stop picturing Elaine, how lovely and congenial she was, and Michael, his innocent, chubby little face, his comically impish smile. Why did Kenny allow this into his life? Just then, every question, every condemnation Martin had leveled against his son, came crashing down, like a ten-story building, onto Martin! He was guilty of everything he was accusing Kenny of; Martin himself, he realized, was gambling with his own good fortune, wagering Janelle and Beth against a future that, even on the best of days, was risky, maybe hazardous, unable to pull himself back from a decision with potentially ruinous results! Even Falco warned him about Noreen's world, that it was not to be trusted, yet Martin was prepared to ignore the portentous advice.

"What are you gonna do, Kenny?" Martin asked, calmer now, unavoidable thoughts still colliding near the back of his mind, harmless, soundless thoughts, orphaned from Martin's immediate attention.

"I'm seeing a therapist again," Kenny said, then added nothing more, as if Martin should know what he was talking about.

"You're blocking things out?" Martin said, wishing he could be face to face with his son.

"Yeah. Like for days. I don't know how many. I'd get home from work and find the note Elaine left me over a week ago, and think she'd written it that day! Then I tried to call her to find out what was wrong. Luckily she didn't answer or she'd really think I'd lost my mind..." Kenny sniffed a few times, trying to compose himself. "I'm scared, Dad...."

"You want me to fly out?" Martin said, feeling stupid he asked. Why make Kenny decide?

"Thanks. I appreciate that. Really. But it's probably best you don't. I'm seeing this therapist, a really nice woman, three times a week. And I'm hoping to open a dialogue with Elaine soon, and... man, what a mess..."

The hesitancy in Kenny's voice made it sound as if he had more to say. Martin waited for his son to empty his thoughts.

"But I don't know what I'm going to do," Kenny said. "Vickie feels the same as I do, and... I care about Elaine, and... the new baby, and Michael... God, I miss him so much... but I don't know how I can just turn my back on Vickie... not again, not like I did in high school..."

Martin paused, about to interject, but knew he had nothing constructive to add; to Martin's mind it wasn't really a decision—go home to your beautiful wife and amazing son, and prepare a loving place for your new daughter on the way.

"...I know this must sound crazy to you, me with this wonderful family and still having these kinds of feelings for a girl I knew from high school... and Tess, she's wonderful—"

"Tess?" Martin said, not recognizing that name.

"My therapist. She just listens, Dad, never judging me. Like... she advocates for *me*, but not against Elaine, or Vickie, that's the great part. I know I haven't figured anything out yet... but I feel like I can, eventually, at least Tess believes I will... I'm sorry to lay all this on you."

"Don't apologize, Kenny. I'm just glad you found someone you trust—"

"Hold on..." Kenny said, with a bit of urgency.

Martin waited, listening to muffled discussion, as if Kenny were speaking to someone with his hand over the phone. After a few moments, Kenny came back on, "Dad, I have to go into a meeting. Can I call you back tonight?"

"Sure. I love you, Son."

"Love you, Dad. Talk later."

Martin placed his phone on the table and glanced up, beyond the buildings, the blue sky streaked with wisps of clouds, which he often found reassuring, but now, with a strange buzzing in his veins, it was as if the entire world were made of static, connections sparking, shorting out, surging haphazardly, dangerously, tremendous voltage arcing across lives, across continents, threatening to cleave apart the very atmosphere, shock the planet off its axis and send it hurtling off into absolute darkness.

Martin's breath caught.

He took in air slowly, deliberately, then, after picking up his phone, walked toward his Taurus, sorting out his plans, leafing through a photo album behind his eyes of everyone that mattered in his life, picturing Kenny, then Elaine and Michael, Janelle and Beth, then finally, Noreen. Why was everything so much simpler in Noreen's reality? Martin tried to reason with himself that he wouldn't be leaving Kenny behind; he would see his son from time to time, coming back to this existence, flying out to New Jersey even. Or he'd call Kenny, talk on the phone, make sure his son was bearing up okay with the difficulties in his marriage. Martin could do that quite often without upsetting the balance of things in Noreen's paradigm, or recommitting himself to Kenny's. But Janelle and Beth; he couldn't fool himself on that count; his leaving would mark the end of his life with them. And he couldn't explain to her where he was going. To Janelle, he would just be gone, vanished, like so many missing persons in the world. How hard would that be on her, especially given the turmoil her daughter was about to endure?

Misery gripped him, not like pain from a moldering disease, but an abrasive discomfort in his heart, grinding away at his resolve, inescapable and unrelenting. And mental torture as well, doubt battling reason; he knew Noreen's reality was an illusion, a perfectly complete world much like a dreamscape, though one he knew wasn't real. Yet, through some magic of his own, Martin had managed to stop believing what he knew to be real. He would go there and live, and maybe in time, would even tell Kenny, and somehow, if it were possible, take him along, so Kenny could see his mother once again, and Noreen see her son a grown man.

Chapter Forty-One

Nothing had prepared Kenny for the news he just received. He sat in his office, his door locked, and cried into his palms, his body quaking. Amy had broken into tears several times while speaking with Kenny on the phone, until finally, so upset, and needing to end the call, had said, "I'm sorry, Kenny... I have to go," sobbing, and then added, "Vickie's funeral's in three days... if you can make it..."

The call ended. No click, only empty space filling Kenny's head. His hand shook as he placed the receiver into the cradle. Another line had lit up while he'd been talking with Amy, and was still blinking, but Kenny couldn't answer it, unable to convince his mind that Roiter beat Vickie to death one night as she was coming out of the floral shop. It had been after hours, Vickie trying to update some new items on the website, and had spoken with Roiter on the phone. Roiter just wanted to talk with her, see if they could settle his share of their floral business without going to court. Vickie had been uncomfortable with the idea of meeting him, and had called Amy. Amy told her under no circumstances should she agree to meeting Roiter at the florist shop or anywhere else. "That's why we have a lawyer," Amy had told her. "Yeah, I felt the same way," Vickie had said. "I told him no. I just wanted to make sure it was okay with you that I said no." Amy asked if she was still at the shop, and Vickie said she was just finishing up with the website. Amy then said, "I'm going to drive over. Keep the doors locked until I get there." Vickie said, "That's not necessary, really, Amy. I'll call you as soon as I get home, okay? I don't want you to worry." Amy regretted that she had agreed, and that was the last time she'd spoken to Vickie. Evidently Roiter waited behind the shop for Vickie to come out to her car. According to a few neighbors in apartments above the storefronts, the meeting between the two escalated quickly into a shouting match, when the man exploded into a rage, slamming the young woman with his fists. Vickie tried to escape into her car, the man pulling her back, throwing her to the pavement and kicking her to death. The man, according to eyewitnesses, then squatted next to the woman's lifeless body, slowly sinking to his knees, hugging himself, rocking back and forth, weeping, until the police arrived.

Someone knocked on Kenny's office door. He wiped his eyes. "Yes?" he called toward the visitor, not wanting them to see his red swollen face.

"A meeting in about ten minutes in the conference room, Mr. Moffett," the woman said through the door. "Mr. Cooper wanted to make sure you knew."

"I'll be there, Sharon," Kenny said, finally recognizing her voice. "Thank you…" What he really wanted to do was call his dad. They hadn't spoken in weeks, maybe two or three, maybe more, he wasn't sure. Kenny called the number but it went to voicemail. He called Tess, his therapist, hoping to schedule an appointment that afternoon, as soon as the meeting ended. He needed to talk to someone. The call to Tess also went to voicemail. Something that was already frayed inside him, was now unraveling, leaving him shredded, coming undone. Vickie was in every thought, every cell of his body, a holographic reckoning of sorts, each fragmented part of him reflecting Vickie whole, alive, her smile, her touch, her smell. It wasn't possible that she was gone. He found himself pleading to a deaf and unrecognizable god, one reserved for agnostics in their time of grief, a lesser god that didn't require faith, or promise results, and seemed to be somewhere in the ether tallying the hardships of poor, suffering souls. It wasn't that Kenny didn't believe in God, it was just that he never gave the matter much thought. Now, however, Kenny's beseeching did nothing to lessen his anguish. He went through periods of terror, then a pain so deep he wanted to howl and scream, pound the desk, kick the walls, but instead, succumbed to the groundless tremor in his chest, the intolerable self-pity threatening to consume him, body and soul.

The meeting with his boss and other members of the marketing team might as well have been underwater for all the trouble Kenny had breathing in the claustrophobic room, the voices muted and unintelligible to his ears. Thankfully no one called upon him to answer questions, and he managed, sitting like a zombie, to bluff his way through with a phony half-smile. When it ended, he rushed to the parking lot, calling his secretary from his car, telling her he'd be out the rest of the afternoon. Before driving away, he tried his dad again. No answer. Then Tess, and got her voicemail again.

Using a few of his vacation days, Kenny split his time between Tess and trying to contact his father, and reaching out to Elaine, though he had no idea what he'd say to her. But he wanted to see Michael.

One evening, Elaine invited him over to the house for dinner. It was cordial, in a formal way, and Michael and he played in the living room. Elaine busied herself with phone calls to clients she had listings with. Later, she and Kenny put Michael to bed, and asked if Kenny could stay while she showed a house.

"It won't take long," Elaine said. "I should be back by nine at the latest."

"Take whatever time you need," Kenny said, genuinely at peace to have some semblance of normalcy, even with the strained undercurrent of animosity he felt coming from Elaine.

She gathered up her purse and a leather satchel, her keys jangling in her palm. At the front door, pulling it open, she looked back at him and said, "Michael had fun tonight. He asks about you all the time…" Then, with a sad smile: "He really misses you, Kenny."

"I really miss both of you," Kenny said, wishing he hadn't said it like that, as if he hadn't been the one who'd created this untenable situation in the first place. "I really am sorry, Elaine."

Elaine's face drew tighter. The same expression she wore all through dinner, one of guarded optimism, or maybe affable pessimism. Her discomfort was obvious, regardless of how much she tried to hide it.

"Can we talk when I get back?" she said. "Or do you need to get home?"

"No, I'm free," he said. "I took a few days off..."

Her look turned to one of confusion. "Why?" she said, then glanced at her watch. "Never mind, I have to go. I won't be long."

He busied himself in the kitchen, cleaning up the few pots and pans, ones he knew Elaine didn't like to put in the dishwasher, then turned on the television and stretched out on the couch. Minutes later, tears rolled down his cheeks when he thought about Vickie's funeral. He'd found no reason to go back to Missouri, though he'd given it much thought, had discussed it with Tess, but the only person in St. Louis he really wanted to see would be lying in the casket. Maybe that would have been best, make it real and concrete, but he didn't want to remember her that way. Instead, he opted to replay the tapes in his head from their trip to Toms River, the time they spent together at the Charter House; those few days would have to last a lifetime.

He wiped his eyes and started flipping through the channels, wondering why he couldn't get a hold of his dad. He pulled out his phone and tried again, the call going to voicemail. Odd, after all the failed attempts, that his dad hadn't at least tried to call him back. Setting the phone on the coffee table, he stretched out and started watching Law & Order.

The vibrating ringer woke him. He bolted upright, still partially snagged in a dream, finally answering the call. "Hello?"

At first, he only heard sobbing on the line, then finally, "Kenny? Is that you?"

"Yes. Who is this?"

More sobbing, sniffling, then the woman's voice came again. "It's Janelle, Kenny..." She stopped speaking, as if trying to gather herself.

"What's wrong?" Kenny said, concerned, rubbing his eyes, trying to chase the last bit of sleep from them. "Is everything okay?"

"Have you heard from your father?" she managed to say after a few seconds, as if the words had been hard to dislodge.

"No, I've been trying him and—"

"He's gone, Kenny. I've contacted the police. I've called his work... It's a mess, Kenny... I just... I don't know—" Janelle began wailing over the phone, distraught, unable to continue. Kenny waited, then called her name softly into the phone. A moment later another voice came on. "Kenny. It's Beth."

Kenny could still hear Janelle in the background, moaning in pain, whimpering.

"You haven't heard from Martin in the past couple of weeks?" Beth asked.

"No. I've called him several times but—"

"He's missing. The police haven't been able to find anything yet," she said. "Did you know he got fired?"

"Fired?"

"Several weeks ago. It seems he was missing so much work they had to let him go."

"That doesn't sound like him," Kenny said, hearing the front door open and close. Elaine came in quietly, and for a split second, though Kenny may have imagined it, she seemed happy he was there. He smiled back and she went to the kitchen and set her things on the island, then stared in at him before grabbing a Coke from the fridge. She held it up, as if to ask if he wanted one. He shook his head, then motioned with his hand for her to come over. She sat opposite him in one of the cushy chairs as he mouthed the word, *Janelle*. Then *Beth*, indicating that's who he was talking with.

"I don't understand," Kenny said, setting down his phone and putting it on speaker so Elaine could hear.

"Well, it was kind of weird," Beth said. "He always drove to Chicago to help get the new offices open, or so he said. Of course, that was a lie too!" The last part Beth had stated with a bit of heat, as if perturbed by some apparent deception. "There is no office in Chicago!"

"What!" Kenny said, incredulous, glancing over at Elaine who was puzzled as well. "What do you mean there's no Chicago office?"

"Mr. Petro told my mom they had no branch office in Chicago, so no one is quite sure where Martin has been going all this time... Anyway, the last time he left for Chicago, he asked my mom to drive him to the airport, which was kind of weird. He said he was leaving the car for me so I'd have something to drive while he was gone because he was going to be staying for a few weeks. He's been giving me driving lessons since I got my permit. Anyway, that's the last we've heard from him… My mom's been calling, but the messages just go to voicemail."

Elaine came over to sit next to Kenny on the couch, placing her hand on his arm. Kenny was filled with a kind of empty, floating sensation, no longer anchored by gravity, his mind untethered.

"I'm sorry you had to find out like this," Beth said. "We're worried about him, but it is strange…" Beth paused, and it sounded as though she'd placed her hand over the mouth piece to muffle the conversation she was having with her mother, who seemed to have composed herself somewhat. For several seconds the silence stretched out until the smothered talking stopped, and Beth came back on the line. "Kenny, my mom's in the bathroom, so we have to talk fast because I don't want her to hear this. Have you ever been to your dad's bungalow in the city?"

It took a moment for Kenny to register what Beth was asking. He looked over at Elaine who stared at him with a look of curiosity mingled with anger. "Yeah, a long time ago…"

"He could be there," Beth said. "I can't drive down to his house by myself because I'm on permit, but if you came to St. Louis, we could go down—"

"But he sold that place a long time ago, Beth," Kenny said.

"I don't think so, Kenny," she said with such confidence Kenny wasn't even sure he knew his dad anymore, like they were discussing a stranger who Beth somehow knew better than he did. "I could drive down with my mom, but she's already so freaked out by Martin's lies, this last one could put her over the edge." A pause followed, then: "I didn't tell the police about the bungalow, so they would have no way of—"

Kenny heard Janelle come back into the room and ask Beth something.

"No, mom… Kenny doesn't know anything. He's as surprised as us," Beth said without covering the phone, then said, "Kenny, my mom wants to speak to you again. Give some thought to what I told you, okay."

"Kenny?" Janelle said, sniffing, coughing a few times. "I'm sorry to tell you all this, but I had to know if you'd heard from him… and… I don't know what… oh, Kenn… Kenn…" The crying started again, slowly at first, gaining force, eventually sluicing the meaning from Janelle's tortured words until she became unintelligible.

Beth came back on the line. "Let me know if you plan to come out, okay, I mean, if you can manage it," Beth said, sounding very adult and sober.

"What about the trial? How's that going? Has it started or what?" Kenny said, numb, trying to catch the tag end of some vagrant thoughts passing through the tangle inside his head.

"Yeah, it's a shit-show," Beth said, then away from the phone, saying to her mom that she'd wake her in an hour. "I have an appointment with my therapist tonight. Man is he earning his money now!"

"Are you okay?" Kenny said.

"Yeah, I guess, missing lots of school. So far they haven't called me as a witness, so mostly, just listening to testimony and watching CCTV footage of the..." Beth sniffled, then cleared her throat. "I'm okay, but I have to go. Sorry about your dad, Kenny. We're really pissed off at him... but we both love him. I actually miss him... I hope he's okay. Call me if you plan to come out..." Then, after a few seconds of sniffling: "I miss you too, Big Brother."

When she disconnected the call, Kenny could only glower at the phone on the coffee table as though it were a dead hamster. After a time, he looked over at Elaine. Her expression was a peculiar amalgamation of sadness underpinned with pity and alarm. The processors in Kenny's brain were chewing through the latest developments, trying to arrange the data into manageable, binary units, attempting to transform abstract concepts into acceptable bytes of conclusive information, everything hobbled and malformed, out of place.

"You okay?" Elaine said, affectionately touching his shoulder.

He looked over at her with surprise and guilt, having done nothing to earn even this minimal tenderness. He felt grotesque, displaced and frightened, a man who hasn't yet figured out he's floating in outer space with no way back to the real world.

"Let me get you some water," she said, getting up and hurrying to the kitchen sink, filling a glass. "Here, drink this," she said. Like a robot he obeyed, upending the glass hydraulically until the water was gone. "Do you want something to eat?" she asked. "I have some leftover pizza."

He shook his head. "How could he lie to me about everything?" Kenny said, after long deliberation.

Elaine bit her lips together, rubbing his shoulder, trying to console him, but the kindness of her touch was like a welding torch on his skin; he didn't deserve it. He hadn't meant to pull away, though he did, an involuntary reaction to pain, and grimaced at his wife. "I love you, Elaine. And I'm so sorry. I have to go." He stood like a man who had to be somewhere, but just then, his legs were stone pillars, he couldn't move, had no idea where he was supposed to be. Elaine stood up, taking his hand.

"Maybe you should wait a bit," she said. "We were going to talk, remember?"

He regarded her with curiosity, as if he'd forgotten where he was. "No, I think it's best I go…" He held her hand a few seconds, staring down at their fingers intertwined, as if the hand at the end of his arm belonged to someone else, then released hers and started for the front door.

"Are you going?" Elaine said. "To St. Louis?"

He stopped and twisted toward her, as if the question hadn't fully bled into his brain. A few seconds later, he said flatly, "I guess I should, right?"

She cleared her throat, obviously struggling with her next question. "Will you see her when you're out there?" Elaine said. "Will you see Vickie?"

The corners of Kenny's mouth pulled down, seemingly by some force outside himself, his chin quivering with the disturbing severity of an earthquake. His eyes were instantly brimming with tears, and he looked at Elaine, a swift erosion shifting though him. "She's dead," he stated without emotion. "Vickie's dead."

Chapter Forty-Two

During the drive from the airport, Janelle, sitting across from Beth who was driving, seemed antsy and troubled, but not by Beth's driving; Beth was very good behind the wheel, confident yet careful. No, it was something else bothering Janelle, but no one to that point had steered the discussion toward Kenny's father, Martin. Kenny, seated in the back of Janelle's BMW, was just about to ask about the trial when Janelle spun toward him, her fingers clutching the top of the front seat, her eyes like hot pokers coming at him.

"Does Martin have a second family?" she blurted out, followed by a gusher of tears, her mouth twitching as if unable to brace herself against the answer. Then, quickly added: "Is he one of those men!" She threw her hand over her mouth in horror, as if Kenny had satisfied her worst fears, though he hadn't spoken a word. He had no idea if his dad had a second family, though was fairly certain he didn't; his dad wasn't that way, or least he didn't think so.

"Mom! We talked about that…" Beth said, shooting quick, disapproving glances toward her mother.

"I don't care!" Janelle said, shaking, squeezing her mouth with her closed hand, her eyes red and soggy. "I need to know!" She jerked her head toward Kenny, her eyes firing arrows, then just as quickly, she pulled them back and swerved her attention toward the windshield.

"I don't think he does, Janelle," Kenny said in a rather sheepish tone, not wanting to come off sounding antagonistic. When Janelle didn't respond, Kenny looked at the rearview mirror and caught Beth looking back at him, smiling sadly, trying to ease the tension with her eyes.

The next morning, when Janelle had gone for her walk, Beth told Kenny they should drive down to his dad's bungalow.

"You really think he still owns that place?" Kenny said, finishing his coffee.

"I do," Beth said, scooping up a spoonful of Cheerios. "And something weird is going on at that place. I'll tell you that. Let's go tonight. After supper. Mom has some book club crap. We'll just tell her we're going to a movie or something." Beth looked up at him furtively, as if they needed to be in agreement on the secrecy of the plan. Kenny nodded.

After supper, Janelle left for her gathering. Beth and Kenny headed for the driveway to use Martin's Taurus. "You okay with me driving?" Beth said.

"I don't think you're supposed to drive at night with a permit..." Kenny said. Then, feeling ridiculous as the voice of reason and regulations: "Sure, no problem."

"I don't know how to find it," she said, slipping in behind the steering wheel. "I was only at his place the one time, and—"

"I remember," Kenny said, buckling his seatbelt.

They talked about Martin for a while, until Beth asked about Elaine, and more pointedly, about Vickie. Kenny looked over at her and didn't know what to say.

"I'm sorry," Beth said. "None of my business..."

"It's not that, Beth... Vickie's dead. Her ex-husband killed her."

Beth kept stealing glances over at him, trying to gauge his seriousness, apparently satisfied he was telling the truth when she let the subject drop. Kenny was curious she had not said anything else, but then, what could she say? It was abstract, Vickie's death, and how she'd died, even to Kenny's ears; he was yet unable to parse the event adequately enough to make it real to his own senses. It floated out beyond his comprehension like a mere concept, foreign to him as alien beings from another planet, or God.

"Did you ever meet Falco?" Beth said, slicing through the gloomy silence inside the car.

Kenny felt disoriented, as if plucked from a strange dream, one that made sense while caught up in it, but was ungraspable upon waking.

"Falco?" Kenny said into the darkness, his own voice sounding hollow and distant. "Is that a first name or last?"

"I think it's his last name, but he actually goes by, *Falco the Fantabulist*," Beth said, with a bit of sarcasm. "He's a magician." Then, she added, smirking: "Supposedly."

Kenny didn't know what to say, only that he had never met the guy. A *Fantabulist* he would have remembered for sure, whatever the hell that was. Kenny told her to take a left at the next street. She switched on the turn signal, even though there was not another car in sight, then slowed and made the turn. The bright glow of fire at the end of the street reached high into the night sky. Beth followed the road to the end and pulled into the bungalow driveway.

"Wow, that's quite a shindig they have going on," Kenny said, his attention fixed on the horde of bikers in black leather shuffling into, and out from, the field, the bulk of the gang sitting around the bonfire staring into it like a portal to hell, motorcycles parked everywhere, including on Martin's meager front lawn. The carnival atmosphere poured into the street in front of Martin's house, and all the way back to the railroad tracks.

"The *Renagades*," Beth said, getting out of Martin's Taurus. "Spelled with an 'a'."

Kenny followed her up onto the concrete porch. Beth tried the door knob first, it was locked. She knocked several times with no answer. Beth looked over at the bikers, then knocked on the door one last time. "Okay, come on," she said, obviously headed into the fray.

"Hey, just a second," Kenny said, snagging her arm. "You think that's a good idea?"

"Desperate cases and lost causes," Beth said. "Just like us." Then added, "We'll be fine."

Beth started snaking through the mob, eyes straight ahead, fixed on the fire, Kenny following, not certain that crashing this curious event was a good idea. Beth seemed to be putting them both in an dangerous position, one that could end badly.

It appeared they had arrived just in time for the fashion show, or strip tease, Kenny couldn't be sure. Five women in various degrees of undress danced in a wash of motorcycle headlights, one woman down to a leather thong and vest with nothing under it, it would appear. Men hooted and cheered, shaking their bottles of beer up and down, a thumb over the top, to create obscene, explosive frothing eruptions. Beth appeared undeterred by the spectacle, and the feral bikers, marching forward through them like Joan of Arc, prompting a few whistles and catcalls of her own. Approaching the fire, she started searching the faces, and found one she seemed to recognize. Kenny cautiously idled up next to her, his heart in his throat, his fight or flight response locked into flight position.

"Tarantula?" Beth said, bending at the waist to catch the scraggly-haired man's attention.

He stood up slowly, as if awakening from a trance. "Hey, doll, where do I know you from?" he said, grinning like a circus clown, as if unable to grasp his good fortune.

"Beth," she said, cocking a thumb over her shoulder toward the bungalow. "Martin's step-daughter. Remember, you were hitting on me out by the railroad tracks, trying to convince me to hop a train with you."

"Sure, sure, I remember," he said, his eyes glinting like an alligator, obviously clueless to what she was talking about.

"Is Geronimo here?" she said.

"Well, sure, but... what do we need him for?"

"Information. Is he here?"

Tarantula, a bit dejected, stared at her a moment, then clamped his lips together and sucked air up his nose. He looked around, his narrow reptile eyes scanning the group. "Hey, Ger-on-ee-mo!" he said, stretching out the name comically. "A young lady here to see you." At that, Tarantula turned to Beth and bowed from the waist. "As you wished, Milady! Always at your service!"

Geronimo came over and they introduced themselves, Geronimo guiding Beth away from the shouting and mayhem so he could hear her better. Kenny followed, watching his step, careful not to stumble over anyone and inadvertently spark a melee.

"Does my step-dad, Martin, still own the bungalow?" she said.

"Yeah, but I ain't seen him in quite a while," he said, stopping, as if he wanted to say more but thought better of it.

"Do you have a key?"

"To his place?" Geronimo shook his head sadly, toeing the dirt. "Well, uh, who is this feller here with you?" Geronimo's eyes came at Kenny like shiny brass bullets.

"This is Kenny Moffett, Martin's son," she said, growing a bit impatient.

Geronimo let his head bob up and down a few times, eyes squinting at Kenny, still sizing him up. "What do you want in his place for?" Geronimo said, looking back to Beth.

"Trying to find him… or Falco—"

"Falco! Well hell, I see him all the time," Geronimo said. "Only late at night though. Never during the day. He's an odd one, that feller. Like a damn vampire or something…"

Beth looked over at Kenny and he just shrugged; so far out of his element he felt like a different species.

"Well, do you have the key then?" Beth asked abruptly, shifting back toward Geronimo. Geronimo squeezed his lips together, then scrunched his nose like he was wearing glasses, though he wasn't. When his face snapped back to normal, he said, "You kids wait here and I'll be right back," then shuffled off across the field.

When he was out of earshot, Kenny said, "How did he get that big ass scar on top of his head."

"Tomahawk," she said, rolling her eyes at Kenny.

"Aw, funny. Okay," he said, guessing she didn't know either. They waited on Martin's porch for Geronimo to return, watching the festivities from what felt like a safe distance, but the fashion show was over and a train was approaching, stirring up the bikers like a nest of hornets. Kenny couldn't understand why his dad had told him he sold this place, but more than that, why he was hanging onto it, lying to Janelle, Beth, him.

"So why did you think this Geronimo guy would have a key?" Kenny asked, wondering if he was his dad's friend or something.

"He trusts Geronimo," Beth said. "I think he went with your dad to pick up his motorcycle and they bonded over his Harley or something." Kenny was about to say something when Beth shushed him.

"Check this out. Your dad told me about this," Beth said, wearing a creepy smile. "You'll love this little ritual."

Kenny watched as the bikers got up and hustled closer to the tracks, the beam of the train starting to wash across their faces and jeans. As the train passed, the bikers hurled beer bottles at the passing coal cars, as if through sheer will and collective force, they could derail the train, the whooping and hollering like a rodeo.

"What's that about?" Kenny asked.

"Desperate cases and lost causes," Beth said, shaking her head, leering.

Just then Geronimo came back with the key and handed it to Beth.

"Thanks, I'll get this back to you," she said.

Geronimo lingered a few moments, then nodded and walked away toward the bonfire, his head still working on something, maybe trying to will back an errant thought that had escaped his brain.

When Beth opened the door to the bungalow, it was obvious someone had been living there, and had not bothered to clean up; dishes stacked in the kitchen sink, the futon folded out, the blankets and sheets in a tangled wad, partly hanging off the edge and onto the living room floor, some fruit in a bowl in the center of the table, and an open package of Oreos on the counter. The house didn't smell bad, exactly, but the odor of burned spaghetti sauce mixed with air freshener hung heavy in the kitchen.

Kenny walked through the house, then checked his watch. What was the allure of this dump? He checked the bedroom first, the bed made, the room neat and orderly, then walked into the spare room, the one his dad had called the *Anytime* room, or the *Any-something* room, he couldn't remember. It had been years since he'd been down here. But it looked the same, basically empty, no drafting table, no art supplies or easel, nothing. Just as he was flipping off the overhead light, he heard Beth talking with someone in the living room.

He walked out to see the scraggly biker, the one she called Tarantula, sitting at the kitchen table eating an Oreo, explaining to Beth that he hadn't had anything to drink all night, that he was *on the wagon* because of some issue. "Got to cool the alcohol or I'll lose my job," he said, twisting the Oreo into two halves, a few more cookies stacked like poker chips in front of him.

"Yeah, well, we all have problems," she said, sounding thoroughly unimpressed with his. "I'm helping send my dad to prison for life..." Beth bit into her cookie, standing near the kitchen counter.

Tarantula turned serious and miserable, his tongue working over some molars beneath his cheek. "He abuse you or something?" Tarantula asked, his eyes deep holes, his fingers kneading the skin of his jaw.

"No, he shot some guy four times in the cereal aisle at Dreyburg's," she said, "then put another one in the guy's forehead when he was lying on the floor."

Tarantula bounced back in his seat as if he'd been slapped in the forehead. "Whoa, that's some dark shit! He like, you know, Mafia or something?"

"Yeah, well, you ponder on that while you're trying to picture me naked..." she said, shoving the last of her cookie into her mouth. "He shot that guy for just talking to him!" Then, still chewing: "Come on, let's go."

Tarantula got up and put his last two cookies in his pocket and started to follow Beth to the door.

"Hey, Beth, where're you going?" Kenny said, not comfortable with the trajectory of the evening so far.

Beth turned toward him. "Tarantula's gonna give me a ride on his bike," she said, her face blank. "I'll see you later."

"Beth! Beth, wait!" Kenny said, his eyes shifting back and forth between her and Tarantula. "Can you give us a minute here, ah, *Tarantula?*"

Tarantula folded his lower lip down and thrust out his chin, nodding like a basset hound. "Sure thing, chief," he said, walking past Beth and smiling. "Pick you up out front of the palace, Princess."

Tarantula's chains jangled when he pulled the door open and stepped outside, pulling the door closed behind him. "What, Kenny?" Beth said when Tarantula was gone.

"That fucking guy is like a... jeez, I don't know," Kenny said, not sure how to talk her out of this crazy idea. "Can we—"

"Kenny, thanks, but nothing's gonna happen to me that I don't want to happen, okay," she said. "I can handle Tarantula. And don't wait up for me. I'll see you when I see you. Just don't go back to my mom's without me..."

"Are you sure about this, Beth, I mean—"

"Look, just hang out here until Falco gets back, okay? Hopefully it won't be too late." She leaned in and kissed him on the cheek. "Don't worry, Big Brother, okay? See you soon. I love how you care about me."

When she walked out, she took all the air from his lungs. He stared speechless at the door, the ticking of the oven clock like a bomb. A moment later a loud rumble, next to the house, rattled the windows. Kenny rushed over and pulled the curtain back as Beth, wearing a black helmet, threw her leg over the seat and snuggled up behind Tarantula, wrapping her arms around the mid-section of his leather jacket. The bike eased away slowly at first, Tarantula, his legs like outriggers, walking it away from the house, before drawing his legs back to the foot pegs. The bike surged forward, the front end rising up on the shocks, then roared away up the street, like some growling monstrous beast escaping The Netherworld. Kenny watched from the window a few minutes, though there was nothing to see, thinking how Janelle might react to him letting her go off with this guy. What choice did he have? With nothing to do but wait for Falco to return, Kenny popped an Oreo in his mouth and started rummaging the cupboards for real food, then checked the fridge, finding a clear Tupperware container filled with some kind of pasta. He pried the lid off the container, mac and cheese, then dug a fork out of the drawer and decided to eat it cold.

He hadn't thought about Vickie in a day or so, not obsessively anyway, and hadn't talked to Elaine in almost a week. Everything was out of his control, or so it seemed, spinning, like a tornado, or a perpetual motion machine. He sat down, filled his fork with little elbow shaped noodles covered with congealed cheese and shoved them past his lips; like chewing rubber.

When he finished, he cleaned up the dishes, checking the time, wondering about Beth, why she went off with that crazy biker who looked to be in his forties. His mind shifted to his dad, to Elaine and Michael, then, unable to stop its foray into difficult topics, his thoughts filled with Vickie, images of her flashing up from Toms River, from the hotel room at the Charter House Inn, her on the beach, how she felt lying next to him under the covers, naked and warm, her fingers tracing the creases of his ear, her lips against his. The tears came and he couldn't stop them.

Kenny turned on the television, a hazy snow sizzling across the shows on every channel. It was nearly unwatchable, but after a while, he actually got used to it. He doused the lamp on the end table next to the futon, then toed off his shoes before plumping up the pillow beneath his head. Lights from departing motorcycles slid along the walls, the rumble of engines fading away down the street in a steady procession, merged with the constant drone of voices on the television.

Kenny must have dozed. Someone shook his shoulder, waking him. In the eerie murk of the room, lit only by the radioactive glow from the television, Kenny didn't recognize the ghoulish face staring down at him.

"Hey, Sport, mind telling me who you're supposed to be?" the man said. "You one of Geronimo's less scruffy clan?"

It took a moment for Kenny to remember where he was. "I'm Kenny. Kenny Moffett. Martin Moffett's son. Martin used to own this place. I'm sorry if I—" Kenny was embarrassed, trying to get himself untangled from the blankets.

"Relax. I'm Falco. Your dad still owns the place. I'm like the caretaker now... at least when I'm not traveling." Falco went over and opened the fridge, standing in the glow of the refrigerator light, studying the contents, or the lack thereof. "Did you eat the mac?" He looked over the fridge door at Kenny.

"Yeah. Sorry." Kenny sat up, trying to find his shoes.

Falco shut the door and switched on the kitchen light. Kenny snapped his eyes shut from the sudden brightness, then eased them open slowly. "I guess mac and cheese doesn't go bad," Falco said. "It's been in there a while." Falco rooted around in the cabinets above the kitchen counter, finding some instant rice meal, then digging out a pan from under the sink, adding some water and twisting the burner on.

The man at the stove worked in silence, obviously not put off by Kenny's presence.

"So... you know my dad, huh?" Kenny finally said, tying his shoes.

"Yeah," Falco said, turning once to glance over at Kenny, then back to the water in the pan starting to boil. "Want some?" Falco said, not looking over. "Should be enough for two."

"No thanks." Kenny waited a moment, feeling an odd drift, as if he'd wandered into someone else's world. "Have you seen my dad?"

Falco poured the contents of the instant meal into the sauce pan and started stirring, watching the process intently, as though he were mixing nitroglycerin. He seemed to purposely keep his attention away from Kenny. Beth had implied that Falco was peculiar, or maybe Kenny had inferred it, but Beth had stated, though never gave her reasoning for her assumptions, that strange things were happening at the bungalow.

Kenny, waiting for Falco to answer, felt the pull of this strange man, this supposed magician, as Beth had referred to him. She had questioned his validity as an illusionist, but Kenny could feel something of the sorcerer in this offbeat character, something dangerously protean about him, as if Falco could turn himself into a hawk, or a fox, and vanish from the house without a trace.

Falco moved the pan from the burner, then turned the knob until the flame snuffed out. He looked over at Kenny. "I haven't seen your dad in about three weeks or so," he finally said, reaching up to grab a plate from the cupboard above the stove. He retrieved a fork from the drawer and brought everything over to the kitchen table and sat. Kenny, unsettled, got up and eased slowly toward the empty chair across from Falco, then sat slowly at the table, half expecting Falco to reprimand him for interrupting his meal. When Falco appeared okay with the intrusion, Kenny said, "Was my dad okay? Did he say where he was going? He's been missing for a few weeks…"

Falco sat back in the chair, as if upset, his features tinged with anguish. He set his fork on his plate and stared at nothing for a long, couple of breaths, then brought his eyes to Kenny.

Uncomfortable with Falco's quirky silence, Kenny added, "The police have been looking for him—"

"The police won't find your dad, Sport," Falco said, his eyes blank and dark as tarnished pennies. "And neither will you…"

The air in the bungalow turned faulty, treacherous, as if the molecules of the tiny house were destabilizing around him. Was Martin dead, perhaps stashed away in some unthinkable, undiscoverable grave like Jimmy Hoffa? And for what reason? Who would want to hurt his dad? For nearly a minute Kenny could do nothing but stare at

Falco, whose face was giving off no further clarity about his father, leaving everything to float about haphazardly, disenfranchised particles in the cosmic soup.

Without warning, Falco stood and walked toward the hallway. "Come with me, Sport," Falco said without turning. Kenny stood, oddly and unquestioningly obedient to this stranger, his knees weak, his throat parched. Whatever was about to happen, Kenny wasn't sure he wanted to experience it alone, wishing Beth would get back. At least she'd met this bizarre magician, if that's what Falco really was. Kenny couldn't be sure; the baffling man was difficult to read.

Falco flipped on the light in the *Something* room, or whatever his dad had called it, and drifted slowly toward the closet door at the back. He reached up to the top of the door frame and brought down a key, then looked back at Kenny.

"I spoke to your dad before he left," Falco said, squinting, his head cocked to the side. "He said he'd come out from time to time to see how you were doing, that you were having some marital problems. Have you worked things out?"

It felt odd this stranger would have any knowledge of issues between him and Elaine, but obviously Falco and his father were good friends. Even so, it bothered Kenny. And what did he mean, *before he left*?

"None of my business," Falco said, inserting the key into the door, pausing a few moments without turning it. "I'm not sure I should be showing you this... but I can think of no adequate way to explain where your father is." Then, after a troubled pause: "He's with your mother, Noreen..."

"My mother's dead," Kenny said sternly, as if some record needed clarification. Falco just nodded knowingly at Kenny, as if this wasn't new to him. The peculiar man's mannerisms were maddening to Kenny; he wanted to wrench the damn key from Falco's bony fingers and open the damn door himself. Falco stood motionless, as if he had ossified before Kenny's eyes. He brought his gaze to Kenny, his hand still gripping the key.

"You're a computer guy, right?" Falco said, more as statement than question. "Writing code. Left brain functioning... You may have trouble with this..."

With no further fanfare, Falco unlocked the door and pulled it open, not at all surprised by the blinding light pouring into the room. Kenny looked away at first, then over at Falco, whose features were nearly erased by the dazzling luminescence. Falco stared seemingly unharmed into the bright mist. Kenny shielded his eyes, then forced himself to look into the formless glow, not sure what he was supposed to see. Falco glanced over at him, then said. "It won't ruin your eyes," Falco said, his eyes glinting like those of a madman, his face burned to a glassy white, almost translucent. "Just think of someone you've lost, like your mother... and picture her in your mind..."

A moment later, lowering his shielding hand from his eyes, Kenny watched an image in the void begin to take form. He squinted, and rocked his head from side to side. It wasn't possible. Vickie Kramer, leaving biology class in high school, walking toward him down the hallway, stopping at her locker to put her books away. Kenny looked over at Falco who was still staring into the glare.

"Do you see what I see?" Kenny asked, allowing himself to believe this impossibility for the moment, as if to play along until he learned the crux of the illusion.

"I have no idea what you're seeing," Falco said. "It's only for you."

"Why am I not seeing my dad?" Kenny managed to ask after a few minutes of watching Vickie gather her books from her locker, then talk with a classmate before her next class. They laughed, talking about something or someone, Vickie more beautiful than Kenny could imagine. When Falco didn't answer, Kenny started to pose the question again. "Why am I not—"

"Because he's not dead," Falco stated with such certitude that something snagged in Kenny's chest, maybe a breath, or a heartbeat.

Falco turned abruptly, and started from the room, telling Kenny to close the door when he was finished. A moment later Falco was gone, closing the door to the small room, leaving Kenny alone with the light. It was then that the sound Falco must have reacted to registered in Kenny's mind, the sound of someone coming into the bungalow. Beth. Why did he not want her to see this, whatever it was? With no sound coming from the glowing void as Kenny watched Vickie walking with her friend, he became oddly aware of the conversation between Falco and Beth in the other room, Beth laughing about something, but not like joke laughter, more sarcastic, as if Falco had told her something she knew was a lie. Then the front door slammed and a few minutes later, Falco returned to the small room, then, without a word, walked over to the door and slid it shut, the light vanishing so abruptly, Kenny became unsteady, almost dizzy, as if the light had been holding him up. Falco locked the door and instead of placing the key back on the small ledge of the door jamb, he pocketed it.

"Beth's waiting for you in the car," Falco said, walking from the room.

"Wait a second," Kenny said, rushing after him, grabbing Falco's arm before he sat back down to his rice. Falco glared at Kenny's hand on his arm. Kenny pulled it away, leaving white finger marks on Falco's skin. "Sorry... but I need some kind of explanation..."

Falco smirked. "Who were you watching? Your mother?"

Kenny was uneasy telling Falco about Vickie. "No..."

Falco sat down and picked up his fork, as though continued explanation was pointless unless Kenny divulged who he'd seen.

"Vickie Kramer," Kenny finally said, hating that this man now knew her name, feeling he'd betrayed Vickie in some way to this lunatic. "Someone I cared a great deal about." The next realization hit Kenny like a truck—if Falco indeed was an illusionist, and what Kenny had just witnessed had been an elaborate mind trick, how could Falco possibly have known about Vickie, or that she and Kenny had gone to high school together. Had Martin said something? That was the only explanation. But how could Falco possibly have known exactly how Vickie looked in high school. Kenny's legs fell weak again and he sat down across from Falco.

"How long has she been dead?" Falco said, shoving a forkful of rice past his lips.

"A short time," Kenny said absently, not sure he was even still in the room, or in his own body, his voice echoing out from all directions at once.

Falco nodded and continued eating. After a long, tenuous interlude, Falco said, "The way you saw this Vickie girl, that's the way Martin sees your mother, Noreen."

Kenny still didn't understand. The questions inside Kenny's head tumbled toward him like an avalanche, Kenny unable to separate out the most pressing ones, as if every question was pressing. Falco must have read his consternation. "You could have gone into that mist and been with her." Falco dropped the statement on Kenny with the sober finality of a casket lid.

A new maelstrom of questions, a swirling mire of implausibilities sitting atop a tower of turmoil. Kenny felt an odd vertigo, resting his arms on the cold Formica of the kitchen table to steady himself.

"Your dad is living with Noreen, your mother," Falco said. "Martin has his own design firm there, I think he calls it—"

"The Phoenix Group..." Kenny blurted out, unsure where the name came from.

"Something like that," Falco said. "He's happy... at least for now..." Falco raised another fork-load of rice to his lips, then got up and grabbed a beer from the fridge. "Want one?"

Kenny told him no as Falco was popping the cap off the bottle. Falco belched, nothing loud and obnoxious, yet the involuntary burp seemed out of place, almost comical, considering the gravity of their discussion.

"*At least for now?*" Kenny asked, picking up on the slight derision in Falco's tone in reference to his dad's happiness.

"Let's just say, events in that paradigm aren't always predictable..." Falco said. "Things don't always work out the way you'd like..."

"Is it normal?" Kenny said. "My dad living with my mom, I mean, is it normal, like living with someone in this world...?" The question was so freakish to Kenny's own ears he expected Falco to burst out laughing. And he did. Falco had to stop eating for a moment. He tried to take a drink of beer, but ended up choking on it and jumping up from the table. Just then, Beth came in, asking what all the commotion was about. Kenny just looked at her, then back to Falco, wondering if he should get up and perform the Heimlich.

"Is he going to be all right?" Beth asked, walking over closer.

"Is it *normal?*" Falco said, laughing. "Did it look *normal*, Sport! Jesus, what a question? You are definitely your father's son!" Falco was now propped over the kitchen sink, a hand on either side, looking out the window toward the dark field. A train was rumbling closer, then passed going fast enough to shake the small house. Falco waited as the train passed, then wiped his eyes and turned back toward the table, wearing the last vestiges of a fading smirk. He looked at Kenny, shaking his head. *"Normal!"* Falco said, almost under his breath, then took his eyes to Beth.

Nearly a minute passed before the odd man spoke again. "I meant what I said before," Falco told Beth. "We'd be great together. And you'd have fun, traveling, putting on magic shows, seeing the world… I'm heading to Germany next week, then Amsterdam. Amsterdam… that place alone would mature you by ten years!"

"Yeah, okay, so who will be wearing the tight little red sequined skirt with their ass hanging out," Beth said, smirking at Falco, "and their tits glowing like orbs, and the nose-bleed high heels? Me or you?"

Falco laughed goodheartedly and said, "Well, I can start off with the outfit and my glowing orbs… and you can wear the tux, at least for the first couple of months, and we'll see how it goes!"

Beth scoffed and punched Kenny on the shoulder. "Let's hit the trail, Big Brother," she said. "Mom will be wondering what happened to us. Plus, I've got an early court date tomorrow."

Falco shook his head. "That is completely unreasonable," he said, genuinely sympathetic. "After all that trial business is over, you should really consider going on the road with me."

"What about high school?" Beth said.

"I have just three things to say on that subject—G - E - D!"

Kenny stood up, his mind in a blender, stuck on the periphery of Falco and Beth's conversation. How could Falco act so nonchalant toward the mystical, glowing abyss in the other room? Did Beth know about it?

"Yeah, that's exactly why my mom spent thousands of dollars on my privileged education, so I could end up with a *GED!*" Beth spoke the acronym as one word, making it sound slightly comical, as if it were a pimple, or some other unsightly deformity.

"Don't discount my offer so quickly, Ma'am," Falco said with the disarming grin of a crocodile.

"Ma'am?! Yeah, right! I'm seventeen… and you're like a hundred," Beth said, seemingly being lured in by Falco's charm, it appeared to Kenny.

"Come on, Sis, let's go," Kenny said.

"I didn't ask you to marry me," Falco said, unwilling to concede. "Just asking you to join me for the thrill of a lifetime!"

Beth laughed. "Some thrill!" She grabbed Kenny's hand and practically dragged him to the front door. Kenny was still wheeling from the evening's events, disoriented, suddenly noticing the fragrance issuing from Beth, some kind of perfume he hadn't noticed earlier. She released his hand when they got to the front porch and asked if he minded driving home. Beth explained that she had smoked some pot with Tarantula, and was a little woozy, and didn't trust herself behind the wheel.

Chapter Forty-Three

On the ride back to Beth's house, Kenny listened with a fragment of his attention, as Beth related how she had planned to sleep with Tarantula, that she had never had sex before and he seemed like a safe bet, at least from a relationship standpoint, that she figured he wouldn't be clingy, and even if he proved to be, he'd have no way to contact her. It seemed perfect, she'd told Kenny.

"Hey, pull into that convenience store," she said, telling him she needed chips and a Pepsi, then asked if he wanted anything. He said no and waited in the car, trying to process the evening, the dazzling movie playing before his eyes of Vickie going to her locker, seemingly adrift in the spellbinding light, so real it felt Kenny could reach out and touch her. Then the thought broke in, at least according to Falco, that he could have. There was so much more he wanted to know about the strange room: if Vickie would know him in that alternate reality? why couldn't she see him when he was looking right at her? and could he ever come back out? Obviously, he could, as Falco had related about Kenny's dad saying he'd come out to call Kenny on occasion. But how did that work? The coming and going? Kenny was deep into imagining the mechanics of the light room when Beth jerked the door open and threw herself into the front seat. He jumped, startled, but she was smiling, munching on chips, oblivious to his pallor and alarm.

Sipping her Pepsi, Beth continued where she'd left off with the details of her evening, as if she hadn't even left the Taurus to buy snacks, assuring Kenny she wasn't about to have unprotected sex with Terrence, explaining that Terrence was Tarantula's actual name, then laughing at some joke only she was privy to.

"I don't know what happened, though," Beth said, suddenly reflective and serious, her shape a foreign shadow in the seat across from him. "We got to his apartment, and jeez, it was so messy and crapped up, I just couldn't even think about taking off my clothes. He seemed to understand when I told him I had to get going. I guess his feelings were hurt, but jeez…" Then, a few minutes later: "I guess I'm a snob."

Beth made no excuses for her disgust with how Terrence lived. "Plenty of opportunities ahead to have sex, I suppose," she said a moment later, as if hanging her thoughts out on a line to study them closer. Kenny had to wonder what the hurry to have sex was all about. It seemed sudden, realizing how frank Beth was being. Maybe it was the weed talking.

They were getting close to home when he felt Beth looking over at him. He glanced in her direction, catching s strange glint coming off her eyes; she wasn't just looking at him, but staring, almost studying him. "What?" he finally said.

"Will you have sex with me?" she said softly, serious.

His heart leapt into his throat and for a moment he couldn't speak.

"We're not really brother and sister, Kenny," she said. "You know… so it's not like we're breaking some law, or violating some unwritten canon or something." Then, without a hint of remorse. "I hope I didn't embarrass you… but, this trial deal, it's freaking me out, and, I know it's stupid, but I have to go into that courtroom tomorrow morning and testify against my own dad! How fucked up is that?" She let that statement float around them for several long seconds, then: "And, so, here comes the stupid part; I feel that I'm entitled, no, that it's almost compulsory, that I walk into that courtroom a woman when I take that stand tomorrow."

"But, Beth, sex isn't the measure of—"

"Don't finish that sentence, okay," she said. "You're sounding preachy. Just tell me you will… have sex with me. Tonight…"

Kenny slowed the Taurus when he came to the driveway, then eased the car toward the garage door, stopping and shutting off the engine. He withdrew the keys, shaky, unable to counteract the yaw and pitch of the evening—Vickie in the brilliant white haze, someone he'd never expected to see again. Now Beth, asking him to make love to her, and his dad, living with his dead mother in some unknown universe, wherever that was supposed to be. The contents of his stomach defied gravity and Kenny threw up outside the driver's side door.

"Holy shit, Kenny!" Beth said, laughing, feigning a bit of hurt. "Am I that repulsive?"

Kenny, still leaning out the door, eased back upright slowly, away from the awful stench. He wiped his mouth, glancing toward Beth, shaking his head. Her expression was sour, much like his stomach. "That's not true," he said, "...that we wouldn't be breaking any laws... You're a minor and I'm... I'm—"

"Age of consent in Missouri is seventeen..." she said.

"What does that have to do with it—?" He felt bad about barking at her, then dialed down his anger and added sheepishly, "It's just wrong, Beth... okay..."

Without a word, she leaned over and pulled him to her lips. He pulled away, embarrassed by the taste in his mouth—as well as an emotion he couldn't quite puzzle out. She drew him back, her hand behind his neck. She took his hand with her free one and guided it to her breast. He knew he should withdraw gently, but he couldn't, caught in a disorienting vortex of confusion, loneliness and anger, at Vickie, then his dad, his dead mother, even Falco; this new anger frothy and hot, seemingly without bounds, until he jerked his hand back, tucking them both together in his lap, ashamed to look at her, to look at anything.

"Hey, I'm sorry, Kenny," she said, reaching over to touch his arm. He looked at her and noticed the tears running down her face. "It's just that..." she said, her lip quivering. "I don't know..."

They sat in silence, neither of them ready to discharge the spell, and unwilling to move toward it. She held his eyes, and for a moment, he only saw Vickie looking back.

"I want my first time to be special," Beth said with a gentleness he had not heard from her. "And I can think of no one more special than you to share this moment with. To share myself with..."

Kenny couldn't parse any of this. It was madness, and he couldn't understand what had come over her. He was about to speak though there was nothing to say.

She scooted across the seat and got out on the passenger side, pushing the door shut. Kenny sat a moment behind the steering wheel, dizzy from the oscillation of the evening, as if the pull of the universe rushing at over a million miles per hour through the black void of space was dragging him along, stealing his breath, throwing off his balance. He couldn't get his bearings, the impossible pull of circumstances drawing him deeper into a bottomless morass. When he looked up, Beth was standing at the open driver's side door, near his vomit, extending her hand toward him. "Come on, Big Brother," she said. "You don't look so good."

When they walked into the house, Janelle was seated at the kitchen island, reading a novel. "I was just getting ready to go to bed," she said. "How was the movie?"

"It was okay," Beth said. "But I think Kenny had too much buttered popcorn and Milk Duds." Beth turned to Kenny. "You should go to bed, Big Brother." Kenny looked over at Janelle, then at Beth, still unsettled over Beth's proposal, not wanting to reject her, but knowing he couldn't fulfill her desire, then feeling bad about that, the evening swamping him like a raging black river.

He smiled, and told Janelle that tomorrow he planned to visit some of his dad's friends, and talk to some of the employees at Petro, that maybe they had some insight into where Martin might be.

"Are you worried... about your dad?" Janelle asked.

"No. No, not at all," he said, trying to sound reassuring, but he had no idea what the hell was going on. "I mean... I'm sure he's fine..." Kenny could say no more, the vertigo taking him over again.

"Thank you, Kenny," Janelle said, closing her book and getting up. "I'm going to bed." Then, looking at Beth, with tears in her eyes: "We have a long day tomorrow, sweetheart." She reached out and took Beth's hands in hers, then mouthed to her daughter, almost inaudibly, shaking her head softly, remorseful, "I'm so sorry."

Beth gave her a sad smile, and with her eyes said it was okay, not to worry, then turned to Kenny, "Goodnight, Kenny..." She stared into his eyes a moment, as if to add something more, but turned to her mom and walked her mother back to her bedroom. Kenny stood alone in the kitchen, listening to Janelle's bedroom door shut, then the bathroom door, Beth getting ready for bed, and Kenny wasn't sure why he was here, in St. Louis, in this house, in this kitchen, his surroundings suddenly foreign, elements that carried no weight in his life. Just then he pictured Elaine, and Michael, as if at any moment they'd walk out from the guest bedroom and ask if he was coming to bed, Michael asking for a bedtime story, Elaine wearing her pajamas, her realtor makeup removed, revealing her natural beauty—dark eyebrows like tattoos, perfectly full lips— remarkable without any cosmetic help.

Kenny was in the guest bedroom reading, trying to settle himself when he noticed the house was completely still, only the low hum of the refrigerator kicking on. He set the book down on the nightstand, knowing that when he turned off the light it would feel like a hangover; the room would spin like a dervish, a barrage of thoughts and impressions spilling through his brain. But it wasn't like that at all. The dark solitude sluiced through him like a warm drug, and he would have probably slept through the night if he hadn't been awakened by Beth's naked body straddling him. She leaned down close to his ear and whispered, "I'll leave if you want me to."

What a pitiful, pathetic wretch I am, Kenny thought, picturing himself with this seventeen-year-old girl perched atop him, maybe not breaking actual laws, but certainly laws of morality that went without stating for any person with a proper navigational system, his hands on her rib cage just beneath her breasts as he entered her, the sensation excruciatingly, mind-numbingly intense, with the hermetic quality of a dream, and that's what he told himself; it's just a dream.

Chapter Forty-Four

B eth took the stand, swore on a Bible, perspiration dampening the spaces beneath her arms. At the table for the defense, her father looked on with empty eyes, his face ashen and gaunt, like a prison camp survivor, though he'd yet to spend a single day behind bars. He would never make it in prison, Beth knew with certainty, the realization stretching a grim tightness across her chest. She knew most of the questions the prosecution was going to ask, as they had gone over much of what they needed from her. And while the questions, and her answers, would be truthful—which the attorneys for the prosecution had stressed to her repeatedly, to be as truthful as possible—the questions themselves didn't seem to be that damning to her father, at least in her mind. Beth's mother was seated near the center of the courtroom, already with a handkerchief to her nose, her eyes red from the drive to the courthouse.

With every breath, Beth felt everyone in attendance could see how afraid she was. She tried to calm her breathing, slow her heart rate, quell her nervousness. Kenny had offered to attend, had asked if it was okay, but Beth wasn't sure she could bear seeing him there; it would be hard enough watching her mother, not to mention her father's face as she answered questions that could seal his fate. It would be too embarrassing for her knowing Kenny might be judging her, what she was doing to her own father.

Dr. Carl Drake had been charged with second degree murder, first degree murder, and manslaughter, the prosecution hoping to ensure a jury would find one of these charges befitting this unnecessary and heinous crime. What Beth hadn't counted on, or had even considered, was Naomi, Dr. Geoffrey Nevins' daughter—who had been in the cereal aisle when her father was shot, had witnessed the entire ordeal —being in the courtroom today. She had not been there for any of the earlier proceedings, and as far as Beth knew, would not be testifying unless things were not going well for the prosecution, but today, there she was, seated behind the prosecution table with her mother, a beautiful woman, though not bearing up quite as well as her daughter it seemed, her eyes stained red from tears. Naomi on the other hand, now thirteen, or fourteen, Beth wasn't sure, appeared strong and mature, sitting up straight, her chin forward, her eyes clear, as if she'd done this a thousand times. Occasionally Beth's attention drifted toward the young girl, who sat expressionless, though her quiet intensity made it impossible for Beth to hold her gaze for long.

The prosecution started out slowly, laying out why Beth was testifying today, explaining to the jury that it was important, even though it was her own father on trial, to make clear Dr. Carl Drake's intentions, and how Beth Drake had interpreted her father's reasons, and how she herself felt about her own safety in public, about her father owning a gun, carrying it on his hip.

"Did your father ever tell you why he bought the gun, Ms. Drake?" the prosecuting attorney, a tall, graying woman in her fifties, asked.

"Protection," Beth said, following their direction to answer as simply as possible.

"What was Dr. Drake afraid of? Did he ever tell you?"

Beth hesitated a moment, glancing briefly at Naomi. "He was bothered by the woman who was killed in the parking lot at the West Town Mall a couple years ago," she said.

"Do you recall why that bothered him?"

Beth swallowed. "He said... he said that poor people became dangerous when they came into proximity with the wealthy..." Then, as if to clarify: "I don't feel that way, that poor people—"

"Objection," the defense attorney said. "No one asked for Ms. Drake's opinion."

"Overruled," the judge said. "You may finish your answer."

Beth knew she shouldn't have said anything about how she felt. "I just... I don't feel that poor people hurt others because they're poor..."

The courtroom fell silent, the prosecuting attorney waiting a moment. "But wasn't there another reason your father, Dr. Drake, purchased the gun and carried it in a holster on his hip?"

Beth closed her eyes a moment, then opened them. "He, uh, had been harassed by some teenagers, I think, when he came out of his office a couple of evenings, but I don't think they ever did anything but yell stuff. They might have painted some graffiti on the walls outside in the parking lot."

"So, Dr. Drake had every right to be afraid?"

Objection," the defense said. "Calling for speculation on her father's emotions."

"Sustained," the judge said.

"Did your father tell you he was afraid at his office?"

Beth stammered a moment. "No, not really. Not that I recall."

"Did you ever visit your father's dental practice?"

"Yes, numerous times."

"Were you afraid?"

"No, it always felt pretty safe to me, but—"

"Thank you, Ms. Drake," the prosecution said. "So on the day your father shot Dr. Nevins, were you with your father?"

"Yes."

"Were you afraid when Dr. Nevins started shouting at your father?"

"A little, I mean it was unnerving at first, but then..."

"But then?"

"Well, Dr. Nevins was saying everything I wanted to tell my dad about that stupid gun, but I just couldn't...!" Beth started crying, angry over the incident, angry at her dad's callousness. Angry he had put her in this position.

"The truth is, you were embarrassed by your father's gun, to be seen in public with him, correct?"

"Objection. Leading."

"Sustained."

"Ms. Drake, were you embarrassed to be seen with your father when he was wearing his gun?"

"Yes. It just seemed so ridiculous…"

"How old are you?"

"Seventeen."

"Did you feel safer with your father when he started carrying the weapon?"

"No. Actually… I was more afraid… like it could draw aggressiveness to us. You know. It stood out. People looked at us. Without the gun, we were just a dad and his daughter shopping, or getting ice cream…" Beth tried not to look at her father, but when she did, he seemed crushed, not that what she was saying was damning, but maybe that he was sorry she'd felt more afraid with him than by herself.

"Did you ever feel your father was in danger from Dr. Nevins' confrontation?"

"Objection! Calling for speculation to her father's emotional state."

"Sustained."

"Did you ever feel you were in danger from Dr. Nevins' confrontation?"

Beth looked at her father, then at Naomi, then back to the prosecuting attorney. "No… not really…"

"Can you speak up, Ms. Drake?"

"No. I was never afraid of Dr. Nevins."

"But he was yelling and moving his arms in an animated fashion, at least according to the CCTV. Didn't that frighten you?"

"No, it was unusual, but he never seemed dangerous. His arms moved the way they would during a conversation… he seemed… he seemed more like someone who talked things out, who was willing to debate topics, make himself heard. He stood up for what he believed, but he never seemed violent, like he could hurt someone, and then…"

"And then?"

"Well, then… his daughter. She was so lovely and calm, as if she knew exactly what Dr. Nevins meant, as if she'd heard this speech about non-violence before and believed in her dad. It never seemed as if he meant to hurt anyone. He was just passionate about guns, I guess, ridding society of guns…"

"Did it frighten you that Dr. Nevins was black?"

"No. Absolutely not. The school I attend is racially diverse. That was important to my mother."

"Not to your father?"

Beth shook her head and shrugged. "I guess. I don't know, we never talked about it."

"Was your father prejudice?"

"Objection! Calling for speculation to her father's beliefs."

"Sustained."

"Did your father ever say things to you that sounded like prejudice?"

"Objection! Calling for speculation."

"Overruled. The witness may answer."

"I can't say. I don't really know."

The prosecution attorney walked back to her table to retrieve a document. "It says here, that when your father brought up the woman who was murdered at West Town Mall, that he referred to the killer as a 'black man.' 'A poor black man, probably a drug addict.' Is that true?"

"I can't recall exactly how he said it. Maybe something like that."

"Were the youths, the ones who shouted at him coming out of his office, also black?"

Beth looked over at her father, then at her mother. "I think so."

"Did your father ever demonstrate this same fear or animosity over white assailants that may have popped up in the news?"

Beth sighed. "Not that I can recall."

"Thank you, Ms. Drake. No further questions."

The defense attorney for her father stood up, then asked her father something before approaching the witness box. "I'll be brief, Ms. Drake. I know you're missing school today, so we want to get you back in class as soon as possible."

Beth smiled weakly, hating every second.

"Does your father love you, Ms. Drake?"

She leaned forward toward the microphone. "Yes, very much."

"Yes, of course he does," the defense attorney said. "And do you believe he would do anything to protect you?"

"Yes, I believe so."

"Do you believe that it is your father's responsibility to keep you safe?"

Beth nodded.

"Could you *speak* your answer, please."

"Yes, of course."

"And isn't it true that parents, in their parental zeal and responsibility to keep their children safe from harm, do things that at times that might embarrass their children, such as, keeping you from attending a certain movie with friends, or going to an unchaperoned party at someone's home?"

Beth couldn't believe the attorney knew about the unchaperoned party. Her father must have told him, and, that she had not been allowed to go. "Yes."

"Yes, of course. Parents are often tasked with making tough decisions when thinking of their children's safety and well-being." Then, after perusing some papers in his hands: "You're a very good student! 3.9 GPA. Very good. Your parents send you to a very good school, racially diverse, as you mentioned. Did your father ever balk about you going to your current school?"

"Balk? Like complain about it or something?"

"He let you go, right? Encouraged you to attend your racially-diverse school, correct?"

"Yes," Beth said, understanding that the defense attorney was building a case for her father's supposed open-minded acceptance of other races, though Beth wasn't sure that was necessarily true. Her father never used racial slurs, or pointed the finger directly at African Americans or Hispanics, but some unspoken bias existed. Beth felt it from her father, though nothing she could attest to, an intuition at best.

"Thank you, Ms. Drake," the defense attorney said, smiling, then turned and walked back to the table and sat next to her father. Beth had just looked over at the judge, wondering if she was done, when the prosecuting attorney hurried out from behind his table.

"Glad to hear you're doing so well in school," she said, "but it wasn't that way at first, was it, after the shooting? Can you tell the court what happened to your studies after the shooting?"

Beth looked at her, the memories flooding back, stubborn tears forming at the bottom rims of her eyes. She sniffed. "I couldn't focus, and I guess, my grades started to suffer…"

"Yes, your GPA dropped to 2.1. And you had to stay out of school for a while, isn't that correct?"

"It was hard… I just couldn't focus…"

"You started seeing a psychiatrist, isn't that correct?"

"Yes."

"Had you ever had occasion to see a psychiatrist before?"

"No."

"And he prescribed medication for your depression, isn't that correct?"

"Yes."

"Do you think it was the medication that made it hard to concentrate?"

"Well, that was part of it…" Beth said, knowing where Ms. Batch was going with these questions. They had gone over all of this in the deposition.

"What else was bothering you?"

Beth hesitated, letting her eyes slip past the people seated in the gallery, pausing only a second on Naomi Nevins, whose features were unchanged, solemn. Beth cleared her throat, knowing that as soon as she spoke, the tears would come.

"I couldn't stop thinking about Naomi Nevins, Dr. Nevins' daughter, who was standing right there when her father was killed." Beth brought her hand to her mouth, sickened by the recollection. Ms. Batch was silent, letting Beth gather herself. "Every time I closed my eyes I saw Naomi's face, terrified, unable to scream… the air gone from her lungs… her mouth open… her cheeks drenched in tears. I'd see her over and over, falling to her knees, soundless, her face twisted in horror… she was in shock, I guess, as was I…" Beth paused, unable to look at Naomi, unable to look anywhere but down, ashamed. "I wanted to help her, somehow, but I couldn't move… I just stood there, the blood draining from my body, shaking, like I was about to puke…" Then, after a slight pause, she added, "And every time I saw Naomi in my thoughts, the realization of what we'd done, my father and I, was like being kicked in the stomach… because of us, Naomi would grow up without a father… it wasn't fair!" Beth put her hands over her face, sobbing. The courtroom was silent, everyone waiting for Beth to compose herself, Beth feeling the weight of all the stranger's eyes upon her. She sniffed and wiped her eyes. "Sorry."

"It's okay, Ms. Drake," Ms. Batch said. "I'm sorry to have to put you through this, I really am. Naomi Nevins, nor you, should never be subjected to what you both witnessed that day in the grocery store, nor to anything as grueling as this trial. That's why it's so important the jury understand the grave fallout from such an act." Ms. Batch hesitated a moment, then continued: "I'm sorry to have to drag you through these memories again, but that wasn't all, was it? I mean, after Dr. Drake shot Dr. Nevins in the chest four times, then stepped forward, and with Dr. Nevins lying on the floor, most likely already dead, Dr. Drake, your father, shot Dr. Nevins in the head. What happened when he did that?"

Beth shook, the courtroom disappeared; the sound and images playing behind her eyes the only reality now. "Naomi yelped!" Beth blurted out, watching it all happen again. "As if she'd been shot, then fell to the floor and curled into a ball, sobbing, shaking… it was horrible…" Beth turned to face her father, saying, "I'm sorry, Daddy! But it was hideous… monstrous!" then broke down crying.

"Objection! The witness may not address the defendant!"

"Sustained," the judge said.

"No further questions," Ms. Batch said, handing Beth a clean handkerchief before turning to go back to her table. For several long moments, the judge, as if waiting for Beth to calm herself, as well as allowing the jury to feel the full impact of damage this unnecessary violence caused, watched, as time stretched forward, before he told her she could step down. She wiped the tears with the handkerchief, then glanced briefly at the judge before taking her eyes to the gallery. Naomi and her mother were gone. Beth stood, steadied herself, then looked at her mother, who was still sobbing quietly, her hand covering her mouth, her eyes red and staring at nothing.

Chapter Forty-Five

K enny had wanted to attend the trial, but Beth had been emphatic about him staying away, telling him it was too embarrassing, that she felt so ashamed. Kenny tried to talk to her, tell her she had nothing to be ashamed of, but she was quick to remind him that she had done nothing when her father bought the gun and started wearing it everywhere they went. It was *obscene!* she told Kenny, lying next to him in the guest bedroom. "I could have refused to go with him," she told Kenny, obviously angry at herself, believing she could have made a difference, blaming herself for the murder as if she'd pulled the trigger. Kenny let it drop, and just held her. After a short while, she got up and put her pajamas back on, then came over to the bed and kissed him on the lips.

"Please don't ever regret this night," she had said with sad sincerity. "Promise me, Kenny. Being with you like this meant so much to me..." He had nodded, feeling horrible and shocked by what they had just done, and could hardly recognize this *guy* who was like some unknown character playing him in this life, a life he no longer recognized. He felt as if someone, or something, some foreign presence had inhabited his body. She glanced back one last time before closing his bedroom door softly behind her. He heard the door to her bedroom shut, then silence all around, except inside his head, where a riot of unruly thoughts and regrets banged and broke glass and set fire to all that was sane and meaningful.

As if the night with Beth hadn't been unsettling enough, Kenny had already decided, if he wasn't attending the trial, he was going back to the bungalow, to the *Anything* room, as if to test the boundaries of the illusion. Falco. Was this unlikely trickster capable of such a convincing mirage?

When Kenny stepped onto the porch of his dad's little shack, he wasn't even sure how he'd get in. A train whistle echoed from some-where in the distance, rolling, it seemed, along the underbelly of the slate gray sky out beyond the field. Kenny tried the doorknob—locked —then knocked on the door. A moment later the door swept open, surprising Kenny, Falco in a T-shirt and boxer shorts. "Hey, Sport, come on in."

"I didn't think anyone would be here," Kenny said, going in as Falco walked from the door. Kenny closed the door behind him, then looked at Falco, who was seated at the kitchen table drinking coffee and reading a paper.

"I was supposed to be in Europe, but the tour got cancelled," Falco said without looking up. "Coffee?"

"No thanks," Kenny said, not sure how this was going to work with Falco around. If he walked into the *Anything* room and opened the locked door and saw nothing—no blinding light, no Vickie—he'd feel like a fool. And he didn't want to sit down with Falco.

"I guess I should go…" Kenny finally said, figuring he'd come back another time; the whole thing suddenly seemed ridiculous. What had he been thinking? Falco put the paper down and looked over at Kenny, his eyes intensely black, looming, caught in the shadow of his brow.

"You want to go in, right?" Falco said. "The door's unlocked."

Falco stating Kenny's intentions without flair or even a hint of ridicule sent a shiver up Kenny's spine. "I guess," Kenny said. "Any-thing I should know?"

Falco held his eyes on Kenny, as if to burrow directly into his brain. Then, a moment later, said, "Whoever you're trying to meet, imagine them at the time you want to be with them."

Maybe Vickie had appeared in high school because that's where

Kenny had imagined her when Falco had opened the door. But was that where he wanted to be with her now? In the middle of his thought process, Falco broke in.

"Just know... you can't change their death," Falco said, his legs crossed, his foot bouncing up and down. He went on to explain a few other quirky aspects of the paradigm, Kenny nodding, not really taking it all in. Falco held Kenny's eyes a few moments longer, then picked up his paper, but then, as if needing to clarify something, looked back and said, "Oh, and if you come down when I'm not here, there's a brown rock next to the front porch with a key. Just let yourself in." Falco went back to his paper. Kenny nodded, though Falco was oblivious to his presence now, it seemed.

Kenny went to the *Anything* room, then walked to the door at the back and stood. Nothing felt peculiar or out of place—everything solid, gravity holding—except for a low-grade current bristling through Kenny's veins. Where did he want to be with Vickie? He turned the knob and opened the door slowly, the light streaming out, filling the room, spreading through the darkness inside his head. Details gradually sharpened, Vickie in the Charter House Inn hotel room, coming out of the shower. Kenny entered the light, glancing over his shoulder to see what it looked like behind him, if he could see the *Anything* room. But nothing was as he'd imagined it would be, more dream than reality at first, the light sealing up around him, and he felt himself giving over to this other reality. Nothing frightening, or disorienting, just serenity. Plenty of air to breathe, gravity that felt natural, sensations of walking on the carpeted floor, the faint fragrance of air freshener and clean towels, the sweet smell of Vickie's freshly shampooed hair. When she saw him, she let her towel fall away and ran to him, throwing herself into his arms, wrapping herself in him.

"God, I thought you'd never get here!" She kissed him on the lips, on the neck, and pulled him to the bed, undoing his slacks, his shirt, then kissing him again, pulling him down on top of her. Kenny lost all doubt around the veracity of this new world, becoming fully present when they made love, then afterward, lying in each other's arms. When Vickie spoke, it was her voice, the one he knew so well. The smell of her skin, the way she smiled, the way she touched his face, the way her eyes merged with his. Every sensation was so familiar, so utterly authentic, that Kenny lost all apprehension over where he was, what he was doing.

"I'm famished," Vickie said, sitting up. "Let's eat."

Kenny sat up, unable to take his eyes from hers. "I love you so much..." he said, tears filling his eyes.

She leaned in slowly, pressing her lips to his, then, drawing back, wiped away his tears. "Don't be sad about anything," she said. "We're together... and that's all that matters..."

They went out for an early dinner, then went to a movie. Kenny tried to stay focused, but this reality, Vickie's reality, was populated with normal people, doing normal things—shopping, eating, crossing busy streets, driving their cars—and Kenny recognized every street, the buildings of Newark, mostly, yet some very different, an aspect Kenny couldn't quite puzzle out. Many buildings he didn't recognize, for sure, but not so many as to make him feel disoriented, or concerned. And Vickie was different as well, not in a disturbing way, but something unusual about her, as if she knew things, or now saw life in a very different way; as if she possessed knowledge of her own fate, as well as some understanding that Kenny was not of her world. She had not even bothered to ask why he'd been crying in the hotel room when he'd told her how much he loved her, as if she already knew the source of his sadness; losing her to a brutal attack. Did she know she had been killed? Did she know she was dead? A frenetic panic shot though him and he felt himself shuddering, until she rested her hand on his arm. When he looked over at her, she gave him a warm, reassuring smile, as if nothing could hurt them now. That's when the oddest thought broke in; *I'm dead too!* Walking into that light, I died! His mind frantically shuffled through accounts he'd heard or read of NDEs, people who'd died and came back to life, reporting that they walked into a bright light and were met by deceased family members or friends. What has he done?

When the movie ended, Vickie turned toward him. "Are you okay? Did you not enjoy the show?"

"No, yeah, it was good." He forced a smile, then started to get up when she pulled him back down. "Kiss me," she said, waiting for him to lean toward her. When their lips met, her tongue pushed past his lips, sending a tingle through the skin of his cheek, that vibrated through his flesh, a slight ticklish quiver. No other woman, not even Elaine, with just a kiss, had aroused such an involuntary and pleasurable sensation in him before.

They left the theater and walked back toward the hotel, stopping off at a coffee shop, sitting at a table near the window that looked out on traffic, the lights of Newark reflecting in the Hudson River. They talked about Vickie's flower shop back in St. Louis, Kenny somewhat surprised that it existed, unsure how Vickie's reality was constructed. Certainly, Amy couldn't be her partner, Kenny realized, thinking back to some of what Falco had told him about the oddities of this reality, that everyone in it had died, or maybe never existed in the first place; Amy wasn't dead.

"You're running it by yourself?" Kenny said, curious what she'd say.

Vickie gave him an odd look, her mouth caught in half smile. "No, it's just an idea we're talking about, Francine Tilden and I," she said, as if he should already know that. "I thought I told you that already." Francine Tilden. He knew that name. She'd been killed in their junior year when her drunk boyfriend dozed off, it was believed, then ran off the highway into the median, coming out into oncoming traffic on the other side. Killed instantly, both of them, the reports had said. Kenny recalled pictures of Stew's Chevelle SS 454 convertible; a mangled tangle of metal and chrome, that even now, recalling it, stole Kenny's breath.

"You knew her, didn't you?" Vickie said, sipping her latte.

"Sure," Kenny said, the image spilling out over Kenny's thoughts, Francine hanging on Stu at dances. They'd been inseparable. "Is she still with Stu?" Kenny asked. Vickie chuckled in a way that made Kenny uncomfortable, as if he'd said something ridiculous and out of place. It was a dumb question, especially given that Kenny didn't really care about Stu or Francine.

"No, don't you remember?" Vickie said. "They broke up after junior year."

How was that even possible? They'd been killed in their junior year! Falco hadn't mentioned anything about disjointed timelines and malformed histories. "Don't try to make sense of it, Sport," Falco had told him a few hours earlier, the magician's finger's fiddling with the edges of the newspaper, as if looking for something by touch. "It doesn't fit any of the rational boxes you might try to tick. Just observe and accept. The only way to stay sane."

"I didn't know her that well," Kenny said, hoping they could drop this conversation about old high school classmates. It made him uncomfortable not knowing the background stories in Vickie's reality.

Vickie smiled, obviously content to end the discussion, reaching across to hold Kenny's hand. Kenny squeezed her fingers gently, taking his eyes past the glass and neon sign in the window, spying a building he'd never seen before, one that couldn't possibly exist. But it was more than disconcerting; it was inconceivable. Twisting in her chair to see what had captured his attention, Vickie's eyes followed his gaze to a lit building on the bank of the Hudson, across the street from the coffee shop. *Flanders Medical Assistance Center.*

"You've never seen that before," Vickie said. "It's amazing."

Kenny could only stare. *Flanders.* His mother's maiden name. He remembered telling Beth about his idea a few years ago, when they'd met for the first time in St. Louis. Until then, he'd never told anyone about his dream, how he'd envisioned a medical help center functioning purely on advanced intelligence, completely computerized, state-of-the-art technology, that didn't yet exist even today. It had just been an idea, something he pondered often, a place that could have saved his mother had it existed decades ago, where she could have gotten more personalized and skilled care, free of charge, a social benefit to all citizens, exempt from the greed creeping into the existing medical apparatus, which was making care so expensive, driving up insurance, making it nearly impossible for many to receive even adequate care. It seemed monstrous to Kenny, that in a society as robust and forward thinking as this one, people could be made outcasts of the medical system, rejected based on income. But why was the Flanders Center here, in Newark? Why did it exist at all? Then, as if any question he asked would be answered, The Phoenix Design Group came to mind, his dad's dream studio that he never made into a reality. But according to Falco, his dad was running that design group now, in his mother's reality. Just then, in a swirling mash up of dismembered thoughts, the strangest notion broke free inside Kenny and took precedence over all others; was Vickie's reality nothing more than a phantasm of Kenny's own imagination? That anything he could envision, had dreamed—his desires and thoughts, his wants and most guarded and secret wishes—could exist here, no questions asked, no boundaries too rigid, even those of a limited technology, or adverse political machinery. It was preposterous, and unnerving, and Kenny felt like some of his cells had begun to dissipate, as if at any moment, Vickie would look over at him in horror, screaming that he was dematerializing.

"Hey, you okay?" she said, taking his hand in hers, making him nearly solid again.

He stretched a weak smile over his discomfort, feeling the blood slowly creep back into his extremities, sounds returning—the buzz of the neon sign, the discordant rush of the espresso machine behind him in the cafe. He brought his eyes to Vickie; she seemed so real it made him dizzy, as if he could suddenly feel the rotation of the earth, his molecules struggling to remain intact. His mind was not constructed for such leaps from logic. Vickie's reality was winning the battle against rational thought. But it wasn't Vickie's reality after all, or so it seemed now to Kenny—it was *his*. His reality, his creation, a construct of his mind, she was just in it, but that wasn't correct either. All the others, who populated the streets, who worked in the buildings and drove the cars, were, according to Falco, dead. And Francine? Kenny barely knew her; she had no purchase in his sphere of reality. Falco had told Kenny many things earlier that evening, most of it sounding like gibberish. Then Falco said something to Kenny that upon first hearing sounded as though it made sense, but under further scrutiny, the concept seemed to fall apart, at least in Kenny's mind. "When faced with the unknowable," Falco had told him, "...we rush to introduce an explanation that, while feeble and flawed, at least satisfies some need within us to hold the world intact. When you do that, Sport, *rush to introduce an explanation,* and you will, at least make it one that entertains you."

"I have to go," Kenny said, shooting up from the table.

Vickie stood stiffly, sliding her jacket from the back of the chair and pulling herself into it. "You mean back to the hotel? Don't you want to see the Flanders Medical Assistance Center first? With your knowledge of computers and software, I think you'll be impressed..."

Kenny, without a word, turned toward the door of the coffee shop, purposely keeping his attention away from the bold, glowing letters over the entrance of the six-story building, as if merely glancing at it would turn him to stone.

When they got back to the hotel, Kenny tried to sit and watch television with Vickie, attempting to normalize the events of the evening, but his mind was unruly, jouncing about like a car with square wheels, all the machinery in his chest shaking and threatening to fly apart.

"I have to go, Vickie," he said, bolting up to grab his jacket. She came over as he was zipping it up. Then, bringing his eyes to hers: "I'm sorry. I just have to go..."

She smiled and kissed him, holding her lips to his, then drew back slowly, her smile returning. "I loved seeing you," she said, warmly. "It was so wonderful." Her statement was strangely free of animosity or disappointment. "I love you, Kenny."

Kenny nodded, anguished, unable to continue. His smile, forced and unnatural, probably came out like a grin, or worse, a grimace. He wanted to tell her he loved her too, but couldn't, suddenly unsure how he could get back to his reality. In that moment, he saw the door to the *Anything* room, like an apparition, and looked at Vickie, wondering if she could see it too. It was obvious she couldn't, which further flummoxed him.

"Goodbye," he said, rushing toward the door, and through it, looking back, watching Vickie walk across the hotel room in her bare feet, then stretch out on the bed. Kenny carefully—unable to stop staring at her, wondering if Vickie even questioned where he had just gone— pushed the door shut, as if a wrong move in this moment could result in dire consequences, the light sucking back through the narrow opening until it vanished completely. He locked the door and placed the key on the door frame above it, then walked to the kitchen. Kenny had no idea what time it was. With it now dark outside, he fully expected Falco to be seated at the kitchen table. But the house was quiet, the kitchen clean, dishes stacked in the drainer, already dry.

"Where were you?" a woman's voice asked.

Kenny startled, his heart thumping wildly, like a bird trying to break free, slamming against his ribs. Beth, who appeared to have been asleep, slowly rose up from the futon, her eyes half-lidded. She yawned, covering her mouth, then, a moment later, bringing her drowsy eyes to meet his, said, "I've been down here for a couple of hours waiting for you. I saw your car, so I figured… you know…" She yawned again, her eyes fluttering at the edge of sleep.

Kenny looked at the clock on the stove. Two in the morning. How was that possible?

"How did you get down here?" Kenny asked.

Beth waved her hand toward him, her head turned away as if battling another yawn, then, after succumbing, stretched her eyes open. "My mom's car," she said. "After today, I think my mom would let me have anything I wanted." Then, after rubbing her eyes trying to come fully awake. "I could have probably driven your dad's Harley and she wouldn't have said a thing!"

"Rough, huh? Today?" Kenny said, starting to feel the gyro inside normalizing, as if the past several hours hadn't happened.

Beth pointed at his cheek, smiling fiendishly. "You've been busy," she said, a bit snarky.

He rubbed his cheek, his fingertips coming away smudged with lipstick. He shook his head; no point trying to explain. "You ready to go home?" he said.

"Yeah." She sat fully upright, placing her bare feet on the coffee table. "Do you see my sandals?"

Her feet reminded him of Vickie, her toes plowing softly through the deep pile of the hotel carpet. "Here." He walked over to the door, bringing back her shoes.

"Thanks." She slipped them on, fastening the straps. "How about we leave the Taurus down here and you drive us home in the Beemer. I'm wasted."

"Are you stoned?"

"Maybe a little. Tarantula was by earlier…" She grinned, her eyes on her toes. "That guy walks around like he's stoned even when he's cold sober." Then, after a moment's thought: "He should probably avoid drugs all together." She laughed a little, then stood abruptly, and turned to Kenny. "Let's hit the road, Big Brother."

Kenny walked her out to the car, making sure to lock the front door behind him, the night beginning to swirl again, the otherworldliness of it, detached from any version of the reality he was familiar with. He opened her door and she got in, then closed it and walked to his side. After starting the engine, he backed out slowly. Before they got to the highway, Beth was asleep again, and Kenny, hoping to hear how the trial had gone, was actually glad to have this time to himself, even as confusing and disorienting as it was.

Chapter Forty-Six

If Falco was to be believed, there was no point in looking for his father—Kenny knew where Martin was, yet, with no way to explain it to Janelle or Beth, he could do nothing but keep pretending to look. And keep lying.

It had been nearly two weeks since he arrived in St. Louis, and every day Janelle and Beth attended the trial, Kenny feigned searching for his father, reporting back in the evenings that he'd had no luck so far. Most days he spent drinking coffee in small, neighborhood bistros, scouring want ads, looking for an IT job, and had gone on several interviews, though no takers yet.

When Kenny explained to his employer in Newark that he may be stuck in St. Louis for several weeks looking into his father's disappearance, his supervisor, after relaying his deepest sympathies, regretted they'd have to replace him. Kenny apologized, and said he understood, and was relieved in some ways; he really didn't want to go back anyway, except for Michael, and Elaine. He and Elaine spoke on the phone several times since Kenny flew out to St. Louis, Elaine asking if he was coming back to New Jersey, that she had heard he quit his job, wanting to know where their marriage stood, trying delicately to broach the subject of Vickie, suggesting in a roundabout way that since she, Vickie, was out of the picture, Kenny might now be clearer on what he needed in his life, what he wanted. Elaine even suggested that she might be open to moving to St. Louis, that it would be fun to be near Janelle and Beth, especially since they'd gotten along so well.

"This would be the time for us to make such a move, Kenny," Elaine had said. "Before Michael starts school. Maybe even before the baby is born."

That would be in the next two months. Was that even possible? Could Elaine find a place in St. Louis in the upcoming weeks she felt comfortable enough with to leave Jersey behind, as well as her job, her friends at work, Michael's child care, which she had researched for weeks? "It's not like this is the only real estate job in the country," she'd said to him, almost flippantly. "St. Louis seemed to have a healthy supply of houses to move!" Then, after a beat or two: "And I'll find a nice preschool for Michael."

Elaine had changed, her entire central nervous system rewired, or so it seemed to Kenny. Her willingness to uproot everything and move a thousand miles across the country, just to be a family again, took Kenny by surprise, and made him feel guiltier than ever.

Then there was Vickie.

Though Elaine figured Vickie to be out of Kenny's life forever, as had Kenny, Vickie had become once again a joyous but prickly presence in his reality. He hadn't been back to the bungalow in over a week, not since his initial journey into Vickie's domain, or whatever it was; Kenny had yet to introduce an explanation that had meaning for him, much less one that *entertained*, whatever Falco had meant by that. But Kenny planned to go back. Soon. Maybe even later today, still grappling with his hesitancy. It had been great hearing Elaine's voice, and Kenny wished she'd been able to put Michael on the line during their last call, but Michael had been asleep, battling some kind of cold or something. And Kenny was missing it all. And just as he'd veered his thoughts back onto Elaine's highway, Vickie became a side road he couldn't avoid. The push and pull was maddening, debilitating.

A few days after his last conversation with Elaine, Kenny was invited for a second interview with an investment firm on the Riverfront, not far from where his dad had worked at Petro. Kenny loved that area, the smell of the river, the old newness of the landing; old factories transformed into funky upscale offices, old riverboats reshaped into shiny, bustling casinos. Steel and glass rising above a jetty of period cobblestone and rusted mooring bollards, the mingled pong of dead fish, grilled kabobs, perfume and exhaust. Over two-hundred years of history, and a muddy, eddy-swirled river that never stopped rushing toward the Gulf. Kenny loved St. Louis, and was glad to be back.

The second interview seemed to go well, the woman telling him that the firm had a few other candidates they were considering, but confided that he, Kenny, topped the list. After leaving the interview, Kenny strolled along the cobblestone levee watching the river slip past, thinking about his life, but more pointedly, about Vickie. He wanted to tell her that he was in a good position to land a high-paying position at a prestigious new firm, though most likely, the news would mean nothing to her.

That evening, Kenny, Janelle and Beth went out to dinner, Kenny telling them about his job interview, excited that he might know some-thing as soon as next week. Beth smiled and told him that was great, that she didn't even know he'd been considering moving to St. Louis.

"I've been thinking about moving back ever since I graduated from Rutgers," he said, looking at Beth, wondering how she felt about his news, then over at Janelle, who chewed her food solemnly.

"What about Elaine and Michael?" Janelle finally said, not both-ering to mask her brusque tone. The comment took Kenny by surprise, though it probably shouldn't have. Maybe it was the anger she'd spoken the words with that had been unsettling. Beth looked down at her plate, then over at her mother, giving her a non-committal glance.

"We're talking," Kenny said, trying to remain upbeat. "They may be moving here… to St. Louis…"

Janelle, her head hung, shifted her eyes upward, like a bull about to charge. "Really?" Janelle stated flatly. "She didn't say anything to me about it and I talked with her yesterday."

"Mom…"

"And what's with the new job interview?" Janelle said. "I thought you were supposed to be finding your father?"

"Mom… let's don't—"

"No, Beth!" Janelle aimed her fury at her daughter. "No, let's do get into it. While you and I are sitting in that damn courtroom all day, where is Martin? Where is—?"

"I told Kenny not to come," Beth said, making her eyes firm. "I didn't want him in the courtroom. I was just… just too ashamed…"

"Ashamed! Sweetheart, you have nothing to be ashamed about!" Janelle's eyes turned damp and shiny, her chin beginning to quaver. "Martin should be ashamed for not being here to support you! And Kenny, with his new job interview, should be embarrassed for thinking only of himself, abandoning his family in New Jersey. And your ridiculous, stupid father, he should be ashamed for putting us through this outrageous trial in the first place! No, dear, you have nothing to be ashamed of… you… you…" Touching Beth's wrist, Janelle was unable to speak, her head lolling back and forth, tears rolling down her cheeks. She stood and dropped her napkin on the table, then huffed from the restaurant without a word. Kenny and Beth sat quietly, looking at each other, waiting for the charged air to lose some of its amperage. Heads which had turned toward the commotion, were now reset back to their original position, people eating, conversing, sipping wine, a pleasant calm settling over the room again.

Beth shook her head, her hands in her lap, then brought her eyes up to meet Kenny's. "I am so sorry," Beth said. "Mom didn't mean any of that. I know she didn't. She's going to feel horrible she said those things."

"She's right, though," Kenny said, feeling more mortified than ever. "My dad should be here. And I should be in New Jersey with Elaine and Michael, and—"

Beth took hold of his arm and squeezed gently, saying, "Stop. Please," as if in pain. Her eyes red, at the edge of tears, she loosened her grip and gently caressed his skin with her fingertips. "No one can fix what's happening. And if anyone's responsible for this colossal mess, it's my dad. Not you. Not Martin." Then, after sniffing and running the edge of her finger under her nose, said, "I don't blame Martin for getting out of the way during this trial. I don't want to be in that stupid courtroom day after day, so why would Martin want to. And yours and Elaine's problems are your own, and none of my mom's business to judge or accuse. And I am so sorry that she doesn't know about Vickie, and your loss, even though I know she wouldn't understand anyway…" Beth released his arm and picked up her fork, then held it suspended over her plate.

"I don't want you to go..." Beth said, tearing up again, "but maybe you should head back to Jersey, get away from all this crap." Beth put her fork down and furtively wiped her eyes, working desperately not to build on the scene her mother had started. After a few moments, she turned to Kenny. "Can I come to your room tonight?" she whispered.

Kenny didn't know what to say, his insides doing somersaults, the compass in his head spinning out of control. "I need to go to Kansas City for a few days," Kenny said, knowing that even if Beth knew he was lying, she'd accept it and never question him on it. "My dad has relatives in KC... He could be there... Plus, I need some time to think..."

Beth smiled and touched his arm, then stood and picked up the leatherette binder with the check.

"No, let me get that," Kenny said.

"I have my mom's card," she said, smiling sadly, but lovingly. "We'll get this. Really." Beth held the binder, then leaned over and kissed Kenny on the lips, slowly drawing back after a few seconds. Then added: "Meet you in the car, okay. I'll drive home if you don't mind."

Kenny watched her walk to the front register and pay the bill. He waited, then followed her out. The BMW's engine was running, Janelle seated in the backseat, Beth behind the wheel.

"Sure you don't want to sit up front with Beth?" Kenny said, opening the front door.

"No, Kenny," she said, her tone more conciliatory. "Please, just get in."

As Beth pulled from the parking lot, Janelle spoke into the thick silence. "I'm really sorry about before," she said, clearing her throat. "It has been so stressful lately. I shouldn't have taken it out on you..."

Kenny wasn't sure what to say, then: "You were right, though. My dad could have been here for the trial... and... I should probably—"

"No, Kenny," Janelle said. "Your situation with Elaine, whatever it is, is hard enough without my two-cents worth of judgmental witchery. I feel terrible. I hope you'll forgive me."

They rode in silence, music on the radio playing softly into the hum of the highway, when Kenny said, "Would ice cream help get us through these difficult times?" He wasn't sure if the joke was ill-timed and stupid, but Beth smiled, switching on her turn signal.

"I know just the place," she said. "Frozen custard, Mom?"

"Sure, baby. That's sounds good."

A few moments later, Kenny felt Janelle's fingers on his shoulder. She squeezed him gently from the back seat, then said, "I'm glad you're here."

"Me too," he said.

Chapter Forty-Seven

He felt terrible lying to Janelle and Beth, but was fairly certain Beth knew he wasn't headed for Kansas City. Beth walked him out to his dad's Taurus carrying a care package of homemade cookies —that her mother had made—and a sandwich for the trip. "What is that, about a five-hour drive?" she asked, smirking, her eyes slowly rolling up. "Just be careful, okay. With those *relatives* from Kansas City."

Kenny hugged her to him and didn't want to let her go.

"I'll be back in a week or so, maybe less," he said, drawing back, though not releasing her hands, like teenagers on a first date.

"You don't have to report to me," she said. "Just make sure you come back, okay."

He got in the car and rolled down the window. "I hope the trial is over soon," he said, the comment sounding lame. She had said it might only last another few days, and he did want it to end for her, but felt stupid saying it, as though it were an inconvenience to him. "You know what I mean..."

"Yeah, don't sweat it," she said. "I'll miss you Big Brother."

"I'll miss you too, Beth."

He was easing backward down the driveway, twisted in the seat, when Beth hurried up next to the driver's side window. He glimpsed her from the margin of his vision and stopped the car. "What's wrong?" he said.

She regarded him for several seconds, her expression blank, then said, "You know where your dad is, don't you?"

Heat wrinkled up under his shirt along the skin of his back. He wanted to give her something other than lies. "Why do you think that?"

"Because at the restaurant, you told me that my mom was right, and that your dad should be here." Beth waited, watching his eyes. "It seems odd to pass judgement on your dad, saying he *should* be here, if you had even an inkling that he could be hurt... or worse. It feels like you knew Martin made the choice to leave..."

Kenny opened his mouth to speak, but could say nothing, though he wanted to tell her so much. He wanted to tell her about the Flanders Medical Assistance Center, how his idea had become a reality, that he couldn't wait to tour the facility, to see if it functioned just as he'd envisioned. He wanted to take her there, show her what he could only try to make her see through her imagination. He wanted to tell her about the *Anything* room, that his father was living with his deceased mother, that Vickie was also there, that she still loved him, that he still loved her, that he had never been so confused in all his life as he was right now...

"You don't have to explain," Beth said. "Just be careful, okay." She kissed him on the lips, then turned and hurried up the driveway, not looking back, disappearing into the house like a fleeting thought.

Kenny arrived at the bungalow just before lunch, snacking on the cookies Beth had packed for his drive, figuring to stow the sandwich in the fridge. He hoped to avoid Falco if possible, gathering up some things and his duffle bag from the back seat of the Taurus, unsure if he'd be able to take his stuff into Vickie's world. It was worth a try. He knocked on the front door, waited, then knocked again. He tried the knob; locked. He stretched to look over the edge of the concrete, see if he could spot the faux stone with the key in it. Falco said it was brown. Kenny hopped down off the porch and turned over a few rocks, looking for a secret compartment, finally finding the one with the key.

Once inside the bungalow, he called out to Falco, just in case, then stuck the sandwich in the refrigerator. A faint judder shook through his chest, erupting soundlessly behind his ribs. Nerves, he figured, glancing toward the doorway of the *Anything* room, wondering if it would work. During the drive down to the city, Kenny's mind was hounded by thoughts of delirium, psychotic breaks with reality, mental disorders and schisms, questioning his own sanity, as well as Falco's.

Kenny entered the *Anything* room, his eyes fixed on the plain wooden door at the back—the dark wood rectangle hard against the soft white walls, like a marker, a monolith, no hint of light behind it.

He slung the duffle bag strap over his shoulder and approached the door, feeling a sudden oily fatigue in his legs, his muscles doughy, insubstantial. He reached his hand toward the knob, his fingers closing on the smooth metal object, the world slowing on its axis, an uncomfortable elasticity of Time he could feel in his veins, making him queasy, the pressure palpable, electric. His fingers tightened on the cold knob and he turned it, expecting it to be locked, but it wasn't. As he drew the door open, stepping back with it, light flooded from the gap, filling the room, even the corners and edges that should have been in shadow; no discernible source of the dazzling brilliance rushing past him, circling him like a vortex, images coming into focus, a room, a hotel room, a person seated at the desk, a woman in a burgundy dress, barefoot, Vickie, leaning forward, reading a book, unaware of Kenny's presence.

He stepped into the light, a frenetic current swirling round him like the eddy of a river. His breath caught and he moved forward, like walking through syrup at first, as if this reality had density, requiring penetration, a sensation he wasn't aware of the first time he was here. This time, though, he was hyper-alert, more mindful of this extraordinary ether, and just as he breached, Vickie looked up, a smile breaking across her face as she jumped up to meet him, taking him in her arms, kissing him passionately, then drawing back to take a loving inventory of his hands, his arms, every feature of his face, as if he were a returning soldier, as if she hadn't seen him in months.

"I'm so glad you're here," she said, her eyes bright, sparkling, as if amazed.

Kenny could never quite anticipate the euphoric intoxication, like a powerful potion, that surged through him when she smiled, as if witnessing it for the first time, as if he had never experienced the sensation of enchantment before. He melted, pulling her to his chest, breathing in the fragrance of her hair, taking her into his lungs, holding her like a prisoner.

"Do you know what the best day of my life was?" she said, her head resting against his chest.

He couldn't imagine one better than this.

"The night of the reunion," she said, squeezing him closer. "Making love in your car, all of humanity a million miles away, the universe ours alone, every star in the sky shining just for us."

The warmth and intimacy of just a second ago drained from Kenny's body, a sickening unease filling the vacuum left behind. In that moment, something inside him, some life-sustaining components went out of sync, lurching and swaying, the system breaking down. She shouldn't have knowledge of that night, Kenny thought, waves of shock pulsing through him, but she does, confusing him further about the rules of her paradigm. He could have sworn that Falco had told him that the point in time when he met up with whomever he planned to connect with was crucial, that *Time* would begin at that point, sometimes to the exclusion of any personal history. "Will she remember me then?" Kenny had asked Falco, concerned and bewildered. "As long as you knew each other at that point in time before she died, then yes. Otherwise, you'll be strangers." But Time wasn't beginning at her visit to Newark, obviously, the realization baffling. Time, in this reality, Kenny quietly pondered, wasn't linear. It wasn't even *Time*, at least as he knew it. No, this was something far more perplexing, foreign, unpredictable, and the floor beneath his feet started to crumble, his architecture fragile, unmoored, the walls rushing away, a silent, sentient darkness closing around him, enveloping him.

"Kenny. Kenny, are you okay?" Vickie said, kneeling on the floor beside him, tapping him gently on the cheek.

Vickie's words were the first things to breach the void, her features rising slowly to focus, the room around her slowly creating itself from nothing, spreading outward until it filled the entirety of his vision. In that moment he became aware of the rapid thumping in his chest, the tightness of his lungs.

"Breathe, Kenny," she said, slapping him harder this time. He gulped at the air like a newborn, like a creature that had crawled out of the ocean to experience oxygen for the first time. She leaned over him, pressing her lips to his forehead, the warmth penetrating his skin, past his skull, dispersing slowly through his body.

Kenny sat up, disoriented at first, coming back slowly from a dark, shapeless void. He sat a few more minutes, Vickie talking, her words smeared together with a dampened underwater quality, her meaning unintelligible, gradually becoming sharper, more distinct, then: "What happened?" she said, the question coming at him like a siren. "One minute you were holding me, then you just, like, melted to the floor..."

"I'm sorry," he said, struggling to get to his feet. She held his arm until he regained his balance. Then, with gravity restored, the blood pumping through his brain again: "That was weird. I've never fainted before..."

"Let's get out of this room," she said. "It's stuffy in here."

"Yeah, sure," he said, still getting his bearings.

The night air seemed to calm him, though he was shocked it was night already, but said nothing, realizing if he was going to survive in Vickie's world, he had to accept this strange domain with all its idiosyncrasies, or he'd go mad trying to figure it out.

"Let's get coffee," she said. "I know it's late, but we don't have to be anywhere tomorrow, right?"

"Sounds good," Kenny said. "How about that place near Flanders Medical Assistance Center?"

"What place?"

Kenny looked at her, as if she were kidding, but it was clear she wasn't. "Don't you remember, we were having coffee by the window and—" He broke off the explanation when her features seemed to constrict. Then: "There's a coffee shop across from Flanders Medical Assistance Center. Do you know it?"

Vickie shook her head. "Have you gone to Flanders Medical Assistance Center before?"

"No, I thought maybe we could sometime."

"Sure!" she said. "It is an amazing place. I think you'll especially love it, you know, with all your computer knowledge..."

"Maybe tomorrow," Kenny said.

"Why not tonight? Like, right now?"

"It's late. Will it even be open?"

Vickie laughed. "Wow, you really aren't from around here, are you!"

Kenny knew she was joking about him being a stranger, but there was an off-putting awareness to her statement, as if she *knew* on some level that he was an interloper in her world, while not consciously certain she knew it. This place had a dizzying effect on Kenny's psyche, as if his mind kept constantly trying to tune itself to the odd elements of this existence.

"It's open all the time... anytime! Twenty-four-seven! That's one reason it's so awesome. Come on, let's go now." She grabbed his arm and practically dragged him toward the rather plain building.

They entered through glass and steel revolving doors, into an artful foyer filled with sculpture and pottery, warm and reassuring tones, with a softness that seemed to exude health itself. They took the elevator to the sixth floor.

"Why the sixth floor?" Kenny asked, wondering how different this place would be from what he had imagined. He had never seen it as needing six floors, but then, he hadn't puzzled that detail out in his head before, painting his vision with very broad strokes as far as the interior was concerned.

"No reason," she said. "All the floors are the same, I think. I've never been to the sixth floor, though."

When they stepped off the elevator, it seemed at first as though they had stepped outside, until they both realized that most of the floor was enclosed by a glass dome.

"Wow, this is more amazing than I ever realized," Vickie said.

Kenny let his eyes rove the spaciousness of the rotunda, almost as if it weren't enclosed at all, a series of plain doors circling at the center of the enclosure. "What are those?" Kenny asked.

"Those are examination rooms," Vickie said. "I guess that's what you'd call them. Come on." Kenny fell in behind her, surprised by his own imagined innovation, never quite envisioning the space to have the mingled ambience of art and spirit, an airy design which produced a welcome calming effect.

Vickie walked up and opened the door, then went in, looking back to make sure he followed. Kenny stopped behind her and closed the door.

"Welcome, Ms. Kramer, how are you feeling today?" The female voice was soothing, mellow, with none of that mechanical tonality associated with computerized vocalization.

"Very well, this is my friend—"

"Hello, Mr. Moffett," the voice said. "This is your first time with us, isn't it, Kenny?"

Kenny could only nod, the actuality of the facility surpassing his wildest expectations.

"Well, would you like to go first, Vickie?" the voice said.

"Is Curly here?" Vickie asked.

"By all means," the voice said, changing to a man's voice when it spoke. "Hello, Vickie. It's been almost a year! You must be doing very well."

"I am," she said, stepping into a cylindrical booth, the door closing around her, almost like a vertical MRI machine, except that her face and head remained completely exposed above the enclosure; none of the claustrophobic characteristics of the magnetic imaging equipment Kenny was familiar with. This was perfect, Kenny thought, bringing him nearly to tears. Beth was suddenly in his head; he wanted to bring her here to see his most amazing vision, one that he had only shared with her. Not even Elaine, or his dad, knew of his dream.

The room was silent, lights scanning Vickie, her body fully clothed. She even talked to Kenny while she was being scanned. It was then Kenny noticed the music playing in the background, and the artwork on the walls, depictions of the cosmos, planets and quasars, waterfalls and forests, mountains and sunsets, images almost magically morphing into new images, three dimensional images that appeared to spill beyond the limits of their frames.

"Well, Vickie, it would seem congratulations are in order," the voice said when the scanning ended.

"Healthy as a newborn colt, right?" Vickie said, exiting the round enclosure, smiling, giving Kenny her warm eyes.

"Well," the man's heartened voice said. "Newborn is a good way to describe your health, Vickie... you're pregnant!"

The color drained from her face. "Pregnant?"

"Just a few weeks, but yes... would you like to know the sex of your child?"

"Uh…" She glanced at Kenny, her face ashen. "I, uh… I don't think I could be pregnant, Curly," she said to the room. "Could it possibly be a mistake?"

"No… is there a problem?" Curly said, with concern in his voice. "You have nothing to worry about. It's early, but the fetus is perfect. I performed enzyme and chromosome screenings, as well as DNA analysis. Even if we found some abnormality, we'd fix it. It wouldn't be a problem; nothing to be concerned about."

"Yes, of course, Curly," Vickie said, the color absent from her face. "Thanks, we're going to go." Vickie headed for the door.

"Would you like a checkup, Kenny?" Curly said.

"No. But thanks, Curly," he said, following Vickie to the elevators. They rode to the ground floor in silence. Vickie turned back toward the hotel. Kenny caught her arm. "Coffee?"

She brightened, as if awakening from a daydream. "Yeah, wow, what was I thinking? Absolutely." She wrapped her arm through Kenny's as they crossed over to the coffee shop.

"Hey, let's sit outside, okay?" she said, finally herself again, her complexion glowing, full of life.

They went in to order, then waited, Kenny pensive and introspective wondering how Vickie could be pregnant, more confused than ever. After the barista placed their drinks on the counter, Kenny grabbed them and carried them to a table outside. They sat, unspeaking, Vickie testing the temperature of her coffee by sipping it. Kenny, unsure what to say, was eventually salvaged from his dismay when she spoke first.

"It's amazing, isn't it!" she said, smiling, reaching across the table to hold the tips of his fingers.

Kenny was dumbstruck, unable to muster even the lightest spark of excitement over Vickie's pregnancy. He couldn't even understand how that could be possible; she's dead! How can the dead bring new life into the world? Any world? Even a world lacking logic and discernible guidelines?

"Don't you think so?" she said, bringing both of her hands to his.

"What are you talking about?" Kenny said, bristling, annoyed with her Polly Anna attitude.

"The Flanders Medical Assistance Center," she said. "Didn't you find it amazing?"

He had even felt intoxicated by its profound similarity to his own dream, and the impossibility of it, how the facility transcended current technology, prevailing belief systems as well as politics, even reaching beyond the societal ills of greed and power. It was staggering, the implications, how easily it had assimilated into the culture, until *Curly's* pronouncement that Vickie was pregnant. That's when the gears stopped, the lights flickered, and everything turned to smoke and ash.

"How do you even know so much about the place?" Kenny asked, with a trace of antagonism. "You've been in Newark, what, two days?"

Vickie's expression darkened, like a fortune teller who had foreseen a terrible event. "There's one in St. Louis," she said, calmly, but with reserve. "That's where the first one was built. Now they're all over the country." Then, after trying to regain her smile: "What's wrong, Kenny? You seem angry?"

"No, not angry, just..." Kenny wasn't angry, exactly, but he was uncomfortable, baffled by the idea of this pregnancy. The thought of raising children with Vickie was something he'd considered often, even in high school, had seen himself and Vickie growing into a family together, imagined how it would feel to go to the park, celebrate holidays, painting the children's rooms, his mind playing through decades of living with this incredible woman, watching their children grow up, going off to school, graduating, their children getting married themselves, having grandchildren—and Kenny had found nothing but joy and pleasure in his journey into their potential future together. Nevertheless, this situation was something altogether different, beyond different, perplexing, untenable, unnatural...

"This is about the baby, isn't it?" Vickie said, as if they'd already discussed her pregnancy, but Kenny, somehow, hadn't been present for their previous conversations.

"Aren't you concerned?" Kenny said, thinking about Elaine, his daughter Elaine was carrying in her stomach, his son, Michael, the family he already had in his world, the one that could be living with him in St. Louis in a matter of weeks. His chest tightened, and it was becoming harder to breathe. He tried to calm his mind, his thoughts unspooling, degrading into unintelligible fragments, drifting out of reach, new thoughts spilling forth, unmanageable as agitated molecules.

"Not really, but I can see you are," she said. "If this isn't something you want in your life right now, I totally understand..."

"You *understand?* I don't get it! You're pregnant! That doesn't bother you?"

Vickie smiled, maybe a bit confused by his reaction. "No, Kenny, it doesn't. I love you. I think it's the greatest thing that could have happened. But I know you have other commitments..."

This threw him completely. Did she know about Elaine? Michael? What the hell was going on? "I have to go," he said, hating that he was gruff, unable to draw upon even one extra ounce of tolerance and patience.

After they walked nearly a block, she wound her arm through his and rested her head against his shoulder. He had planned to stay a week, maybe longer; now he couldn't stay another second. When they got to the hotel, he started putting his things into his duffle bag. She went in to brush her teeth. When she came out, he was standing near the hotel door, though that wasn't the exit he was going to use. The *Anything* room door floated near it, like some nefarious omen, waiting.

When she smiled, her teeth glistened like a new day. Buoyant, seemingly light as air, she drew closer to him and took him in her arms, resting her head against his chest.

"Don't worry about anything," she said softly, Kenny feeling her words penetrate his skin, echoing in the hollow of his chest. "I love you so much, Kenny. Everything's going to be fine. Really." She drew back and kissed him on the lips, holding the embrace for several seconds before easing away, her smile never dimming. He tried to smile, but turned away before he could manage it, then disappeared through his private doorway, glancing back one time to see Vickie walking back into the room. When Kenny was safely back in his world, he slid the door shut, extinguishing the radiant light, the way a storm cloud darkens a shining day.

Conflicted didn't come close to describing his state of mind. Wrecked, was more accurate. Mangled. Butchered. Kenny stared a long time at the door, knowing he could open it back up, join Vickie in her hotel room, as if nothing before had happened. He was sure of it. What he wasn't sure of, was, if she would still be pregnant. He sighed, his legs slowly becoming solid, stronger. He wanted to get back to Beth's house, hear Beth's voice. Maybe he could explain some of this to her, but how? Embarrassment shifted through him like a fever when he realized what he was considering. Unloading on a teenager in the middle of a trial, her father's fate hanging in the balance, her own finger on the scales? *Jeez, Kenny, grow the fuck up!* In that moment, Kenny despised himself for even contemplating such a stupid notion.

Almost to the front door of the bungalow, Kenny stopped when someone spoke to him. He spun around to see a stranger sitting up on the futon, a bedraggled bum with a scraggly beard and shabby clothes. The man looked as if he hadn't bathed in weeks. At first Kenny thought he might be one of Geronimo's biker friends. The guy didn't look dangerous, but he smelled, his eyes so ravaged they looked like blood-filled holes.

"What are you doing here?" Kenny said, holding onto the front door knob in case this guy became animated, though it seemed unlikely.

"Kenny," the man said, his mouth misshapen, rough, as if he'd forgotten how to smile but was trying. "You look good, Son..."

Chapter Forty-Eight

K enny helped his dad get cleaned up, then took him to dinner, checked into a hotel, his father staring straight ahead, seemingly mute. A few times Kenny looked over at him; Martin's tear-damaged eyes glinting like broken glass, red and bruised, as if crying had become his new hobby.

"Dad," Kenny said, reaching over to comfort him. Martin, lifeless as a lamp, sat on the edge of the bed, oblivious to anything other than some drama playing inside his head. "Do you want to talk about what happened?" Kenny asked when Martin didn't respond to touch.

"I'm so sorry, Kenny," he said, clearly contrite. "I shouldn't have just left... it was selfish..." Martin's face darkened unnaturally, as if a part of him hadn't returned from his misadventure, or the memory of it was too painful to keep remembering. His head turned slowly toward Kenny, as if not under his own command, his eyes looking at nothing, his mouth sagging at the corners as though the tendons had become impaired. It was painful to regard his father in this new state, the gray, putty pallor of his skin, the looseness of his flesh, as though his muscles had turned to jelly.

"Get some sleep, okay," Kenny said, helping him under the covers, getting the pillow beneath his head. Martin stared at the ceiling, his eyes shiny as chrome. Kenny had to look away, situating himself in the other bed across from his father's. Maybe they could talk in the morning, after a good night's sleep, and Martin would be more communicable. Right now, his father looked like a mental patient whose prognosis wasn't good. Kenny had so many questions, but they could wait, they'd have to, until Martin found his mind again.

In the morning not much had changed. Kenny, lying awake, listened to the toilet flush, the bathroom door open. Martin shuffled out like some prehistoric creature and dragged himself across the hotel room, then dug back under the covers, a mole shunning light. Kenny rolled his head to the side and could see only a squatty lump of blankets, no movement, no sound, no sign of human life in the other bed.

After dressing, Kenny started the coffee maker in the room, then rode the elevator to the lobby and brought back a few Danish rolls, two paper plates and utensils. Martin hadn't moved, still buried in a hummock of blankets. Kenny thought the smell of coffee might roust his father, but Martin seemed vulcanized against the outside world, living entirely in his mind now. Was that the effect the *Anything* room portal had on its visitors? Falco had issued lots of warnings, but never mentioned anything about madness.

Kenny sat at the desk, nibbling on a Danish roll and thinking about Vickie, missing her, feeling like an ass about how he'd reacted to her pregnancy. At moments like this, Kenny was able to push away the impossibility of Vickie's universe and could process events through normal filters, could measure his reactions against a landscape of logic and reason. Then, without warning, the veil of credibility came crashing down, his mind tossed and rolled like a small boat caught in a vast, violent sea, lost in a storm of imponderables and muddle. Kenny's stomach clenched. He set the pastry down on the paper plate and looked over at his father's bed, at the mounded cocoon of blankets and sheets. As if stirred by Kenny's observation, the mound moved, like the awakening of a long-dead mummy; Kenny watched his father unearth himself from the curious grave. Martin sat up and looked around, his sleep-tousled hair sticking out like ruffled feathers, a fledgling in a strange new world.

"Kenny?" Martin said, then shifted his attention to the hotel room, swiveling to survey the space before bringing his attention back to his son. "Kenny, what are we doing here?"

Kenny said, "Trying to regroup." He poured coffee into a Styrofoam cup, then brought it over to his dad. Then: "I have some Danish here, if you're hungry."

Martin took the coffee and sipped it, his mind finally awakening to the present.

"How long were you at the bungalow?" Kenny asked, picking up his pastry and nibbling at the edge, still uncertain if his stomach was ready for food.

Holding the coffee in his left hand, Martin used his fingers like a thresher across his scalp, scrubbing his hand back and forth through his hair to bring himself more fully into the world. Then, after giving thought to Kenny's question, said, "I don't know... three days, maybe a week... I've lost all track of time..."

Kenny was confused. How was that even possible? Kenny hadn't been with Vickie for even a full day, much less a week! Without further consideration, Kenny dropped the conundrum like a hot coal, unwilling to keep beating his mind against the rock of rationality. Just accept the impossible, Falco had said, or something to that effect, or you'll make yourself crazy. Kenny looked over at his dad again; Martin's eyes far away, uncoupled from his brain, his mind adrift, his eyes unmoving.

After several minutes, Martin asked if there was anything to eat. Kenny brought him a pastry on a paper plate, then went back to the desk and sat down. Martin ate like a man who suddenly remembered he had an appetite. Kenny brought him the last one and Martin devoured it in four bites, then got up to use the bathroom. When Martin returned, he refilled his coffee cup and went over and slid his legs under the covers.

After a few minutes of silence, Martin, articulate as a minister, said, "I know you have a lot of questions... and I have a lot for you, but I need to get my motorcycle from Janelle's house."

Chapter Forty-Nine

Martin wanted to know everything that had happened after he'd left, glad that Kenny wasn't pummeling him with questions about where he'd been. How could Martin explain the portal to Kenny, or Janelle, anyone, for that matter? Over the past several days, before Kenny had rescued him from the bungalow, Martin, during his more lucid moments, had been trying to reconstruct a feasible explanation while ignoring the implausible facts, tiptoeing a tightrope between what Janelle would never believe and what she'd accept. Martin wanted to focus on the present, the future, see if anything was salvageable from his and Janelle's marriage. It was selfish, he knew, to even entertain a desire for such a reunion, not to mention foolhardy to think she'd ever take him back, especially since he couldn't conjure even the barest of justifications for his absence. But he was going to try. Had to move forward. Pin his hopes on anything but the past, still unable to parse how Noreen had broken his heart. Falco had told him the portal could be cruel; nevertheless, Martin, ignoring Falco's warnings, was certain he could beat the odds—their love, Noreen's and his, was indestructible, could only be vanquished by death, and not even death. For eleven years after she was killed, he'd never stop loving her. Even now, Martin had a hard time admitting that he'd been wrong about their love, seeing a side of Noreen for the first time he'd believed impossible.

"What do you want to do if Janelle and Beth are home?" Kenny said, pulling into the subdivision.

"You thought they were still attending the trial, right?" Martin said, antsy, his heart hammering as they got closer. He needed to get his motorcycle and retreat, feeling he would get one chance to speak to Janelle, and he didn't want to blow it.

"Yeah, but..." Kenny said. "It could have ended already."

Martin looked over at his son, unsure why Kenny was so uncertain about everything; not so much from what he was saying, but the hesitancy in his voice.

"You could just drop me off and take the Taurus," Kenny said.

"What are you going to do, walk to the house from here?"

Kenny pulled to the curb. "Yeah, it's only like two blocks."

"It's not about the distance, Kenny, it's about your skittishness. What's going on?"

Kenny shook his head. "Dad, Janelle is really pissed, and I'm afraid if she sees you, she's gonna blow a gasket..."

Martin nodded, then said, "She has every right to be." Then, after giving the situation a bit more thought, said, "Just drive me to her place. If she's home, then I'll face the music."

Without a word, Kenny slowly pulled from the curb. They rode to the house in silence. Kenny pressed the garage opener. The door rattled up slowly. No Beemer in the spacious garage, Martin's Harley parked off to the side, toward the back.

Martin started to get out, then looked over at Kenny. "You coming back down to the bungalow?" Martin said. "We haven't had much chance to talk..."

After pondering the question a few seconds, Kenny said, "I'm going to hang here a day or so, see how the trial's going. I'll come down tomorrow, or the next day, okay? I really do want to catch up."

Martin smiled, then leaned over and hugged his son, kissing him on the cheek. "Sounds good, and thanks, for coming to look for me... and getting me back on track..." Then, with a tear in his eye: "I love you, Kenny."

"I love you too, Dad," Kenny said. "I'll see you soon."

Martin nodded, then jumped out and closed the door, hurrying to the garage. He strapped on his helmet and started the Harley; the

engine rumbled beneath him, giving him a sense of being, of belong-
ing, a welcome back to a universe he had missed. He clicked the
engine into gear and slowly eased forward, toward the garage opening. Kenny was standing in the driveway next to the Taurus.

"See you soon!" Martin said, smiling.

Kenny smiled back as Martin eased past, then turned the shiny big
bike onto the street, the world aligning along predictable planes, the
wind angling toward him fresh as a sea breeze, the thunder of the
engine bringing him fully back to life.

Halfway back to the city, Noreen was in his head, Martin fighting
against images which refused to leave. As if the events unfolded in
present time, Martin's chest locked, his heart straining to beat, all the
sensations rushing back of walking in on Noreen in bed with the loan
manager. It was a terrible blow, seeing her with another man, her back
upright and straight, naked, straddling Carter Richardson. "Martin, I
didn't expect you home so early," she said, calmly. "I'm sorry. Will you
give us a moment to get dressed?"

Martin had been going out of his mind, waiting in the kitchen,
Carter finally leaving almost ten minutes later. The young man, maybe
late thirties, waved to Martin as he shambled past the kitchen, clicking
down the hallway in his Florsheim shoes. Noreen came in a few
minutes later, walked over to Martin and kissed him on the cheek.
"How was your day, Sweetheart?" she asked, going to the fridge,
pulling the door open. Martin was speechless. She looked distressed as
she inspected the shelves, bending over, moving jars around. "I think
we're going to need to go out to dinner tonight," she said, still holding
the refrigerator door open. "What sounds good? Thai?"

Martin could feel himself boiling over. "Thai food! Noreen! What
the fuck was that!"

She slowly pushed the door shut and walked over to the table,
sitting across from him. "I'm sorry you had to see that," she said,
genuinely perplexed. "But I had no idea you were leaving work early
today, or I would have—"

"This isn't about you fucking the loan manager so it doesn't inter-
fere with my schedule, Noreen! Why are you fucking him at all?"
Martin could feel the flywheel in his chest starting to lose cohesion, in
danger, at any moment, of coming loose and wrecking every organ in

his body. "What is happening here? I thought we were happy, just you and me… I just don't—"

"We are happy," Noreen said, moving smoothly into the chair next to his to be closer to him, taking his hand in hers, her eyes soft and warm. "I couldn't be happier! I love you so much! You're happy, aren't you, Martin?"

Martin felt as if his mind had been cleaved down the middle, neither half able to process what he was hearing, Noreen spewing some kind of demented gibberish. Was she purposely trying to drive him mad? What was the game?

She leaned over and kissed him on the cheek, then said, "I'm sorry if that bothered you. I would never want to make you uncomfortable…"

"*Uncomfortable!* I'm… I'm fucking incensed, Noreen!" He started to shake all over, praying for her to drop the charade and tell him how she really felt, that she hated the sight of him, and was tired of his blathering on about how much fun he was having with his own studio, how creative he felt now, how happy! "I am so sick of living with you! It's such a drag!" he expected to hear, her features a road map of disgust and loathing. And then she'd tell him to leave, and that she never wanted to see him again!

"Let's get dinner," she said after a tense, impossibly quiet interlude, smiling weakly, gently sliding her palm over the hairs on his arm. "Can we talk about this more in the car?"

"Dinner? Talk in the car? Are you crazy?"

Noreen sat upright, drawing her hand from his arm and tucking it into her lap with her other hand, like a scolded child. Her smile faded, her eyes shifting down toward the table. Martin felt bad about what he'd said, outraged at himself that he should feel bad about anything. He wasn't the one fucking the loan manager in their own bed! Martin sat as long as he could, the air stifling, growing ever harder to breathe.

"I have to go, Noreen," he said, getting up from the table.

"I wish you wouldn't, but I understand," she said, rising, moving closer to him and kissing him on the lips. Then, pulling back from him: "Where will you go?"

"Fuck, I don't know. Anywhere but here!" A part of him wanted her to start crying, apologize, beg him to stay, tell him she'd make it up to him somehow, that it would never happen again. Her indifference sent him into a maddening rage, Martin suddenly feeling as if he could hit her, a notion which had never crossed the threshold of his thoughts, no matter how angry he might be. He turned and hurried toward the hallway, glancing back once when he got to the front door, expecting her to be waiting at the edge of the living room, remorseful, pleading with him to give her another chance. But she was nowhere to be seen, the brutal vacuum sucking his breath away. Did she not understand he was really leaving?

Martin turned the motorcycle into his neighborhood, twisting the throttle until the big bike lifted gently and roared down the street, picturing himself driving past the bungalow, through the field, and, if the universe complied with perfect timing, into a rumbling, oncoming, earth-rattling freight train. Martin hit the brakes partway into the weeds and brought the motorcycle around, bringing it to a halt in the decrepit driveway next to his house. He had just unstrapped his helmet when a locomotive rolled by, shaking the ground beneath his feet.

Chapter Fifty

Kenny was seated in the living room watching television, eating a sandwich he'd made, a family-size bag of potato chips on the lamp stand next to him, when Janelle and Beth entered through the garage entrance into the kitchen. Janelle rushed in first, her eyes flashing like red lasers. "Kenny!" She appeared panicked, as if she'd just realized someone had broken in and stolen all her furniture.

"Is everything okay?" Kenny said, setting the can of Pepsi down on the coffee table.

"The motorcycle!" she said. "It's gone!" Then, as if she hadn't fully expressed what was bothering her, asked: "Do you know anything about that? Where is it?" Then, after another moment: "Was Martin here?" Janelle rushed over closer to Kenny. Beth trudged into the living room after her, her eyes, and the skin around them, pink, as if she'd been crying.

Kenny wasn't sure what to say. Janelle, impatient with his lack of response, wrenched the remote from the coffee table, spun around briefly to switch off the television, then dropped the remote on the table, the small plastic device bouncing a bit before tumbling from the edge onto the carpet.

"Well, was he? Was Martin here? Who took the motorcycle?"

Kenny glanced over at Beth, who gazed at him noncommittally, unwilling to show her fealty for either side of this exchange. "Can we sit down and just talk?" Kenny said. "You know, calmly?"

Janelle bristled at the suggestion, her face turning red, her eyes tightening at the corners. She shifted her head, looking for the best place to sit, then asked Beth to get up so she could take the chair across from Kenny, as if that would give her the best vantage point to detect untruths. Beth shifted to the other end of the sofa, placing herself against the arm rest opposite Kenny, just a few feet away, but clearly not aligned with his camp.

"Yes, I drove him out this morning so he could get his motorcycle…"

Janelle's chest heaved, her back arching oddly, as if she couldn't catch her breath, then, after giving this news a moments' considera-tion, shot up from the chair and rushed from the room as if the pronouncement had crushed something inside her.

"That went well," Beth said a moment later, kicking off her shoes to fold her legs under her.

Kenny screwed up his lips and looked in the direction of Janelle's exit. "I don't know what to do. Lying hasn't worked, and I'm afraid the truth won't be much better."

"Lying has definitely not worked," Beth said, chortling a bit, a sarcastic yet sympathetic laugh, as if she understood his dilemma. Beth got up. "I'm going to bed, Big Brother," she said, heading for the back bedrooms.

"Kind of early, isn't it?"

"Not if you had my day?" She leaned over and kissed him on the cheek. "It would be tremendous if you could hold me tonight," she whispered, letting her fingertips trace the flesh of his arm. It gave him a chill. Kenny put his hand to his mouth, squeezing his lips into a twisted dark hole, unwilling to meet Beth's eyes. About twenty minutes after Beth left, Janelle came back, more composed, it seemed to Kenny, sipping a drink, probably Scotch, and sat down across from him again.

"I'm sorry about before… it's been a day… a month…"

Kenny felt terrible for her. "No need to apologize," he said. "None of this can be easy."

Janelle teared up and shook her head as if to clear it, then took a long draw from her glass, leaving a small reserve of alcohol at the bottom. She looked at Kenny, as if he should just continue where he'd left off. Then, before he could speak, said, "The truth, Kenny, no matter how horrible."

Horrible wasn't the adjective that came to mind. *Unfathomable* would have been more suitable. Kenny gave it some thought, replaying what Beth had said about lying, that *lying had definitely not worked*. But how would the truth be any better? It would sound like the worst kind of lie, the kind that tries to makes an ass of out of the listener, as if Janelle was so stupid that she'd believe anything.

"The truth is..." Kenny started, wading into the shallow end, allowing himself to acclimate to the water. "The truth is, Janelle, that my dad reconnected with someone he had loved years and years ago, long before he ever met you. The meeting was unexpected, and to my dad, spelled a second chance, as if fate had brought them together again after all these years. Martin saw a chance, no matter how wrong, to explore a relationship with this woman that had been clipped short by circumstances beyond his control. He'd loved her deeply at one point in his life, and... well, decided to seize the opportunity, conflicted as he was about you and Beth, yet certain this situation would never present itself again..." Kenny stopped a moment to gauge Janelle's reaction. She sat like a statue, her face stone, her mouth a carved line across her features. Even her eyes failed to reflect light. "I know he loves you, Janelle, that much I'm sure of," Kenny said. "And I know he wished things had been different, and that he is truly sorry he hurt you, and Beth, and feels miserable about how everything played out."

Janelle allowed herself a deep breath, as if before this moment it was best not to take in the fouled air—like a dust-filled, collapsed mineshaft—until it was safe to breathe.

"Where is he? Why didn't he tell me this himself?" she said, at the edge of tears again, it seemed, but maybe too angry to actually cry.

Kenny thought a moment before he answered. "To be honest, he's a wreck. Last night, when I found him at the bungalow—"

"The bungalow!" Janelle bellowed like an air raid warning. "You mean that crappy little shack down in the city? That's not possible. He sold that years ago!"

Kenny cleared his throat. "He didn't sell it..." Kenny felt like a cowardly conspirator, turning on his dad.

Janelle covered her mouth, pushed back in the chair as if some invisible force had wedged itself against her chest.

"Everything's been a lie," Janelle mumbled, her face wrecked with betrayal, as if the words had originated somewhere else and she had only witnessed them coming from her lips. Kenny wanted to comfort her, tell her that that wasn't true, but kept his opinion locked down, knowing, to her ears, his assertion was meaningless. She brought her eyes to his, tears slipping down her cheeks, questions written across her face. She voiced none of them, deciding instead to get up and leave and headed toward her bedroom.

Kenny sat staring at the blank television screen, wishing he'd had a chance to talk with Beth alone, wishing he had just lied about the motorcycle, but what would the lie be? What could he have told Janelle? Martin had assured him she would never notice it missing and now Kenny felt awful. He switched on the television, and took the sound to a whisper, staring at nothing, his mind a busy airport, thoughts leaving, thoughts landing, the traffic unending.

After a few hours, he got up, brushed his teeth and went to bed. He wasn't sure what time it was when he was awakened by Beth slipping in next to him. She pressed up against him, her back to his chest, pulling his arms around her. She said softly, "Just hold me."

Kenny was relieved she was wearing her pajamas, but nevertheless was drawn to the sweet smell of her skin, unable to fight the urge to place his lips against the bare spot of neck. She allowed his overture, melting closer to him. She placed her palm on top of his hand. "That was quite creative what you told my mom," she said without turning toward him. "Using your situation with Vickie to explain your dad's absence." Then, caressing the back of Kenny's hand: "Well, sort of... I guess..."

Kenny was about to protest. That wasn't at all what he'd done, yet, upon replaying the explanation he'd given Janelle, he could under-stand how Beth might have come to that conclusion.

"I'm sorry about bringing up Vickie," Beth added, turning in Kenny's arms to face him. She brought her eyes close to his, her lips a breath away. Then: "Do you miss her?"

Kenny held Beth's gaze for a moment, then closed his eyes, wanting to redirect the conversation. "How's the trial going?" he asked, drawing his hand up to the side of her face.

"Should be over soon," she said, easing back to create more space between them, her expression all at once gloomy. "My dad testified today, well, actually, yesterday I guess now..." She shook her head back and forth. "It was pathetic... him talking about the prevalence of crime and violence, how it was one's duty to protect themselves, that the police couldn't be everywhere at once—he could go free..." She paused on that notion, then: "I realized that sitting in that courtroom, listening to him, looking over at the jury..." then, taking Kenny's hand in hers under the blankets, "The prosecution questions him next... he's going to have a rough time..."

"Isn't that good news, though?" Kenny said. "That your dad could go free?" Kenny's eyes were beginning to adjust to the dark. Beth's features tightened, or so it seemed to Kenny, unable to read her expression fully in that moment.

"He killed a man in a grocery store! Carl killed a little girl's father for talking to him in the cereal aisle! Why should Carl go free and Naomi have to bear the weight of his stupid decision for the rest of her life?" Even in the dark, Kenny could see the tears beginning to spark in her eyes.

Kenny said, "I'm sorry, I just—"

She leaned in and pressed her lips to his, pulling him closer, her tears wetting his cheeks. Her body began to shake in his arms. When she pulled away, her face was twisted with sadness, her world collapsing. "It's all wrong," she whispered. "Everything's all wrong!" Then, as if some valve released, her features went slack; every cell in her body surrendered. She rested against his chest, leaving her head to rise and fall with his breath.

Chapter Fifty-One

M artin couldn't sleep. He put on his robe and went outside. The night sky was starless, scuffed with faint clouds giving it the look of a poorly erased blackboard. Finding his lawn chair leaning against the house, he unfolded it, sat down and stared out across the empty field. When his eyes adjusted to the dark, he could just make out the mounded white rocks lining the railroad tracks rising above the weeds, the stones reflecting what little light was present. The faint glow from the rocks created a ghostly path that swept off into the distance in both directions, like a pale, mythical serpent lying in wait for its prey.

It hadn't ended the afternoon Martin came home to find Noreen having sex with Carter, the loan officer at her bank. Well maybe it had, but not for Martin. Not that day, anyway. Martin had left Noreen's reality, returning to the bungalow for a few days, trying to understand what was happening. He then went back to their home, needing clarification, attempting to talk to Noreen, to make her understand. And she listened, sitting at the kitchen table together, him voicing his outrage, her nodding in appreciation of his pain, offering no rebuttals or excuses. At first Martin had been grateful not to have been subjected to lies and lame justifications, but after a while it seemed Noreen truly had no clue she'd done anything wrong, as if Martin's revulsion over her actions was an issue which he alone must deal with. As if the fault lie with him and his inability to accept the situation fully, though she ascribed no blame nor leveled condemnation. She just listened. Night after night. Martin talked incessantly, wrung his hands, shook his head, wearing himself down, trying to get beyond his hurt. Noreen sat quietly, patiently, regarding him with the disinterest of a robin on a windowsill.

This went on for a couple of weeks, Martin trying to break through her defenses, Noreen seemingly immune to shame or remorse. At times, when Martin's thoughts left him and he fell silent, she would offer to make them dinner, or order take-out food and have it delivered. One night, when he had completely exhausted himself with his tirade, she smiled and touched his hand. "Maybe we should watch some television for a while," she said. "You seem miserable."

The comment threw him into a rage and he stormed from the house, taking refuge in a motel not far from their home, avoiding the bungalow, not wanting a chance encounter with Falco—he wanted to be alone. When he returned to Noreen a few days later, he found her and Carter in the bedroom again, both of them naked lying on the sheets. Martin could only stand in the doorway and shake his head.

Noreen got up and put on her robe, then turned to Carter and asked him to leave. Carter got up and dressed and walked past Martin, blank-faced, without a word. Noreen took Martin's hand as she led him toward the kitchen. She offered him something to eat or drink as he sat at the table. "No, thanks, Noreen," he said weakly, the strength gone from his body. She brought over a glass of water and sat, then sipped from the glass before setting it down.

She took a deep breath and brought her eyes to his, giving him a warm, empathetic smile. If Martin had had any fight left in him at that point, it would have touched off another irate shouting spell, but he was spent. Completely numb; he couldn't even muster the slightest hint of annoyance.

"Don't ever doubt how much I love you, Martin," Noreen finally said, her eyes as lovely and kind as the day they'd met. "But you don't belong here…"

That was it. He'd been cast off. Banished from paradise.

The memory crushed him, but he was empty of tears. Past all thinking.

A train in the distance, a myopic leviathan—with one brilliant orb flopping insanely from side to side, the laser eye of a deranged cyclops —rumbled toward him like thunder, monstrously shaking the earth. For a fleeting moment—through some trick of perspective and refraction—the train appeared to have autonomy, as if it had left the tracks it depended upon, and was charging—an incensed bull—straight for the bungalow. Martin felt the hairs on his neck and arms rise like Lazarus, his body instinctually pushing back in his chair, until the beast was so close he could feel its steamy breath, or so it seemed. He bolted from the lawn chair and cut a mad dash for the safety of the street. A second later the iron demon roared past the field behind the house, that glowing lone eye slapping at trees and shrubs crowding the tracks, blazing a brilliant trail through the desolate neighborhood. In seconds, still clattering and screeching, the shadowy body and tail of the locomotive writhed away, a dark specter fleeing the night.

"Hey, Sport, you okay?" Falco said, getting out of a taxi, handing the driver some bills.

Martin swiveled his head toward the voice, then back to the train, which was little more than a toy now, scratching along the earth, fading into the distance. Martin felt dislodged, expelled from Time and Space, adrift. Though he recognized Falco immediately, at least thought he did, for a moment, he couldn't speak.

"Hi," Martin finally managed, startled by the sound of his own voice, as if it had issued from somewhere else. Falco moved closer to Martin and stared into his eyes. Martin straightened slowly, hydraulically, his shoulders pulling back from Falco's, his shoes cemented to the pavement.

"You don't look so good, Sport," Falco said, raising an eyebrow and squinting at Martin like a pirate. "You should come inside. I'll make you some tea."

Martin followed—the world swelling and receding like gelatin— feeling a bit of nausea. Falco switched on the lights and waited for Martin to find his way across the room. He started to sit on the futon but Falco instructed him to sit at the kitchen table. Like some cult initiate, Martin obeyed, absently shuffling over to sit facing the stove. Falco filled the kettle with water, twisted the burner on, then brought down a box of tea from the cupboard above the stove.

Waiting for the kettle to whistle, Falco spun toward Martin, leaning forward over the table, balanced on his splayed palms planted on the Formica surface. "When did you come out?"

Martin shrugged, trying to rewind Time, unable to locate either end, his mind trapped by the Möbius loop in his head. A number finally emerged from the dark cellar of his brain. "Three days... I think. Maybe more. A week?"

Falco nodded, his expression grim, fixed. "You need to take it easy for a while. Another week. Maybe two. Give your body a chance to readjust to reality." Then, after the kettle shrieked and Falco pulled it from the burner, he spun his head back toward Martin. "Have you seen your son?" Falco said. "Kenny's in town..."

Yes! Kenny, that's right, Martin thought. He hadn't imagined him after all. "I saw him yesterday, I think, or... I don't know when, but he drove me out to Janelle's to get my motorcycle."

"Have you spoken to Janelle?" Falco said, bringing a cup of tea over and setting it in front of Martin.

"She hates me, I'm sure," Martin said, morose, thinking of everything he'd lost.

"Plenty of time for that later," Falco said, sitting down. "Let's call Kenny and have him down for dinner one night this week."

Martin nodded, sipping his tea.

"Are you hungry?" Falco said. Martin shook his head. They sat without speaking much of the time, Falco occasionally asking Martin a question about Kenny, or the Harley, telling Martin he'd like to learn how to drive a motorcycle. Martin nodded, finishing his tea, feeling sleepy. He stood up and said he needed to get to bed.

"Good idea," Falco said. "I'll whip us up a nice breakfast in the morning."

Martin shambled toward the hallway, turning back toward Falco at the last moment.

"How can I explain to Kenny about the portal, where I've been, his mother, all of it?" Martin said, remembering Noreen, how she'd looked when she told him he didn't belong in her world. Just then he felt the same hot, molten iron filling his chest, weighing him down, sucking at his air.

"Not tonight, Sport. Just get some sleep."

Except for the pain, Martin felt dead to this world, dead to reality, a husk. "We need to do something about the portal," Martin said with the shaken but restrained urgency of man trying to rid his home of rattlesnakes.

"We'll figure it out, Martin. We will, just not tonight..."

Martin nodded and lumbered off, slightly less dismal than a second ago, as if the great curative aspect of sleep promised relief; if only he could get his mind to stop spinning back on itself, if only he could make it quiet.

Chapter Fifty-Two

Kenny was relieved to get the call from Falco a few days later. It had become awkward being at Janelle's home now, especially with no reason for him to be there. Martin's disappearance, which had been a mystery, and cause for concern and angst, imagining something awful had happened to him, was no longer a puzzle. Kenny's presence seemed to now cause Janelle distress, as if Kenny was now the reminder of Janelle' worst fears about where Martin had gone. Another woman. Another family. Another wife or significant other. Janelle and Beth didn't spend much time at the house in the mornings, grabbing a quick breakfast, then back to the courthouse. Over the past few nights even Beth had become a stranger, not coming to his room at night, and too exhausted in the evenings to spend communal time watching television or just chatting, preferring to be alone in her room, listening to music, or maybe just sleeping, or maybe staring at her ceiling. Janelle, like a predictable satellite, spent her evenings orbiting the usual rooms, the kitchen to put away dishes—she refused any help from Kenny—then the bathroom to clean the sink and toilet, then the living room to vacuum and tidy up magazines and cushions—which never fell into disarray—then to the deck to have a cup of decaf by the pool, then to bed.

Janelle had already gone out to the garage, yelling back to Beth to get a move on, that they were running late. Kenny was seated at the kitchen island finishing his cereal when Beth came running past, harried and oblivious to Kenny.

"Hey, Beth," Kenny said as she hustled by. "I hope things go smoother today. I'm going to be gone when you get home."

She stopped at the garage entrance off the kitchen, then walked back toward him. "You're leaving? Why?" Her expression was concerned, almost grave.

"It's weird being here now, you know, with my dad back and all," he said. "And your mom, I think, hates me more and more with every sunrise…"

It was hard to read Beth's expression, but she almost looked sad, or hurt.

"I thought you'd be glad to see me go…" Kenny said.

Beth came over slowly to his chair and kissed him passionately on the lips, tears in her eyes as she drew back from him. She shook her head. "Wow, when you get it wrong, you're like off the charts!" She wiped her tears. "I don't want you to ever leave, and my mom, she wants to see Martin so much, but she's afraid to ask you to talk to him. She can't take another rejection, but she misses your dad, believe it or not. She still loves him… and so do I…"

Kenny wasn't sure what to say.

Just then Janelle stuck her head in through the garage entrance door and screamed," Beth, for Christ's sake, let's go!"

Beth brought her eyes to her mother's. "Kenny's leaving today," she said.

Janelle's face fell. She eased herself into the house. "You don't have to leave, Kenny," Janelle said. "We love having you here. I know we've been distracted, but… and I'm sorry for that, but… the trial will be over soon, hopefully, and things will get back to normal…"

"No, it's okay," Kenny said. "I completely understand. My dad invited me down for dinner, and I thought I'd hang with him a few days, then probably head back to New Jersey…"

The air changed suddenly, pregnant with unspoken desires and regrets. Each of them regarded one another without speaking, until Beth broke the truce of quiet desperation. "I guess we should get going, Mom."

"Yes, sweetheart," Janelle said, the urgency to leave gone from her voice. Janelle came over and hugged Kenny, then gave him a smile filled with unsaid words before turning toward the garage entrance. Beth glanced back at her, then came to Kenny and hugged him. Janelle waited at the door for her daughter. "I love you, Big Brother," she whispered, then turned away to go with her mom.

"Do you want to see Martin?" Kenny said. Both of them turned to look at him. "I think he'd like to talk with you if you're open to that."

Janelle sniffled, clearing her throat softly, as if pushing down some larger emotion. "Yes, I think we should," Janelle said. "At least talk…"

Kenny nodded, holding Janelle's eyes until she spun away, disappearing through the garage door. Beth smiled at him, pursing her lips as if to lessen the gloom of their parting. A second later she was gone, Kenny sitting alone at the kitchen island, listening to the garage door rattling up along the white ceiling of the garage. The BMW backed out, the garage door rattling back down, the chain-driven mechanism indifferent as a stop sign. Then, silence.

Kenny packed up his things and hurried out to the driveway, to his dad's Taurus, the interior bringing back the night of the reunion, he and Vickie making love in the front seat, the fragrance of her hair, the smell of her skin. Escape was impossible. No matter which direction he faced, he could see nothing but another insoluble situation; Elaine and his family, Vickie and her pregnancy, and now Beth. It was disorienting, everything in motion. He was unsure what to think of Beth. She would say she loved him, come to his room at night, then call him Big Brother, as if to restore the boundary lest he get the wrong idea. And Elaine, Michael, his new daughter on the way, Elaine's willingness to move to St. Louis, as if they could make it work again. But most confounding was Vickie—even in her present form, whatever that was, his heart lifted just picturing her, and beat a little faster having her close, some weird helium high that made him feel weightless, indestructible, clear-headed and euphoric at the same time.

Reflecting on these three women in his life—if it was even fair to think in those terms, that he was somehow romantically entwined with each—was exasperating. And embarrassing to feel as fickle as a weathervane, his heart helplessly, hopelessly, pointing in the direction of the prevailing wind.

Disheartened, he started the engine and headed for the bungalow,

Vickie now curating all the thoughts in his head, nothing allowed to enter without her stamp. He had to see her, that was certain, unsure if he was ready for the kind of commitment it would take to live in her world.

Kenny pulled into the driveway and saw his dad and Falco in the backyard grilling something on the barbecue pit his dad had bought years ago out of some domestic need to make himself more neighbor-hood-ready. Kenny walked back to join them, Falco pushing a beer into his palm. Kenny nodded, appreciative of the warm reception. Martin came over and hugged him, holding him a long time before bringing his arms back to his sides.

"I'm glad you came," Martin said.

"Of course I came," Kenny said, grinning over at Falco, who no longer radiated warmth, tending the burgers with the focus of a lion tamer.

Kenny and Martin sat next to each other, not speaking to one another, Falco sharing stories about the magic shows he'd been performing all over the country. "I'm still looking for an assistant," he said, flipping the burgers. Then, looking back at Kenny. "How about that stepsister of yours, Beth? She'd make a fine assistant."

Kenny shook his head. "She's barely seventeen," he said, feeling awful for sleeping with her, Beth not even out of high school, Kenny with a wife and a child, another on the way. At times, Kenny couldn't believe what a mess he'd made of his life.

"Seventeen comes and goes... like everything else," Falco said. "How's the trial?"

"They hope it wraps up this week."

Falco nodded, sipping his beer.

"Are they doing all right? Janelle and Beth?" Martin said, sheep-ishly, as if he had no right to know, and was ashamed to ask.

"Stressed, but hanging in there," Kenny said.

"How about you?" Martin asked, low enough Falco couldn't hear. "You and Elaine and... Vickie, that's her name, right? Vickie?" Then: "What's going on with her, if you don't mind me asking?"

"It's complicated."

Over the next few days Kenny filled his dad in on everything that had been happening with Beth and Janelle, the trial, he and Elaine, leaving out his journey through the *Anything* room into Vickie's world. He hadn't even told his dad Vickie was dead. And even though his dad was intimately familiar with the otherworldly phenomenon, Kenny kept it to himself out of some misplaced sense of self-preservation, not wanting any negative feedback from Martin's experience, not wanting to hear anything that might deter him from forming his own decision about going back, about staying with Vickie. Martin never offered any explanation of what had happened between his mother and him, and judging by what a mess his dad was—Kenny could hardly recognize his own father, as if Martin had been the recipient of shock treatments, or botched brain surgery—it was clear the experiment ended badly. And in some gated part of Kenny's brain, he didn't want to know.

During the day, Martin was often gone from the bungalow by eight in the morning, leaving with a loud rumble on his motorcycle, not retuning until after supper. Falco would pass through the space like an apparition, day and night, sometimes staying only long enough to grab something from under the futon, or stop off in the bathroom, or cook soup in a sauce pan and eat from the pot. They hardly spoke, he and Falco, but one afternoon Kenny asked him if he'd told Martin about Kenny's visit to Vickie's world.

"None of his business, Sport," Falco said, hungrily searching the fridge like a frat brother. "None of mine either if you must know, but..."

Kenny waited for the perplexing magician to finish his thought, then growing impatient, finally said, "But...?"

Without looking over, Falco said. "You and your old man have a lot in common. I'm sure you realize that. You should tell him what you're up to. He could probably help."

"Help?"

Falco shut the fridge door with a hermetic thump, shooting his bullet eyes at Kenny. "You're playing with fire, Sport, and nobody knows that better than your old man."

Kenny frowned, chagrined by Falco's admonishment. What was he going to do, force himself to forget about her, if that was even possible? Leave Vickie to deal with the pregnancy alone? Abandon her? When the words echoed back in Kenny's head, something buckled in his chest. "What about Elaine?" a sterner voice in his mind said. "And Michael? Don't they count? You abandoned them!" Kenny shot up from the futon, needing air.

"I'm going for a walk," Kenny said to the bungalow. If Falco heard him, that was fine, but Kenny didn't feel he had to explain anything to the magician.

Kenny walked to the railroad tracks, Elaine and Michael tangled in his riotous thoughts. Staring past scrawny trees and weeds, Kenny winced from the hot tar stench of creosote rising from the deadmen securing the rails. Just then, from the glum rubble of his mind, Vickie stepped forward like a flesh and blood dream, like a breeze, full of light, the sweet scent of her hair suddenly in his nose. His body went slack, the sensation like bone and muscle turning to putty, the afternoon losing coherence. He couldn't help how he felt about Vickie, how he'd always felt about her. What was he supposed to do? Maybe he should never have married Elaine, lived as a hermit, nourished himself on the remote, implausible possibility Vickie would somehow come into his life. "Life is messy," his therapist had told him. "No one gets it right, no matter how crazy they make themselves trying." But did they get it *this* wrong? Time and time again?

"Kenny?" someone said, walking up behind him. He spun around, his rumination evaporating like steam.

"Dad? I didn't hear the bike pull up."

"It's at the shop," his dad said. "Routine service. Warranty stuff. Took a cab back."

"You should have called—"

"Cabbies got to make a living too…"

Kenny smiled at his dad, wondering about what Falco had said, about them having so much in common. Kenny was leaning toward telling him about Vickie, how he'd ventured into the *Anything* room, when Martin reluctantly brought up Janelle. "You really think she'd take me back?"

"It's certainly worth a conversation," Kenny said.

"I thought maybe I'd call her tonight, you know, after she gets back from the courthouse."

Kenny knew his dad was not himself right now, overly cautious, insecure, or maybe just scared, unable to deal with rejection. "When do you get the Harley back?" Kenny asked.

"They told me to come back around six this evening," Martin said. "I thought I'd grab something to eat on the way home, then call her around eight or so."

Kenny nodded, thinking about Vickie, wanting to see her, and wanting his dad to be out of the picture for a while. Though the suggestion Kenny was about to proffer felt selfish, it didn't mean it was without merit. "How about I drive you to the dealership at six. You can grab a bite, then drive out to Janelle's house. You'll be waiting on the porch when she gets home."

Martin's features sunk toward the center of his face like quicksand, the corners of his mouth pulled in anguish.

"It'll send a message," Kenny quickly added, seeing his father's vexation. "That she's important to you. That you're contrite. That you're serious about reconciliation if she'll take you back."

"And if she shows up with a new boyfriend and doesn't want to see me?" Martin said, his face already twisted with humiliation. "What message will that send?"

"That you're a crazy stalker bastard and she's lucky to be done with you!"

Martin eyes narrowed, glinting like steel, the flesh around his eyes reddening. It took several moments before he softened, then started laughing, shaking his head. "Yeah, you're right. What do I have to lose?"

"She wants to see you, Dad," Kenny said. "Don't forget, you left without a word, rejected her without any explanation... worried her, then enraged her... and she still wants to see you, so..."

"Maybe she just wants to kick me in the nuts!"

"That could make for a nasty ride back down here on the Harley..." Kenny said, grinning, relieved to see his dad laughing again. They stared at each other a few seconds, smiling, on the verge of a hug when Martin turned toward the horizon, all at once gloomy, obviously seized by a confounding thought.

"Why haven't you asked me where I've been, Son?" Martin turned toward him, his eyes ringed with tears. For the past several days they had done such a masterful job of avoiding this conversation. Why now?

"When you're ready," Kenny said. "I'm just glad you're safe."

Martin gave him a smile so brief it could have just been a facial tick, then squinted his eyes out past the railroad tracks. He took a deep breath, scrunching up his lips as if in discomfort, then told Kenny, "I appreciate the space." Then, after a short pause. "I hope Janelle is that gracious."

Kenny had explained to Martin everything he'd told Janelle, and Beth, with her powerful bullshit detector, hadn't rejected Kenny's account outright, and actually thought it was kind, and plausible, though he could tell she doubted its veracity. "I don't think she'll press you on it, Dad. If she does, just tell her the truth, at least the version I told her."

Meeting Kenny's eyes, Martin regarded his son with a glossy countenance, a kind of revelatory burnish to his face, as if caught unawares by a disturbing realization. "How did you come up with that scenario, the one you told Janelle?"

There it was. Martin stumbled upon the chink in Kenny's story; Kenny supposedly had no idea where Martin had been, or that he'd been with a woman at all, especially a woman he'd loved long before he'd met Janelle; that stretched coincidence beyond the breaking point. Up to this point, Martin had been satisfied just knowing Janelle had left a tiny opening in her heart for him, the rueful supplicant, to crawl through. Before Martin could ponder too long on the implausibility of his narrative, Kenny spoke up. "I used my situation with Vickie," he said, hoping this was enough for Martin to release his skepticism. "It seemed credible… it's what happened to me."

Martin looked over at Kenny, flashed him another fleeting facial-tick smile, not completely sold, but sold enough to let it go. Martin checked his watch. "Let's grab something to eat. Then you can drop me at the dealership, okay?"

"Sounds good, Pop," Kenny said, putting his arm around his dad's shoulders. They strolled across the weedy field. Kenny brought his arms to his sides, slipping his hands down into his pockets, all at once giddy, upbeat and confident, knowing he'd see Vickie tonight.

Chapter Fifty-Three

Already he'd spent four days in her world, this time in St. Louis, and couldn't have been happier. Kenny chose to start their adventure after the second night of the reunion, after they'd left the luau, sitting at Denny's, Kenny careful to picture a time after they'd made love in the Taurus. Unlike the real version of that evening, when they left Denny's after pancakes and sundaes, Kenny had taken her to her apartment, and spent the night with her. And every night thereafter. Roiter didn't exist in this world; no vicious ex-husband to contend with. Roiter was in prison in the *real* version of Kenny's life, not dead, so he didn't exist in Vickie's sphere. Which made Kenny wonder if that would change the conditions of her death. Falco had warned him about that, that her death could not be prevented. That was a rock-hard rule, supposedly, according to the magician anyway. Without Roiter, though, Kenny couldn't help but feel that the facts surrounding her death would have to take a different tack, maybe cease to exist at all.

And it would seem Vickie was no longer pregnant, an intended consequence of avoiding their lovemaking in the parking lot of the country club, even though Kenny had wanted to relive that incredible moment. Vickie, radiant and lovely as ever, came from the bedroom wearing a tight black dress with spaghetti straps and high heels, ready for a night at Powell Hall with the St. Louis Symphony Orchestra performing Nicolai Rimsky-Korsakov's *Scheherazade*. It was Vickie's night off from the restaurant, and they'd wanted to do something special. Since he had no formal wear, Kenny rented a three-piece suit, plain but tasteful. The limo picked them up at five-thirty. After dinner, they asked the chauffeur to drive them around downtown St. Louis, Kenny and Vickie drinking champagne in the back, making out, then making love before they attended the performance.

At intermission, amidst the murmur and prattle of other concert goers, Vickie and Kenny each held a glass of champagne, gliding on the splendor of the evening. Willingly and completely, Kenny had given himself over to Vickie's world, adrift in the heady illusion that everything before him was true and real and lasting.

"This was a great idea, the concert, the limo…" Vickie said, glowing, her eyes sparking with light when she moved her head.

"Did I tell you how amazingly gorgeous you look tonight?" Kenny said. She smiled and he raised his glass to toast her. "To new beginnings!" he said, clinking her glass with his. He held her eyes, but her smile faded slightly, as if unsure about what he'd meant by, *new beginnings.*

Vickie fell quiet, introspective, and he was about to ask her what was wrong when the house lights flashed. He took her glass, then returned both to the bar before they went back in to find their seats.

The concert ended with rousing applause, some of the audience showing appreciation by standing. Vickie looked over at Kenny and shrugged, her face bright, inviting, then stood to join others around them, Kenny following her lead, both of them clapping and laughing. Out on the sidewalk, Kenny looked for their limo. While they waited, people bustling by, Vickie pushed toward Kenny and kissed him. "A perfect evening," she whispered, drawing back only a few inches from his face. He was about to reengage the kiss when a scraggly man approached.

"Can you spare a few bucks?" the man asked. In his grubby hand, not bothering to hold it up, was a sign that said War Vet printed on a piece of cardboard. The man didn't appear old enough to have been in Vietnam. Maybe the war in Bosnia, or the Gulf War. Even with his disheveled hair and beard, he looked to be Kenny's age. Kenny was about to reach into his pocket for his wallet, sending his eyes to the street for the limo. From the margin of his vision, Kenny saw Vickie starring at the indigent man, not afraid, but curious, yet more than curious, intent.

"What war?" Kenny said to the man.

"Listen, pal, for two bucks I'm not gonna stand here and give you my fucking life story," the guy said, a peculiar confidence and energy in his voice Kenny hadn't expected. "If you want to help me out, cool." Then: "Look, I'm not Dylan Thomas, pal. I ain't looking to *rage, rage against the dying light*. I just wanna go numbly into that good night."

Dylan Thomas. Kenny was familiar with the Welsh poet, but had never read any of his work. He reached into his jacket pocket and brought out his wallet, just as the limo pulled up and waited in the first lane of traffic for them. Vickie was still staring at the man, the man trying to avert his eyes from her, holding his hand out to Kenny. Kenny placed a couple one-dollar bills in the man's grungy palm.

"Sean?" Vickie blurted out. The man's head whipped around toward her, his eyes burning into hers. "Sean, is that you?"

The man held her gaze a moment, then reluctantly said, "Vickie?"

"What happened to you, Sean?"

"Nothing. Between opportunities."

What about your job at Semco? You were a line supervisor, the shop steward!"

Sean shrugged, shoving the bills into the breast pocket of his dirty shirt. "People die on your watch because you came in stoned, well, even the union can't dump you fast enough." Sean looked over at Kenny. "Thanks for the..." Sean patted his shirt pocket and looked toward the street. "Your carriage awaits, your excellency!" Sean turned with a weird smirk and walked away.

Kenny looked after the disheveled man a moment, then at Vickie who seemed shocked. He took her arm and guided her toward the limo. The driver asked where to. Before Kenny could think of some-where to go, Vickie said, "Home, please," then gave him the address.

They rode in silence for a while. Vickie spoke first. "Sean is my ex-husband. Years ago, Kenny. Big mistake."

The disclosure flipped some alarm switch in Kenny's head, brought him back to the confounding reality he'd been basking in the past several days. How could she have a history? Kenny thought. At least one that didn't include himself. Kenny was more confused than ever. If Vickie and her world consisted of mere byproducts of his own buried desires and dreams, why would this Sean character even exist?

"You didn't know Sean," Vickie said. "He went to a different high school. He was a few years ahead of us. I met him at a school dance. Back then he was a beautiful young man. His brother, Rory, though, was a monster in the making, but Sean—even though he and Rory had been twins—didn't share any of Rory's ugliness. Until we got married…"

Kenny's head was in full spin cycle now. He remembered a pair of notorious twins named Sean and Rory, how their untimely deaths became the grist of urban legend in every school in St. Louis, how the brothers had been *mulched* attempting to hop a freight train. Officials believed that one of the brothers managed to get into an opened box car, and then tried to hoist the other brother in, when the boy trying to get up into the train got his legs tangled with a signal box along the tracks, which sent him swinging beneath the train cars, pulling his brother from the box car, both of the young men dragged for almost fifty yards beneath the train. But this couldn't be the same Sean.

"Sean Roiter?" Kenny said, unable to believe his own question. "Tommy's older brother?"

"I don't know a Tommy, but yes, Sean and Rory Roiter. I think Rory's in prison. And Sean, I just can't believe what's happened to him…"

Back in Vickie's apartment the evening was mostly quiet, Vickie not wanting to talk about her marriage to Sean. "Was he mean to you?" Kenny asked.

She gave him a horrible smile, then pressed her head against his chest, wrapping her arms around his waist, pulling him as close as she could.

Five days later, leaving the restaurant after her shift ended, Vickie was beaten to death in the dark parking lot behind the building. Police had no clues to her attacker, and no eyewitnesses. Kenny was shattered. After the police left Vickie's apartment, Kenny escaped back to the safety of his father's bungalow. He stayed just a day, trying to sort things out, before returning to Vickie's world. Trying to meet her at different times, thinking back to the toast he'd made to her the night of the concert at Powell. "To new beginnings!" How strangely Vickie had regarded him. Did she know even then how many *new beginnings* he would attempt before he finally gave up. No matter what he did, when he started with a new beginning in St. Louis, their time together always ended tragically.

Kenny had lost count of all the attempts at Vickie's world, had lost track of time in his own reality. Each time he returned to the bungalow, he fully expected to find his father, or Falco, but the shack was always empty. He wondered how his dad was doing, if he and Janelle persisted in trying to make it work, if the trial had finally ended, how Beth was faring in the wake. Kenny had almost hoped Falco was around, pick his brain about what was happening, but didn't really want to be called Sport and listen to a bunch of admonitions and dire prognostications. After all, what did Falco really *know* with concrete certainty about the phenomenon?

After a couple of days of sitting in the field behind the bungalow watching trains go by, and drinking beer till midnight in a bar down on the Landing, Kenny decided to return one last time to Vickie's world. This time back in New Jersey, at the Carriage House Hotel. For some reason that version seemed less cluttered with awful anomalies than the ones in St. Louis, Kenny recalling one night when Vickie had been killed by a hit and run driver, while Kenny, still on the curb, could only watch, unable to do a thing. They'd experienced no such calamities in New Jersey.

Chapter Fifty-Four

Vickie was elated when Kenny entered the hotel room, never asking how he came through the locked door, never suspecting anything odd or disturbing. Either she was aware of what was happening, at least peripherally, or had no way to apply logic or reason to the situation. On the third day of his visit, while sitting at an outside café having lunch, Vickie looked up at him and said, "Do you miss her? Elaine?" Before he could answer, she added, "And Michael? You must miss your son terribly…"

Disarmed by her knowledge of Elaine and Michael, Kenny stupidly stared at her forehead, his voice muted, his brain scrambling for traction.

"It's none of my business," she said, smiling, taking his hand across the table. "I'm so glad you're here with me."

After they finished eating, they walked along the Hudson, then back to the hotel room that evening. The next day they visited the Newark Museum, then attended a dance performance at the New Jersey Performing Arts Center. Vickie wore her black dress, the same one she'd worn to the Powell Hall the night they rented the limo, the night Kenny met her ex, Sean Roiter, the memory a looming storm front on the horizon of Kenny' mind. Being with Vickie now felt as if they walked on a tilted world, everything slipping away down a precarious slope.

A few days later, at Branch Brook Park, they stopped at one of the lakes and sat on a bench. For several minutes they just watched the ducks swimming along the smooth surface, some of them waddling up through the mowed grass, quacking methodically, moving closer to beg food, evidently accustomed to being spoiled. Vickie held out her empty palms and smiled, apologizing in soft, sweet tones, letting them know they hadn't planned ahead for snacks.

The ducks, maybe disapproving of the poor planning, ambled back down the bank and slid smoothly into the water, as if the oversight had been forgiven. Vickie set her palm on Kenny's thigh, then turned toward him. "Hey, you, where are you today?"

He brought his eyes toward her, realizing he'd been like a zombie for the past few hours. "I'm really sorry," he said, gripped by a sadness so deep it nearly brought him to tears.

"What's going on?" she said, her lips soft, her features pleasant and lovely, involuntarily responding to some simple, inner happiness.

Kenny didn't know where to start. He knew he could not stay with her, not in this way, knowing her end was coming soon, when she returned to St. Louis, maybe by that madman Sean Roiter, or some other thugs, or a hit and run driver, or a stray bullet, or whatever ungodly perversion would be leveled on this lovely woman who didn't deserve any of it. And yet, he couldn't turn his back on this opportunity to be with her again? He'd done that once, and had regretted it his entire life. Now he was given a second chance to spend his life with her, or some odd semblance of a life, and for the next few days, before she returned to St. Louis, she would be all his. But then, another death. Another new beginning. How many *new beginnings* could he endure?

"Do you have to go, Kenny?" she said, her shoulders slumping, though her smile remained untouched.

He turned toward her, unsure of her meaning. "No, I'm fine. We can walk some more. It's still early. We'll grab dinner on the way back to the hotel."

She let her soft eyes sink into his, as if mining his thoughts. "Do you have to go, Kenny, back to Elaine? To Michael?"

He hadn't felt like he could cry, but tears slipped down his cheeks. He gently rocked his head back and forth, not wanting those words in his head, not wanting to think about going anywhere, not wanting to leave Vickie ever again. But how could this be sustained, this parody of life they continued dreaming through, he and Vickie, moving with each day, Kenny knowing the eventual outcome, always tense, braced against impending doom? The thoughts never left now, the image of Vickie being run over by the hit and run driver, her bloodied, broken body tangled and lifeless in the damp street.

"I understand if you do," Vickie said, holding his arm, then bringing her palm to his cheek. "I love you, just know that. Never forget how much I love you."

"No... no, I can't do this," Kenny said, his red eyes pointed at Vickie. "I can't leave you..."

A couple walked by and glanced at Kenny crying, then continued on without words, pointing at the ducks, throwing scraps of bread in their direction as they strolled along the path.

"I think you're going to have to," Vickie said. "This is no place for you, Kenny. You have an entire life waiting for you, a beautiful son, a daughter on the way... your father, everything..."

Kenny wasn't sure anything or anyone was waiting for him anymore. He felt hollow, a horrible death taking over inside him. What was the point? Vickie had been his fantasy for all those years, the source of so many *What ifs*, and, *If onlys*. She was the answer to every question in Kenny's muddled life he'd had no answers for until he saw her for the first time. And now, he was just going to leave her, and her love, behind? For what? A reality built on logic? A more predictable existence? One he at least had the rule book for?

"What about the baby?" he finally said, wiping his tears.

"What baby? I'm not pregnant," she said, bewildered.

"Are you sure?"

Her confusion turned to concern. Kenny had tried to imagine what happened to Vickie when he departed her world, did her life just continue as it had for his dad, or Falco, or Beth? Would Vickie eventually have their baby and raise it on her own? How about Elaine? She was raising Michael on her own. And their new daughter? Would Elaine end up raising her alone as well?

Vickie suggested, if it would help with Kenny's consternation, they could just go find out. So they did, driving back to Flanders Medical

Assistance Center. They took the elevator to the sixth floor and silently went into one of the examination rooms. A woman's voice greeted Vickie and Kenny, then asked what she could help with today.

"I just need to know if I'm pregnant," Vickie said.

"Oh, isn't that wonderful!" the woman's voice said. "What a lovely potential. Let's find out."

Vickie stepped into the cylinder, smiling over at Kenny as machines hummed and whirred, lights flashing inside the metallic apparatus, shining oddly on Vickie's features. After several minutes, the voice said, "Congratulations, Vickie and Kenny! How much would you like to know about your beautiful new baby?"

Vickie smiled over at Kenny, her face radiant. "Do you want to know more, Kenny?"

He could only shake his head. She nodded. "It's okay for now," she said. "Thank you so much!" She stepped out of the cylinder and closed the door behind her.

"That was some hunch you had, Mr. Moffett!" she said, slipping her arm around his waist. "But it doesn't seem to have lifted your spirits much…"

He ushered her out to the rotunda, finding a bench near the huge windows where they could sit and talk. He sniffed, and cupped her hand between both of his. "I don't know what to do," he said. "I wish clarity would come, that answers would become obvious."

"What if I weren't pregnant?" she said. "Would that make it easier?"

Nothing would make leaving her easier, contemplating a decision that might curse his future happiness forever, if it hadn't been already.

"I can't stay here…" he said.

"I know…" she said.

"But I can't leave you here knowing you're pregnant with our child…"

"That's not a problem, Kenny…"

"I don't think you understand," he said. "All through high school, and at Rutgers, that was all I could think about, raising a family with you. I know it sounds weird, that some teenager would have his mind on having a family, but it wasn't about *any* family… it was about you, having one with you!"

She smiled and pressed her free hand on top of his. "You know that's not even possible, right? Pregnant or not, I don't think we can have that..."

He sniffled, unsure what she meant, but could only think she was referring to her own death in the next few weeks, or days. Her baby would most likely die with her. Just then the most unsettling notion shot forth; had Vickie been pregnant with his child the night Tommy Roiter beat her to death behind *Floral & Party?* New tears sprouted and ran down his face.

"Hey, I'm not exactly sure where your mind has just taken you, but there is a beautiful solution to all this..." she said, her lovely features unfazed by his dread. "Come on." She stood and took his hand and led him back into the examination room. Inside, she opened the cylindrical chamber and stepped in.

"Vickie, Kenny, want to know more about the baby?" The voice was upbeat and effervescent.

"No, but I can't keep it..." Vickie said, smiling over at Kenny.

Kenny rushed up to the chamber and pulled the door open, taking Vickie's hand in his, pulling her away. "No, Vickie! No abortion!"

The woman's voice spoke calmly into the charged space of the room. "Kenny, it's okay. We don't perform abortions anymore. That ended decades ago. We'll perform an FT, a fetus transfer. Vickie's and your baby will be transferred to the most compatible host. We have thousands of women waiting for a baby. It will only take a moment to secure an approval from the awaiting mother."

Vickie pulled him closer to her and kissed him, then: "It will be fine, you'll see. The baby will have a wonderful, loving mother, growing in her womb."

A few minutes later the woman's voice came back. "We're set. Are you in agreement?"

Vickie squeezed Kenny's hand, then said, "Yes. All set."

Kenny couldn't begin to guess how long this would take, trying to picture the process, wondering if he should wait in the rotunda. Envisioning this facility in his imagination, he had never drilled down into the details this deeply, and was now receiving an education about his own creation, as if greater minds had brought this into existence, had worked out all the details, had coded for every possibility, had performed feats of biology he couldn't even imagine. Certainly this center was capable of making infertile women fertile, but maybe not. It was hard to imagine the limitations, if any, that people in this dimension might be subjected to. Obviously, death—though everyone here at one time or another had died—was immutable, could not be prevented, like Vickie, whose death in this realm was inevitable; the concept was too strange to ponder for long. Maybe birth was the same? Infertility a blight to be dealt with through creative means, not one to be overcome through technology or blunt force. There was so much to think about.

"Would you like to speak with the joyous new mother?" the voice in the room said.

"Kenny?" Vickie said, opening the chamber.

"Is it done?"

Vickie walked over to him, her eyes shining, happy. "Yes. Would you like to speak to the new mother?"

Kenny thought on it just a moment, unable to bridge the gaps in logic, weighing the potential ruin to his heart. "No, I can't," he said, feeling a tremulous current rushing through him, as if his mind had become indelibly marked somehow, this moment living forever in his memory, his and Vickie's baby nestled in the womb of a stranger. But it was more than even that, a disquieting unease shifting through him. Trying to parse this dimension in rational terms was impossible.

"Thank you," Vickie said. "Tell her we hope she and her child will be very happy!"

"You can't know what this means to us," the new mother's voice said through some speakers. Kenny could not see her, thankfully. "Thank you so much!" the mother added.

Kenny rushed from the room, unable to suspend disbelief any longer. Out in the rotunda he felt himself shaking, hurrying toward the bench before his legs gave out. Vickie came out a few minutes later. When she sat next to him, he could hardly look over at her.

"I don't know what just happened in there…" he said, never anticipating that his concept could be stretched to these kinds of extremes. He imagined tumors being removed without surgery, broken bones healed in moments, diseases cured at the source, not just treatment of the symptoms, but had never imagined anything like this, the ability to transfer human cells from one person to another over hundreds, if not thousands and thousands of miles. In seconds! No software or technology, no Advanced Intelligence, or innovative coding in his wildest imagination made such a feat possible. It was amazing, truly life altering, and impossible as far as he could imagine.

"Come on," Vickie said, standing. "Let's head back to Charter House."

They drove in silence, Kenny guiding Vickie's car into a parking space in the hotel garage. They rode the elevator to the fifth floor, Vickie unlocking the door to her room. She suggested ordering dinner and staying in tonight. Kenny sat on the edge of the bed, unsure where her world began and his ended, if a clear demarcation existed anymore. If it ever had. Vickie picked up the phone and ordered dinner for them, then undressed and got into her pajamas. Kenny, unable to move from the edge of the bed, looked over at her.

"I have to go," he said, standing slowly, his legs like putty.

"I know," she said. "I love you, Kenny. Maybe in some other life we'll have a chance..."

He felt his face pucker, his lip quavering, the sorrow rising up though him like a ghost. He wanted to speak, but what could he say. The door to the *Anything* room hovered at the edge of the hotel room, vague as a spirit guide, imploring him forward. Kenny was pulled toward the portal, yet fighting against it, his eyes on Vickie. Vickie smiled at him lovingly, watching him until she turned away, finding her robe on the back of the chair and slipping it on, her back to him as he left her world.

He watched her a few more seconds from the Anything room. Unable to look at her any longer, he slid the door back into the jamb, the light evaporating around him, leaving him in darkness.

"Kenny?" a woman's voice said, shaky, cautious.

Chapter Fifty-Five

Kenny was frozen facing the portal door, Vickie fading slowly from his retinas. Without moving his limbs, he turned his head to see a woman silhouetted by the light from the hallway, standing in the doorway of the little room. For a moment he thought it was Vickie, that somehow he had not come back from her world, that something had malfunctioned and he was stuck. The notion gave him a moment's relief, helped to ease the devastating sadness.

"Kenny, are you okay?" The voice came again, soft and vague, as if across Time itself.

Kenny thought he recognized it. "Beth?" he said. "What are you doing here?"

He was still unsure if he'd made it back, the dissonance playing like a shadow across a wall inside his mind. The moment felt ungraspable, an unreachable abstraction, that no matter how much he tried, he would never manage to give it form. Her dark shape waited, defined by the bright light around it, or cast from it, and like a shadow, appeared diaphanous and mercurial. Kenny himself, in this moment, did not yet feel solid.

"Kenny, do you want me to turn on the light?"

He saw her hand reaching toward the switch. "No, don't... please."

"Sure. Are you okay?"

Kenny felt odd, ill-formed, as if some of his atoms had not returned with him. He was hesitant to move, to test his legs for fear they wouldn't work, that maybe they no longer existed. A few moments later, though time felt irrelevant, he sensed a hand on his arm and turned to see Beth's eyes waiting for his. She guided him slowly toward the light of the hallway, to the futon and helped him sit. The living room of the bungalow gradually came together, as if the walls had reconstituted from some other dimension, followed by the ceiling, the furniture, the television, windows, the floor, all coalescing at once around him, all locking into place, steady, sturdy, solid. Blood flowed through his veins once again, his nervous system forging connections, completing circuits, a subtle electricity chasing the numbness from his skin. In minutes he felt like himself again, a corporeal being, his mind processing his world perfectly.

"What are you doing here?" Kenny said to Beth, his eyes roving the small interior for Falco, or his dad. Beth placed her hand on his leg.

"I came down looking for you?" she said.

"By yourself?"

"Yeah... but Falco's here..."

Kenny looked around, then brought his eyes back to Beth. "Where? Where is he?"

Beth told him that Falco was in the backyard, sitting. He and Beth had just watched a train go by when the bungalow started glowing like a 500-watt bulb. "That's when I came in," Beth said.

"What did you... did you see..." Then, after a moment: "What did you see?"

Beth tilted her head, her features squeezed. "Everything," she said. "But Falco had already told me where you were..."

So, she knows? But how... Questions unspooled inside his head. Beth explained that Falco had opened the portal door for her, but she hadn't seen anything, except the dirty old studs inside the wall. She had looked at Falco and laughed, and made some smart-ass remark like, "Yeah, that's some mind-blowing magic... a door that leads into the dusty narrow space of a crappy wall." Falco had thought on the problem for a moment before he remarked to her that since she had never *lost* anyone, there was nothing for her to see. "Someone you know or care about had to have died in order for you to experience the portal," Falco had told her. He'd said it with such gravity, that she almost felt like he was serious, she told Kenny. Kenny couldn't under-stand why Falco had shown it to her at all. What was he up to?

"But then I pictured Dr. Nevins the day my dad shot him," Beth said, "and all of a sudden, this blinding light blasts from the doorway, filling the entire room. I thought Falco had pulled some stunt, and I was about to give him hell, until I saw Dr. Nevins walking down the cereal aisle. Strangely, his daughter, Naomi, wasn't with him. It all looked so real..."

Kenny could only listen, his mind split between the seeming veracity of Beth's presence in this world, and Vickie's in the other, trying to understand why one felt more real than another. Or was that just illusion, like when you're in a dream, and the dreamscape *is* the only world that exists, until you wake?

"Kenny?"

Kenny looked up, finding Beth's eyes in the darkened room, still feeling separate from his body. "Yeah?"

"You ready to go home?"

Kenny nodded and took the outstretched hand Beth was offering. Falco was at the kitchen table having a cigarette, drinking coffee. He looked up at Beth first, then at Kenny, tamping out the butt in the ashtray.

"You okay, Sport?"

Kenny found Falco's eyes and felt dizzy, wanting to ask him so many questions, wanting to know how it worked, if it was real, or if it was the product of some elaborate illusion, induced through some post-hypnotic suggestion, or a kind of narcosis achieved through atomized hallucinogenics pumped into the room through a hidden vent. But then what did it matter; Kenny was never going back, and the realization he'd never see Vickie again left a crater in his chest.

Falco jumped up, sliding the chair toward Kenny just as he started to crumple, catching Kenny before he hit the floor. Beth clamped her hands to Kenny's shoulders to steady him. The room was spinning now, Kenny trying to find his center, the sadness spilling down his cheeks. Beth and Falco talked to one another, their voices low and unremarkable, Kenny hearing the conversation with the ears of a foreigner stranded on an unknown continent.

Kenny must have dozed off, or fell unconscious. When he woke, he was seated on the passenger side of the car, Beth driving her mother's BMW, sailing past the red taillights of traffic on the highway. He couldn't recall how he'd gotten to the car, or leaving the bungalow; the only clear memory left in his head that of Vickie, her soft, lovely face, turning away from him with a sad smile, reaching for her Charter House robe over the back of the hotel room chair.

"Beth? Where are we headed?" Kenny said, taking his eyes out the side window, recognizing some of the buildings rushing past.

"Home. To my mom's house…"

Kenny let his eyes drift past the windshield, picturing his dad, then Janelle, wondering how they were getting on, but not wanting to face them tonight. Then Elaine, and Michael, fragments of his life returning like ships long lost at sea. He spotted a billboard with an advertisement for a motel chain.

"Beth, take this next exit," Kenny said. She looked over at him, then switched on the right turn signal and exited up the ramp. At the light, Kenny told her to make a right and head to the motel. When she pulled into the parking lot, he directed her toward the office. Getting out, he looked back at her, holding the door open, and said he was going to check if they had a room.

"Kenny, wait," she said, leaning toward him across the seat. "What are you doing?"

"I can't go to the house right now. I can't be around everyone. I need time to think…"

Beth's features held a moment, until she pulled up, straightening herself behind the steering wheel.

Kenny returned a few minutes later, grabbing his duffle bag from the backseat, then opening the front door. "I just need a day or two. Can you pick me up in a couple of days, or my dad can, I guess…?"

"Kenny, wait. I need to talk to you…"

Kenny nodded, then said, "Yeah, okay. Room 136. Just pull down there." Kenny closed the car door and padded down the sidewalk to his room, getting his door open as Beth was locking the BMW. He tossed his duffle on the bed, then shut the door after Beth came in. She went to the desk and pulled out the chair. He sat on the edge of the bed and said, "How's my dad and your mom getting along?"

"Rough at first, but better now. My mom has a way to go, but I think she'll make it... Martin has been incredible, attentive and focused, and apologetic, so yeah, I think it will work out..." Beth paused, then: "I hope so, anyway."

Kenny was happy to hear that, then asked about the trial. Beth's face darkened, making Kenny wonder if it was still going on. Beth explained that the trial was over, and that the jury deliberated for almost two days, but finally came back with a verdict. "They let him go free. *Not guilty,* can you believe it?"

Kenny thought Beth would be happier with the outcome, but remembered what she'd told him about Dr. Nevins' daughter, Naomi, how unfair it was to the Nevins family.

"It was an all-white jury," Beth stated with disgust. "So, I guess they felt my dad acted in self-defense... so messed up..."

Kenny was about to offer his condolences, but that didn't seem right either, so he said nothing. The motel room grew quiet, Beth looking down at her hands in her lap. Kenny asked if she wanted a Pepsi or something from the vending machines. She shook her head, then raised her eyes to him, staring into him, it seemed, through him. "Is that where your dad was all that time? In Falco's *portal,* with your mother, Noreen?" Beth wore a sickly expression, a glaucous cast to her skin.

"Falco tell you that?" Kenny said.

"Is it true?"

Kenny gestured with his head that it was. Beth's head tossed gently side to side, the likelihood impossible to grasp, her dismay deepening. After nearly a minute of silence, she eased the words past her lips. "Is that where you were... with Vickie?"

Again, he could only bob his head, his experience forced up against the walls of his own disbelief.

"How is that possible, Kenny? Is it a trick? How could Falco create such an illusion? Tell me you understand how he did it, how he made me see Dr. Nevins pushing his grocery cart down the cereal aisle..."

Kenny cleared his throat, the fear in Beth's eyes coming at him like a virus. "I'm sorry, Beth... I don't have anything for you... it seems it's unknowable... even to Falco..."

Her features hardened against him, as if she'd caught him in an ugly lie, one that made a fool of her if she happened to be stupid enough to accept it. Then, after a strained silence, her eyes pulling at him like magnets: *"Unknowable?* That's it, Kenny? That's all you have to say about it? You sound like that crazy magician! He told me the universe was in flux, oscillating waves and particles of energy, that humans were *multidimensional infinity,* that all *matter* was illusion!"

Beth shot upright as if about to rush from the room, sniffling, then wiped her nose, staring at Kenny. He understood her trepidation, himself feeling as if he'd never again be complete and solid, as if this world he'd been born into was no longer trustworthy, credible, that at any moment a curtain could drop, exposing a fresh version of reality which was incomprehensible.

Beth started toward the door, then spun around, thudding back across the room. She dropped herself back into the desk chair, then sniffed a couple of times, bringing her attention to Kenny. "So, I'm supposed to just accept this?"

Kenny shrugged, wishing he could offer something more than empty body gestures. She got up and walked to the sink, unwrapping one of the plastic cups and filling it with water, downing it, then refilling the cup. She sipped it as she went back to the chair and sat.

"Elaine's been calling," Beth said. "She's worried, Kenny. We didn't know what to tell her when she asked where you were. I told her you were visiting relatives in Kansas City, and she said she didn't know you had relatives there. Then your dad got on the phone and compounded the lie, saying that they were cousins on your mother's side, ones you hadn't spent much time with. My mom was going crazy with all the lying and just wanted us to tell Elaine the truth, that we had no idea where you were. But that sounded like it would make her worry more, so…"

"I'm heading back to Newark in a few days," Kenny said. It was the only thing that made sense, still unsure what he'd tell Elaine.

Beth looked away, then back to him. "What are you gonna tell her?"

"I have no idea," he said. "But don't tell anyone you found me yet, okay. I'm just gonna hang low here a couple of days… then probably just fly back to Jersey."

"Without seeing your dad? Or my mom? They'll be worried."

Kenny thought on it a moment, then said, "Yeah, all right. Tell them

I was at the bungalow, and that I just needed to get back to New Jersey, that I'll call him when I'm back home for a few days."

Beth seemed almost satisfied with that plan and stood up to leave again. She walked to the door and stopped, then turned to look at him, her eyes churning with dark energy. He stood, as if she had a parting shot for him; he wanted to face it standing.

"Falco wants me to join him on the road," Beth said. "Be part of his magic act. He even gave me some books to read. One is really old, about magic and alchemy, like from the seventeen-hundreds…"

The statement shook Kenny, as if she couldn't possibly be considering something so ridiculous. "You're not going to, are you?"

She pursed her lips and swallowed, tilting her head to the side. "I don't know, Kenny. I'm so fucking baffled with everything lately. My parents' divorce, the shooting, the trial, school… which I've missed so much of I don't even feel like I belong there anymore. Nothing makes sense, you know. I can't concentrate. I'm still taking depression meds. It's like the ground opened up around me and I'm still falling…"

"It'll get better," Kenny said. "Things will settle down."

She scoffed. "Really? What about us, Kenny? Making love all those nights in your room, while you were seeing Vickie in the *netherworld*, or whatever you're fucking calling it! Is that going to settle down? Will that get better?"

Kenny walked over to her at the door. "I'm really sorry about that, Beth. I—"

She jerked back, her expression soured and tight, suddenly furious, as if he'd slapped her. "Sorry! You're *sorry*? I'm not sorry, Kenny! I love you! I'm in love with you! I don't want you to be *sorry*! I want you to feel the way I do!"

Before he could speak, she was out the door, hurrying toward the BMW. In seconds she was backing out of the parking spot, spitting a bit of loose gravel as she sped from the motel. Kenny stood in the doorway, watching her taillights burn a hasty crimson path from the dismal lot, disappearing around the corner. Sick to his stomach, Kenny eased the door shut, some device slamming against the inside of his skull, fracturing the night into a million pieces.

Chapter Fifty-Six

Olivia was born six weeks after Kenny returned to Newark from St. Louis. Elaine had a much easier birth with their six-pound four-ounce baby girl than with Michael. The doctor had told them a second birth was often less difficult. Kenny was both relieved and chagrined when Martin and Janelle flew out to help with the children after they got home from the hospital. It was awkward having them around, though it gave Elaine a chance to recuperate, and a window to help acclimate Michael to his new sister. Michael took to Olivia Jordyn instantly, wanting to hold her by himself and show her his toys, making sure she understood she wasn't allowed to play with them, only look, and only when he was in his room with her.

In the evenings, after the children had gone to sleep, a smothering silence often rose between the four of them. His dad and Janelle seemed to be doing very well—frequent displays of genuine warmth and love between them—while he and Elaine pursued solutions to their own problems. His trip to St. Louis to find his dad still lingered on the radar screen, a clumsy blinking blip begging for clarification, which Kenny hadn't managed to provide, a subject no one else was willing to breach. Small talk of the kids and work floated heavy in the room, the spaces between the words charged with the menacing residue of the unspoken. Martin had managed to land a job at a mid-sized marketing firm in West County, mostly working on logos and simplified corporate identity projects, nothing like the comprehensive campaigns he created for huge firms. Janelle was thinking of changing banks. The most disturbing updates revolved around Beth, who had withdrawn since the trial—according to Janelle, who was clearly vexed by her daughter's behavior—and was partying to all hours of the night, not bothering to call or say she'd be late.

"She's talking about quitting high school!" Janelle said with a hint of water in her eyes. Martin just held his lips firm, his eyes cast down, as if he now felt responsible for anything that went wrong in Janelle's or Beth's life. "How can you do anything in this world without a high school education?" Janell added with disgust.

Elaine tried to assure her that it was probably a faze, that maybe Beth was still confused by everything that had happened with her father, the trial. It had to be difficult, Elaine told her, that perhaps Beth just needed time. Elaine shifted her eyes toward Martin, as if for reassurance her observations had been correct. Stolid as Switzerland on the subject, Martin offered nothing in the way of agreement, while Kenny winced, feeling Elaine's input was a bold but hapless attempt to be supportive, especially since Elaine's comments seemed to land directly in Janelle's wastebasket. She was having none of any discussion that ended with her daughter quitting school.

Martin and Janelle hung on for about week—Martin and Kenny having some time to talk amongst themselves, the subject of the bungalow or Falco never coming up—and while Kenny was glad to see them leave, needing time alone with Elaine, it was crushingly sad when they dropped them at the airport; Kenny loved having family close, just maybe not in the next bedroom.

The months slogged past, Elaine and Kenny trying to create something greater than just amenable space between them, desperately trying to build on a foundation other than the bond of children. They both felt mutual respect and caring, as they tried to foster the love they'd felt toward one another before the children were born, Kenny flying dangerously close to the conclusion that too much damage had been done. Like the aftermath of a twister in a trailer park; the mangled tin might still be recognizable as a mobile home, but impossible to make livable again.

They tried counseling, going twice a week. And that was helpful for both of them; Elaine to get beyond the hurt and mistrust, and Kenny for the guilt and shame. Both growing healthier, while at the same time growing apart.

Needing a change, they packed up the kids and drove to St. Louis, thinking the trip could have a restorative effect. On the drive out they talked about moving to St. Louis, both of them almost giddy over the prospect of being near family, Elaine comparing Janelle to the mother she never really had.

"It would be nice for the kids to grow up around her, like a grand-mother. And their Aunt Beth," Elaine said, glowing in a way Kenny hadn't seen in months, maybe years. It all suddenly seemed possible, a way forward. "It's healthy to have family near, don't you think?" Elaine reached over to take his hand on the seat.

One night, during their visit to St. Louis, Kenny was sitting outside by the pool listening to kids beyond the wooden privacy fence in the next yard playing and laughing, when Beth slid open the glass door and asked if he minded company. Up until that moment, it seemed Beth wanted nothing do with him. Kenny welcomed the armistice, not sure how good of company he'd be, his life and heart in shambles. In fact, over the past several months, supposedly working on his marriage with Elaine, he hadn't been able to stop thinking about Vickie. He felt like a phony, the worst kind of bastard. Marriage coun-seling helped to a point, but Kenny's time with Vickie in the portal could never be spoken of, so it sat between them like a washed-out bridge. His guilt and shame over loving Vickie kept resurfacing—the dead body in the room—and while Kenny found it an apt though unsettling metaphor for the numbing cycle he was caught in, it did nothing to help him move forward. And Vickie was still there! Waiting *behind that door*, like some kind of macabre game show of the departed. *"Jay, show us what's behind Door Number One!"* The possibility of being with Vickie again was a constant threat, an option housed in the dark cellar of Kenny's brain. He needed to put her behind him, but so far had not found the inclination nor the will.

"I'm sorry about last time I saw you, you know, at that motel," Beth said, pulling a chaise lounge over closer to his. "That was crappy what I said. So many times I wanted to call you and tell you what an ass I was that night."

"I'm pretty sure I was the ass that night," he said, feeling as if he'd been one every night for the past several years. Beth sat staring at the crisp blue water purling near the diving board. Kenny figured she must have had more she wanted to say. She just sat, so he said nothing. Occasionally the faint odor of chlorine drifted up around them. Kenny liked the smell; it always reminded him of summer, though it was still spring, the water far too cold to swim.

"What's your dad—Carl, isn't it?—what's he gonna do now?" Kenny asked.

"Carl is selling dental supplies," Beth said, with a tinge of disgust. "The jury may have found him innocent, but he knew what he did was wrong. He'll have to live with that the rest of his life."

"How do you know that?"

Beth spun her head, her eyes charging him, almost incredulous that Kenny would question her conclusion. "He got rid of the gun!" she scoffed. "He knew he fucked up. He got lucky in that trial."

Kenny was on dodgy ground with Beth this evening; everything he said seemed to be wrong, or just stupid, according to her facial cues. Maybe she was jittery, still pondering the primary topic she wanted to discuss with him. He had no idea what could possibly cause this much angst; she didn't ruffle easily.

After a few minutes she said, "I'm going to do it, Kenny." She stated this as if they'd been discussing *it*, whatever *it* was, for the past twenty minutes. Before he could press her for clarification, she said, "I'm going on the road with Falco! I'm gonna join his crazy fucking magic show!"

Kenny bit back so many rebuttals he was starting to choke on them, then finally came out with, "You can't! It's insane! He's insane!"

Her eyes came at him again, calmer this time, but with no less fury. A sneaky smile crept across her face. "You jealous?" she said, now grinning, as if she'd trapped him in a box with holes punched in the lid.

He scrunched his face, scoffing away her ludicrous question. "No, it's just... Falco. He's mad, Beth. And you're mad to even consider it!"

She twisted toward him, her face bright as a carnival, laughing. "Oh my God, you really are jealous!"

He wasn't jealous, that much he knew, but he was concerned. Falco had to be in his fifties, and was definitely not to be trusted. And he was weird and sometimes creepy, with his metaphysical machinations on existentialism and the current state of humankind, not to mention his incomprehensible ramblings on science. And what did he want with a teenage girl anyway? What was his game? Would they travel by car? By plane? Where would they stay on the road? In motels? Hotels? Would he take her down the road to alcohol? Drugs? Kenny pictured Beth gaunt, dark rings beneath her eyes, sprawled half-naked on some grimy motel bed overdosed and unconscious.

"You can't! You just can't!" Kenny shouted, his face turning red. Beth leaned toward him, then reached up and wiped a tear from the bottom of his left eye, her expression softer, concerned.

"Hey, it's okay," she said. "I'm not going to do it until I finish high school. Ben insisted I finish high school first..."

Kenny wiped his other eye. "Who's Ben?"

"Ben Falco. Benjamin. He's okay, Kenny. He really is kind of sweet once you get past that wacky outer crust."

"You've been hanging out with him or something?"

"Yeah, I've been down at the bungalow several times, working on magic stuff. He's been showing me card tricks, sleight of hand. It's kind of fun."

Kenny felt sick again, everything changing so fast, like he was standing still, or on a conveyor moving backward, while the world and everyone around him was rushing toward the sun at light speed. He felt alone, desperate, struggling to keep his universe right-side up. "Does your mom know?"

Beth shook her head. "She doesn't know about Falco, or that he's teaching me his magic act." Then, a few seconds later. "She wouldn't understand, Kenny. I told her I was thinking about quitting high school and she about had a brain hemorrhage. It's just, I don't fit in at school, and I have no direction. But this magic stuff excites me. And Falco is like some exotic, mythical creature. I've never met anyone like him... I think it's a way to find myself, you know?"

With head in hands, Kenny closed his eyes, trying to make the freight train in his skull stop. Vickie appeared for a moment, smiling, so full of life she seemed more than a product of imagination, more than chemicals sluicing through his brain, tricking his olfactory glands with her scent, leaving phantom traces of her on the flesh of his tongue. Then she was almost gone, the kids in the next yard screaming, crying, their mother calling them into the house. The odor of chlorine removing the last residue of Vickie. Kenny felt Beth's hand on his back, the warmth of her breath on his cheek.

"Do you miss her?" Beth said softly, lovingly.

It was as if Beth had read his mind, and he didn't bother questioning it. "I can hardly breathe."

For the longest time Beth said nothing, rubbing gentle circles along Kenny's shirt, then: "I hope someday you'll trust me enough to tell me everything about being with Vickie in that room... what it was like living in her world, or however you say it. And why you left. I want to know everything, Kenny. I do."

Beth stood, bringing her fingers across his shoulder, then to his cheek, letting them linger on his skin just a moment. "I love you, Kenny."

When Beth disappeared into the house, Kenny was in free fall, his stomach squashed to a fist. Vickie was back in his thoughts, the uncanny properties of her reality, as if it were constructed on the premise that everyone in it had a purpose, a *role* to play, like Sean, most likely the one who had beaten her to death behind the restaurant. Sean was meant to see her coming out of Powell that night, was meant to go to her place of work and wait in the parking lot. And the hit-and-run driver, probably ran over Vickie and never looked back. Probably went home to have dinner with his or her family. Because that's what they were *ordained* to do, expected to do, leaving no reason for concern or anger, arrests or trials or jails. Even the police, they did their job, but probably never even searched for Vickie's killers, any of them, unless compelled by some grander scheme than police work, as if every event, every nuance, was orchestrated, and nothing happened by chance.

Was that how it was in this reality, too? Everything predetermined, while he pretends to have control over his life? Does destiny reign, even while he acts as though his choices, his decisions, have weight?

Chapter Fifty-Seven

E laine and Kenny moved to St. Louis several months after Beth's birthday, and found a nice house a few miles from Janelle and Martin. Martin was so happy to have his son back in town, and Janelle was over the moon being grandmother to Michael and Olivia, though issues between Kenny and his wife stood unresolved. The couple hoped a fresh start in a new city might be the catalyst to melt the stagnation, though Martin wasn't so sure that would work; they were amicable, and certainly still fond of one another, but the passion had faded from their hearts. Nevertheless, Martin remained positive, wanting Kenny to have love and happiness in his life.

Beth had stopped talking about dropping out of school, which gave Janelle a huge relief, but Beth had withdrawn after the trial, spending a lot of time away from the house, Martin unsure where she was going. She dropped sports, and didn't seem to spend much time with friends, and when she was home, she stayed in her room and read. Martin had given her his Taurus, so she'd have a vehicle to get back and forth from school, while Martin used his Harley to get to his new job, which was a grind, working with marketing folks, his mind looping back to Noreen's world, to his Phoenix Group, the attention to graphics and pure design, typography, kerning and fonts, logos and annual reports and corporate identity, with concern for the *quality of line*, not the *bottom line*.

Janelle insisted they go car shopping before summer was out. "You can't ride that motorcycle through the winter!"

Not St. Louis winters, Martin knew, but Janelle planned to pay for his new automobile; he was broke, having gone through what savings he'd had juggling Noreen's world and Janelle's. The guilt was crushing, knowing he'd blown everything feeding the odious deception. He had yet to sell the bungalow, which would easily afford him a new car, which would be the honorable move, but since Janelle wasn't bringing it up, he chose to ignore it as well. The truth was, which he could admit to no one, not even Falco, Martin missed Noreen. He couldn't see himself going back to her world, but knowing she was there, just beyond that door, was enough for now. In time, he hoped her imprint would fade, that he would only remember the times they had before she died, that he would truly put her behind him, a memory which would eventually lose traction but never wane completely.

After the Christmas holidays, Kenny and Elaine went through a short separation, divorcing soon after, Kenny finding his own apartment. Having difficulty finding work, Kenny would have been eligible to receive money from Elaine, who was thriving in the St. Louis real estate market, but Kenny said he'd be fine living on the settlement he and Elaine had come to, and would find a way to pay child support. Kenny was losing weight, his hair graying unnaturally, the job market unresponsive to his skills and knowledge. Martin got him an interview for a consulting gig at the marketing firm, which worked out well.

"This should tide you over for a while," Martin said. "They love what you're doing."

"I really appreciate it, Dad. It's great to be doing something constructive."

Martin wanted to tell him that Janelle and he considered starting their own firm, and if they did, they'd need an IT guy. Janelle had tired of the bank, and was ready to exercise her marketing savvy again, but wanted to hold off embarking on such a venture until Beth graduated high school.

Their creative enterprise was on permanent hiatus, it seemed, Janelle beside herself when Beth announced after graduation that she was going on the road with Falco.

"A magic show!" Janelle screamed. "Are you insane! Who the fuck joins a traveling magic show? NO, young lady, you're going to college. I don't care what you study, or how many times you change your major, but you are not going on no goddamn magical mystery tour!"

Beth just looked at her, disarming her mother with her uncompromising, unemotional conviction. "I'm sorry you can't be happy for me, Mother. But I am going."

Janelle screamed about Falco being an old lecher, a pervert, a profligate. "What kind of man takes a young girl on the road with him? Jesus, Beth, have you lost your mind?"

"You don't even know him," Beth said, then turned and walked away.

Janelle was frozen in place, rattling like an off-balance washing machine, slobber and tears dripping from her chin. When she turned her burning eyes on Martin, he bowed his head, unsure what to say.

"Talk to him, Martin," Janelle finally said, using the backs of her hands to wipe the mess from her face. "You know this Falco character. Talk sense into him! There must be a law against this. It doesn't sound right!"

Martin tried to remain calm, knowing that Beth was eighteen. No law existed stopping an eighteen-year-old girl from taking a road trip across the country with anyone she pleased. Martin agreed to speak with him, knowing it was futile talking with Falco; he was an enigma, outside Time and social constructs, forsaking all codes of ethics; he was a goddamn *magician*, for chrissakes! But Martin couldn't say that to Janelle.

The talk with Falco was fruitless, though Martin enjoyed catching up, Falco explaining that Beth had been working extremely hard on learning everything, "A brilliant student and quick study!" Falco said, beaming like a proud father. Martin could not detect anything nefarious or untoward from Falco, just an unbridled excitement to have such a delightful and intelligent assistant. "It's given me new life, Sport!" Falco said, holding his beer bottle up to Martin's for a toast.

Martin clinked bottles, certain to never mention anything about this *salute* to Janelle. Falco was like a kid with a new bicycle, pulling out his itinerary, showing Martin all the cites they planned to tour.

"I bought a bus! *Falco the Fantabulist and his assistant, Freya,* in this bold script painted down the sides." Falco shoved the design toward

Martin, who was impressed. It was tastefully done and Martin fought the urge to ask who'd designed it for him.

"*Freya?*" Martin said.

Falco's features sagged. "You don't like it, Sport? Too much? Beth thought of it..."

Martin nodded, smiling to himself, realizing how much these two oddballs belonged together on this mystical undertaking, *Freya* with her sagacious old soul and unflappable spirit, and Falco with his shamanistic multidimensional view of the *continuum*, as he called it now, unable to refer to it as the *world*, or *universe*, which, to his thinking, suggested that the *world* had material substance, that it existed beyond illusion. Falco then rejected his own assessment, pointing out that *continuum* wasn't even correct, that that word suggested a linear construct, events laid out in sequence. "But they aren't, Sport," Falco told him. "The past, present and future exist equally in the same instant, all at the same time, if Time existed." Then, as if needing some name for this construct, Falco now referred to it as, "The *Infinity.*"

Martin didn't understand any of his bewildering explanation, wondering what some of these conversations on the bus would be like. Beth could handle it all, though; she had a nimble mind, and a robust bullshit detector.

Martin told Janelle that he felt she had nothing to worry about with Beth and Falco, not mentioning Beth's new moniker, or Falco's latest musings on the *continuum*. The summer marched on, much of the time Beth at the bungalow helping Falco finalize details, in the evenings at home battling Janelle, rolling her eyes, silently pleading with Martin to referee. By the fall, Beth was on her way to destinations unknown, at least to Janelle. Janelle had called her lawyer again, and Martin pleaded with her to drop it. "She'll be okay, Janelle. I know it," Martin told her. Janelle gave him a, *You don't know shit!* look but never said a word, just spun away and huffed off to the bedroom and slammed the door.

Beth's leaving took its toll on their marriage for a while, but as the weeks and months peeled off—Janelle received letters or postcards every week from Beth—Janelle started to talk about her and Martin's new company again, the two of them banging out details over lunch or dinner. Some evenings they'd go for motorcycle rides before it turned cold. Michael and Olivia came to the house at least once a week, Janelle usually picking the children up to give Elaine some time to herself. Kenny took the kids every weekend, expanding his consultant work, doing much of it from his apartment over the Internet. When Kenny traveled for work, Martin and Janelle were more than happy to take the children.

Janelle received a postcard from Beth saying she and Falco would be in St. Louis for a few weeks between gigs. "I'd like to spend some time at the house if that's okay," Beth said on the phone one night.

Janelle was thrown. "Aren't you going to spend the entire two weeks here? I don't understand."

"Mom, I don't want to fight, okay. I really want to see you and Martin, but I've arranged other accommodations in St. Louis."

Janelle agreed, reluctantly. When she disconnected the call, she flopped down on the couch and sobbed into her hands, her shoulders heaving, shuddering. Martin regarded her like a lethal reptile, giving her plenty of space before asking questions.

"She's only staying here a few days, Martin!" Janelle blurted out through snot and tears. "She's made *other* arrangements..." the offending word slurred over a new swell of tears. Janelle talked about it for days, unable to accept her daughter's sudden independence.

"Sudden? It's hardly sudden, Janelle!" Martin said, needing to set the record straight. She eyed him with revenge, then hurt. "Ever since I've known your daughter," Martin added, "she's followed her own path. I think she came out of the womb independent!" Janelle laughed a little, like a hiccup, fighting back the slightest hint of cheer, not quite ready to be consolable.

Beth stayed only two nights with them, the time together pleasant and affable, no one willing to dig too deeply into the past several months and what was going on with her. The next afternoon Beth said she had to get going, that she had things she needed to do.

"Will I see you again before you leave St. Louis?" Janelle said, her eyelids flickering, chin trembling, battling back the million questions clawing at the inside of her chest. Beth hugged her.

"I love you, Mom. I'll be back in St. Louis before you know it."

Janelle, heroic in her attempt to stifle the raging emotions, succumbed to a sobbing fit, trying futilely to direct them away. Beth hugged her again.

"Hey, I've got an idea," Beth said, drawing back from her mother. Janelle's eyes brightened, as if powered by a rheostat. "Falco and I are going to be in Vegas for two weeks in June. Why don't you and Martin come out? It would be fun."

Janelle soured, mouthing the word, *Vegas?* as if her baby could not possibly mean *Sin City.* "That's the soonest I'll see you?" Janelle finally said, obviously battling back the horror she was imagining.

"Mom, it's only a few months away."

Janelle, lip quaking, said, "I already missed your birthday! I feel like I'm missing everything!"

Beth smirked and kissed her mother, then hugged and kissed Martin, and true to a magician's assistant, vanished.

The next few months were busy, Martin and Janelle finding office space, buying equipment, Janelle making phone calls, lining up new accounts, Martin setting up the graphics department, interviewing local college graduates for an intern position, Kenny helping him in the evenings, getting their computers upgraded to the latest software.

"Did I tell you that Janelle and I are heading to Las Vegas to see Beth and Falco in a few weeks. We're driving out on the Harley. Taking Route 66!"

"That's fabulous, Dad. Yeah, actually I'm gonna be out there as well. Beth invited me to come, and asked if I could bring the kids, which I wanted to talk to you and Janelle about."

Kenny explained that he had a new client in Vegas, and that he might need a sitter for a couple of hours.

"No problem, Kenny. We'd love to take the kids. It sounds fun!" Martin was relieved. Kenny sounded so much better, as if he'd finally managed to move on from all the loss in his life.

Chapter Fifty-Eight

W hen Martin and Janelle arrived in Las Vegas, they rumbled down the strip before checking into the hotel, Martin feeling like he was on top of the world, revitalized by their motorcycle journey across the Midwest. After parking in the garage, they rode the elevator to the seventh floor. Kenny had made arrangements to be in the same hotel, though Martin wasn't sure what floor he'd be on. They couldn't wait to see the kids. Martin left a note for Kenny at the front desk, telling him what room they were in, that they wanted to grab dinner together before the show, that Beth had left tickets for all of them.

When the knock came at their door, Janelle bounded gazelle-like across the hotel room.

"Look at you two!" Janelle said, squatting down to hug Michael, then taking Olivia in her arms. "Oh, I've missed you both so much!" Carrying Olivia, Janelle took Michael's hand and led him into the room.

Martin hugged both children and asked Michael how the flight was? Michael said his belly felt a little funny, that maybe something sweet might help. Always the manipulator, Martin thought. Martin led Michael to a muffin on the desk. "Would that do it?" he asked. Michael nodded, his eyes blossoming.

After dinner, they walked to the venue, Olivia starting to get a little fussy. "I can take her back to the hotel, Kenny," Janelle said.

"No way. You can't miss your daughter. If Olivia gets too cranky, I'll take her back. You go see Beth. We'll be fine." Michael, a bit forlorn, asked if he had to go back, too. "Not if you behave," Kenny said. Michael smiled up at his father, then over at Martin, taking his grandfather's hand, as if an ally would help to fortify his chances.

They found their seats near the front, in the center, facing a huge deep crimson curtain. The orchestral pit was less than thirty feet away. Michael sat next to Martin, asking questions about Aunt Beth, if she was behind the curtain, and why did they need a curtain; was it a big window? And who were the people with the horns and drums? Kenny shushed him a few times. Martin was relieved Janelle had not seen the poster out front for *Falco the Fantabulist and his lovely assistant, Freya;* she would not have liked the frothy moniker Beth had chosen.

When the lights dimmed, a suave man wearing a sleek black tux came out on stage, a single spotlight illuminating a circle where he stood.

"Ladies and gentleman, we have a little change in our headliner this evening, but I assure you, you won't be disappointed!" Martin glanced over at Kenny who shrugged, Olivia fidgeting in Janelle's lap. Janelle seemed to miss the update, busy with Olivia. A few grumbles and moans idled over the hushed crowd. The emcee was still grinning, as if waiting to find out the new itinerary himself.

Then, with a flourish of his arms, like a conductor, said: "Ladies and gentlemen, without further ado, I present to you for the first time on any stage, the *amazing,* the *spectacular, Freya the Fantabulist!* The curtain went up and Beth glowed like a neon doll in the spotlight, wearing a red tuxedo and sparkling top hat, her hair hanging to her shoulders. When her legs scissored across the stage, her red tights sparkled as if embedded with diamonds. The orchestra played heroic music, solid and marching, large kettledrums giving way to mysterious and haunting strings. Without a word, Freya motioned toward the wing, assistants in black pushing out a huge glass aquarium into the center of the stage. Within minutes, an enormous satin cover came down from the ceiling over the eerily lit water, hiding it completely from the audience. The music built as Beth rounded the covered structure, occasionally lifting the edge of the satin cloak to peek underneath, smiling mischievously toward the crowd. She tapped the glass as she went around and when she reached the front, water began sloshing out the sides beneath the cover, spilling out onto the stage. Beth feigned shock and fear, dancing away from the deluge on her spiky heels, followed by a quick flourish of her wand. With the kettle drums beating like a frenzied heart, the cover jerked up and away, revealing an enormous shark swirling and splashing in the aquarium, its jaws spread, biting at its own reflection. A collective gasp spread across the auditorium, people leaning back in the seats, bracing their feet against the floor. Then applause, a little at first, then more, people rising from the seats. Janelle was in tears, surprised to joy, pointing Olivia's attention toward the stage, saying, "Look, Olivia, it's Aunt Beth! Aunt Beth! At least I think it's Aunt Beth!" She was laughing now. Olivia was laughing too, though she probably wasn't sure why. Janelle's face was bright with pride and awe at her daughter; Martin had never seen her beam with such vitality, not even at Beth's graduation.

In moments the crimson satin shroud lowered back down from above, covering the shark and tank, the commotion subsiding, as if the shark had quieted, like a bird with a towel placed over its cage. Beth came front stage, the large covered tank behind her. The music quieted, people retaking their seats, the applause dying out. Stage hands dressed all in black busied themselves with mops behind her, cleaning up the water.

"Thank you all for coming! I'm Freya. I know you expected to see *Falco the Fantabulist*, and he will be along shortly, but until he arrives, let's see what we have under this shroud!" The moppers fled the stage, the music building majestically as Freya briskly circled the tank once again, clapping her hands methodically as if to initiate an event. Stopping with her back to the audience, facing the tank, the lights dimmed as she slowly bent down to take the corners of the satin covering, jerking it free of the tank with the flourish of a matador, letting the satin fall to a rumpled pile on the floor at her feet. Inside the backlit tank, the water now an incandescent yellowish-green, swam a dark creature, a silhouette, slowly gliding about like a tailless newt. It appeared to have arms and legs, with enormous fins for feet, and some kind of headgear, perhaps to aid its breathing, but not connected to machinery of any sort. Martin was transported back to Terrell's explanation of how Falco had opened the portal that stormy night, how the lightning had struck the rod on the telephone pole, the freight train roaring past at that precise moment, the tank filled with water exploding with the light of an atomic bomb. Just then, in the theater, the floor began to quake beneath Martin's feet, the music now the rumble of a locomotive.

An unnatural hush fell over the audience, the orchestral pit completely silent; the rumble of the train coming from somewhere else, some unknown source shaking the floor, the seats. Flashes of blinding light exploded behind the tank, casting Freya and the tank into silhouette, the sallow greenish water beginning to glow. Booming thunder echoed in Martin's chest, lightning bursts flashing with greater regularity, wind starting to rustle Freya's hair, though she stood perfectly still, back to the audience, arms raised, as if invoking unseen gods. The sound in the auditorium was deafening, the explosions of light melding to a strobe-like blinding glimmer, when suddenly the tank of water appeared to explode, a chaotic, sparkling cloud rising almost intact, the dark, undefinable creature writhing in the middle, as if caught in the swell of particles, rising toward the ceiling, disappearing from view.

Then utter silence. It seemed no one was breathing. Martin felt his chest tighten, then release as he stole a slow quiet breath, the hairs on his arms standing erect. Freya, with her back to the audience, slowly lowered her arms and turned toward them, her expression blank. Behind her on the floor was the crimson shroud in a heap. Impossibly, the stage appeared completely dry. Freya stared out at the onlookers, a smile breaking slowly across her face as the mound of crimson velvet on the floor behind her began to stir. Just then, bolting upright and shrugging away the cloth, Falco, dapper in his black tuxedo, spread his arms triumphantly and smiled, then looked over at Freya, taking her hand to thundering applause. The house erupted, people on their feet, whistling, howling, cheering.

Martin was stunned, his hands clapping slowly, inaudibly, like a mime, trying to parse what he'd just witnessed, remembering back to the night Falco had walked in front of the speeding train, how the brilliant locomotive's headlamp had erased his features, how the iron behemoth had seemingly erased his life in one fleeting, unimaginable moment.

The adulation lasted nearly five minutes, the air so charged people refused to sit back down. Falco and Freya both bowed numerous times, smiling, holding hands, then smiling over at each other. When the auditorium was finally restored, people adjusting themselves back into the seats, Falco released Freya's hand and the two of them began to scurry around, the lights and music coming up, frenetic and playful, as they began their next magic trick.

That evening, back at the hotel, Martin was still mesmerized, as if in a trance, spellbound by Falco and Beth's mind-bending illusions. Beth joined them an hour later, back at the hotel in Martin and Janelle's room, so Beth could see the children. Kenny waited with champagne on ice. Janelle talked nonstop, astounded by Beth's theatrical prowess, then about the magic, remarking how she'd never seen anything like it before. Janelle sustained a permanent smile, getting Olivia ready for bed, then helping Michael brush his teeth, Beth helping her, talking to the children. Janelle had told Kenny they'd keep the kids that night, give Kenny a chance to explore Las Vegas. Martin sat with Kenny, sipping champagne, shaking his head, still flummoxed.

"It was remarkable," was all Martin could say, wanting to tell Kenny about the portal, the weird parallel of Falco's performance to Terrell's story from several years ago. He hated that he couldn't talk about it. Once Olivia was down for the night, Janelle and Beth came out to sit with Martin and Kenny, Michael beginning to show signs of travel fatigue, falling asleep in a chair by the window.

Martin was dying to ask Beth about the mechanics behind the illusions, but knew she would be tight-lipped; the magician's code.

"Why did you take the name, *Freya?*" Janelle asked.

"It sounded good with *Fantabulist!*" Beth said, her happiness abundantly obvious. Martin had never seen her so enraptured, but no one broached the subject of some romantic entanglement between her and Falco. Their mutual affection seemed apparent, at least to Martin.

"Benjamin should have joined us tonight," Janelle said.

"He's pretty spent after two performances a day. The truth is, so am I," Beth said. "We have to start early to get everything set up for the afternoon show."

Janelle reached over and took Beth's hand. "You look so happy, sweetheart."

"I am, Mom. I truly am."

A short while later Kenny finished his champagne and stood up, setting his glass on the table. "I think I'm going to call it a night," he said, smiling at everyone. "Thanks for watching the kids tonight," he said to Martin and Janelle. Then to Beth: "Spectacular show, Beth." She smiled up at him, then got up and hugged him.

"Thanks for coming," she said.

"Wouldn't miss it for the world."

Chapter Fifty-Nine

Back in his room, Kenny changed out of his clothes and slipped into his white hotel robe, remembering back to Vickie at the Charter House Inn. Kenny had to remind himself that that had happened in this reality, not in Vickie's world beyond the portal door. He was glad to recall that detail; it made the memory more real, more meaningful and satisfying somehow. He had just settled down on the bed when a knock came at the door. He got up, switching off the television, then cinched his robe and walked across the carpeted floor to answer it. When he pulled the door open, Beth was standing there.

"You going to bed?" Beth said, walking past him into the room. She kicked off her shoes, and started undoing her blouse.

"Not without you," Kenny said, retrieving her robe from the bathroom hook. When he returned, she was standing naked near the bed. Kenny handed her the garment, which she tossed onto the bedspread, then undid the belt of his robe, pressing her body against his. "This was all I could think about all day," she said, melting into his arms. "Ben kept asking me if I was all right. I couldn't concentrate... and it's all your fault!" She pulled him toward her pressing her lips to his. She eased his robe off his shoulders, letting it fall to the floor, then pulled him toward the bed. They had just gotten beneath the sheet when a knock came at the door.

"Holy shit," Beth said, laughing quietly, covering her mouth.

"It's like fucking high school," Kenny said to her in whisper, smiling. He got up and grabbed his robe from the floor, tightening the belt around his waist. Beth got up and strode naked into the bathroom, slowly closing the door behind her. Kenny pulled the hotel room door open.

"Dad, what's up?"

"Sorry to bother you, Son. Michael wants, no, *needs*, his giraffe!" Martin said smiling. Martin stepped inside the doorway while Kenny rummaged through Michael's little backpack, coming up with the stuffed animal.

He handed it to Martin. "I didn't think he'd wake up again tonight," Kenny said. "He's pretty zonked."

"Yeah, he was asking where Beth was, disappointed she wasn't around when he woke up." Then, fiddling with the stuffed animal: "He's okay now, though. Janelle's reading to him."

Kenny nodded, then scratched his head. Martin nodded back, smiling. "You okay, Son?"

"Sure. Why wouldn't I be?"

"Oh, just that you're all alone out here... I worry about you..."

Kenny scoffed. "Don't, okay. I'm fine." Kenny thought he heard Beth sniggering in the bathroom.

Martin hugged Kenny. "Goodnight, Son." He turned and walked down the hall. Kenny heard his dad's door shut, echoing loudly in the hallway, then closed the door to his own room. Beth rushed from the bathroom, tugging at Kenny's robe, pushing him naked toward the bed.

After sex, they lazed in the suffuse light of the room, nestled under the sheet, Beth's head tucked against Kenny's chest. "Falco would like to meet us later for a drink," Beth said softly.

"Sure. Sounds good. How's he doing?"

She got up on one elbow to look into Kenny's eyes. "He's vegetarian now!" She smiled victorious.

"No way!" Kenny said, recalling how Falco had been putting on weight every time Kenny had visited Beth on the road, which was quite frequently over the past year; Falco had fallen into disrepair, smoking too much, not exercising, eating too much greasy food, and consuming too much alcohol. "Is the drink a good idea?"

"Yeah. He just has one beer, then switches to club soda with lime. He's doing great."

Kenny thought he had looked better tonight, slimmer, more energetic. "When are we going to tell your mom and my dad that we're married?" Kenny finally asked, coming up on his elbow to meet Beth's eyes.

Beth smiled sadly. "I don't know," she said, sitting up, the sheet slipping down to her waist. "She's just getting used to me being on my own, traveling with Ben and all." Then, a moment later: "What do you think your dad will say?"

Kenny wasn't sure. He figured Martin would be shocked at first, but ultimately, okay with it. Would it be strange? Probably, but Michael and Olivia had gotten very used to Beth, Kenny often bringing the kids with him when he traveled to meet her. However, Janelle, she would have a more difficult time, especially concerning Elaine; she and Elaine had grown extremely close since they had moved to St. Louis. And Elaine would be beside herself, wondering how long Kenny had been sleeping with Beth. It was a big mess in the making, for sure.

"Your mom and Elaine will have the hardest time with it," Kenny finally said.

Beth looked down at her hands resting on the sheet across her lap. "Yeah, but we have to, eventually. Well, we don't have to, I guess… but I want to, Kenny! I want to be open about it. I want you to travel with Ben and me, especially now that you can do most of your consulting work over the Internet. You could just get rid of the apartment in St. Louis, travel on the bus with us. We'd be nomads, live like rock stars!"

"You're already a rock star!" Kenny said, leaning over to kiss her. Since leaving with Falco, Beth stayed at Kenny's apartment any time she visited St. Louis. They had outfitted it with her things; a spare toothbrush, clothes hanging in the closet, underwear and socks in the dresser, her fuzzy penguin slippers under the bed. It would be hard to trade that in to live on a bus, out of a suitcase, no permanence. And Falco. He liked Falco, Ben, but could never quite align himself with the magician's ideas about life, about reality, never comprehending the portal, how that was even possible, at times, doubting it had ever happened, convincing himself it too had been an illusion, like the elaborate one Falco and Freya performed. Yet Kenny knew it wasn't, that he had touched Vickie, her skin convincingly real, indulged in the sweet scent of her hair, could almost smell it now, had felt the warmth of her body next to his, his brain still at war with itself over the bizarre riddle.

"Do you still think about her?" Beth said, bringing her eyes to Kenny.

"Who?"

Beth scoffed, smirking at him.

"Not really," he said. "Occasionally, I guess. It's just weird, you know. The bungalow, the door..." He turned toward her, the air unmoving between them, the moment static and silent, fixed in time. "What's wrong?"

Beth hesitated a moment, then said, "Falco still talks about Mitzi. He longs for her, Kenny. Some nights he's so miserable he considers going back in, trying a different approach..." Beth's expression hardened, eyeing Kenny, shaking her head.

"That's not me, Beth," Kenny said. "You know how much I care about you, right?" Kenny felt sick to his stomach, wishing she could read his heart, but maybe she had, and maybe she saw something that gave her pause; it scared him that she may be able to see something even he wasn't aware of, that she could know him better than he knew himself.

"I love you, Kenny," she said, reaching over to touch his hand. "I always have."

Chapter Sixty

The *Renagades* had grown rowdy, shouting and laughing, celebrating their annual Thanksgiving pig roast in the field behind the bungalow, ignoring the low gray clouds rushing soundlessly by above them. Beth, Janelle and Kenny, when they heard the 4:28 from Carbondale in the distance, left the bungalow and started through the fray. Janelle didn't think it was a good idea, taking Beth's arm before they reached the edge of the weeds. "Let's go back to the house. Martin and Ben may need our help," Janelle said. "Anyway, this looks like a private affair."

"Come on, Mom. It'll be fun!" Beth said, moving forward. Kenny followed, helping assure Janelle it would be fine, though around this crowd he could never be sure. But Beth didn't want her mom in the house while Martin and Falco worked.

Bikes and bikers and women in tight jeans everywhere, drinking beer, playing lawn darts, horseshoes, music playing, more dancing in a cleared spot in the field. At the center of the activity was a makeshift cinder block pit, built up from the ground, blocks stacked on top of blocks three high, smoke pouring out the sides, a biker in jeans and leather vest stoking the coals with a long metal pipe through a space in the blocks on the ground. Kenny couldn't see the actual pig, but guessed it was under the cover of thick aluminum foil he could see just beneath the top row of blocks. He marveled at their industry and pagan zeal.

Walking now in single file through the throng, with Janelle taking the center position, Beth took the lead, Kenny bringing up the rear, nodding at partiers as he walked past. Halfway through the wild bunch, a spontaneous chant began with just a few at first, quickly building to a crescendo when bikers saw what was happening. "Freya! Freya! Freya! Freya!" they cheered in unison, like conquering Danes welcoming a returning sorceress, coming to their feet, raising their arms. Beth raised her arms playing along. The shouts continued, Beth slipping off her blue leather jacket, revealing a skimpy black studded leather vest with a plunging neckline and nothing underneath. Janelle gasped, her eyes shifting nervously through the horde, amidst new guffaws and shouts and whistles, the chant "Freya! Freya! Freya! Freya!" growing louder. Kenny stooped to pick up Beth's jacket, knowing she had planned this little exhibition before they left the house that morning. Beth and Falco's traveling magic lollapalooza was common knowledge to the inhabitants of Yurning Place and their friends.

As the locomotive approached, the chant died down, but the shouting continued, bikers all moving toward the tracks. A couple bikers strolled up to Beth and Janelle and handed them unopened bottles of beer. Janelle refused at first, until Beth took it for her, then handed it to her. Kenny laughed, glad to be in on the ritual for a change.

"I'm not going to drink this," Janelle said, holding the bottle out to Beth.

Kenny walked up next to Janelle, holding a bottle someone had pressed into his palm.

"It's not for drinking," he said, laughing, the cheering and shouting almost deafening combined with the rumble of the approaching train. Janelle regarded him curiously, looking at the bottle, then back to him. Beth had moved a little closer to the tracks. Kenny nudged a reluctant Janelle forward, nodding toward the tracks, imploring her to move closer to Beth.

Everyone was lined up along the edge now and the engineer, in the spirit of the holiday, or maybe trying to discourage what was about to happen, gave three long blasts on the horn, the cheering and screaming growing manic, the coal cars approaching fast, bottles flying through the air, exploding against the iron cars, beautiful plumes of beer and glass, almost like fireworks. Janelle was frantic, caught in the hoopla, trying to understand what was happening when Beth reared back and let her bottle fly, the amber projectile cartwheeling through the air, landing solidly with a great splash, shards and beer-spray sucked along in the draft of the train. In the din of whistling, hooting and hollering, it was hard not to get swept up in the momentum of the riot. Kenny cocked his arm and gave it all he had, the bottle nearly going over the train, finally catching the upper lip of the car, the blast of beer and glass particulates swiftly carried away by the speeding train.

With the end of the 4:28 from Carbondale getting closer, and the rabble making it impossible to hear, Beth looked over at her mom and mouthed, NOW! THROW IT NOW! Janelle brought her worried eyes to Kenny, who was laughing, miming a throwing motion with his arm, encouraging her to get rid of her bottle. A few other bikers chimed in, urging Janelle to throw it before it was too late.

Janelle, now frantic and jumpy, obviously doing battle with every proper impulse in her brain, brought her arm back, her fingers gripping the beer bottle neck like a hatchet, then swung it forward. The bottle rotated cleanly, like a saw blade, toward the escaping train, catching the last car squarely, a violent, gorgeous detonation, the glass vaporized, the spray absorbed into the ether. The bikers remained on their feet, cheering, shouting, a few of them dispersing back to their games, or the pig pit to tend the fire.

Falco had said that Geronimo and a few other bikers had started building the pit the night before, getting the fire going, and had stayed up all night in shifts, tending it and the pig. By morning, Falco had said, "It was almost like Woodstock for Harleys." People had been milling around, sleeping on the ground wrapped in blankets, using the portable toilets brought in for the occasion, playing music on their guitars. One guy had a trumpet. Another an electronic drum set he plugged into a receptacle on the back of the bungalow.

As Kenny, Beth and Janelle walked back toward the house, Kenny spied what was left of the cord of firewood the bikers hauled in for the roast. Tarantula came up to Beth and asked how she was doing. Beth introduced him to her mom. Janelle was gracious, gave him an edgy smile, then hurried back to the bungalow.

Beth dispensed Tarantula fairly quickly, then slipped her jacket back on and walked with her arm through Kenny's back toward the bungalow.

"So, what do you think?" Kenny said. "Should we tell everybody tonight that we got hitched? Maybe before dinner?"

Beth sighed. "Too soon," she said, almost apologetically. "My mom is finally settling into me being gone all the time, and…"

Kenny spun toward her, cradling her face gently in his palms. "Is that the only reason?"

"Well… Elaine…"

"Look, Elaine will have to deal with this situation no matter when we tell everyone," Kenny said. "And she'll be fine. She's moved on. She's seeing someone now, and it seems serious, so…"

"Does that bother you?" Beth said.

"No. Of course not. I'm crazy about you, *Freya!*"

"Ha ha, Muppet!"

"*Touché.* No more monikers then. But I like *Freya*…"

"I promise we'll tell them soon, okay…" Then: "Does the other thing bother you, you know…?"

Kenny hesitated, knowing the decision had brought him a moment's distress, but it was silly, thinking of losing Vickie forever. She was gone, had been for a long time. Falco had given him time to think on it, but there was nothing to ponder; the happiness Kenny had known over the past months with Beth had no rival. "No. Not in the least."

Chapter Sixty-One

With Falco's help, Martin had nailed up the wooden lath the week before Thanksgiving, both of the men wearing welding goggles to remove the door, then nail in extra studs for the lath. Martin had plumbed the wall, making sure they had a proper vertical surface, then placed the wooden keys along the lath. Falco mixed the cement for the rendering coat, Martin instructing him on the consistency of the plaster. They had worked together, Martin demonstrating how to use the trowel properly, getting the surface uniform and smooth as possible. Falco, under Martin's tutelage, scored the rendering coat with the edge of the trowel, preparing it for the float coat. The float coat would have to cure before the finish coat could be applied.

But before any of this work commenced seven days earlier, they had both sat at the kitchen table, a twelve pack of beer between them, contemplating their decision.

"Are you sure about this, Ben?" Martin had said, calling Falco by his first name now, since he was almost like family, Falco and Beth together all the time, touring America in their bus. There was even talk of a European tour. Martin wasn't about to ask, but it was still a subject for discussion between he and Janelle as to whether or not Beth and Falco were romantically involved. Janelle could barely suffer the possibility of her eighteen-year-old daughter with a fiftyish man, especially

Falco. "My God, she'll end up being his damn nurse in a few years!" Janelle would yelp, then grimace with disgust.

Falco wasn't that bad, Martin thought, and seemed healthier now than he'd been since he'd known the odd man. However, Martin said nothing to Janelle about that, having so many misgivings about the crazy trickster to begin with, his mercurial nature, his mastery of deception. That's what magicians do—*Deceive. Distract. Divert. Lords of the smokescreen.* Falco was nice enough, as a human being, when he acted human, but his ruminations on life and the universe were troubling at best, and at worst, downright taxing.

After a lengthy and troubling span of silence, Falco had finally said, "Yes, I think it's for the best." But he hadn't been very convincing, his eyes dark, alchemical, or maybe it was his hooded, thick black eyebrows that made it seem he was always brooding. "It should not stand. I'm sure of it now."

"And Mitzi?" Martin had said, finishing his third beer.

"Aw, come on, Sport!" Falco said, knocking back his beer, quickly popping the tab on a fresh one. He jumped up with his new can and walked to the window, and for a moment, Martin thought he might be sobbing. The strange man stood solid as a post, unmoving, his back to Martin. After several minutes, he returned to the table and sat, taking a long pull from the can. He eyed Martin like a thief, then finished his beer. "I can't allow the world to keep taking her from me," he said, drawing another beer from the cardboard packaging.

That made more sense to Martin than anything Falco had ever said, helping Martin to conquer the demon whispering in his own ear about Noreen, the nagging little voice trying to convince him that the next time through the gateway into Noreen's world would be different.

Martin and Falco agreed to finish the patch on Thanksgiving Day.

Martin had come down on the eve of Thanksgiving just to hang out with Falco and share a few beers. They sat out back and watched Geronimo and his friends construct the pit for their pig roast, watching other bikers join in and make camp in the field, or just bundle up in a blanket on the ground near the fire pit. Once the fire was blazing, a truck pulled up and three men hauled the dead pig to the grill and set it on, covering it with thick foil. Martin was amazed by the enterprise; never had he witnessed such a spectacle. Then, without prompting or prelude, Falco said, "Memory and expectation are the illusions that seduce us from the present moment." The pleasant night, which had gathered itself around the two men like a cordial companion, suddenly fizzled, an experiment gone wrong. Martin unsure how to respond, said nothing, as was often the case when pitted against Falco's philosophical musings.

The next morning, Martin had slept in, while Falco started working on Thanksgiving dinner. Beth, Janelle and Kenny arrived sometime around two o'clock, everyone helping Falco with preparations, cutting up vegetables, stirring sauces, preparing dessert. Falco and Martin knew it wouldn't take long to apply the *finish* coat, both of them privately weighing the consequences of their decision to make this final, both of them pondering if, in fact, this momentous resolution could be undone, both of them dreading that it might be possible, at the same time hoping it wasn't.

The biker crowd beyond the bungalow was gathering steam, the noise shaking the windows at time, or so it seemed. When the 4:28 from Carbondale made itself known with a loud blast from its whistle, Beth and Kenny convinced Janelle, after much cajoling, to come outside with them. Janelle, having seen the leather-and-blue-jean mob when they'd pulled up wasn't in the mood for *socializing*. When the three of them finally left the bungalow, Falco and Martin hurried to the *Anything* room to finish what they'd started. The welding goggles were no longer necessary, the brilliant luminescence trapped behind wood lath and the first two coats of plaster. Martin checked the float coat while Falco mixed cement for the finish. Falco was just bringing the plaster over when the muffled cries of, *Freya! Freya! Freya!* bled through the walls of the little room. Martin smiled over at Falco, who either didn't hear, or was so preoccupied with memories of Mitzi he didn't respond.

The train was closer now, the yelling and whooping like a rock concert. Martin held his concentration on the trowel, spreading the finish coat, the vibration from the locomotive spreading through the ground, shaking the earth beneath the smallish house, bristling up though the walls, rattling the glass in the window, as if the light buried in the wall was fighting to get out. The hairs stood up on Martin's arms. He glanced over at Falco, who, evidenced by the vacancy in his eyes, had sent his mind to another universe. Martin ignored the peculiar man, smoothing the trowel over the creamy plaster, regaling himself in its texture, the train a monstrous, invisible force crushing the air beyond the thin walls, tossing the world, testing the planet's resolve. Falco was frozen like a mosquito in amber, his eyes fixed on nothing, the shouting and cheering shifting through the small house like the howls of demented souls, Martin swallowing unconsciously, his hand troweling absently, his legs weak, the wall trembling, and for the briefest second, it looked as if the fresh plaster was being melted from the inside, dripping down to the floor, a trapped god, a terrifying authority unwilling to be imprisoned.

Just as Martin was applying the last few strokes to the fresh plaster, the roar of the locomotive began to fade, the trembling in the flimsy house abating, the train rushing away through the barren landscape like a startled beast. The plaster was smooth now, final, as if nothing had ever been there before but wall. Martin cleaned the trowel, scraping the last vestiges of plaster into the leftover dregs.

"Falco? Ben?" Martin said softly, not wanting to startle the perplexing man standing behind him like a statue. Falco was unresponsive, as if something inside him had died, or had been buried alive. "Falco?"

Falco, like spontaneous combustion, sprung suddenly to life. "That it, Sport? I need to check on the tofu turkey roast. I hope it's good. It's stuffed with wild rice."

Falco removed his gloves and walked from the room. Martin, while cleaning up, heard Falco talking to Beth about the vegetarian turkey or something. Janelle exclaimed that it looked delicious, then they all started laughing about something Kenny was sharing, everyone but Falco. Martin felt sad for the man, as if Falco's mind battled his heart for jurisdiction over any possibility of true happiness. But then, maybe Martin was no different. He looked at the floor, planning to clean up the rest of the mess later, pick up the drop clothes, carry the dried plaster out to the trash.

About to switch off the light in the *Anything* room, Martin removed his gloves and took his eyes to the fresh plaster along the seamless wall, imagining the wooden door, the blinding light, recalling how Noreen would be vague at first, her visage sharpening slowly in her hospital bed, her face brightening when he walked in, telling him how happy she was to see him.

"Marty? Sorry to bother you. Dinner's on the table."

Martin turned toward the voice. "No bother, Beth."

He smiled as she turned away, then heard Janelle ask Beth if Martin was coming, what was he doing in there? Beth assured her mother everything was okay. A few seconds later, muffled conversation came from the kitchen amidst the clink and clatter of people passing platers, scooping food onto plates.

Martin took his eyes to the blank wall, told Noreen goodbye, then switched off the light.

About the Author

Lonnie Busch is an award-winning author whose short fiction has appeared in *Southwest Review, The Minnesota Review, The Baltimore Review* and other magazines. Among his awards for fiction are the Clay Reynolds Novella Prize for his novella, *TURNBACK CREEK*, finalist in the Tobias Wolff Award for Fiction, the *Glimmer Train* Very Short Fiction Award, and others. Busch is the author of several novels, *CARGO HOLD 4, PROJECT ÜBERMENSCH, ALL HOPE OF BECOMING HUMAN, THE CABIN ON SOUDER HILL and THE BALDWIN HOTEL,*

Busch is also a painter, animator and illustrator, and has created artwork for numerous corporations, ad agencies and institutions, including the "Greetings from America" and "Wonders of America" Commemorative Stamps for the USPS.

See Busch's short story collections, *PUSH ME, and TURNBACK CREEK: A NOVELLA & SIX STORIES.*
https://lonniebusch.com

www.ingramcontent.com/pod-product-compliance
Lightning Source LLC
Chambersburg PA
CBHW051515250626
47156CB00001B/99